BENEATH A Christmas Sk

ALISSA CALLEN

JANET GOVER • JACQUIE UNDERDOWN
JULIET MADISON • NORA JAMES

FICTION
HQ

Contents

Under Christmas Stars   1
Alissa Callen

Christmas at Coorah Creek   103
Janet Gover

The Christmas Wish   247
Jacquie Underdown

Above the Mistletoe   353
Juliet Madison

His Christmas Feast   463
Nora James

Also by Alissa Callen

The Bundilla Series
Snowy Mountains Daughter
Snowy Mountains Cattleman

The Woodlea Series
The Long Paddock
The Red Dirt Road
The Round Yard
The Boundary Fence

Under Christmas Stars

ALISSA CALLEN

To Luke

Chapter 1

'Are you sure you're not moving into Santa's workshop?' Amusement curved Ella's mouth as she passed Freya a plastic crate heavy with Christmas paper, gift bags and tags.

Freya smiled at the blonde vet whose friendship had helped ease the ache of loneliness when she'd left the city to teach at Reedy Creek's one-teacher bush school. 'As my mother always said, you can never have too much Christmas.'

'Let's hope there's not too much Christmas for my car boot.' Ella caught a roll of festive ribbon that slid out of the crate Freya was wedging into the back of Ella's four-wheel drive.

Freya slammed the door in place to secure the full load of luggage and Christmas items. 'Too easy.' Laughter threaded her words as she gave Ella a high five.

After the heartache of the past year, it felt good to laugh again. She turned towards the small house across from the schoolyard that had become her new home.

'There's two more Christmas boxes to put in my car and I need to throw some clothes into a bag, then we're good to go.'

Ella also turned towards the cream weatherboard building. A frown stripped the vibrancy from her brown eyes as she stared at the left side of the house. Tarpaulins covered the gaping hole where once a door, window, fuse box and laundry had been.

'I'm glad you were in town having coffee with me this morning when that wheat truck made an off-road detour.'

'So am I. I'm also glad it's school holidays and the kids weren't in the playground. I still can't believe the driver walked away.'

'He's very lucky. According to Edna, Fliss read him the riot act about fatigue management.'

'It would be a foolish man to ignore a Dr Fliss safety talk.'

Fliss and her cowgirl sister, Cressy, had also become good friends. Fliss lived in a bluestone homestead not far from where Cressy lived on a farm with her bull-riding fiancé, Denham. Freya banished a tug of loneliness. If life hadn't unravelled last Christmas, she too would be living with the man she'd loved.

As if sensing her sadness, Ella touched her arm. 'Let's finish loading your car and get going before we lose the light.'

'Good idea.'

Freya led the way towards the damaged house. It was no surprise Ella could read her pain. They'd bonded over having had their hearts broken and not being willing to risk investing in another relationship. While Woodlea and the tiny village of Reedy Creek fixated on Cressy and Denham's late autumn wedding, Freya and Ella made the most of their single status. They'd enjoyed pamper weekends in Dubbo, travelling film festivals and long lunches at food and wine events.

'So,' Ella said, as Freya held the screen door open and the vet walked through. 'Are you going to tell me where you're moving to or is the big secret you're setting up a Christmas shop in Woodlea's Main Street?'

'Now there's a tempting idea.' Freya smiled and followed Ella inside. Without the hum of the air-conditioner the house remained airless and hot. 'I loved that Christmas shop we visited in Mudgee when we went to the readers' festival. It's not really a big secret where I'm staying.' She paused as she remembered the intent stare of masculine dark-blue eyes. 'Drew just asked me to keep it quiet.'

Ella stopped in the narrow hallway and turned, her mouth open. 'As in Drew Macgregor? You're staying out at Inglewood with dashing and distant Drew?'

'Yes. His goddaughter Hattie is in kindergarten and he says offering me a place to stay is the least he can do to say thank you for making sure she's okay.'

The shy six-year-old had become an orphan earlier that year when an explosion on their farm had killed her parents. Her mother had been with her father when he'd refuelled the farm truck and the fuel pump had failed. Hattie now lived in town with her mother's sister and husband and their twin sons. The tragedy had rocked Reedy Creek and Woodlea and both close-knit communities continued to mourn the loss of a much-loved young couple.

'Poor little Hattie. This Christmas will be hard for her.'

'It will be but she's surrounded by people who care for her so I hope she'll be okay. She's a brave little girl.'

'She is. She loves that stubborn pony of hers. I've bought him a red Christmas halter and reindeer ears so she can dress him up.'

'Panda will look adorable.'

'He will.' Ella stared at Freya and shook her head. 'Drew Macgregor ... wait until Edna hears where you're staying. Tanner and Drew remain the top contenders on her future-husband list for Bethany. It goes without saying that if things don't work out at Drew's, there's a bed at my place for however long you need it.'

'Thanks. All should be fine. Drew said he'll hardly be home because of harvest. Inglewood isn't far from here so I can still run my Christmas craft classes in the Reedy Creek hall. He also isn't the most ... *social* of men so I'll have my own space.'

Ella grinned. 'Now that's an understatement. He isn't named distant and dashing Drew for nothing. He's more reclusive than a hermit. I used to think he was a figment of Edna's imagination until one of his stockhorses went through a fence in a storm. Even when I was there, he wasn't exactly talkative.'

'Tell me about it. The only person I've seen him speak more than two sentences to is Hattie.' Freya fanned her face before taking the band around her wrist to tie her heavy hair into a ponytail. 'I'd better get my bag packed before we sweat like we did in that sauna and steam room.'

She turned to head into her bedroom before Ella realised the flush colouring her cheeks had nothing to do with the heat. The pale skin that went with her red hair revealed her every emotion and she didn't need perceptive Ella to realise that at the school Christmas concert she'd done more than a little observing of Drew Macgregor. There was something about the dark-haired, broad-shouldered cattleman with the rare smile that made it impossible to stop thinking about him.

She threw clothes into a duffle bag. Her fingers stilled on a pretty deep-red dress hanging in her cupboard. The moment she'd tried on the sleeveless lace dress she'd known it would be a perfect Christmas Day outfit. Her fingers clenched. But thanks to discovering her fiancé's definition of 'Christmas drinks' involved him and his latest intern naked on his desk, the dress remained unworn.

She pushed aside the anger and hurt and uncurled her fingers. Never again would she render herself vulnerable by trusting. Never again would she allow her tunnel vision to blind her. Never again would she allow her soft heart to lead her astray. She slipped the dress off the hanger and folded it to pack in her bag.

Yes, she did speak quietly and preferred to keep the peace. Yes, her small stature gave the impression of fragility. Yes, she did prefer to blend into the background. But the side of her she'd always tempered to avoid conflict had been liberated. When Charles had called asking for a second chance, she'd cut him off mid-sentence in a dismissive tone worthy of any courtroom opposing counsel. She now lived life on her own terms. And she'd continue to do so by making this the best Christmas ever, for herself, for sweet little Hattie and for the still grieving Reedy Creek community.

Bag packed, she headed out to where the sun dipped towards the horizon. A pair of galahs trilled as they swooped overhead to land in the cedar tree. A gentle evening breeze brushed the heat from her skin. She stopped and smiled. She loved this time of day. The schoolyard and surrounding bush came alive as birds and wildlife emerged from the shade to eat and drink. The wallabies that lived beyond the school fence grazed on the green patch of grass where the sprinklers overshot the lawn.

Ella too stopped to look at the wallabies. She adjusted her hold on the large box of craft supplies Freya would need for her workshops.

'Now that's something you wouldn't see in the city,' the vet said, voice serious as she glanced at Freya.

She knew what Ella was really asking. The Reedy Creek School might only have nine students, but between a handful of challenging boys and the isolation, parents had become used to seeing teachers come and go.

'No, it isn't, and I'm glad to say it's a sight I'll see many times. My city days are behind me. I'm here to stay.' Freya studied her half-demolished house. 'Even if I have nowhere to live and even if I have to spend Christmas with a man who I'm sure won't hang a single bunch of mistletoe.'

Drew Macgregor returned to a farmhouse that should have been dark. Instead, pale light spilled from the east wing. Freya

George, the composed, quiet teacher with the serene smile, had moved in.

He parked his ute in the shed. Even when the engine noise died he remained in his seat, staring at the light. Today had been like any other harvest day, intensive and exhausting. But for some reason fatigue bit even deeper than usual. When he'd heard the wheat truck had ploughed into Freya's home he'd been surprised by his reaction. Concern had coiled around his chest and pulled tight. Before he'd made the conscious decision to check she was okay, he'd realised he already had the UHF radio in his hand to call his workman to take over driving the header.

Drew rubbed at his chin and his stubble rasped in the silence. He still didn't know what he'd been thinking asking Freya to stay. When he'd arrived to see her assessing the damage, standing so still and so silent, an unexpected protectiveness had stirred inside. A tendril of hair had escaped her usual neat bun. He hadn't been able to keep his attention away from how the vibrant red contrasted with her flawless skin. He was yet to look into her grey-blue eyes and not feel like he'd surfaced after holding his breath under water for too long.

He pushed open the ute door. He should have used Freya's hesitation when she'd asked if he was certain about having her stay as a way out. But no, he'd made some excuse about him needing to repay her kindness to Hattie. He sighed and left his seat. He had planned to do that with a large box of handmade chocolates, not by inviting her into his home.

He unloaded the esky from the back of his ute. The last time he'd had someone stay was years ago after his parents' funeral. He knew exactly how Hattie felt losing her family. He briefly closed his eyes. As tired as he was, his grief and his guilt still had the power to wound him.

Home from university for the summer, he was supposed to have driven to the coast to inspect a mob of cattle. But he'd been making the most of the district's social scene and had become distracted by a bubbly blonde he'd met at the picnic races. He hadn't made it back from her place in time, so his father had elected to fly his light plane and his mother had offered to keep him company.

Drew's steps dragged as he made his way towards the back kitchen door. A violent storm had ensured they'd never reached their destination. From that day onward he'd never allowed himself to be distracted again. Not by a pretty face, not by a social event or a holiday like Christmas and especially not by his own needs. Inglewood was his life. He'd work around the clock to honour his parents' memory. He'd work himself to the point of exhaustion so he wouldn't have time to think or feel.

A wet nose touched his wrist and he ruffled the head of the liver-coloured kelpie that appeared out of the darkness. The dog whined.

'I know, Bailey. We don't normally have company but everything's okay. I hope you minded your manners when our guest arrived. Freya's a city girl. I'm sure where she comes from dogs don't roll in anything dead or lift their legs on everything within reach.'

The kelpie licked his hand.

'I'll put this inside and feed you and Panda. I'm surprised he's not trumpeting the house down. All he thinks about is that stomach of his. Hattie will have to let the girth out another hole when she rides him.'

As Hattie now lived in the Reedy Creek village and not on the farm where she'd grown up, Inglewood had become Panda's new home. The six-year-old had already lost so much, she didn't need to also lose her beloved pony.

Drew continued through the garden that consisted of a thick lawn, established shade trees and a hardy bed of purple irises. Gardening wasn't high on his priority list. He kept the lawn short and removed the weeds to make sure the garden wasn't snake friendly, otherwise all his energy went into running the farm. It wasn't pride or ego that had driven him to purchase two neighbouring properties to expand his holdings, just his vow to fulfil his father's dreams.

At the kitchen door he tugged off his boots. While time had removed the gloss from the extensive house renovations required after a bushfire, his mother's life lessons remained. No farm boots inside. Full stop.

He entered the kitchen. It was just how he'd left it that morning. Neat and tidy, just how his mother would always leave it. But now a faint floral scent filled the air and over on the island bench sat a bottle of red wine tied with a fancy gold Christmas ribbon.

Drew crossed the open-plan kitchen to the pantry, which housed a deep freezer. He opened the lid to put in the ice bricks from his esky. Pink and purple plastic containers added colour to a basket that had earlier been empty.

'I hope it's okay I put some things in there?' a soft voice said from behind him.

He spun around, conscious he had grease down the front of his navy shirt and his hair hadn't seen a brush in weeks. That's what the cap he'd left in his ute was for, to make him look halfway respectable when out in public.

In contrast, Freya with her black skirt and pale pink blouse looked fresh, clean and so beautiful his lungs strained for air.

He rubbed the back of his neck and searched for the right words to prove she hadn't come to stay with a Neanderthal. He didn't need the charity ball in a converted cotton gin he'd briefly attended last spring to remind him his small talk needed work. He could speak to his workmen and their wives with ease but he was sure

Freya didn't want to know about how many bags of wheat he'd stripped per hectare today.

'It's more than fine.' His voice emerged deeper than he'd intended. 'Please make yourself at home.'

'Thanks, I will, but I'll also stay out of your way. I know how busy this time of year is.'

Her smile failed to reach her thick-lashed eyes. She was as wary of him as he was of her. The knowledge, and her words, lowered the tense line of his shoulders. She'd keep to her wing of the huge house and the only area they'd need to interact in would be the kitchen. He'd hardly know she was there.

He left the pantry. 'Thanks for the wine.'

She moved away to let him pass. 'You're welcome.'

He hesitated. He was out of practice entertaining a guest. 'Would you like a coffee, or tea? I'll put the kettle on before I feed the animals.'

'No, I had a cuppa earlier. I hope it's okay but I fed your kelpie and that noisy pony of Hattie's. I gathered from the way he kicked the gate it was dinnertime.'

'Thanks. I'm home a bit later tonight. You found the food?'

'Yes, the kelpie ran to the shed door so I gathered that's where it would be. I have a feeling I might have given Panda too much. He looked at me as though Christmas had come early.'

'I bet he did. He usually gets half a scoop of lucerne chaff.'

'Oops.' He glanced away from where Freya bit the fullness of her smooth bottom lip. 'I gave him two. He acted like he was starving.'

Drew chuckled as he leaned back against the sink, surprised the sound came so easily. 'He's such a greedy guts. I'll lunge him tomorrow so he can work off his dinner. Bailey will be fine with whatever you gave him.'

'He's a great dog.'

He briefly turned to flick on the kettle. Her tone had been genuine. He'd expected her to not appreciate Bailey's youthful kelpie energy.

'He can be a little full-on.'

She smiled and this time her eyes warmed. He folded his arms, thankful Freya wore her conservative clothes and practical hairstyle. Usually she was surrounded by students, but now it was just the two of them, there was no escaping the way she made his pulse kick. If she affected him dressed like the sensible schoolteacher she was, he didn't want to imagine how his testosterone would react should her heavy auburn hair fall down her back and her clothes hug her gentle curves.

'Just like any young dog. I might have grown up in Sydney but we had a family dog and I did ride horses. Some of my favourite memories are attending pony camp on a property outside Bathurst. I'll be right to lunge greedy little Panda tomorrow.'

The kettle switched off and Drew didn't move. He nodded, jaw tight. He'd made a mistake and misjudged Freya. Not only was she comfortable around farm animals but she was far from fragile.

There was an angle to her small chin he hadn't seen before and a steadiness to her quiet stare. No wonder the Reedy Creek parents were in awe she'd sorted out the youngest Ridley boy within three weeks of school starting. Two other boys who'd preferred pigging to being in the classroom had also returned to school and caused little to no trouble.

She hid it well, but for all of her apparent gentleness, she possessed a will as strong as the curved steel in his wheat silos.

Mouth dry, he collected a coffee mug from the shelf beside him. So much for quiet and unassuming Freya not disrupting his life. It wasn't enough her beauty drew him to her, her spirit did as well.

Chapter 2

The days at Inglewood settled into an easy routine. Freya would hear Drew leave early and would then briefly see him when he returned dusty and tired for a late dinner. The conversation they'd had the night she arrived remained their longest.

He'd insisted she not cook for him but it didn't feel right not doing something to help at such a busy time and to thank him for having her to stay. So she'd taken to leaving a meal in the fridge and muffins or slice on the bench to pack in his esky for morning smoko. She'd also made sure she fed Bailey, if he hadn't accompanied Drew into the paddocks, and Panda.

She clucked to encourage the fat black and white pony dawdling at the end of the lunging lead as he walked in a circle around her.

'Come on, Panda Bear, I know you can walk faster. Hattie's coming over and might want a ride so I don't want you misbehaving. You don't fool me. The glint in your eye tells me you know plenty of tricks.'

The Shetland pony flicked his tail and increased his pace.

Freya smiled across to where Bailey lounged in his favourite spot in the shade of an old jacaranda tree. Everywhere she went the young kelpie followed. As she'd predicted, she mightn't have Drew's company but between Bailey and Panda she didn't feel alone.

Her smile slipped. It didn't seem to matter whether she saw Drew or not, she kept thinking about him. Especially late at night when she heard the splash of water as he took a swim in the large pool at the back of the homestead. She focused again on Panda and not on imagining what muscled and tanned Drew would look like wet and shirtless. He already distracted her enough dressed in ripped jeans and covered in dust.

She lunged Panda in the opposite direction before returning him to his shaded pony paddock. Hattie mightn't ride after all. The temperature already soared. No birdsong sounded and no blue-and-black wrens flittered around the sparse garden. The only sound that disturbed the hot silence was the ceaseless drone of cicadas. Out in the summer-bleached paddocks, heat waves shimmered, distorting the dark shapes of Red Angus cattle. Today wouldn't provide any respite from the heatwave predicted to last until Christmas.

She returned to her wing of the house to change into a loose white blouse and a denim skirt. Her jeans, long-sleeved pink cotton shirt and the cowgirl boots Cressy had gifted her for her birthday protected her fair skin when outside but weren't practical inside. She kept her heavy hair in its quick and cool top knot.

She was adding the last detail to the design template for the felt Christmas tree her class would make in the upcoming craft workshop when tyres crunched on the gravel driveway. Hattie had arrived. Her aunt needed to take the energetic twins to Taylor at Woodlea to have their hair trimmed and Hattie had asked if she could visit Freya and Panda. Drew was going to try to come home at lunch so he too could see her.

Hattie's small hand slid into Freya's as they stood on the veranda steps and waved goodbye to her aunt and cousins. A plume of red dust followed the white sedan along Inglewood's gum tree–lined driveway until it reached the tar road.

Freya always maintained a professional distance between herself and her students. But with her teacher hat being shelved for the summer, she could be what grieving Hattie needed—an adult who understood and cared. She smiled at the six-year-old.

'So what should we do first? Make Christmas cookies or visit Panda?'

Hattie's solemn heart-shaped face broke into a smile. 'See Panda.' She pulled an apple from the pocket of the purple shirt she wore with shorts and cowgirl boots. 'I brought him a treat.'

'He'll love that.'

Bailey trotted beside them as they headed for the pony paddock behind the stables. As soon as Panda saw Hattie he nickered and cantered over.

Freya smiled. 'That's the fastest I've seen him move.'

Hattie giggled as the pony flung his head over the gate and neighed. For all his energy, when Hattie sat the apple on her flat palm, Panda ate with care. Hattie leaned in close to hug him and play with his white forelock. Panda sighed with bliss. The pony adored his little rider as much as she adored him.

When the heat flushed Hattie's cheeks, they headed inside for a cool drink and watermelon Freya had cut into Christmas trees. They busied themselves with making cookie dough and rolling it out onto the floured, grey granite bench. Hattie's face became a picture of concentration as she pressed out Christmas shapes with the cookie cutters.

Freya helped slide the last tray into the oven when tyres again sounded on the driveway. Bailey's excited bark said Drew had come home. Hattie's bare feet made no sound as she sped over the floorboards to the back kitchen door.

Freya took her time to wash the cookie dough from her hands. There was no reason for Drew's arrival to trigger a flurry of nerves in her stomach. Laughter sounded as Drew piggybacked Hattie into the kitchen. Freya glanced up and her hands stilled beneath the trickle of warm water.

She'd witnessed the deep bond between Drew and Hattie at various school functions. But she'd only ever seen them together when she'd been working and busy. Now there was nothing stopping her from fully seeing the depth of their connection.

Hattie's brown eyes sparkled and her blonde hair fell about her face as she giggled and clung to Drew's broad shoulders. But it was Drew who Freya barely recognised. From their two-minute conversation that morning she knew his jaw was clean shaven and his aftershave contained a woody-citrus note. She also knew he wore his usual faded navy work shirt and jeans.

What she wasn't prepared for was the happiness that relaxed his face. His grin flashed and his eyes turned the deep, dark blue of a moonlit sky. No longer did grooves bracket his mouth or reserve close his expression. Unsmiling, Drew Macgregor had the power to hijack her thoughts. At ease and playful, he took her breath away.

No wonder Edna had him on her marriage list for Bethany. Freya ignored a twinge of unease at the thought of Drew's single days possibly being numbered and finished washing her hands. He loved Hattie so much and deserved to one day have a family of his own.

Drew and Hattie approached. She smiled, hoping her strain didn't show.

'Something smells good,' Drew said, glancing at the stainless steel oven.

Even his voice sounded different, lighter, less rigid, as though it came from a part of him he always kept hidden.

'Yes, sugar Christmas cookies. They'll be ready in about ten minutes.'

Drew turned his head to grin at Hattie who remained on his back. 'Time enough for a swim.'

Her squeal was only matched by the wideness of her smile. Drew lowered her to the floor. She skipped over to scoop up her pink backpack and continued towards the guest bathroom where she could change into her swimmers.

Drew's eyes met Freya's. She wasn't surprised seriousness tempered his happiness. The way he'd folded his arms now they were alone reflected her own wariness. 'Would you like to come for a swim too?'

She'd shaken her head even before he'd finished. 'Thanks, but no. Apart from not packing any swimmers …' She lifted a pale arm. 'This Irish skin of mine isn't designed for the outback sun.'

The gravity in his eyes eased as he smiled. 'I wondered where your colouring came from.'

'My maternal grandmother emigrated from Ireland when she was ten. My sister has the same colouring.'

Drew's attention focused on Freya's hair. 'I've never seen such a shade. It's very … pretty.'

She thought she caught a flare of something in his eyes before Hattie appeared at the kitchen doorway dressed in a colourful swimsuit and holding a beach towel. 'I'm ready.'

Drew grinned at his goddaughter. 'I'd better hurry up then.'

He gave Freya a brief nod before he strode down the hallway to the west wing. Freya could only hope the hot colour in her cheeks hadn't betrayed her reaction to his words.

Her red hair had been called many things, not all complimentary, but never had a comment elicited such a rush of feeling. For some reason it mattered that Drew thought her hair … pretty. She pushed aside her contentment to concentrate on making sure Hattie had sunscreen smoothed all over her young skin. She hadn't started a new life only to risk her heart again.

A splash sounded and she and Hattie looked through the oversized kitchen window to where Drew resurfaced after diving into the pool. Sunlight caressed planes and chiselled hollows tanned by the summer sun. Smooth, corded muscles flexed as he tunnelled his hand through his wet hair. Freya swallowed. Her imagination could never have done justice to the masculine perfection that was one Drew Macgregor.

Shoulders tight and eyes gritty, Drew drove over the cattle grid to head for home. It'd been one of those days. A bearing had gone in the auger and now the header steer tyre had blown, all before lunch. So he was off to Woodlea to collect a new tyre. The closer he drove to the homestead, the more his tension increased.

He couldn't get used to Freya being there to greet him. He couldn't let her warm smile or the way she always left him homemade treats for his morning smoko trigger longings he'd suppressed. She'd soon be gone and the kitchen would no longer smell of cinnamon or gingerbread.

He'd already crossed the line by complimenting her on her hair. The way she'd stiffened and now looked at him with caution ensured that he wouldn't blur the boundaries again. But as much as he needed to keep things casual between them, the urge to spend time with her proved too strong.

He parked the farm ute in the shed. Bailey bounded over to him and he rubbed the kelpie's neck.

'I know, I'm home again during the day. I must have had too much sun.'

He removed his boots at the kitchen door and continued inside. Freya came out from the living room, a book in her hands. She'd pulled her hair into a high ponytail and wore the short-sleeved green dress he'd seen the night of the Christmas concert.

'Everything okay?'

He blanked out the concern in her voice and the way her eyes searched his. Her worry wasn't personal. Freya had a kind heart. He'd seen how she'd cared for a student after the little girl had skinned her knee at the sports carnival. She'd also gone out of her way to make sure Hattie received the support and help she needed.

'Yes, all good. I have to go to Woodlea to pick up a header tyre.' He rubbed a hand around the base of his neck. 'You said last night you needed more craft supplies ... I wondered if you'd like to come with me.'

Her smile was instant. 'Yes, please. I'll grab my bag.'

Instead of taking the farm ute, Drew led the way towards the garage and his white four-wheel drive. They'd be more comfortable with the stronger air-conditioning. Freya gave Bailey a farewell pat before climbing into the passenger seat.

Silence settled between them until they reached the tar road. As they passed a neighbour's mailbox entwined with red tinsel Freya turned to get a better look.

'What a great idea. Hattie would love to decorate your mailbox.'

Drew looked away from where a chaser bin moved in tandem with a red header to catch the golden flow of grain. The unharvested wheat rippled as a breeze danced by. The unseasonable spring rain had resulted in bumper crops right across the fertile Bell River valley.

'I'm sure she would. I'll see if I can get some tinsel while in town.'

'It's fine. I have plenty and in lots of colours.'

He sent her a quick look which she met with a smile.

'No, I'm not a crazy hoarder. I just like Christmas.'

'I didn't say a word.'

She laughed softly. 'You didn't have to. Just be warned your mailbox is going to be very sparkly very soon.'

He nodded, fighting to keep his expression from changing. Freya's husky laughter reached inside and thawed places he'd never known were frozen.

She looked out the window as they passed a windmill decorated in rainbow woollen scarfs. There was a reason Woodlea was called the town of windmills. The closer they got to town the more circular blades they'd see spinning in the wind.

'I can't wait to see what the guerrilla knitters do next. I wonder what they'll do to Main Street for Christmas?'

He too glanced at the colourful windmill. 'I have no idea but whatever they do the tourists will love. The yarn bombers have been great for business.'

'They've also been good for the kids. I've had students ask me to teach them to knit and crochet and it's been so nice to get them off their electronic devices.'

'Hattie showed me the scarf she's knitting me for Christmas.'

'It's coming along really well.' She paused to look at him. 'I hope it's okay to ask … sometimes she asks me things and I'm not sure of the answer … but how did you know Hattie's parents?'

'It's fine. I'm happy to fill in the blanks. Brett was my best mate. We went away to school in Sydney together, then when my parents died in a light plane crash while I was at university his family looked out for me.'

'I'm so sorry to hear about your mum and dad.'

The care and concern in Freya's quiet voice had him meet her gaze. Sadness made her eyes appear more grey than blue.

'Thanks.'

'Do you have any cousins or other family you spend Christmas with?'

'No. My father was an only child like me. He met my mother when he went on an agricultural exchange to Canada so my mother's family are all over there. I usually went to Brett's for Christmas.' He risked another glance at Freya, knowing if she looked close enough she'd see the rawness of his grief. 'What about you?'

'It's just my father and my sister. My mother died of stomach cancer when I was at school. My father's overseas this year for Christmas and my sister's spending it with her fiancé's family. I'm welcome to go there too but ... I want to spend the holiday season here.' A small smile twisted her mouth. 'I'm not sure what the rumour mill said about me coming out west but I'm guessing there are many conspiracy theories.'

'Just a few.'

As he'd hoped, his light tone eased the shadows in Freya's eyes. He guessed she hadn't enjoyed being in the public spotlight.

'The truth, and the short version, is that I was engaged to a man I should never have believed I'd be happy with. He cheated on me last Christmas so I accepted the first job that would take me as far away as possible.'

'He was a fool.' He made no attempt to hide the disgust edging his words. Freya was special. Any man should have treasured and valued the relationship he had with her.

'Yes, he was.' The composure in her reply signalled she'd moved on. 'Even though I was devastated, it actually was a blessing as we weren't compatible. So here I am very happy to be in the bush, and even happier being single, with no plans to change my relationship status anytime soon.'

'I second that.' Drew grimaced. 'Even if Edna thinks I'd make Bethany a perfect husband.'

Freya's soft laughter wrapped around him.

He slowed as they reached the Woodlea town limits. After making plans to meet at the Windmill Café in an hour, Drew dropped Freya outside the craft shop. Knitted woollen stars and candy canes adorned the lampposts along Main Street. The yarn bombers were already dressing the town in the red, white and green of Christmas.

With a sweet smile and a wave, Freya disappeared into the craft shop. Drew's gaze lingered on the doorway. Even with the faint scent of flowers reminding him that Freya would soon again be beside him, the passenger seat felt too empty.

For the next sixty minutes he focused on running errands, collecting the header tyre and doing a grocery shop. When he entered the Windmill Café, Freya sat at a corner table chatting to the shop assistant, Sally.

When the university student saw him she gave him a cheeky grin. He knew full well his name around town was dashing and distant Drew, a fact confirmed by it being six months since he'd last called in for a coffee. He usually didn't come to Woodlea to socialise.

'Hi, Sal.'

'Hi, Drew. Your usual?' Her smile grew teasing. 'I think I can remember what it is.'

'I'll be happy with anything as long as it has caffeine in it.'

Sally giggled. 'I know, it's harvest time. I'll make you a takeaway.' She smiled at Freya. 'Your usual too?'

'Yes, please.'

Drew had only just slid into a seat when the door opened and the distinctive smell of overpowering perfume alerted him to who had entered.

'I thought it was you, Drew,' Edna Galloway said, voice higher-pitched than usual as she bustled over. 'I can't believe I've finally caught you in town.' She looked at the spare chair between Freya and Drew. 'May I?'

Without waiting for a reply she sat and waved at Sally. 'I'll have my usual, dear. Oh, and a piece of your caramel slice. Dr Fliss isn't here to see what I eat. My cholesterol's just fine.'

Drew didn't miss the smile tugging at Freya's lips before she spoke. 'Edna, you know you can't hide if you haven't been eating properly. Your next lot of blood test results won't lie.'

Edna sighed. 'Freya, you're always so … sensible. Sorry, Sally, hold that slice order.' She turned to him, her blue gaze sharp. 'Now, Drew, about coming for dinner …'

Sally brought over his coffee and two hot chocolates which granted him a brief reprieve from Edna's matchmaking. Sally's sympathetic glance suggested she'd made their order as fast as she could.

Before Edna's focus could zero back in on him, Freya smiled gently. 'Edna, I'm so glad I've seen you as I've something I'd like your expert opinion on.'

Drew hid a grin as he took a swallow of coffee. He could add diplomacy to Freya's considerable list of skills.

Edna's hand fluttered over her chest with false modesty. 'Of course. Ask away. I'll be happy to help.'

'This Christmas will be tough for Hattie, as well as the Reedy Creek and Woodlea communities, and I've been trying to think of a way to lift everyone's spirits.'

Edna nodded.

'I wonder if something like a mailbox decorating competition might be fun? There's only two weeks before Christmas but it will be enough. We could have different categories like best light display, most creative, most rural, best decorated, so that way there's a few prizes given out to reward people's efforts.'

Edna's smile contained real warmth. She patted Freya's hand. 'That's such a good idea. I already know some businesses who'd be happy to donate a prize. And it goes without saying, I'd be the best person to judge the contestants.'

Drew spoke while he could get a word in. 'I'd be happy to also contribute a prize.'

Freya's smile thanked him more than her words could have.

Edna got to her feet, her takeaway cup in her hand. When there was a crisis or event to be organised, there wasn't any better person than Edna.

'Right. Leave this to me. I've got donations to collect. Freya, I'll call you tonight to finalise details but I'd like to make a formal announcement in the *Woodlea News* tomorrow. The sooner people get decorating the better.'

Freya stood to hug Edna. 'Thank you.'

The surprise widening Edna's eyes confirmed she wasn't used to being on the receiving end of such a gesture. 'You're welcome.'

Drew came to his feet.

As Freya stepped away, Edna looked between the two of them, her eyes narrowing.

'Freya, you'll be happy to know I spoke to the builder working on your house and he said you'll be able to move back in by the end of the week.' The high-wattage smile she beamed towards Drew made his teeth clench. 'I said to Mrs Knox when I saw you at the ball last spring that the time would come when you'd realise you can't work all the time. Freya will soon be gone and you'll be all alone in that huge house of yours, so I'll make sure my Bethany calls around. How does Monday sound?'

Chapter 3

'I missed you too,' Freya said between laughter as Bailey did a happy dance around her.

She shifted the box balanced on her hip to a more secure position. The way the young kelpie bounced as though he'd scoffed too many red jelly beans meant she was likely to trip over him. She carefully made her way along the paved garden path. Afternoon shadows dappled the lawn and the heat had lessened but it wouldn't truly be cool until the moon had risen.

After giving the liver-coloured kelpie a last pat, she used the spare key to unlock the kitchen door. She returned the key to the left boot of the pair that sat on the rack at the back door. From the age and style of the boots, she guessed they'd been Drew's father's.

She checked the messages that had accumulated on her mobile while she'd taught her first Christmas craft class. It had been a fun afternoon filled with laughter and friendship. Hattie had sat next to eight-year-old Zoe and they'd swapped pony stories while making their felt Christmas tree decorations. Zoe was a leukaemia survivor and displayed a wisdom and empathy beyond her years.

Freya's first message was from her builder. Despite his reassurances to Edna, his words confirmed there was no way Freya could move back in until the new year. The supplies he needed wouldn't be available until after the Christmas break.

She listened to three more messages and when she was done dialled Fliss's number.

'Hi, Freya, how did your craft class go?'

'Really good. We had a table full of people, young and old, and when we weren't making a mess, we were eating. Taylor brought a gingerbread brownie that I'm sure I ate half my body weight in.'

Fliss laughed. 'I'll have to ask her for the recipe. Speaking of all things sweet, and not so sweet, I called earlier to say thank you. Sal said you came between Edna and a piece of caramel slice.'

'Let's just say a gentle reminder about logical consequences can work as well with adults as it does with kids.'

'I'll have to remember that. Give me a stubborn, hard-headed and risk-taking cowboy any day. I can't seem to get through to Edna.'

'You'd be surprised how much she does listen to you. If she didn't, she'd still have eaten the slice.'

'Maybe. Ever since I supposedly dumped Rodger at school I haven't exactly been her favourite person.'

'Yes, the day I met her, she did happen to mention you broke her son's heart when you were both twelve. She also said it was Woodlea's lucky day when you decided to return to town.'

'Really?'

'Yes, really, and she meant it. But don't worry, I've joined you in her so-called bad books. She hasn't come out and directly said anything, but she doesn't approve of me staying with Drew.'

'No, she wouldn't. It's not that she'd think your reputation's at risk. The whole district knows Drew's a gentleman like his father. It's just that she's been biding her time waiting for a sign that Drew's ready for a social life again. His invitation to have you stay could be seen as proof he's realised there's more to life than his precious cows.' Fliss paused and when she spoke her tone had lowered. 'Freya … don't worry about Bethany. She isn't Drew's type.'

Heat filled Freya's cheeks and she was glad this wasn't a video call. There was no point misunderstanding what Fliss had said. Fliss's intelligent hazel eyes saw too much. When she'd come to the school Christmas concert, Freya had felt Fliss's gaze on her when she'd briefly talked to Drew. 'Thanks. I won't.'

'Great. Drew's one of the good guys.' To Freya's relief, Fliss changed the subject. 'Your mailbox idea has caught on. Apparently the grocery store has sold out of tinsel.'

'That's wonderful.'

'It is. Now before I go, don't forget Christmas lunch is at Cressy's and, if you can, bring Drew. We'd love to see him.'

'Will do. I'll mention it. Talk to you soon.'

Freya ended the call and stared at her phone. Why had Fliss reassured her that Bethany wasn't Drew's type? Was it so obvious he intrigued her?

Indecision held her still. Now that she knew her house wouldn't be habitable again until after Christmas, should she continue to stay? Self-preservation warred with practicality. Drew already affected her far more than he should and she wasn't the only one to have noticed. The sensible thing would be to remove the risk to her heart by leaving.

But her conscience wouldn't allow her to go. Drew had offered her a bed when she'd needed one. He'd given Panda a home so Hattie wouldn't have to part with her childhood pony. He didn't deserve to be by himself at Christmas. She hadn't missed the loss etched on his face when he'd talked about Hattie's parents and his own. If it still suited him, she'd remain at Inglewood.

By the time Bailey and Panda were fed and the aroma of roast chicken filled the kitchen, shades of crimson and gold streaked the sky. The engine of Drew's farm ute sounded and Freya glanced at the kitchen clock. He was home a little earlier today. He entered the kitchen, his royal blue work shirt and jeans dusty and a streak of grease on his cheek. She glanced away before the tight stretch of his shirt made her pulse race. She didn't need any reminder of the hard-packed contours that lay below.

He set the esky on the bench with a tired grin.

'Inglewood's harvest's officially done.'

'That's great news.' She crossed the kitchen to collect the bottle of wine she'd sat on the bench the night she arrived. 'I think that calls for a celebration. You get your life back.'

The corner of his mouth kicked into a grin. 'I do ... for a day or two. We then start harvest on the other farm. But I'll still drink to being finished here. Well ... I will as soon as I'm clean.'

It wasn't long until he returned, his dark hair shower-damp, feet bare and wearing worn jeans and a black T-shirt. The woody scent of his aftershave seduced her senses and she fought to keep her appreciation from showing as she placed two wine glasses on the bench. It hadn't mattered how expensive Charles's cologne had been, it had never made her toes curl.

She glanced at the kitchen table and only realised her brow had furrowed when Drew stopped uncorking the wine bottle to look at her.

'I'm guessing you haven't eaten yet. It's okay. We don't need to sit at the table, the bench will be fine.'

She hoped her nod didn't communicate her relief. Sitting around a bench would be far less intimate and formal than sitting across the table from each other. 'Sounds good to me.'

The wine was poured and chicken and vegetables heaped onto two white plates. Drew sat on the other side of the island bench,

leaving a wide space between them. Before he ate, he lifted his glass
to clink against Freya's.

'Thanks again for the wine and also for dinner. My stomach's
not going to appreciate going back to my own cooking next week.'

'You're welcome.' She took a sip of wine. 'It turns out I won't be
able to move back home in a hurry. My builder left a message with
the bad news this afternoon.'

Drew's casual expression didn't change. 'Stay as long as you like.
Not that I'd tell Edna, but I've enjoyed having some company and
I know Bailey and Panda have too.'

As relaxed as Drew's words were, his tight hold on his cutlery
suggested he wasn't as comfortable as he appeared.

'Are you sure? The only thing is I mightn't be able to move back
until the new year.'

'It's all good. I'll just be working.' Drew sliced off a piece of
chicken before his eyes searched hers. 'That's if you want to stay
until then? I understand if you'd rather go elsewhere.'

There was just something, a faint rasp in his words, a flicker of
darkness in his eyes that reassured her she'd made the right decision.
It wasn't right for him to be alone over Christmas with only his
grief for company.

'No, there's nowhere else. I'd like to stay.' She smiled. 'Besides,
Hattie and I haven't decorated your mailbox yet. Now everyone's
getting into the Christmas spirit, we also might have to go a little
bigger than planned.'

He groaned. 'Go bigger? As in what the Knoxes have done to
their mailbox and front entrance? There's hay bales made to look
like reindeer and fairy lights strung everywhere.'

'Exactly.' She didn't try to hide the enthusiasm in her voice. 'But
if Woodlea's already out of tinsel it's not looking good for finding
what we need to go big.'

To Freya's surprise he set his knife and fork on his plate and came to his feet. A smile lit his eyes. 'I have something to show you that might help with your go-big vision.'

For a second she thought he'd hold out his hand to help her manoeuvre herself off the high stool. But then he slid his hands deep into his jeans pockets and turned away.

'Where are we going?' She wriggled off the seat to follow him along the hallway and into the west wing.

'You'll see,' he said over his shoulder.

He stopped in front of a door.

'You know how I said my mother was Canadian?'

Freya nodded.

'Well, you both have something in common.'

He opened the door.

'She too loved Christmas.'

If Drew had been an artist he would have captured the moment Freya's face registered the room before her was filled floor-to-ceiling with Christmas items.

Golden reindeers sat in open boxes, ornaments filled clear storage tubs and wreaths hung from hooks along the picture rails.

'No way,' she breathed.

He nodded and braced himself should she hug him like she'd done to Edna. There was a joyous brightness to her eyes as she turned to smile at him. Instinct warned him that having Freya in his arms once would never be enough.

But instead of hugging him she stepped into the room and placed her hands on her cheeks. 'There's … so … much … stuff.'

'That's why this room's known as the Christmas room.' He touched the head of a nearby Santa Claus. 'It was always my mother's favourite time of year and she went all out to celebrate.' He reached for a red box decorated in gold scrolls. 'Much to my teenage embarrassment.' He removed the lid and took out a photo. 'At twelve Fliss might have been dumping Rodger, but I was still having photos taken with Santa.'

Freya laughed softly. She leaned in close to see the picture nestled in the ornate frame. Her sweet floral scent replaced the mustiness of a room whose door hadn't been opened in years. 'You look so … solemn.'

'That's a nice way of describing my expression … I think a more apt word would have been scowl. Needless to say, if Mum had the photo out and Brett was coming over to ride motorbikes, I'd hide it.'

Freya stared at the picture. 'You know … the scowl doesn't reach your eyes. I think what this photo says is that you loved your mum and wanted to make her happy.'

'Yes. I did.'

Freya touched his hand where he held the frame. 'There's nothing wrong with that.'

Then before he could examine her expression, she moved away to run her fingers over the snowy roofline of a gingerbread house. 'Many of these things are too good to use outside. Maybe I could decorate the living room and put up the tree I can see over in the corner? We can then put our presents for Hattie under there?'

'That's a good idea. It's been so long since anything was used … Feel free to decorate more than just the living room.' He dipped his head towards a box of Christmas lights. 'I have a camping generator that could provide power for anything we might want to use for the mailbox display.'

The smile she flashed at him was so beautiful it dazzled him more than any string of fairy lights. '*We?*'

'Yes. If there's one thing my mother taught me, it's never say no to a woman wearing a poinsettia apron and whose arms are full of tinsel.'

'I would have liked your mother.'

Drew turned to hide how much Freya's words moved him. With her generous heart and empathy, his parents would have liked her too.

'We'd better finish eating. I just wanted to show you what's here so you won't have to worry about not having enough decorations.'

As they ate, and their wine glasses were emptied, they discussed plans for the front entrance. Every so often Freya would glance down the hallway and he knew she couldn't wait to take a closer look at the Christmas room.

When Freya rested her fork and knife together he collected their plates and carried them over to the dishwasher.

'I'll bring in a ladder from the shed. Give me a yell if there's anything you still can't reach.'

'Will do. I take it you'll be over there doing whatever secret men's business Cressy says happens in sheds and usually takes hours.'

He didn't know if it was the wine or the way Freya's teasing eyes held his, but his man-cave was the last place he wanted to be. 'Yes, I'll make a start on the jobs I need to do over the next two days so I have some time to help you and Hattie decorate the mailbox.'

Freya smoothed wisps of loose hair behind her ear. 'Anything I can help you with?'

He smothered the urge to reach over and slide his hands through her heavy hair. The need to set it free so it tumbled over her shoulders kept him awake at night. 'No, thanks. Many of the jobs are just maintenance to make sure we're harvest-ready, like blowing down the header with the air compressor to reduce the fire risk.'

'Okay.' She rubbed her palms together, smile wide. 'I'll leave you to have fun in the shed and I'll get busy seeing what treasures are hiding in your mother's special room.'

It was only when an owl disturbed the silence that Drew realised how late it was. He should have known he'd lost track of time when Bailey headed off to his kennel beneath the old plane tree. Drew turned off the shed light and stepped outside. Stars glittered overhead, their pinpricks of light reminding him of the star-shaped fairy lights that would soon illuminate his front gate.

The temperature had dropped and a stiff breeze delved beneath his shirt collar. He slowed his stride to enjoy the respite from the summer heat. A frog croaked from over near the rainwater tank. He wasn't the only one making the most of the cool darkness before the sun rose.

Restlessness coursed through him, along with an unfamiliar reluctance to spend the new day working like he normally did. He'd only ever wanted to follow in his father's and grandfather's footsteps. He was happiest out in the paddocks, mustering his cattle or fixing machinery in his shed. Inglewood had sustained him these past years but now something felt … missing. Maybe Edna was right, maybe he did need a social life?

The kitchen lights were off when he entered, but even in the gloom he could see the shimmer of red tinsel and the glitter of gold. His steps slowed. He hadn't realised how much he'd missed seeing the house reflect his mother's love for all things Christmas. While driving the header, and even fixing the windmill, his father's quiet presence was embedded in the memories of when they'd worked side by side. But his connection to his mother hadn't felt as strong. Until tonight.

A scrape echoed down the hallway and drew him towards the living room. The wash of light beyond the doorway said Freya was still awake. He walked through the doorway and stopped. It wasn't the explosion of Christmas items that held him still, but the woman with her back to him.

A woman who wore a pair of grey pyjamas that were little more than shorts and a singlet top. A woman whose long red hair fell down her back to the sweet curve of her waist. A woman who was so beautiful it made his chest ache.

He went to back away but the slight movement had her swinging around, eyes wide. Her hand splayed across her chest. 'You startled me. I thought you'd gone to bed.'

'Sorry.' He hesitated before continuing into the room. 'I've just finished in the shed.'

From the front, Freya was all full curves and large eyes, with a mass of tousled hair. The thin straps of her top showcased the delicate jut of her collarbones and the flawless sweep of her porcelain skin. He fixed his attention on the ladder he'd brought over earlier and not on the way her top dipped low at the front.

'I'm guessing the ladder came in handy?'

Even to his own ears his voice emerged husky.

'It has.' Freya hid a yawn. 'I did go to bed but then got up to open one more box. I'll put on the Christmas angel and call it a night.'

He nodded, studying the tree that was decorated in a white and silver theme. Whenever he glanced at Freya, he had trouble keeping his gaze away from her mouth.

Without looking at him, she took hold of the angel dressed in a fake fur-trimmed robe and scooted up the ladder. As Freya stretched to reach the tree, her top lifted to reveal the smooth skin of her lower back. She sighed. 'It's times like this I wish I wasn't so vertically challenged.'

He stepped forward to anchor his left hand on the ladder. 'I can put the angel on?'

'No, it's fine.' Determination firmed Freya's lips. 'It's almost in place.'

As she spoke her fingers slipped and the angel tilted. She grabbed for the top of the ladder as her balance wavered.

Without thought Drew placed his right hand on her hip to steady her. Instead of the thin cotton of her singlet, his fingers encountered satin-soft flesh.

'Thanks.' Her cheeks flushed. 'I'm not going to bed until this is on.'

Drew only nodded. Beneath one palm he felt the cold, hard steel of the ladder. Beneath his other hand, he could feel Freya's soft warmth and the way her fine muscles rippled as she stretched even further.

She spoke through gritted teeth. 'Is now a good time to admit I do have some obsessive tendencies, like finishing what I start?'

Despite the tightness of his jaw, he smiled. 'I'd never have guessed.'

As the angel slipped into place, he released the breath he'd been holding. Freya moved down a step and when he was sure she was stable, he removed his hand. Cool air replaced the heat of her skin. He folded his arms to prove to his testosterone he wasn't touching her again, even if mistletoe hung beside them.

She stopped on the step that allowed her eyes to be level with his. In the grey-blue depths he saw a smile as well as an indefinable emotion. Colour continued to paint her cheeks.

'That was close. If I'd fallen I could have ended up in the emergency department. I'd prefer Dr Fliss didn't know ladders and I aren't always compatible.'

'So you've almost come off second best before?'

Smile sheepish, she moved down another two steps. 'A time or three. I blame my father for my sometimes single-mindedness. There's a reason why he's on his own at Christmas in Salzburg embracing his Mozart obsession. Just like why my doctoral thesis was on the social assimilation of high-functioning Asperger's children in

the mainstream classroom. My sister and I might have inherited our
mother's red hair but there's still a little of our father in us.'

'Which is understandable. I inherited my dad's workaholic gene.
So you're Dr Freya?'

'Yes.' She descended the last step and the tension locking his
shoulders eased when her mouth moved out of kissing distance.
'But no one knows. I'm also a little obsessive about just being seen
as Miss George. My hair colour already draws enough attention and
I'd prefer not to be singled out.'

'Your secret's safe with me.'

'Thanks.' She stifled another yawn. 'That's why I told you. Now
I'd better get to bed.'

She made no move to leave. Her gaze dropped to his mouth and
when her eyes again met his, he knew what the emotion was that
he'd seen earlier. Uncertainty. Vulnerability.

He wasn't the only one experiencing the intensity of their
connection or feeling out of their depth. He reached out to cup her
jaw and to reassure her.

'Yes, you had, Dr Freya. It's bedtime for you, you're almost asleep
on your feet.' His thumb brushed the petal-softness of her cheek
before he lowered his hand. 'Sleep tight. I'll see you tomorrow for
some more Christmas chaos.'

She nodded, her gaze steady and her irises a clear grey.

'Night.'

He stayed where he was until he could no longer hear her
footsteps, then he dragged his hands through his hair. He didn't
care about the cool night breeze that rippled across the pool, he
needed a cold swim.

Chapter 4

The call of a too-cheerful kookaburra penetrated Freya's deep sleep. It couldn't be morning yet. She pushed the bedsheet away from her chin and, eyes closed, used her fingers to rake hair away from her face.

Her exhaustion had nothing to do with staying up late to decorate the Christmas tree. Thoughts of Drew had stolen her sleep. Everything had changed. Last night there'd been a recognition that something sparked between them. There'd also been physical contact. She opened her heavy eyelids and frowned at the white ceiling.

Drew touching her had been so much more than a physical connection. His firm, strong hold on her hip said he wouldn't let her fall. The gentle, tender brush of his thumb across her cheek reassured her he wasn't a man out to hurt her. And with two such simple messages, the armour had fallen away from around her heart.

She was supposed to not trust a man again. She was supposed to be protecting herself from heartbreak. But when it came to Drew she was already heading down the smitten path. And she had to do a U-turn, both for herself and for him. Grief still held Drew tight within its grasp. What he needed this holiday season wasn't complications, just friendship. He was already in the crosshairs of

Edna's matchmaking. So as much as Freya's hormones disagreed, she'd do the sensible thing and make sure things remained platonic between them.

She flipped the sheet off her legs and cold air rushed over her skin. The thermostat in the air-conditioner had switched the wall unit on. It was going to be another scorcher or she was awake later than usual. She grabbed a lightweight white robe that fitted in well with the dreamy guestroom. A white wrought-iron bed had been paired with a soft rose-pink wingback chair and curtains. She'd taken photos on her phone the night she'd arrived. One day she'd like a room just like this.

The floorboards were cool beneath her bare feet. Usually when she went for breakfast she'd showered, dressed and her hair had been tamed. But after Drew seeing her in her pyjamas last night, there was no point maintaining her polished image.

She stepped into the large kitchen and discovered the room empty. The aroma of fresh coffee and bacon and eggs confirmed she'd overslept. A note stuck to the fridge said there was bacon warming in the oven and asked if she'd like to go for a ride before the day heated up.

She bit her lip. The rational choice was to stay inside and continue decorating. Her attention strayed to the rural view through the window above the sink. The green of the lawn gave way to rolling paddocks, framed by hills that backed onto a distant high ridge. A tree line meandered through the golden wheat stubble. Since she'd arrived she'd planned to take a walk to the river. In the still of dusk she often heard the calls of cockatoos and saw the glitter of white as they flew amongst the red river gums.

She slipped on the bear-themed Christmas oven mitt that read *Have a Beary Christmas*. The need to feel the wind on her face trumped any need for self-preservation. It felt like a lifetime since she'd experienced the freedom of being in the saddle. Charles had never understood her love of horses or her appreciation for all things country. She'd once taken him to the Royal Easter Show and he'd ended up at the bar with a university friend while she'd walked around the showground. She opened the oven door. She'd have a quick breakfast, shower and see Drew to accept his offer.

After breakfast, dressed in jeans, boots and an emerald work shirt, she headed over to the shed. As she walked, she settled a broad-brimmed cream felt hat on her head. The practical hat had been the first thing she'd bought in Woodlea when she'd started her new life. The long-sleeved cotton green shirt the second. She'd plaited her hair and it slid over her shoulder as she bent to pat Bailey, who'd slid to a stop in front of her.

'Morning, Mr Hypo.'

The kelpie's exuberant wiggles never failed to make her smile. After he'd had his normal morning pat, he dashed over to the shed. Freya followed, her steps slowing as she drew a calming breath. She was as bad as Bailey. The thought of seeing Drew made adrenaline zip through her.

He looked up from where he stood working at a bench. For a moment his eyes remained grave and then he smiled. 'I take it that it's a yes for riding.'

'Yes, please.' She wasn't sure but she thought a muscle worked in his jaw as his gaze swept over her. 'If it's not too late.'

He wiped the grease from his hands with an oily rag. 'It's all good. If we get going now we'll still beat the midday heat.'

It wasn't long before Drew had the horse gear loaded in the back of the farm ute and Freya had packed shortbread and water bottles for their saddle bags. As they drove into the paddock beyond the house yard, in the side mirror Freya could see Bailey's happy grin as he rode on the trayback. The ute negotiated a ditch in the track and she grabbed the door handle as she was thrown about in her seat.

Drew shot her a quick grin. 'Sorry, grading the road again is on my after-harvest list.'

'I can imagine there's quite a few things on that list.' Freya glanced over her shoulder to check Bailey remained on the ute. The kelpie wagged his brown tail. 'Bailey doesn't mind. He thinks this is more fun than a show ride.'

Drew smiled and Freya snuck a sideways look. Apart from his seriousness when he saw her, he didn't appear to treat her any differently after what had happened last night.

'So where are we riding to?'

'I need to check the cattle and instead of driving around them, I thought we could ride. The horses could do with the exercise. They're starting to think they're nothing but paddock ornaments. If it doesn't get too hot we could also go down to the river.'

'That sounds wonderful.' She looked to where the track wound through a cluster of gum trees to a grazing paddock carpeted with thick, bleached grass. 'Panda would love it here.'

Drew chuckled. 'That's why he's back at the house. He has a history of laminitis so it's for his own good he's in a smaller paddock, especially in spring when the grass has a high sugar content. Since he's arrived, he's slimmed down, lost his cresty neck and his feet haven't given him any trouble. Ella's pleased.'

'I bet Hattie is too, she can ride him more.'

'Exactly. The plan is for her to be confident enough to go on the mountain trail ride next year.' Drew glanced at Freya. 'I spoke to Hattie's Aunt Cath and Hattie's at Alice's today so will come over tomorrow to help decorate the mailbox.'

'Great. I'll keep thinking about more things we can do.'

Drew raised a dark brow. 'More?'

'Yes. I know we came up with a few ideas over dinner, and even though we're not entering to win any prizes, our display has to be spectacular. Hattie doesn't deserve anything less.'

Drew nodded as they reached a double set of steel gates.

'I'll open them,' she said, unclipping her seatbelt before he could lower his hand from the steering wheel to release his belt.

She swung the left gate open and looked around for the horses. All she could see was a group of grey kangaroos dozing beneath the spreading canopy of a gum tree. She smiled and breathed in the scents of dust, warm earth and eucalyptus. Above her the sky stretched in a brilliant blue, while over in the tops of the distant river red gums white cockatoos gleamed. Bailey barked and wagged his tail as the ute drove by.

Drew's gaze lingered as she slid into the passenger seat, and she realised she was still smiling.

'You look like you like it out here.' His tone sounded quiet, deep.

'I do. The colours are so vivid and the air's so fresh. I might be a city girl but I've always had a country heart.' She angled the air-conditioning vent a little more towards her. 'Even if the heat makes me feel like a snowman about to melt.'

As if she'd answered an unspoken question, Drew grinned before he parked the ute beneath a nearby box tree.

He left the driver's seat and his whistle sounded. Even before Freya had her door open, two brown shapes flashed to the left. Hooves pounded as the horses topped the rise and thundered over, their black manes and tails lifting in the wind.

The bay mare slowed to a trot as she drew near, while the larger gelding bucked and flung his head high. Freya remained standing by the ute. It wasn't fear that held her still as the gelding reached Drew, but Drew's expression as the horse nuzzled his hands.

Just like when he was around Hattie, the darkness in his eyes ebbed and the tension that chiselled grooves beside his mouth eased. Again Freya could see the open, warm-hearted man beneath his reserve. A man capable of feeling deep emotion. Freya swallowed and looked away. A man she was supposed to be insulating her heart against.

'How are you going with Liberty's girth?' Drew asked as he pulled Ace's girth one hole tighter.

He made sure he didn't look across to where Freya was saddling the mare. When she'd entered the shed dressed in fitted jeans, boots and wearing her hat, his hard-won self-control had slipped. Last night, when her heavy hair had hung down her back and her pyjamas had revealed more than they hid, he'd been thrown. But seeing her as a country girl winded him far more than a kick from the wild steers Brett had bought to trade last spring. Today Freya looked right at home in his world.

'All good now she's not inflating like a party balloon.'

Drew nodded. Freya had put on Liberty's bridle and saddle with quick and efficient movements showing she more than knew her way around horses. She now led the stockhorse around one way and then the other to make sure the girth didn't pinch.

Chest tight, Drew walked Ace over to where Freya readied herself to mount Liberty. That Freya clearly enjoyed and had adapted to bush life didn't bring him any relief. All it did was stir long-buried yearnings and dreams that had no place in his workaholic world. It was bad enough he'd indulged his restlessness by taking time off this morning to ride. Inglewood had to remain his sole focus.

Freya held the stirrups up to measure them against her arm. Once their lengths had been adjusted, she gathered the reins in her left hand. She hesitated. Drew could understand why. Liberty was over fifteen hands high and Freya wasn't particularly tall.

'Here.' He looped Ace's reins over his neck. The placid gelding would stay where he was. 'I'll give you a leg up.'

'Thanks. My flexible days are long gone. I don't even think I could get my boot in the stirrup.'

She bent her left leg as he closed the distance between them.

'Okay.' He placed a hand on her knee and another on her ankle. 'After three. One … two … three.'

Freya jumped at the same time he hoisted her upwards. She laughed as she almost flew over the other side of Liberty.

Against the cloudless sky, Freya's irises shone blue as she settled herself into the saddle and slid the toes of her boots into the stirrups. 'I don't think you'll have any trouble moving those hay bales we need for the mailbox makeover.'

'That's what the hay fork on the tractor is for.' He chuckled as he swung into Ace's saddle. When he was around Freya, the burden of his grief didn't press quite so hard. 'I have a feeling my back isn't up to the challenge. I'm certain the amount of bales we need since we last spoke have doubled.'

Freya just smiled.

He led the way through the trees to a gate that would allow them to enter the cattle paddock. Liberty fell into step beside Ace. The relaxed way Freya held her reins and the curve of her mouth all communicated how happy she was to be back on a horse. She wasn't the only one enjoying the ride. Bailey loped beside them, his ears pricked and amber eyes bright.

Drew opened the single gate from Ace's saddle and before long they rode around Inglewood's prized breeding herd. He kept a close eye on the young kelpie but Bailey showed no sign of dashing after either a cow or a kangaroo.

Drew studied the cattle around them. While mothers rested in the shade and chewed their cuds, calves hung together in small groups. All were doing well on the grazing oats crop.

He glanced at Freya as she watched two calves play beneath a tree. Red dust lifted as the calves butted heads, the larger calf determined to push the younger calf backwards.

'Your father might like Mozart, but my father and grandfather liked Red Angus cattle. Around here Black Angus cattle are more popular, but I confess I also have a soft spot for Red Angus.'

'I like them too. Their colour looks ... familiar.' She dipped her head to where a lone cow grazed not far from the calves and appeared to be the designated babysitter. 'I feel like I'm back at school and that poor cow is on playground duty.'

Once they'd ridden around the paddock, Drew glanced at Freya to see how she was holding up. Despite the wide brim of her hat, her cheeks were pink from the strength of the sun.

'We can either head back or keep going to the river.'

She answered without hesitation. 'If you have time, can we go to the river, please?'

He turned Ace towards the line of red river gums to hide his pleasure and his respect that she wanted to keep riding despite the heat. 'Sure.'

Soon the hills gentled into the alluvial flats of the valley floor. The green of the oats gave way to the golden hue of wheat stubble before the land dropped away to where the Bell River flowed. Drew followed a narrow animal-made trail that would take them the easy and safe way down the steep bank.

Once under the shade of the ancient trees, their mottled bark swirled with shades of brown, the temperature cooled. The raucous calls of cockatoos echoed overhead as the birds took flight. Bailey was the first into the river, his liver-coloured coat turning dark as he swam and lapped at the water.

The horse's hooves clattered on the pebbles as they walked side-by-side into the shallows to drink. Drew opened his saddle bag and handed Freya a water bottle and a slice of shortbread.

'Thanks.'

The pale skin of her throat moved as she drank. She passed him the water bottle before she unwrapped the shortbread. While she ate, her attention focused on the high ridge beyond the riverbank.

'I bet the view's stunning from up there.'

'It is, but that's a ride for a cooler day.'

Her eyes met his. 'After harvest?'

He nodded and couldn't let go of the feeling he'd just agreed to far more than a second ride.

Freya snapped photos on her phone while the horses and Bailey continued to splash and play in the river. When Ace's front hoof pawed the water, Drew headed him towards the shore. The gelding was notorious for rolling and despite the heat he had no desire to get wet.

They left the cool of the river and retraced their steps, keeping their pace slow but steady.

One minute Liberty was walking beside Ace as they re-entered the cattle paddock and the next she'd stumbled. From the corner of his eye he saw Freya struggle to remain in the saddle. Heart pounding, he twisted in the saddle and turned Ace. Freya might end up in the Woodlea Hospital emergency department yet. Her bones would be no match for the hard summer-baked ground.

As Liberty regained her footing, Freya righted herself, only to kick her feet free of the stirrups and slide to the ground. As Ace fully turned, Drew understood why. Liberty held her right front hoof off the ground. He too left the saddle.

Freya's wide eyes met his as she stroked the mare's neck. 'What happened?'

He glanced at the ground. Beneath the long grass, a rabbit had burrowed a hollow the perfect size to catch a horse's hoof.

'Rabbit hole.'

He ran his hand down Liberty's leg, over her knee and past her fetlock to her hoof. There wasn't yet any heat or swelling, but they would soon come. He straightened to loosen the mare's girth and to strip off her saddle and saddlecloth to make her cooler.

'Come on, Lib, let's see if we can get you over to the shade and I'll be back with the horse float.'

Freya stepped away as the mare hobbled the short distance to the gum tree, her head bobbing as she took slow steps. When the cool shade covered her, he removed her bridle. She wouldn't be going anywhere. He draped the bridle over the saddle Freya had rested against the tree trunk. Bailey flopped on the ground beside the stock saddle to watch them.

Freya smoothed her hand over the mare's shoulder. 'I'll stay until you get back.'

He shook his head. Heat shimmered around them and the sun's rays burned through the cotton of his faded red shirt. Freya's cheeks were now a deep pink.

'That's a good idea in theory, but it's too hot.' He rubbed Liberty's favourite spot high on her neck. 'She's a sensible old thing and will be fine.'

'I'll have my water bottle.'

'Freya, I've had sunstroke and I wouldn't forgive myself if you ended up with it too.'

She frowned and glanced at Liberty's hoof that she rested on the ground but didn't put any weight on. 'Okay. I won't waste time arguing. The sooner we get going the sooner we can get her home and Ella can look at her.' Freya's eyes locked with his. 'I am coming back with you.'

'Of course.' He collected Ace's reins. 'Ready?'

He knew the moment she realised he intended for her to ride on Ace with him back to the ute. Indecision flittered in her eyes before her chin lifted. 'Yes.'

He swung into the saddle and held out his hand. Freya locked her wrist around his and, using his foot for leverage, clambered up behind him. He thought she wasn't going to hold on to him but then her hands settled on his waist. He fought to keep his muscles relaxed so she wouldn't feel his reaction to her touch. His jaw clenched. Or how much he wanted her arms wrapped tight around him.

'All good?' he asked over his shoulder. Freya was so close the scent of flowers filled his lungs.

'Yes.'

Ace walked forwards, showing no sign that the addition of Freya's weight caused him any concern. Bailey trotted sedately by his side, his normal liveliness sapped by the heat.

Drew concentrated on scanning for any more rabbit holes and not on the way Freya's grip tightened as Ace increased his stride to a fast walk. His self-control hung by a single, rusted wire. The ride to the ute couldn't end quick enough.

Chapter 5

'Okay, cover your eyes.' Freya smiled as Hattie placed her small palms over her face. Freya pushed open the living room door. 'Open them.'

Hattie's gasp made all the hours Freya had spent decorating the large living room worth it. She'd wanted to bring a smile to Hattie's solemn face. She'd even lit a candle to fill the air with the scent of pine and hidden candy canes deep in the Christmas tree. The boxes filled with Christmas items Ella had helped lug to her car were proving invaluable.

Hattie rushed through the doorway to where Freya had set up a picturesque Christmas village. Freya moved to flick on the power. The village came to life. A miniature train circled an old station. A Santa in a sleigh flew in a small arc above an old-fashioned two-storey house. Lights twinkled and music played as a carousel spun. Hattie's eyes widened as she moved in close to see the details on the tiny horses. One of the ponies resembled black and white Panda.

The six-year-old went over to where Freya had clustered a family of golden reindeers.

'This one's my favourite.' Hattie touched the back of the baby reindeer.

Freya picked up the reindeer to hand to Hattie. 'I thought you'd say that. She can stay with you today if you like.'

Freya didn't hear any sound to indicate Drew had returned from the shed, but something made her look up.

He stood at the doorway. Her throat ached at the sombre darkness in his eyes as he surveyed the room. Hattie wasn't the only person missing their parents at Christmas. She too missed her mother, but she'd been able to make the most of what time she'd had left with her. Unlike Drew and Hattie.

When Hattie realised her godfather was there, she raced over to show him the reindeer. Excitement quickened her words. 'I'm playing with her all day. I'm going to call her …' The six-year-old gazed around until her attention fastened on the knee-high snowmen that jiggled when switched on. 'Snowy.'

'That's a great name.'

Freya snuck a sideways glance at Drew. She curled the fingers of her right hand into her palm to stop her awareness of him from showing. Fine sawdust covered his blue shirt and she caught the scent of wood. He'd spent the morning making Christmas trees out of old pallets. Stubble blurred his jawline and his hair sat in soft spikes from where he'd run his hand through the front after removing his farm cap.

Ever since he'd doubled her on Ace yesterday, his eyes hadn't held hers for as long as they usually did. And ever since she'd grasped his waist and felt the heat and power beneath his shirt, she'd been glad he didn't look at her too closely. The need to reach under his shirt and smooth her hands over the hard ridges below was fast becoming her new obsession.

His gaze briefly met hers. 'There are two trees at the back door ready for you and Hattie to decorate. I'll hose down Liberty's leg again and then can start on whatever project's next.'

Ella had visited yesterday afternoon and confirmed the stockhorse had pulled a tendon. With care, rest and time, the gentle mare would recover.

'Thanks. It's mainly the hay bales and lights we'll need help with.'

Hattie skipped over and handed Drew and Freya a candy cane each. 'Here you go.'

As Drew and Hattie grinned at each other and peeled away the plastic to eat the sweet peppermint, Freya slipped her candy cane into her pocket. So much for being level-headed and patching her composure. Seeing Drew's softness with Hattie still made her heart flutter. She busied herself with turning off the fairy lights and Christmas village.

Once Drew left to take care of Liberty's injury, Freya threw two old sheets over the floor in the laundry. Armed with a hot glue gun and boxes of red, green and gold Christmas balls, she and Hattie decorated the trees Drew had made. When they were installed at the front gate, they'd weave Christmas lights through the gaps between the pieces of recycled wood.

When the last ball had been glued in place, Freya sat back on her heels. 'That's it. I think we're done. Thank you for your help. They look good, don't they?'

Hattie failed to return Freya's smile. 'Yes.'

Freya moved to put her arm around her thin shoulders. The little girl's voice had emerged quiet and miserable.

'What's up, Hat? Are you missing your mum and dad?'

She slowly nodded.

Freya held her close. 'Just because they're not here this Christmas doesn't mean they're not still *here*.' She touched Hattie's forehead. 'And also here.' She pointed to Hattie's heart.

Hattie leaned against her as she nodded. Freya kissed the top of her head, which smelled of strawberry shampoo. Boots sounded on the veranda before the door opened. Hot air rushed in to invade the cool of the laundry. When Drew registered Hattie's sadness, his brow creased. His eyes met Freya's and an understanding passed between them. They needed to keep everything upbeat.

'Anyone for a swim?' he asked, voice cheerful.

'Sounds like a good idea to me. You and Hattie cool off, I'll find something for us to eat. Decorating trees has made me hungry.'

While Freya made a platter of sandwiches, she told herself she only stared through the window at Drew and Hattie to make sure the little girl didn't still look upset. From her squeals as she jumped off the diving board and splashed with Drew, Freya had no doubt she was having fun.

Despite her best intentions, her gaze kept returning to Drew. Tomorrow the house would be silent when harvest started again. Even if it had only been for two days, she'd enjoyed having him home as much as Bailey had. Drew's slow smile and companionship filled her with a contentment she'd never experienced in all her years with Charles. Drew picked up Hattie, his muscles flexing and rippling as he carefully threw her into the air. When Freya realised she'd put the cheese in the pantry and not in the fridge, she banned herself from looking in his direction again.

To her relief, Drew and Hattie soon left the pool. After the sandwiches disappeared, Drew headed back to the shed. It was too hot outside to decorate the mailbox so Freya put on an animated Christmas movie. Hattie snuggled against her side while they sat on the living room lounge. They'd only watched half the show when Hattie's soft breaths told Freya she was asleep.

Drew appeared at the doorway. Relief eased the concern in his dark-blue eyes when he saw Hattie sleeping.

'Thanks again for everything that you do for her,' he said, voice low.

'Anytime. She's a special little girl.'

'She is.' Drew glanced at the Christmas village on the far table. 'And thanks for setting all this up. It actually feels like Christmas this year.'

'It goes without saying I've had fun. I'm not sure what you've planned for Christmas lunch but Fliss says you're welcome to come to Cressy's too.'

Drew folded his arms. 'I think I'll just have a quiet day like I usually do.'

'If you change your mind let me know.'

Drew nodded and, with a last look at Hattie, left the room.

Freya bit the inside of her cheek. It was as though the shimmer of the living room dulled. The sheen of the golden reindeers appeared less bright. The glitter on the tree ornaments sparkled less. Christmas Day without Drew wouldn't feel like Christmas at all.

Air-conditioned air filled the tractor cabin along with the scent of peppermint. Freya had handed Drew and Hattie a candy cane before shutting the tractor door. Hattie had already finished hers and they hadn't even made it to the hay shed.

'Is Snowy having fun?' he asked.

Hattie's hands were wrapped around the golden reindeer in her lap. Her beaming smile answered him. It wasn't only helping decorate the mailbox making her happy; she'd always loved riding in the tractor with Brett.

Drew drove into the large timber-framed shed and speared the closest round bale with the twin hay forks on the front of the tractor. He then turned to drive along the driveway to the front gate. To make the hay snowman they'd need one round bale and two large rectangular ones. They'd also need a large and small tyre for his hat.

They drove past the shed where Freya was using red spray paint to write a Christmas message on a piece of tin that lay on the ground. Dressed in jeans, boots and a pink shirt, she gave them a wave. Bailey lay beside her. He lifted a hand in return, glad of the dusty tractor window between them. It was becoming harder to hide how she affected him.

When she'd suggested he accompany her to Cressy's for Christmas lunch, a rush of pleasure had been quickly crushed by the weight of reality. He had no time to be led off track by his emotions. He had a farm to run. Spending Christmas by Freya's side would only fuel the longings that refused to return to the shadows, longings that had only intensified after spending time with her over the past two days. At least tomorrow would be business as usual with harvest starting on the other farm. He'd soon be too tired to think or feel.

Beside him, Hattie giggled as Panda trotted along the fence line, following the hay. Liberty remained where she was under the shade of a tree.

Drew grinned as Panda let out a loud neigh. 'It's not Christmas yet, Panda. Besides, I think Santa has a carrot for you, not enough hay to feed you all winter.'

Once the round bale was positioned to the left of the white forty-four-gallon drum mailbox, Hattie left the tractor cabin to help Freya. Drew returned to the hay shed. This time he used the hay fork to pick up a large rectangular bale. Panda again trotted along the fence line as he drove to the front entrance.

Drew delivered the rest of the hay and on the final return trip drove his four-wheel drive to the gate instead of the tractor. When he arrived, Freya and Hattie had hung bunches of artificial mistletoe from the Inglewood farm sign and smothered the mailbox in red and gold tinsel. The *Happy Christmas* sign on the corrugated iron leaned against the right side of the white fence that flanked the cattle grid. Already the round hay bale resembled a snowman as Freya spray painted the front white.

Hattie slipped her hand in his.

He smiled at his goddaughter who looked more like Brett with every birthday. 'Shall we make Snowy a reindeer forest?'

'She says yes.' Hattie's smile shone as bright as the golden reindeer she held up for him to see.

Together they arranged the trees Freya and Hattie had decorated. He hammered star pickets into the hard, dry ground and secured the two tall trees at the back and the smaller ones in the front.

When the afternoon sun cast long shadows, the Christmas display was almost complete. The round bale snowman now sported black circles for eyes and buttons, a big red scarf and his tyre hat. The frame for the lights had been secured and only needed the lights to be strung across the steel rectangle he'd welded earlier.

After Hattie smothered a second yawn, he swapped glances with Freya. Each time she knew what he was thinking, it triggered a dangerous tide of warmth inside him. He couldn't get used to Freya understanding him without having to say words. Come the new year he'd be back talking to himself and Bailey.

He walked over to where Hattie sat on a small hay bale wearing her pink cowgirl cap. 'Time for you to go home, Miss Hattie.'

She frowned. 'Now?'

'Yes. I know the lights aren't finished but tomorrow night you can come for a drive and see them when they're on. I'll talk to Cath.'

By the time Drew returned from dropping Hattie home, dusk cloaked the Christmas scene.

Freya smiled from where she stood on the ute trayback lacing the fairy lights over the frame. 'Perfect timing. All we need to do now is hook this up to the generator and, fingers crossed, we're done.'

'Too easy. I'll move the ute before I switch everything on. Do you want a hand getting down?'

'No, thanks.' She jumped to the ground.

He opened the ute door and Bailey leapt inside to sit on the passenger seat. Drew parked at the front of the display and the kelpie licked his hand.

'I know, buddy.' Drew tickled behind his ears. 'You're very happy with your front row seat.'

He left the ute to plug in the lights. Before he flicked on the switch he looked over to where Freya had climbed onto the bull bar so she too would have the perfect view. 'Showtime.'

He turned on the lights.

Freya clapped. 'It all looks so wonderful.'

He walked over to lean back against the bull bar, making sure he left an arm's length between them. She'd removed her wide-brim hat now the sun had disappeared and the fairy lights brought out the vibrant red highlights in her hair.

She half turned towards him. 'I hope Hattie's pleased when she sees everything all lit up.'

He made the mistake of responding to the concern in Freya's voice by meeting her gaze. 'She will. That's one high-wattage display that will brighten anyone's day.'

Despite his reassurance, her brow remained furrowed. The wind rushed by, tugging at the tin sign he'd secured to the fence and blowing strands of hair across Freya's face.

It was an automatic, simple reaction to smooth the wisps away from her cheek. But when his fingers brushed her soft skin, and tangled in her silken hair, the need that kicked deep inside wasn't simple. His hand lingered on her cheek.

Freya didn't move or look away at the lights that mirrored the stars above them. Her intense stillness and the way her eyes held his said she wanted what was about to happen as much as he did. He took his time to close the distance between them and to lower his mouth to hers. His tender kiss was supposed to say they'd take things slow. His restrained touch was supposed to prove to himself he was in control.

But then her lips parted and the world as he knew it fragmented. There was nothing but urgency and a heat so intense it consumed him. Freya's passion burned as bright as her hair and fuelled his own raw need. She filled his arms like no other woman had and unlocked emotions he'd kept off-limits. He moved away from the bull bar to step between her legs. She smiled against his mouth, her hands slipping beneath his shirt, pressing him even closer. His lips followed the creamy, smooth arc of her neck as she tipped her head back.

The squeal of a car horn delivered a jarring reality check. He lifted his head. The world zeroed back into focus.

'Drew.' Her breaths were as rushed as his. 'It's okay.'

He shook his head. How could he have been so unguarded? He'd just put Freya in the gossip firing line. He went to ease himself away but she held him fast, her hands remaining splayed across his shoulder blades.

'Freya ... that was a farm ute and would have been someone local. I give Edna fifteen minutes and she'll be calling. I've just caused trouble for you.'

'No, you haven't. I'm a single, grown woman who can kiss who I want, when I want.' She slid her hands out from beneath his shirt and ran her fingertips along his tight jaw. 'I've been wanting to kiss you since you walked into the schoolyard and smiled at me.'

The need in her large eyes and the huskiness of her voice had him kissing her again to let her know he'd shared the instant awareness between them. This time he made sure he remained aware of his surroundings. When he heard another car engine, his mouth left hers.

He went to speak.

She placed a finger on his lips. 'You don't need to say anything. I know ... it's not a good time for things to get out of hand. This will just be a one-off ... for now.'

Car headlights approached. He framed her face with his hands and gave her a last quick kiss before turning away so he wouldn't be seen holding her again.

Just like the fairy lights shining before him, Freya had imparted warmth and brilliance to his life. But the acknowledgment didn't bring him the joy it should. His heart grew heavy. No longer was he distant Drew. He'd become a liability. He'd become distracted Drew.

Chapter 6

'So how does it feel to break the Woodlea grapevine?' Cressy asked from across the Inglewood kitchen table as her knitting needles clicked.

Freya stopped crocheting. 'I think the grapevine's much like the internet. It's impossible to break.'

Cressy raised her eyebrows. Like Fliss, she had expressive hazel eyes and dark hair. But unlike her older sister, she had fair skin and she'd missed the height gene. This morning the no-frills cowgirl wore her usual jeans, boots and blue work shirt. But today she also wore her engagement ring and the diamond glittered whenever her hand moved. After the tragedy of losing Brett and Sarah, locals were looking forward to autumn when the bell in the historic Woodlea stone church would ring out in celebration.

'Is that all everyone's really talking about today?'

'Sorry, it is. Drew being seen kissing you has caused quite a stir. Everyone's been holding their breath waiting to see who'd crack that workaholic bachelor shell of his. I'm surprised Edna hasn't been over to find out what's going on.'

'I must admit I was expecting her to call. But so far there's been nothing.'

Freya concentrated on crocheting her red star. At the rate she was going she'd never have a finished example for her next Christmas craft class. If it wasn't thoughts of how perfect it felt to be moulded against Drew distracting her, it was her guilt at sabotaging his anonymity. The last thing Drew needed, especially at this time of year, was extra attention and scrutiny.

Cressy spoke softly. 'Of course, Fliss and I always knew it would be you.'

The cool air-conditioned air had no hope of stripping the heat from Freya's face. 'Has it been that obvious, at least from my side, that I've been drawn to him from the beginning?'

'No, not at all. We knew from Drew. We've known him all our lives. When he mentioned your name twice, and then invited you to stay, we hoped you'd be the one.'

'I'm not so sure I've cracked that hard shell of his. We had a moment … but that's all it can be for now. This is his first Christmas without Brett and Sarah and harvest's still on.'

Cressy slipped the delicate white star from her knitting needle before looking at Freya. 'That moment you had shouldn't be underestimated. You've done what no one else has been able to do. You've reached him.'

Freya sighed. 'Time will tell.'

The regret in his dark eyes after the car horn had blared remained with her. It didn't matter that his touch had communicated that the kiss had meant something to him too. She still wasn't sure he'd let her in at all.

'It will.' Cressy glanced at her engagement ring and smiled. 'And when it does, it's more than worth the wait.'

Freya smiled too. Cressy had filled her in on the demons Denham had to fight before he and the cowgirl could finally be together.

Cressy held up the knitted white star. 'This pattern's a success and won't be too hard for the knitters you have coming. How's your star coming along?'

'I'm almost done.'

Cressy stretched and looked out the window to where Liberty dozed beside Panda beneath her favourite tree. Before they'd started their craft projects, they'd hosed down her injured leg.

'It's a hot one again today,' the cowgirl said. 'I don't envy Drew being out harvesting. I'm glad we've finished at Glenmore. Last night was my first full night's sleep in weeks.' She glanced at Freya. 'Any luck getting Drew to come to Christmas lunch?'

'No, but I'll ask him again when harvest's over.'

'I'll give him a call, too. It'd be good for him to come to the Woodlea Christmas party next weekend even if he won't come to lunch.'

'He hasn't said anything about the party, even when Ella mentioned it when she came to treat Liberty.'

Cressy nodded as she used a large needle to weave and secure the loose end of her star. 'I think the last town Christmas party Drew went to I was telling him about some out-of-towners trying to ride Reggie. That was years ago now.'

Freya smiled. The Brahman-cross bull Cressy had rescued from the long paddock as a calf was the size of a mountain. His size and strength was only equalled by his reputation as being a bull with attitude. When around Cressy and Fliss, Freya had also seen how gentle and docile he could be. 'I'm guessing Reggie's getting carrots for Christmas?'

'That goes without saying. He loves his daily carrots. You know, there's one thing not so well known about Reggie. He's a good judge of character. Ask Fliss. If he met Drew I've no doubt he'd like him.'

Before Freya could discover the reason for the sudden twinkle in Cressy's eyes, her mobile rang. Drew's name flashed on the screen. They'd swapped numbers on their trip to Woodlea but this was the first time he'd called. She bit the inside of her cheek.

The wheat truck hitting her house had illustrated that this time of year could be hazardous. As well as fatigue, the high temperatures and dry, windy conditions only added to the high summer bushfire risk. A local header had caught on fire when harvesting chickpeas thanks to the flammable crop dust.

'Drew, is everything okay?'

Across the table, Cressy stopped knitting her second star. The cowgirl was a volunteer member of the State Emergency Service and always ready for a call-out.

'Hi. No, everything should be fine. I just wanted to give you a heads up—I saw Edna's four-wheel drive go past. She'd be on her way to Inglewood. I'll be home soon.'

The phone line magnified the deep, husky timbre of his voice and reminded Freya how much she missed not having him close to home today. 'No, it's okay. You don't need to come back, you're busy.'

Drew didn't immediately reply.

The line crackled and she spoke again. 'Drew?'

'Yes, sorry, it's patchy reception here. No, I'll still come. Edna will be in fine form.'

Freya used her best Miss George voice. 'I can handle Edna, you stay on that header.'

He chuckled. 'I have no doubt you can. I'll finish this row and check in again to see if you need any backup.'

The line dropped out before she could say she'd be fine.

'I take it we're about to have a certain visitor,' Cressy said, tone wry. 'I knew Edna wouldn't stay away.'

'We'd better brace ourselves.' Freya stood to remove the plate of vanilla cupcakes decorated with white icing and sprinkled with candy cane fragments.

Cressy laughed. 'You're a wise woman.'

'I'm just picking my battles.'

Freya put the cupcakes in the pantry and flicked on the electric kettle. A plume of red dust along the driveway said Edna would arrive in the next few minutes. As if on cue, Bailey barked as Edna's four-wheel drive appeared and then slowed to park beside Cressy's battered silver ute.

Edna's walk was brisk as she covered the lawn to the front door. Freya smoothed her hands down the skirt of her floral print dress, thankful Edna wouldn't be seeing her in her farm clothes. She needed to appear just like she usually did, otherwise Edna would know that moving to Inglewood had changed more than what she wore.

'Anyone home?' Edna's strident voice sounded from the front of the homestead. Freya shared a look with Cressy who mouthed 'good luck' before Freya set off along the hallway.

She opened the door to the strong fragrance of Edna's distinctive perfume. Dressed in her power outfit of a crisp white linen blouse and navy skirt, her grey hair was freshly styled and pearls hung around her neck. No wonder Edna hadn't put in an appearance earlier, she'd been seeing Taylor at the hair salon.

'Morning, Freya.'

'Morning, Edna. What brings you out this way?'

'Let's just say I'm here on … town business.'

'That sounds intriguing.' Freya stepped aside to let Edna into the cool of the house. 'Have you time for a cuppa or a cold drink?'

'Of course.'

'Perfect.'

Freya led the way to the kitchen, conscious of Edna scrutinising every room they passed. She paused at the open doorway of the living room. For a moment her eyes softened and then her lips pressed together.

'You have been busy since you moved in.'

Freya smiled sweetly. 'I'm Drew's guest, remember. I haven't exactly moved in.'

Edna's only response was the slight lift of a pencilled brow.

In the kitchen Freya busied herself making Edna a cup of tea the way she liked it, milky with two sugars.

As soon as Freya slipped into her seat, Edna got right down to business.

'So, Freya … the reason for my visit is that I'm concerned about you and Drew. Last night you were seen kissing at the front gate.'

'Yes, we were.'

Edna's gaze sharpened. 'You admit it.'

'It's not a crime. We're both single adults. Really it's no one's business but our own.'

'I'm sure Drew had no problem with the kiss,' Cressy said with a grin to lighten the strain.

Edna frowned. 'Cressida, that isn't helpful.'

'It wasn't meant to be. It's the truth. Edna, you tell me one single man in Woodlea who wouldn't like kissing a woman like Freya beneath the stars.'

Edna pursed her lips.

Freya spoke. 'Edna … I know Drew just lost his best friend and is busy running the farm. I'm not here to cause trouble for him or anyone else. We had a moment. That's all it was. I'm not in a rush to have my heart broken again and I'm sure Drew isn't in a rush to have his broken either.'

Bailey barked again. Cressy met Freya's eyes. They both knew whose diesel ute had sped along the driveway.

Drew took the veranda steps two at a time. He shouldn't be leaving his workmen with the brunt of the harvest work, he always led by example, but he couldn't allow Freya to face Edna alone. He had no doubt if Freya could handle the youngest Ridley boy she would be more than a match for Edna, but he hadn't been raised to shirk his responsibilities. He'd instigated the kiss and he now had to make things right for Freya. Small towns could have long memories. He tugged off his boots and entered the kitchen.

Freya flashed him a calm smile from where she sat to the right of Edna. Across the table, Cressy gave him her you-are-so-busted look he remembered from school. Edna stared at him through narrowed eyes before her face broke into a smile. In front of her sat an untouched cup of tea.

'Well, hello, Drew, this is an unexpected surprise.'

He nodded as he took the chair beside Freya. 'Let's just say it's going to be another one of those days.'

Edna nodded sympathetically. 'I know what they're like. This harvest Noel's had so many breakdowns, I'm always going to town for parts.'

Amusement tugged at Cressy's lips. 'Noel's lucky you enjoy the trip so much.'

They all knew Edna needed no excuse to go to town.

'Yes, he is,' Edna replied, not taking her attention from Drew. 'Now, Drew, we were just discussing last night's … incident.'

'Edna,' Freya's quiet voice sounded, her tone firm. 'I believe we've established that Drew and I are both adults, it's no one's business but ours and your concerns are unfounded. We're not about to break each other's hearts.'

Drew held Edna's gaze, letting her see he'd not stand for the kiss to be turned into an issue. 'I think that covers everything.'

Edna took her time to answer. 'I'm so glad we had this talk. You've relieved my concerns. But other people might not be so understanding.' She played with her pearls. 'I know you'll be going to the town Christmas party, Freya. Drew, why don't you come too? People will then see there's nothing to the rumour that Freya's expecting and you'll be married by the end of summer.'

Cressy almost choked on her sip of water while Freya's cheeks lost all colour.

'Edna …' His voice emerged low, hard and uncompromising. 'Call Mrs Knox now and set the record straight. This is not a game. These are people's lives you're playing with.'

Edna blinked but instead of displeasure sparking in her eyes, he only saw admiration. His brusqueness hadn't cost him his place on her potential-son-in-law list.

'My, my … I'd forgotten how strong the Macgregor will can be. It would be my pleasure to correct any wrong assumptions.'

'Thank you. And yes, I'll be at the Christmas party.'

Edna left the kitchen, her phone in her hand to call Mrs Knox.

Cressy came to her feet. 'I'll hose Liberty's leg again.' She smiled at Freya before squeezing his shoulder as she passed. 'Well played, both of you.'

When he and Freya were alone, he faced her.

'Thanks for coming home.' Worry pinched her fine features. 'To think one kiss started all of this? All eyes will be on us at the Christmas party.'

'It'll be okay. Having everyone watch us will be perfect to disprove the rumours.' Edna's steps sounded in the hallway. But before he stood, he gave in to the need to comfort Freya. He slid his fingers into her hair and pressed a kiss to her forehead. 'But just like you said, what happens when no one is watching is our own business.'

Her smile stayed with him for the entire drive back to the neighbouring farm.

The days after Edna's visit blurred into a haze of harvest exhaustion and sleep deprivation. But the drive to get the wheat off wasn't why sleep eluded him. Thoughts of Freya gave him no peace. As strong as she was, knowing that people talked about her wouldn't be easy. She'd already flagged she didn't like any extra attention. Now, wherever she went, people would be watching and whispering. He had to silence all rumours they were together. Even if an irrational part of him wished they were true.

He scraped a hand over his face as he walked in the darkness towards the kitchen door. Bailey had given him a sleepy welcome and then returned to bed. A light shone from the kitchen and when he stepped inside, he saw Freya reading at the table.

'Bad day?' she asked as she came to her feet.

'Just the usual.'

The aroma of lasagne wafted through the kitchen and a foil-covered dish sat on the bench.

He busied himself with putting the ice bricks in the freezer. He needed a chance to lock down his self-control. It was bad enough that Freya waiting up for him stirred his loneliness. He also couldn't look at her mouth and not have need twist inside. He'd already caused enough damage by kissing her.

'Do you feel like dinner first or a shower?' she asked.

He sat the esky on the bench so it would be ready to be refilled next morning. 'Dinner smells great but sorry, I ate earlier when I had to go to town. I did text but the message mustn't have made it through.'

'No problem. What part did you need this time?'

'Header rotor belt.'

She nodded and slid the lasagne into the fridge. When she turned she glanced out the window. 'It's finally cool outside and even though it's late I thought I'd go see some of the mailboxes.' She paused. 'I know going out again would be the last thing you'd feel like doing, but you're welcome to come. I'll drive.'

He ignored the fatigue that dug deep into his muscles. If he went to bed he wouldn't sleep anyway. 'Actually … that sounds great.' He grinned. 'But I'll drive. If we're supposed to be fire-hosing rumours, we'd better not be seen together in your fancy city car.'

'True. Luckily every man and his dog has a white four-wheel drive around here.'

'Exactly. Give me ten minutes to take a shower.'

He soon returned and they headed out to see the Christmas displays. A comfortable silence was interspersed with small talk as they slowed to take in the decorated mailboxes.

Freya laughed softly when they reached little Zoe's farm. 'How did I know their decorations would have something to do with horses?'

Horse wreaths decorated the sides of the cattle grid while a huge tinsel-wrapped horseshoe glittered around the mailbox.

At the Walshes a nativity scene had been set up complete with a sturdy stable and real hay, while at the Lawsons a life-sized Santa sat in a tinnie as though he would soon be off fishing.

Drew adjusted his high beam as another car drove by. He smiled across to where Freya sat relaxed in the passenger seat. 'I've never seen so much traffic this time of night. Everyone's out looking at the displays. There's no doubt your plan to raise everyone's spirits has worked.'

'I hope so.' She looked over her shoulder as they passed psychedelic fairy lights flashing pink, blue and green. 'I don't know how Edna will choose the best decorations. There's so many amazing ones.'

'Knowing Edna she'll have a checklist on her clipboard.'

'I bet Denham's done something spectacular,' Freya said as she leaned forwards in her seat to see the entryway into Cressy and Denham's farm.

'We'll soon find out.'

Drew slowed as Glenmore's mailbox came into view. He chuckled as the ute's headlights revealed a large steel sled decorated in red bows and tinsel. 'He's been welding.'

Freya smiled as two dogs barked from inside the sleigh. 'He has. Tippy and Juno approve.'

Drew pulled over. Glenmore was on a back road and he and Freya would be safe to leave the four-wheel drive to chat to Denham. No passers-by would see them together.

The bull-rider greeted Freya with a kiss before shaking Drew's hand.

'This looks great,' Freya said as she patted the older kelpie and exuberant young poodle-kelpie cross.

'Thanks.' Denham dipped his head towards the four large reindeers that were constructed out of lights. 'All I need to do is put these in place and I'm done. Cressy hasn't seen any of it yet. She's over helping Fliss wrap presents so it's a surprise for when she drives home.'

Denham's deep tone and tender smile said how much he loved Cressy. Was that how Drew looked when he spoke about Freya?

They gave the two dogs a final pat and left Denham to finish his display.

Freya stifled a yawn as darkness pressed against the car windows. 'Thank you. That was fun.'

He reached for her small hand and she smiled as she entwined her fingers with his. As simple as her gesture was, it still had the power to move him. Emotion ached in his throat, leaving him in no doubt that when he spoke about Freya he shared Denham's expression. He fought to keep his reply casual.

'It was.'

Soon the lights of their own display lit up the night. His chest tightened as he drove across the cattle grid to the only place he'd ever call home. A home that, without the beautiful and warm-hearted woman beside him, would never feel like a real home again.

Chapter 7

The summer heat showed no sign of abating on the afternoon of the Christmas party. Freya secured her hair in a neat twist that left her nape bare. She'd contemplated wearing her special red dress, but as the plan was to keep a low profile she'd opted for a white lace dress with capped sleeves. She finished putting on her crystal Christmas tree earrings as she entered the kitchen.

Drew stood with his back to her as he slipped a bottle of wine into the gift bag she'd found earlier in her Christmas stash. When he turned and saw her, he stilled. His eyes darkened.

'You look beautiful.'

She smiled, hoping the flutter in her stomach didn't make her smile shaky. The huskiness in his voice said that perhaps she had reached him. When he'd kissed her forehead the day of Edna's visit, she hadn't imagined the concern in his touch. She worked hard to keep her words light. 'Thank you. You don't look too bad yourself.'

Drew wore a blue and white checked shirt she hadn't seen before, brown leather belt, jeans and town boots. The woody notes of his aftershave tempted her to step in close and trail her fingers over his clean-shaven chin.

'Just as well you didn't see me twenty minutes ago.'

She laughed softly and went to the fridge to collect the pumpkin and feta salad she'd made for the party. 'So what's our game plan?' she asked over her shoulder.

'Separate cars and conversations and never mention the word *baby* or *wedding.*'

Even though his words were teasing, she didn't smile as she sat the salad on the bench. 'Thanks for taking the afternoon off. I know you're only doing this for me. You don't care what people think. I wish I could be more like you.'

He moved closer, expression serious. 'No, you don't. I used to not care. But you've shown me ... life isn't meant to be lived alone, without friends and company.' He tucked the hair that had slipped onto her cheek behind her ear. 'And I want to show you that not all men are careless. I kissed you, so it's my fault we'll be the main topic of conversation tonight. I need to fix things.'

'Thank you but ...' Her breathing grew shallow as she focused on his mouth. 'I kissed you back so it's not all your responsibility.'

'Freya ...' Her name was more a groan than a word. 'One thing us men have in common is we're only human. And if you and I don't leave now we both know we won't make it to the party.' He lowered his head to press a kiss to the sensitive point where her neck and shoulder met.

Her fingers curled into his hair and when he straightened, she smoothed her hand down his neck, over his shoulder, to rest against his heart. His large work-roughened hand covered hers. Beneath her palm she could feel the strength of his heartbeat. For a second she wavered, the need to kiss him short-circuiting all common sense. Then she slipped her hand free and stepped away. Drew was doing all he could to look out for her and she needed to do the same.

Uncaring her face would reflect her struggle, she met his gaze. 'Let's get this party over with and when harvest and Christmas are out of the way, we can revisit this … conversation and see where it leads.'

His grin flashed white. 'You have yourself a deal, Miss George.'

Freya followed the traffic as a convoy of cars turned past the drystone wall entrance of Claremont. Three cars ahead, Freya could see Drew's four-wheel drive as the traffic slowed to a crawl along the poplar tree–lined driveway.

Even now her heart beat too fast and her face felt too hot. Just as well she was staying away from him, as how she felt about the broad-shouldered cattleman would be obvious. Her strong feelings weren't just a quirk of her sometimes obsessive nature. They were true, deep and real. She knew now she'd never loved Charles. Their university friendship had developed into a convenient, practical relationship that hadn't ever been based on any genuine emotion.

Her sigh filled the car. But as for Drew … she wasn't sure what he felt. Was it loneliness or chemistry that pulled him to her? Did he feel the same? All she knew was that now wasn't the time to discover the answers, no matter how much she wanted to.

A historic homestead materialised out of the trees. With a wide wraparound veranda, sprawling Claremont sported eight chimneys. Home to the Rigby family for generations, Denham's Aunt Meredith and her husband Phil now lived in the main house since Denham had left to live with Cressy. Tanner came and went, depending on if he was out droving or staying local and training horses.

The park-like gardens and modern stables provided a picturesque venue for the town Christmas celebrations. A towering fir tree in the front garden had coloured lights strung almost halfway up its ancient branches, while over to the right the stables were festooned in fairy lights. Hay bales provided plenty of seating and trestle tables were already laden with food.

A slashed paddock beyond the stables provided a designated parking area. Freya drove to the end of the last row, making sure she parked nowhere near Drew. Her phone beeped and she answered Ella's text telling her to have a good time. The vet had received a call-out and wasn't going to make it. Freya collected her salad and as she walked across the soft grass she was pleased she'd worn wedges instead of heels. Her city-girl ways were long gone.

Hattie gave her a wave from where she ran between the garden beds filled with white roses. Zoe and another student, Alice, ran beside her. All three girls wore flashing reindeer antlers.

''Tis the season for reindeer antlers,' a masculine voice said to her left and she turned to see Denham, a smile in his blue eyes.

'It sure is.' She returned his smile. 'So where's yours?'

'Hidden away in the same cupboard as my suit and tie.' Denham's expression sobered. 'Cressy's filled me in on Edna's visit. If you have any issues this afternoon let me know.'

'Thanks. I will.' She glanced to where he favoured his left leg. 'What have you done this time?'

'Nothing bad like falling off a bull.' His grin turned sheepish. 'Don't tell Fliss as she'll put her doctor hat on. I was reliving my glory days and climbed the fir tree to put up the lights. I obviously weigh more than I did at fifteen and a branch broke.'

'Ouch.'

He grimaced. 'Who knew the soft lawn would be so hard.'

She looped her arm through his so when they walked his limp wouldn't be so noticeable. Together they entered the throng of people congregated outside the stables. She saw Drew talking to a group of men near the round yard. His dark head turned and while he appeared to not be looking in her direction she knew he was making sure she was okay. The knowledge warmed her and stirred emotions she was supposed to be hiding.

When Denham stopped to talk to a neighbour, Freya excused herself. She added her salad to the delicious array of food. Smiling at people as she walked, she made her way over to where Fliss sat at a small table painting a little boy's face. Two other children stood waiting.

Her shoulders relaxed. Other than a few curious glances, no one appeared to give her any special attention. So far she hadn't seen any sign of either Edna or Mrs Knox.

'Need a hand, Fliss?'

Fliss nodded her head so hard the pom pom on her Santa hat bounced. 'Yes, please. I need all the help I can get. This is supposed to be a Christmas tree.' She smiled at the little boy. 'You don't mind if it looks more like a monster, do you?'

He grinned, showing his missing bottom tooth. 'Nah.'

Freya settled herself into the second chair and busied herself turning the two waiting girls into Christmas angels. When she'd finished painting the last white wing, her two little angels skipped away.

'They look so good,' Fliss said with a sigh.

'Thanks.'

Fliss glanced over to where Drew was now speaking to a different group of farmers. 'Before I forget, Cressy's booked the last timeslot for the horse-drawn Christmas lights tour tonight. There's plenty of room for you and Drew and, as it's the stage coach, if you sat inside no one would see you.'

Freya had heard Hattie and Zoe talk about the carriages that went down Main Street and around Woodlea to see the lights.

'That sounds wonderful. I'd love to go. I'll text Drew.'

'Great.'

The two girls whose faces Freya had painted were now surrounded by other children. The oldest girl turned to point to Freya and little feet started running towards her.

Fliss chuckled. 'There's no chance of you being seen with Drew now. You're about to be mobbed.'

Drew looked over to where Tanner and Freya sat on a hay bale laughing as they enjoyed the buffet dinner. Even though he knew their closeness stemmed from friendship, he couldn't stop unease from writhing inside.

Freya was so out of his league. Beautiful, compassionate and clever, she could have any man she wanted. What did she see in him? Edna might think he was a perfect match for Bethany, but he wasn't under any illusion Edna valued who he was as a man over his acres.

As for the awareness that had burned between him and Freya in the kitchen, he hadn't been joking when he said one false move by either of them and they wouldn't have made it to the Christmas party. His willpower was stretched to breaking point. He remained thankful harvest had kept him away from her as much as it had.

He took a swallow of beer and nodded as the farmer he spoke to talked about what rotation crops he'd sow next winter.

Edna's voice sounded above the hum of conversation. Heads turned and noise died as she stood at the front of the stables. She needed no microphone to announce the winners of the mailbox decorating competition. After a heartfelt tribute to Brett and Sarah, and a brief mention of thanks to Freya for the competition idea, Edna ran through the winning farms.

As families went up to claim their certificates and prizes, the clapping and smiles said how much the competition had helped the community through what was a difficult time. When Denham won the prize for the best overall display, the crowd whistled and cheered.

Once the awards had been announced, Drew watched Edna make a beeline for Tanner and Freya. He hadn't missed the way she'd glanced at them while she'd been presenting. Edna said something to Freya who nodded and came to her feet. With a smile at Tanner, she followed Edna over to a group of older ladies.

Tanner joined Denham and both men walked towards Drew. The pregnant wife of the farmer he'd been talking to gave Drew an apologetic smile as she asked her husband to help with their toddler who had green icing smeared through her blonde curls.

'Fancy a road trip to the rodeo yards?' Tanner asked.

Tanner's expression grew strained as he glanced at the parents with the uncooperative and noisy toddler.

'Sure. I've been waiting to see these yards of yours.'

'Great.' Denham grinned. 'It just so happens I left my ute out the back in case we needed a fast getaway. Tanner, don't look now but Edna has you in her sights.'

Tanner shuddered. 'Babies and Edna, that's the stuff nightmares are made of.'

They wove their way through the crowd and ducked into the lengthening shadows to reach Denham's ute. Once they'd piled into the Land Cruiser they followed a dirt road through the paddocks to where Denham had custom built a set of rodeo yards. Even though he now lived at Glenmore, he still bred rodeo bulls on his family farm.

Denham looked at Tanner and then over his shoulder to where Drew sat. 'Edna won't be impressed I've whisked away her two favourite bachelors.'

Tanner grimaced. 'I'm sure she has a GPS tracker with my name on it. Every time I go into town I bump into her.'

Drew and Denham laughed before Denham spoke, 'Just be thankful Bethany has headed to the city this weekend or Edna would have found a way to throw you all together.'

'Tell me about it,' Drew said. 'I must have walked under a ladder as I drew the short straw and got the charity ball gig last spring. I was just thankful Bethany's city boyfriend turned up and I could leave.'

'What you both need,' Denham said, 'is a better half.' He turned to wink at Drew. 'Even though you and Freya have been avoiding each other, my gut tells me you're sorted, but you, Tanner, had better hurry up as soon you could be the only eligible bachelor left on Edna's list.'

Drew smiled while Tanner groaned. The contentment that filtered through Drew said he hoped Denham's gut was right. Once harvest was done he and Freya would have a chance to address what was going on between them.

As the ute approached the steel yards a mottled-grey bull lumbered towards the paddock gate.

Denham shook his head. 'Even when it isn't Christmas Reggie eats more carrots than Santa's reindeers. He's already had half a bucket today and now he wants more.'

Drew took in the muscled power of the bull's shoulders, his athletic stride and the white gleam of his eyes. 'I can see why you'd want to breed bucking bulls from him. He has the right confirmation and temperament.'

'Exactly,' said Denham. 'You can join our Reggie-is-a-bad-ass team. Cressy and Fliss swear he doesn't have a mean bone in that massive body of his.'

Drew chuckled as Reggie reached the gate and pawed the ground. Red dust puffed into the air. 'Let's just say that look he's eyeballing us with isn't going to win him any awards for playing nice.'

Denham stopped the ute and leaned over to open the glove box. He pulled out a withered carrot. 'Cressy always keeps an emergency supply in here.' He unclipped his seatbelt. 'Fliss and Cressy have this thing they call passing the Reggie test. They don't know that I know about it, but basically if you feed Reggie a carrot you're man enough for them. They are serious when they say he's a good judge of character.'

'It's all right for you,' Tanner said, tone dry as he looked at Denham. 'You passed. I fail every time.' He reached for the carrot. 'Come on. I'll show you.'

Denham was already laughing by the time he left the ute. Tanner hadn't even made it to the gate when Reggie bellowed, spun around and presented him with his rump.

Drew grinned where he stood slightly apart from Tanner and Denham. Reggie turned to glare in his direction. The bull snorted before ambling towards him.

'No way,' Tanner said, tone disgruntled. 'He likes you and you don't even have the carrot.'

'We'll see.' Drew held up his right hand and Tanner tossed him the carrot. He broke it into chunks and walked to the fence. Reggie moved closer to accept the treat Drew offered. He scratched the grey whorl high on the bull's forehead.

Tanner shook his head. 'That's it. I'm going to be on Edna's hit list forever. I'm not man enough for anyone.'

Denham slapped his back in commiseration before Reggie ate the last of the carrot from Drew's hand.

By the time they'd continued on to look at the rodeo yards and then driven back to the party, empty parking spaces indicated that tired families had headed home.

Drew helped with the clean-up and as he carried a trestle table over to the main house he saw Freya helping Meredith in the kitchen. He'd answered her text about the carriage ride and said he'd meet her in town beforehand, just in case the rumours about them hadn't become old news.

He followed the boys into Woodlea and met them at the Royal Arms. Over a quick beer, he promised to meet them again for a longer drink after harvest. They all then made their way to the old train station that housed the library. It was from here the two horse-drawn carriages left for their Christmas lights tour.

By now darkness blanketed the hills and the first glimmer of starlight could be seen. Children smiled and cameras flashed as the four waiting horses were treated like celebrities. The first carriage, an open-sided wagon, filled with three eager families. The second carriage, a replica of a Cobb & Co stage coach, offered more privacy as well as seating.

Denham waved as Freya, Cressy and Fliss walked across the road to the coaches. The first carriage set off, the two horses' large hooves clopping as it passed by. They all took their places on the waiting stage coach. Tanner sat with the driver, Denham and Cressy on the outside front seat, which left the inside seats for Drew and Freya. He held the door open and she thanked him with a sweet smile as she climbed inside. He joined her on the far seat. The coach jolted into action and as Freya pitched forward she grabbed his leg. He put his arm around her to hold her steady.

She tucked herself against him, her silken hair caressing his jaw. 'Don't let me forget to take a photo for my dad. He's just sent me one of the horse and carriage ride he went on in Salzburg.'

Drew nodded as the two draft horses picked up pace and their feet clipped out a steady rhythm. Happiness curved Freya's mouth as she looked out at the lights decorating the front house yards. He spent as much time watching the delight play across her expressive face as he did the displays.

Children dressed in Santa hats and pyjamas waved from their driveways or rode scooters along the footpath, racing the horses. Christmas wishes were exchanged as people on the street yelled 'Happy Christmas'.

All too soon the horses had completed their loop through town. When the coach rolled to a stop, Freya brushed his mouth with hers. 'Thank you for coming with me, that was magical.'

'Anytime.'

If Freya noticed his voice sounded deeper than usual it didn't show in her expression. He could spend a lifetime looking at Christmas lights with her by his side and it would never be enough.

As the stage coach emptied, goodbyes were said and car lights lit the way out of town. Drew travelled behind Freya and smiled as she slowed to look at any decorated mailboxes they passed.

A workman had fed Bailey, Panda and Liberty, so when Drew arrived home there were no jobs to be done. Bailey rushed over to give him and Freya an exuberant welcome and then sprinted off to keep chewing on the bone the workman had given him as an early Christmas present.

Freya led the way along the garden path. Drew looked away from the sway of her hips beneath her white dress. He didn't need any reminder of how gorgeous she was. After holding her close in the stage coach he already needed a cold swim if he had any hope of sleeping tonight.

At the shoe rack Freya bent to collect the spare key from his father's boot. She opened the door but didn't walk into the darkened house. Instead she turned to face him. From where he stood on the second step, their eyes were almost level.

He wasn't sure what she was about to say, all he knew was that as she stared at him, her lips parted. Awareness sparked between them.

He didn't know who moved first. Her hands were in his hair and her mouth on his even as he pulled her hard against him.

In her kiss was all the desperation, need and hunger that burned within him. He couldn't remember when his hands freed her hair or when she'd unbuttoned the top buttons on his shirt. He dragged his mouth from hers and cupped her face to look deep into her eyes. She knew what he asked even when no words were said.

The beauty of her smile and the steady palm she placed on his cheek gave him all the answers he needed. There was no more waiting for a sensible or right time.

His hands found her waist and as he lifted her, she wrapped her legs around his hips and her arms around his neck. Heart pounding and emotions running riot, he carried her down to his wing of the house.

Chapter 8

As much as Freya liked her dreamy guest bedroom, she liked Drew's room more. In the days after the Christmas party she only returned to her room to change her clothes. Otherwise she was beside Drew when he woke early and sometimes asleep in his bed when he came back late. He'd agreed to come to Cressy's for Christmas lunch and was working around the clock to get the last of the wheat off. Today, barring breakdowns, would be the last day of harvest. That would then leave one day until Christmas.

Freya used a cutter to round the corners of a photograph she'd scanned and copied for the scrapbook open in front of her. With Hattie's help she was making a memory book for Drew about Brett. She'd gone through Hattie's photos to find ones where he'd been included and in the living room cupboard had found Drew's old family albums.

There'd been pictures of him and Brett as kids holding yabbies and being led on shaggy ponies. As teenagers there were photographs of the pair covered in mud after riding motorbikes and of them wearing big hats while showing cattle at country shows. The later pictures showed them, tall and lanky, with their first utes and wearing big grins as they attended various picnic races. Usually the race photographs pictured them with their arms around different girls, until Sarah became a permanent fixture by Brett's side. In Drew's pictures no girl ever appeared twice.

Freya pasted in the photograph of Sarah holding Hattie with a beaming Brett and smiling Drew behind her. Instead of reaching for the next photograph she checked her phone. Even though the reception was poor where Drew was harvesting, he'd taken to texting her throughout the day. She smiled as she re-read his last text saying this time tomorrow they'd still be in bed.

No words had been spoken about where they were headed, or what would happen once Freya's house was fixed. But for all that wasn't said, there was plenty of non-verbal communication. His kiss made her feel treasured and cared for and his touch made her feel beautiful. When harvest was done there would be plenty of time to talk. If Drew's grief meant he wasn't yet ready for a relationship, that was okay, too. She'd waited so long to find him, she'd do whatever it took to ensure they had a future together.

Her mobile rang and it wasn't Drew's name that popped onto the screen, but Edna's.

'Morning, Edna.'

'Morning. Is now a good time to have a chat?'

'Yes, I'm not doing my Christmas craft class until after lunch.'

'Good.' Edna's tone was crisp. 'Now, it's been a few days since the Christmas party and I want to know if you've made a decision.'

Freya frowned. 'Decision ... about what?'

'Drew and Tanner.'

'Drew and Tanner?'

'Yes, you can't have them both and whichever one you don't choose will still be a perfect man for my Bethany.'

'Edna ... again, not that this is any of your business ... but Tanner and I get on really well ... as friends.'

'Well, you looked to be a little more than that at the Christmas party.'

'Only to you. Some advice … let Bethany choose her own husband. He might be the last person you think of but the best person for her.'

Edna didn't immediately reply. 'You chose Drew, didn't you?'

Freya sighed. 'Edna … that's not up for discussion.'

'Well, I hope you did because he's the right one for you.'

Freya blinked. Even knowing that conversations with Edna could take sudden turns, she was taken aback. 'I'm not sure I understand what you're saying.'

'I've always known you'd be the right one for Drew. Just like I knew he'd be a typical stubborn Macgregor who wouldn't see what was in front of him. Thankfully Macgregors can also be counted on to do the right thing.'

Freya rubbed at her temple as she processed Edna's words. No wonder there weren't any pointed looks at the Christmas party. 'Edna … there weren't any rumours, were there? You came over that day to make sure Drew would come to the Christmas party with me.'

'Well, something had to be done. You're only out there until the new year and it'll take him that long to take a day off let alone to relax.'

'Edna … thank you.'

'You're welcome. You can tell Drew, but otherwise I'd appreciate that this stays our little secret. I have a reputation to uphold.'

'I will … and Edna? I chose Drew just like you knew I would.'

Her phone conversation with Edna stayed with Freya until she reached the corrugated iron Reedy Creek hall. All the time Edna had been meddling and supposedly getting between her and Drew, she'd been matchmaking.

Freya busied herself setting up for her final craft class. This session they were making Christmas crackers and reindeer food that could be sprinkled over lawns tomorrow night for Christmas Eve.

The empty chairs were filled and the hall echoed with fun and laughter. Cressy had come with Taylor, the Woodlea hairdresser. Taylor had once been a dancer and had never lost her love for sequins and sparkles. Her Christmas cracker was soon bedazzled with glitter and baubles. Cressy went for the less-is-more approach, with her cracker sporting a simple sprig of handmade mistletoe.

Freya left her seat to put on the kettle and to arrange the Christmas baking others had brought onto a tray. Cressy came to help her. As the cowgirl opened the container of fruit mince pies she gave Freya a soft smile. 'You, Freya George, have a ... glow.'

Freya couldn't stop her instant blush. 'I suspect I do.'

Cressy laughed quietly. 'I'm so pleased for you both. See, I said you were the one.'

'Thanks ... but it's very early days. When harvest's over we have a few things to talk about.'

'Good luck getting Drew to talk, but I have no doubt this is one time he will.'

The group had started on their second Christmas cracker when Cressy slid back her chair. She reached into the bag at her feet where her phone must have vibrated.

She read the screen and glanced at Freya, her expression grave.

Freya put down the cracker she'd been working on. 'SES call-out?'

The tense press of Cressy's lips didn't ease as she got to her feet. 'Not exactly. Denham texted. There's a fire where Drew's harvesting. His header's already been lost.'

Heart racing, Freya stood.

Taylor spoke from beside her. 'Go, I'll clean up here.'

'And I'll take Taylor home,' Zoe's mother, Kellie, said from across the table.

'Thank you.'

Movements efficient and faces calm, the rest of the class packed up their craft projects. This wasn't the first crisis locals had had to face and support each other through.

Freya grabbed her handbag and followed Cressy outside.

When they reached their cars, Cressy hugged her. 'It's a bad fire, Freya. Go home and wait for Drew there. If you want something to do, cook some meals for the volunteers. Edna will know what to do with them. If I can, I'll text you updates.'

Freya hugged her tight. 'Will do, be safe and tell Denham and Tanner to take care as well.'

Denham and Tanner were both part of the volunteer rural fire service.

She checked her phone as she slid behind the wheel but there were no messages or missed calls from Drew. She texted to say she was there for whatever he needed done and then, after hesitating, sent through a red heart emoji.

She went to start her car when her phone rang. Edna's name appeared on the screen. 'Hi, Edna, I'm just leaving the hall now.'

'Hi, Freya.' Edna's voice was all business. 'Let's hope we don't need you back there cooking meals in the kitchen if this fire turns into an emergency.'

'Let me know if you do.'

'I will. You're on my list. Freya … Drew will be okay.'

'Thank you.'

But the closer Freya got to Inglewood and the darker the black smoke billowing into the sky, the more her nerves tightened. If Drew really was okay, why hadn't she heard from him?

Life hadn't finished delivering knockout blows when he least expected it.

Drew took his time opening the ute door. Even though the fire was out and he was back at Inglewood, he could still smell his header and wheat crop burning. The scent clung to his clothes, his skin and his hair and all he could taste was smoke.

Just like the day Freya arrived, he stayed in the ute seat and stared at the homestead. A bright light shone in the kitchen and said Freya waited up for him. He scraped a blackened hand over the soot and grit on his face. No matter how hard he'd fought the fire over the past hours and no matter how drained he was, the day from hell had one last thing to throw at him.

Muscles protested as he left the ute to reach for his esky on the trayback. Bailey raced over and he rubbed the kelpie's soft neck. 'Just as well you weren't with me today, buddy, it wasn't good out there.'

He continued over to the house that represented the legacy his grandfather and father had created in their fertile corner of the Bell River valley. Drew's steps dragged. A legacy that his weakness had partially burned to the ground.

He looked up at the stars. They seemed to have lost their sparkle, just like Freya's eyes would when he said what he needed to say. Loss barrelled through him and he slowed to prevent himself from swaying.

He'd only reached the bottom step when the kitchen door flung open. Freya rushed down the steps. Despite being still dressed in jeans and a shirt, her tousled hair and bare feet told him she'd been asleep.

She flew into his arms and he held her like he'd never let go. He closed his eyes to savour her clean floral scent and the way her soft curves fitted so perfectly against him. His throat thickened. This would be the last time he'd hold her.

After a long moment she pulled away. 'You're okay?'

Her breathless voice reflected her fear and concern and intensified the anguish thrashing inside him.

'I am. I sent some texts and hoped at least one made it through.'

'Your last one did saying the fire was out. Cressy sent some too.'

Freya settled her arm around his waist and walked with him up the veranda steps. 'Hungry?'

He shook his head.

'Coffee or a beer?'

'No ... thanks.'

She left his side to walk through the doorway and her quick assessment of his face said she'd heard his brittle tone. She took the esky from his grasp and placed it on the bench before turning to unbutton his shirt. 'It's a shower then.'

He covered her hand to keep her fingers still. An aching heaviness settled deep into his bones. He owed Freya nothing but honesty.

'Freya ... the fire was my fault. I got ... distracted.' His words emerged as little more than a hoarse croak.

She slid her hand out from beneath his to touch his whiskered cheek. 'Accidents happen. Harvest's a high risk time. The fire could have happened on any farm.'

'It didn't. It happened on my farm, on my watch, when I was driving the header. I've been working on harvests since a teenager. I have the experience and the knowledge to prevent a fire from starting let alone getting out of hand.'

Freya stayed silent, her eyes never leaving his.

'The hydraulic hose split, spilling oil over the engine ... I didn't react as fast as I should have.' Bitterness rasped his voice. 'Even with steering the header into the stubble and having the fire fighting trailer right there, I couldn't contain the flames. The wind changed at a crucial moment.'

Freya's hand lowered, signalling she'd realised there was more going on than him just decompressing after a crisis.

'You're only human and humans get … distracted.'

He didn't meet her eyes. The passing of time hadn't eased his loss or his guilt at being the reason his parents were no longer with him.

'Well … every time I lose focus … bad things happen. I was supposed to be home in time to inspect those cattle on the coast but thanks to a night out with a pretty blonde I wasn't. My parents should never have been flying through that storm.'

Compassion softened Freya's mouth. 'Drew … you were young and the storm was something out of your control.'

He speared a hand through his dusty hair. 'Well, I'm not young now and that fire was something I could control.'

Freya stilled. 'You were thinking about me, weren't you? That's why you were distracted.'

He cleared his throat, knowing there was no going back from his answer. 'Yes … which is why there can be no … future for us. I put people's lives at risk today, my workmen, the rural fire service volunteers. When I'm not totally focused on Inglewood, I'm nothing but a liability.'

Freya's expression didn't change but her eyes turned a deep, bruised grey. 'My mother used to say you should always sleep on a big decision. Things will look different in the morning.'

He stared through the window to where it would only be hours until the grey of dawn lightened the horizon. 'No. They won't.'

His bleak words fell into the strain between them.

'I understand why you feel like you do. I also know that your grief at losing your parents and Brett and Sarah is still raw, but Drew, tomorrow is a new day. I'm not accepting your decision until you've had a shower and a sleep.' She turned to flick on the kettle and he didn't miss the way her fingers shook. 'And caffeine.'

He crossed the room to draw her against him. She wrapped her arms tight around him and buried her face against his ruined shirt. He kissed the top of her head.

'Freya … I'm so sorry. Being careless with your feelings and hurting you is the last thing I ever intended to do.' He stopped, his words failing him.

Now wasn't the time to tell her how much he loved her. He had to sacrifice his own happiness to keep her safe.

The only thing worse than being responsible for sending his parents into a killer storm would be allowing something bad to happen to the only woman he'd ever want. Every time he looked at Hattie he was reminded that no matter how much Brett had loved Sarah, he hadn't been able to protect her.

Chapter 9

Freya awoke in her own bed in the guest room to a single thought. She couldn't lose Drew. She'd wasted so much time with the wrong man, she wasn't letting the right one slip away.

Light poured in through the gap in the curtains. Somehow she must have fallen asleep. She pressed a hand to her midriff to still her nerves. The silence that surrounded her meant Drew had already returned to harvesting. Tonight was Christmas Eve and Drew would be focused on finishing so his workmen could be with their families.

She headed for the shower. She refused to pack her bags and leave. Her chin lifted. She also wasn't going to sit around powerless and voiceless. She had a cattleman to see.

When they had their after-harvest talk, she'd expected Drew's grief to retain a fierce hold. The social youth revealed by his old photographs showed he wasn't a naturally reserved man; the losses in his life had made him that way. But she hadn't expected there to be no future for them. She'd hoped there would have been a way through whatever barriers stood between them. And there would be. She just had to find it.

Once dressed in a sleeveless blue dress, she headed for the kitchen to grab her car keys from the bowl on the side bench. With the tension roiling in her stomach, breakfast was out of the question.

After finding a pen and paper in a kitchen drawer, she called Cressy.

'Hi, Freya, everything okay?' The cowgirl's husky voice suggested she'd only just woken up.

'Sorry … I shouldn't be calling this early, I know you were up late, but I need directions to Drew's other farm. I have to see him.'

'Everything's not okay, is it?' Cressy's voice was clearer, more awake.

'No.'

'Okay. Give me half an hour and I'll drive you there. I need to visit Fliss and it's not much of a drive from there. Freya … hang in there. Everything will be fine.'

As Freya sat in the passenger seat of Denham's ute, the pounding at her temples said she didn't share Cressy's optimism.

Cressy smiled across at her. 'You're doing the right thing. The longer Drew has to think, the more his stubbornness will kick in and he'll retreat behind that workaholic wall of his.'

'That's what I'm afraid of.'

'He has plenty of workmen so he'll be able to take a break when you arrive. If he's back on the header again, a rest will do him good.'

The scent of the charred ground drifted into the ute cabin. Freya's heart ached as they drove through a flat black landscape devoid of foliage and life. Smoke drifted from the thick corner post of a fence that had been cut to let the rural fire engines access the flames.

Cressy again looked at her. 'It was a fast fire but no wildlife or stock were injured and apart from Drew's header, no other machinery lost.' She nodded over to their right where a header and chaser bin moved through a wheat paddock. 'See, thanks to Drew having a second header, it's business as usual.'

The cowgirl pulled up alongside a Hilux parked beside Drew's farm ute. She nodded towards the man who sat behind the wheel. 'That's old Saul. He used to work for Drew's father so has known Drew all his life. He'll make sure you have a chance to talk to him.' She reached over to squeeze Freya's hands that were clasped tightly in her lap. 'I'll be back soon but if you need me earlier give me a call.'

'Thanks. Will do.'

Freya left the cool air-conditioning to walk towards where the older man spoke on the handpiece of a UHF radio. Heat engulfed her, burning her bare arms and legs. Cressy honked her horn as she left and Freya turned to wave.

Saul opened the ute door and climbed out to greet her. A smile lit up his craggy features. 'You must be Freya. Thanks for all the cakes and slices you've been sending for morning smoko.' He patted his ample belly. 'They were much appreciated.'

'You're very welcome. Sorry I didn't bring any this morning. I just came to … talk to Drew. He doesn't know I'm coming.'

Saul's faded blue eyes flicked between the header to their left and Freya. 'I'm glad you're here. He's been walking around like a horse with a burr under its saddle blanket ever since he arrived.' Saul winked. 'Have you ever been on a header?'

'No, I can't say I have.'

'Great.' He looked down at her sensible wedges. 'I see you came prepared. Hop in.'

While Freya walked around the front of the ute Saul again spoke on the UHF radio.

She slid into the dusty ute seat and Saul started the engine.

He grinned. 'Now don't take any nonsense from that young Macgregor. I want to retire but I can't do that when he's determined to work himself into an early grave.'

Despite the nerves drying her mouth, Freya returned Saul's smile. 'I promise. I won't.'

'Good.'

At the end of the wheat row the header briefly stopped and the door opened. As she left the ute, Saul gave her a thumbs up. All Drew said as she clambered up the header steps and into the spare seat was, 'Hold on.'

She nodded as the header turned.

The rhythmic sound of wheat being stripped filled the cabin as the header followed a straight line. Beside them a tractor pulled a chaser bin in which the unloading auger directed a steady flow of golden grain.

Freya examined the grave cast of Drew's profile. It didn't matter if the reserved man she'd first met had returned, she'd find a way to reach him.

She spoke into the tension. 'So what's this do?' She pointed to a small computer screen.

Drew explained and as she asked more questions about the technology and equipment he used, the tense line of his shoulders lowered.

A third of a way along the row, two falcons dipped and dived in front of the header. The birds' shadows almost made it look like there were four of them.

'What are they after?' she asked, leaning forwards to peer through the window.

'Quails or maybe a rabbit.'

The birds soon disappeared and then it was a kangaroo that bounded out of the way of the header.

A brief smile shaped Drew's mouth. 'It's all happening. Now all we need to see are feral pigs and emus.'

When they were almost at the end of the row, Drew spoke into his UHF radio. 'Saul, can you take over? I'm going to run Freya home.'

'Sure.'

Freya glanced at the muscle that worked in Drew's jaw as he lowered the UHF handpiece. 'Cressy said she'll take me home. We could sit in the shade and talk until she gets here?'

He shook his head. 'It's too hot out there for you. We can … talk on the way.'

'If you're sure?'

He nodded.

'Okay. I'll text Cressy.'

Freya's fingers weren't quite steady as she typed. The fact Drew was worried about her being in the heat didn't usher in any sense of hope. He didn't again look at her or speak.

The strain between them deepened when they headed for home in his ute. Drew's knuckles shone white on the steering wheel and the roomy cabin suddenly seemed too small.

She settled back into her seat. She was determined to finish what she'd started. 'Thanks for taking me home.'

He took a long moment to answer and when he did his bleak voice sounded as though it had come from a dark, deep place inside him. 'Freya … I'm sorry about last night. But as much as I wish it wasn't true … things don't look any different this morning.'

She kept her expression calm and her reply composed. 'I knew they wouldn't. That's why I'm here.'

He shot her a quick glance.

Freya waited until they'd entered the charred remains of his wheat crop before speaking again. 'I think this is the place where we need to talk. Can you please pull over?'

To her relief, Drew did as she asked. He left the ute running so the air-conditioner would keep them cool.

'Drew ... what happened here wasn't your fault. It was just bad luck the wind changed. The fire getting away could have happened to anybody.'

His mouth compressed as he focused on the grey and twisted metal that had been his old header.

If Drew wasn't going to talk, she would. She unclipped her seatbelt so she could face him. 'You thinking about other things besides Inglewood shows you're human and that there's things missing from your life. You can't let your grief continue to shut everyone and everything out, because the reality is then you're only living a half life. And I think deep down you know that.'

He waved a hand towards the desolation that carved a black swathe in the paddock before them. 'This is the reality of my life, especially when I don't stay focused.'

She didn't look away from him. 'No, it isn't. Your life could be so much more, even when bad things happen. Do you think your mother and father, and even Brett and Sarah, would want you to grow old at Inglewood, alone and isolated, working yourself into a shadow?'

Drew didn't reply. His hands fisted where they rested on his thighs.

She spoke into the tense silence. 'What we have is real, special, and I'm not leaving, no matter how much you push me away.' She ignored her fears she couldn't breach the wall between them. She wasn't quitting until she found a way in. 'Drew ... nothing's going to happen to me.'

The deepening of the grooves beside his mouth and the torment in his eyes said her suspicions about why he pushed her away could be right.

She placed her hand on his forearm. He didn't move. 'I'm sorry you've suffered so much loss, but cutting me out of your life isn't going to keep me safe. The safest I'll ever be is right by the side of the man I love and I hope cares for me.' The muscles of his arm jerked beneath her touch. 'Together we can look out for each other and handle anything that life throws our way.'

Drew didn't respond at first. Then he moved. His hands tangled in her hair and his mouth sought hers. The tender sweep of his lips and the shudder of his strong body told her she'd finally reached him. He deepened the kiss until their breathing grew ragged. When they drew apart to breathe, he rested his forehead against hers.

'I love you, Freya George. You're all I think about. You're the only thing I need in my life. If I lost you too ...'

She silenced him with another kiss.

When they again parted, he ran the back of his hand over her cheek. 'This obsession with finishing things that you start, is it going to appear often?'

'Only when it comes to Christmas and making sure you live the full and complete life you deserve.'

He grinned, happiness turning his eyes a pure, deep blue. 'In that case I think we'd better head home.'

She smiled and laced her fingers with his. 'Here I was thinking you had a header to drive?'

He stole a heady kiss before replying. 'Saul told me I wasn't allowed back until I'd been well and truly distracted.'

Epilogue

After the heat of Christmas Day, the cool change that breezed through on Boxing Day brought welcome relief. Though still hot enough to swim, it was cool enough to sit beneath the shade as the sun descended.

Freya carried a tray of watermelon outside to place on the large outdoor table she'd found in the shed. After wearing her special red dress to Christmas lunch at Cressy's the day before, she now wore a casual halter-neck black dress. Christmas at Glenmore had been so enjoyable, Drew had invited everyone around to Inglewood for a Boxing Day swim and barbecue.

The homestead that had stood silent and empty for so long now echoed with life and laughter. She smiled as she returned inside and the shimmer of tinsel greeted her. She'd already started planning what decorations she'd put up next year for when her father and sister joined her and Drew for Christmas.

When her house was again habitable, she'd live in Reedy Creek during the school week and then spend weekends and holidays at Inglewood. Hattie had visited on Christmas Eve to sprinkle sparkly reindeer food on the lawn and to open her presents. After she'd gone Drew had wrapped his arms around Freya and they'd stayed up late talking about a trip to Canada to see his extended family. Her smile grew as happiness bloomed inside. It had been agreed that such a trip would also make a perfect honeymoon.

She reached for the cheese platter on the island bench and when Hattie squealed she looked towards the pool. Tanned skin flashed as Denham played against Hattie and Drew in volleyball. Hattie sat on top of Drew's shoulders and her wide smile as she threw the ball over the net said that while there had been tears, her Christmas had also been filled with love.

Tanner had declined to participate in the volleyball match and instead manned the barbecue on the corner of the veranda. His awkwardness around little Hattie explained his reluctance to join in the fun. Freya could only hope he'd soon meet someone who'd help him overcome his fear of babies and small children. As for his fear of Edna, that would only be resolved when she crossed him off her potential-son-in-law list. Going by the invitation he'd earlier received to attend their Boxing Day celebrations, such a thing wasn't happening anytime soon.

Freya took the cheese platter over to where Fliss, Cressy and Ella sat discussing wedding plans. From the loneliness Ella failed to hide, Freya sensed that her relationship with Drew had proved to the vet that it was possible to find happiness again after heartbreak. Freya was certain one day Ella too would find someone who'd make her want to risk opening up her heart again.

Bailey lay beside Cressy, his eyes glazing over as the cowgirl rubbed his stomach with her boot. Over in the pony paddock, the waning sunlight caught in Panda's fancy red Christmas head collar. He hadn't been as impressed with his reindeer ears. Liberty continued to improve and neighed for carrots and apples whenever Hattie visited.

Tanner grinned from over near the barbecue. 'These steaks are almost done. What would you like to cook next?'

'The kebabs, thanks. They won't take long. I'll just get them.'

She returned inside. The footsteps on the floorboards warned her before an arm snagged her waist and pulled her close to a bare, wet chest. She smiled as Drew's mouth covered hers.

She'd arrived in the bush, alone and bruised, only to discover a community that embraced her and a red earth landscape she felt at home in. Her hands curled around Drew's neck. But most of all, under Christmas stars she'd fallen for a man who didn't need any festive mistletoe to show her how much he loved her.

Also by Janet Gover

The Lawson Sisters
Close to Home
The Library at Wagtail Ridge

Christmas at
Coorah Creek

JANET GOVER

For John. Always.

Chapter 1

In the middle of nowhere, Katie Brooks' car exploded.

At least that's how it felt as thick steam burst out from under the bonnet. Suddenly Katie was driving blind at high speed as the steam enveloped the front of her car. She lifted her foot from the accelerator and reached for the windscreen wipers. That only made things worse. The dust on her windscreen turned to mud and was smeared in a messy rust-coloured arc across the glass. Cursing, Katie turned the steering wheel and let the vehicle roll slowly to a stop on the side of the road. She got out and took a step back to look at the car she had owned for a little less than forty-eight hours. She didn't know much about cars, but she didn't need to know much to be certain that the blue Holden Commodore wasn't going anywhere in the near future.

'That'll teach me to buy a twenty-year-old car,' Katie muttered under her breath. 'So much for an "Australian classic". That's the last time I listen to a used car salesman.'

She took a deep breath and slowly turned in a circle.

She was standing in the middle of the longest stretch of straight flat road she had ever encountered. The thin grey line extended to the horizon in either direction, without so much as a building or another car in sight. In fact, she hadn't seen another human being for what seemed like hours. The only living thing she'd spotted was a kangaroo hopping across the road about a hundred miles back. So much space and so few people! Would she ever get used to it?

The geyser pouring from underneath her bonnet was beginning to ease. She opened the door and walked to the front of the car, reaching inside to feel for the catch. Very carefully she raised the bonnet, releasing another cloud of steam that quickly dissipated. She stared at her engine for a few seconds, before admitting it was a waste of time. She had no idea what to do. If she was going to get out of here, it wasn't going to be in the Commodore. She swung her leg to kick the offending vehicle, but at the last minute, pulled the blow. In her open-toed flat sandals, the kick was likely to hurt her foot more than the car.

She walked into the middle of the road and looked back the way she had come. Nothing. She looked in the direction she'd been heading. Somewhere out there was a small town called Coorah Creek. She did remember seeing a sign a while ago, but had no idea how far she still needed to go. And all the road signs were in kilometres, not miles. So even if she knew how many kilometres, she wasn't entirely sure she'd know how far that really was.

As she stood gazing down the road, bits from her reading leaped into the forefront of her mind. The bits about people dying of thirst when their cars broke down. And the bits about poisonous snakes and spiders. There probably weren't any man-eating crocodiles here, a million miles ... kilometres ... from the coast. But weren't the wild pigs dangerous too? Suddenly a whole less sure of herself, Katie leaned back against the car.

'Ow!' She leaped forward as the hot metal burned her thighs through the thin cotton of her skirt.

That was another thing. It was hot here. Really, really hot! Her car's on-again-off-again air-conditioning had barely been worth the name. And now she was standing in the blazing sun in an area desperately low on trees. She wandered along the road a short distance, looking for a tree big enough to give her a spot of shade. Nothing. She turned her face to the sky – a brilliant arc of totally cloudless blue. She could already feel her pale English skin starting to burn.

'Well,' she said to the vast empty spaces, 'I left cold, grey, miserable London feeling burnt out by my job and that I'd lost my way. Now here I am, lost in the middle of nowhere and about to get really burned.'

The frustration building inside her suddenly exploded into a burst of laughter, but she was aware of the undertone of hysteria.

Returning to the car, she opened the rear door and rummaged around in the bags strewn over the back seat. Somewhere in there was a hat. And some sunscreen. Sweat was dripping from her forehead by the time she found them. She stepped back from the car and began slathering the white cream over her nose and cheeks.

'So now what do I do?' she wondered out loud. 'Do I wait with the car like it said in the books? Or do I start walking?'

The only answer was the distant haunting caw of a crow.

Surely someone would come along soon.

She reached for her handbag, and retrieved her mobile phone. Squinting against the bright sunlight, she looked at it with little hope. She'd already discovered that large parts of Australia did not have mobile coverage. Either that or her phone was rubbish, which was also entirely possible.

Grimacing in disgust, she tossed the phone back onto the front seat.

Just a couple of weeks ago, she'd been wrapped in a heavy wool coat, fighting her way through crowds of shoppers in Oxford Street and admiring the best Christmas lights in London. She had cursed those crowds and their armloads of parcels and bags blocking her way. Right now she would give anything to see a few of them walking towards her. She would even offer to carry those parcels for them.

Once more she looked in both directions along the road. Nothing but the distant heat haze shimmering across the grey tarmac. It looked like water, or ...

Water.

She was suddenly dying of thirst.

Katie turned back to her car. She wasn't a total idiot. She'd bought water at the last petrol station.

Ah-ha!

She held the plastic bottle aloft in triumphant. But her joy was short lived. There was only about an inch of liquid left in the bottom. She removed the lid but hesitated. Should she drink it now or wait. Surely she wouldn't be here long? Would she?

Defiantly she drank the last of the water. There! It was done. Now someone had to find her.

She looked down at her arms, trying to see if the skin was already turning pink. It felt as if it should be. For the first time, she felt a real twinge of fear. As a nurse, she knew about the effects of sunstroke and dehydration. But what could she do? There wasn't any shade.

Maybe she could make her own.

She opened her suitcase and eventually found a long, light cotton skirt. She squinted up to judge the angle of the sun then opened both car doors. She tried to spread the skirt over them to form a tent. It didn't work. The patch of shade created wouldn't have sheltered a mouse. Even that little bit of effort had raised a sweat, and she could feel her energy being drained away by the relentless heat.

She looked at the skirt in her hands. It had been a gift from her sister, and she was quite fond of it. But she was also quite fond of being alive. If another car didn't come along for a couple of hours – and that seemed entirely possible – she was in real trouble.

She gripped the skirt firmly and tugged at the side seam. It took a lot of effort, but finally she heard the stitches tear. When she opened the skirt out, she had quite a large piece of fabric to work with. Enough to make some sort of tent. She spread the material between two open car doors, using the windows to hold the edges. After a few minutes work, and a lot more sweat, she had created a small patch of shade between the two doors, under the tented fabric.

Before she sat down, she scrabbled around some more in her suitcase, and emerged with a woolly cardigan – a garment she was unlikely to need in the near future. She put the cardigan down in the small patch of shade. That would give her bum some respite from the rough gravel on the side of the road. Then she lowered herself into her makeshift sun-shelter.

It wasn't cool. Far from it. The heat radiating from the metal of the car was intense, but at least she wasn't in the full blazing sun.

She wriggled about a bit. Trying to get comfortable – or at least less uncomfortable. She tried to stay focused, listening for the sound of an approaching engine. But all she could hear was that damn crow. It was starting to get on her nerves.

She glanced at her watch. How long had she already been here?

Her head was starting to spin and her eyelids fluttered.

No! She had to stay awake.

She shook her head, wishing she still had some water left. Wishing she had never hopped on that plane in London. She had really messed up. Again. The wrong career, and now the wrong place to pursue that career.

Her life wasn't exactly going as she had hoped. If only …

She felt her eyelids starting to close. She took a deep breath and blinked rapidly. It already felt like she'd been stranded for hours. She glanced down at her watch again. Time was moving at a snail's pace.

She must not fall asleep!

Chapter 2

It had to be the most boring stretch of road in the world – this road that led to Coorah Creek. This road that was taking him back after so many years. It was long and straight and flat with no turnings or side roads. Scott Collins wondered if maybe there was a metaphor in that.

He wriggled his fingers on the wheel to relieve the stiffness and the boredom. He'd never thought he'd see this part of the country again. And certainly not of his own volition. But times change. People change. He was coming back to Coorah Creek and he had no idea what was waiting for him there.

He reached out to pick up the water bottle from the centre console. His air-conditioning was going full bore, but he could still feel the sun beating down on his car. He was looking forward to getting away from the relentless heat. And the dull burnt colours. And the rain that thundered so hard on a tin roof that you couldn't hear yourself think. His future was full of lush green places, where rain fell in gentle refreshing showers. He might even get his first white Christmas, if things went well. That could be fun. He'd never seen snow.

At least he would be in a place where there were no memories to haunt him.

But if he was going to escape those memories, there was something he had to do first. He had to return to Coorah Creek.

Somewhere ahead of him, the sun flashed off metal, pulling Scott's attention back to the long straight road. It was easy – and very dangerous – to lose concentration like that. He strained to see through the shimmering heat haze in the distance. There was a dark shape – a car – on the side of the road up ahead.

Scott immediately lifted his foot from the accelerator. He'd been away from the outback for more than eight years, but some lessons are never forgotten. In the outback, you never drove past a stranded car without stopping to see if the driver needed help. Out here, a broken-down car could cost someone their life.

Scott pulled off the road a few yards behind the blue Commodore. He registered its make with a smile. The car was a classic, but getting on in years. He wasn't surprised that it was stuck way out here. Now, where was the driver?

That's when he noticed the fabric stretched between the two open doors. Someone had tried to construct a shelter. He strode quickly forward when he saw a girl apparently unconscious lying half in and half out of that makeshift shelter. He swiftly knelt beside her and reached out a hand to touch her face where the skin was already red. She looked so young and so terribly vulnerable.

'What the …' With a jerk the girl suddenly sat up, her eyes staring wildly around her.

'Hey. It's all right.' Scott sat back on his heels to give the girl some breathing room.

She ran her hand over her face. Slowly her eyes came to focus on him. 'Oh.'

'I saw your car. Are you all right?'

'Yes. I fell asleep. Jet lag.' The words came out as a harsh croak.

'Hang on a second. Don't try to get up yet. You need water.'

Scott rose to his feet and jogged back to his car. The water bottle he'd been drinking from was half empty, but there were two more on the passenger seat. He picked up both of them.

The girl had pulled herself into a sitting position, leaning back against the car. She looked terrible. Scott tried to conceal his concern as he passed her an open bottle.

'Slowly,' he warned as she began gulping down the warm liquid. 'Slowly!' Scott put his hand on her arm and she lowered the bottle. 'If you drink too fast you'll probably throw up,' he told her. 'And we don't have enough water to waste it like that.'

The girl took a deep breath, and nodded. She leaned back and closed her eyes. Scott could see the strain on her face. He waited silently until she was ready to take a few more slow sips of water.

'Do you want to try to get up?'

She nodded.

'Okay. But take it easy.'

The girl really didn't need the warning. She was moving very slowly, and looked quite shaky as she gathered her feet under her. Scott stood up and reached down to help her. She was a small thing – light as a feather and barely up to his chin. She swayed a little, and he kept one hand on her arm until he was certain she wasn't going to fall down again.

She took another smaller drink of water, and finally looked him squarely in the face.

'Thank you.' Her voice sounded much stronger.

'Are you all right?'

'I think so,' she said. 'I must have fallen asleep. It was so hot.'

'You passed out,' Scott said. 'Dehydration and heat exhaustion will do that.'

'I know that,' the girl said. 'I'm a nurse.'

'A nurse? Then you should know better than to come out here without water.'

'In my part of the world, there isn't much chance of dying of lack of water by the side of a road.'

As she spoke, her accent finally registered. 'You're English?'

'I am.'

'Then what the hell are you doing out here all by yourself? And without water? This isn't England.'

'I know that,' she girl said, a touch of anger bringing a spark into her blue eyes. 'I had water. I ran out. I wasn't expecting this rubbish car to break down, was I?'

'It's not a rubbish car.' Scott tried to hide his smile as the girl painfully shook the fist she'd just thumped the car with. 'It's just old. What happened?'

'It exploded.'

Scott raised an eyebrow. Obviously a girl given to understatement. As she sipped slowly from the bottle of water, he moved to the front of the car and checked under the bonnet.

It didn't take him long to figure it out.

'You've probably put a stone through your radiator.'

'I'd figured that out too.'

Scott was pleased to see the girl had produced a hat from somewhere and was now wearing it. The brim wasn't broad enough to give her face much protection, but it was better than nothing.

'So what do I do now?' she asked.

'You're heading to Coorah Creek?'

'How did you know?'

'That's where this road goes,' he told her. 'After the Creek, there's just Birdsville.'

'And after that?'

'The desert. You really don't want to go there – and especially not with this.' He patted the old Holden affectionately.

She smiled at that, and Scott caught a glimpse of the girl behind the stranded tourist. Now that her eyes were no longer wide with distress, they were a lovely shade of blue-grey. Her face was a bit red from the sun, but she was a very pretty girl. About his own age, he thought. And as for that accent – that was just a cuteness bonanza. He couldn't help but wonder what on earth a girl like this was doing heading for the Creek.

'So?'

Acutely aware that he had been caught staring, Scott tried to look efficient. 'I guess I'd better get you into town.'

'Can't I call the … whatever you call the Automobile Association out here?'

Scott smiled. 'No, actually.'

'Oh. No phone service.'

He nodded.

'Well, there must be a garage at Coorah Creek. Have they got a tow truck? You could send them back for me.'

The words froze Scott in his tracks, his face closing down. It wasn't the girl's fault. She didn't know what memories her words had just unleashed to strike him with an almost physical force. She had just turned an impulse into a stark reality. His return to Coorah Creek was no longer something in his future. It was here and now and he wasn't really ready for it. That wasn't a good sign. He struggled for a few seconds to regain an appearance of normality.

'No truck,' he said. 'I've got a rope in my car. I'll tow you in.'

'But I don't know …' The girl's voice trailed off, and Scott saw the apprehension in her eyes. *You and me both*, he thought.

'Perhaps it would help if I introduced myself. I'm Scott Collins,' he said. 'And I promise you I am not an axe murderer or even a car thief.'

That almost wiped the tension from her face. Her lips twitched in the start of a smile. 'Hi Scott. I'm Katie Brooks.'

She held out her hand and he took it briefly. Like Katie herself, it was small and looked far too delicate for life in the outback.

'I'll get the rope.'

Chapter 3

Ed Collins didn't recognise either of the approaching cars. He squinted against the glare outside his workshop. He'd been Coorah Creek's only garage and mechanic for more than thirty years. There wasn't a car within 200 kilometres he hadn't worked on or filled with petrol. These must be tourists, passing through on their way to Birdsville. He studied the blue car. It was getting on in years. It wasn't surprising that it was being towed. He hoped the driver wasn't planning to take it into the desert. People died doing stupid things like that.

The car towing it was interesting. It looked like one of those hybrids. He'd read about them. Never seen one though. The Creek wasn't a place for flash environmentally friendly cars. Workhorses. That's what the cars out here were. It was too much to hope he'd get his hands on the car, but it would be nice to have a look under the bonnet. If the driver seemed a good bloke and was going to be around for a day or two, maybe he'd get a chance.

Ed picked up an old rag and began wiping his hands. The owner of a car like that wasn't going to want greasy handprints on his shiny new paint. As he tossed the rag aside, Ed looked at his hands. The dirt never really seemed to come off. Not that it mattered. There was no one he wanted to impress. He was a mechanic. Always had been and always would be. Mechanics had dirty hands. People just had to accept that.

The lead car angled off the road towards the garage and began to slow. Ed could see the person being towed wasn't paying attention. He knew what was going to happen next. The Commodore clipped the back of the hybrid, shunting it forward. Both drivers hit the brakes and the cars came to a halt about a metre apart.

A girl jumped out of the Commodore. She was young and blonde and pretty. And very distraught.

'Oh my God. I am so sorry!' As upset as she was, her English accent was still very pronounced. She bent over to examine the damage to the back of the hybrid.

'I wasn't paying attention. It's all my fault. I'll pay to get it fixed.'

So, maybe he would get to work on the hybrid after all. Ed stepped towards the open door, but stopped in shock as the driver of the hybrid got out of his car.

Eight years is a long time. In eight years, regret can eat at a man's soul leaving him empty and lonely. In eight years a boy becomes a man. But even after eight years, a father knows his own son.

Shocked to his core, Ed took half a step backward to remain hidden in the dim interior of his workshop.

His son … Scott … wasn't paying any attention to the girl. He was studying the outside of the garage. He wouldn't find anything changed, Ed thought. At least, not the building.

'I feel just so bad about this,' the girl was still apologising. 'After you rescued me when I was in trouble.'

'Don't worry about it.'

His voice was the same. So too was the shock of brown wavy hair. Just like Ed's when he was young. And the way he stood, straight and sure of himself. As a teenager, Scott had always been unwilling to back down or give an inch. It didn't look like that had changed.

But something must have changed, because he was here – in the place he had left, vowing never to return.

Ed's hands were shaking. He jammed them deep into the pockets of his dirty overalls. He had to do something. He couldn't just stand in the shadows looking at his son. But he wasn't ready to face him yet. He just needed another minute.

'I can't say how sorry I am, or how grateful.'

The girl was still talking. Ed wondered who she was. It sounded like she was a stranger Scott had found on the side of the road.

'Anyone would have done the same.' Scott finally turned his attention back to the girl. He dropped to the ground and reached under the Commodore to untie the tow rope.

Now was the time, Ed knew. He should go and speak to them. He wished the girl wasn't there. He would much rather have been alone when he faced his son for the first time after so many years. There was a lot they had to say to each other. Things that couldn't be said in front of a stranger. In front of anyone. But it looked like he wasn't going to get any choice.

He took a step forward.

Outside, he saw Scott stiffen, staring in Ed's direction. Had his son seen him?

'You'll be fine now,' Scott said to the girl, without taking his eyes from the door of the garage. Then he turned, quickly got back behind the wheel of his car. Within a few seconds he was gone.

His son didn't want to see him. Ed's heart was pounding. He wasn't sure what he felt. Relief at having more time to prepare for their meeting. Fear that Scott might leave town without ever talking to him. He wanted to know what had brought him back after so long. And most of all, he desperately needed to know if Scott had ever found what he was searching for.

Outside, the girl was still waiting.

Ed took a deep breath and walked out into the bright sunlight. 'G'day.'

'Hello. I'm afraid my car has broken down. Radiator, I think.'

'I'll take a look.'

Working on cars had always been Ed's great joy. Even at the worst of times, he could lose himself in his work and put his troubles to one side. Not so today. He took a cursory glance.

'Yeah. Radiator. It'll need replacing. I can get one in for you. Take a couple of days though.'

'That's all right. I'm here to stay. I'm going to be working at the hospital. My name is Katie. Katie Brooks.'

'Ed.' There was no need to tell her more than that. 'Lucky for you that bloke was able to tow you in. Is he a friend of yours?'

'No. He found me on the side of the road. Good thing too. I was out of water and starting to worry.'

'A good bloke then?'

'Oh yes. He was just great!'

Ed looked at her face as she spoke. There was a shine in her eyes that told him his son had impressed this girl. Clearly she was hoping to see him again. Ed knew that look. A woman had once looked at him like that. A long time ago. It hadn't lasted long, but how sweet it had been. It had given him a son, but that relationship too had soured.

Ed felt just a small flare of hope deep inside. Maybe he was about to get a second chance.

Chapter 4

Scott felt bad about leaving the poor girl so abruptly. He wasn't normally that rude. She seemed rather nice. She was also very pretty and just a little bit lost. It must be tough for someone so very English to find themselves all the way out here, beyond the black stump. He was normally more than happy to help a lady – especially one with blonde hair and blue eyes, but he'd had to get out of there. He did not want to face the man he'd seen moving in the shadows inside the garage.

He turned the corner and parked outside the pub. He switched his engine off and looked up at the two storey building. It hadn't changed. The paint looked fairly new. It hadn't faded or developed that faint powdery look caused by long exposure to the harsh outback sun. But it was the same colour he remembered. The lovely wrought iron railings still edged the balcony on the top floor, twisting in intricate lacework. He had always loved this old building. So beautiful and elegant. So different from the garage and the shabby house behind it.

Scott slowly got out of the car and turned to look about him. The pub might not have changed, but the rest of the town certainly had.

He remembered the general store, but it was larger now. Had it been extended? The feed store was still the same, but what was that across the road? A ladies' hair salon? That was new. So were the clothing store and the houses that he could see in the distance, either side of the town's other main road – the one that led north to Mount Isa. When he'd last seen Coorah Creek, the Goongalla Uranium Mine was just a topic of conversation and a hope for the future. Obviously the mine had prospered and the town along with it.

He was glad about that.

He turned around and walked the few steps back towards the T-intersection that was the heart of the town. He could see the garage now. Any prosperity brought by the mine hadn't touched that. It was still shabby and dirty. Even more so than he remembered. It occupied the corner opposite the pub. From this angle, he could see the workshop and the petrol bowsers. Eight years had passed since he'd last seen it and to his eyes it looked exactly the same. Nothing had changed. It didn't even appear to have benefited from a new coat of paint in all that time. Over the top of the rusting tin workshop roof, he could see gum trees reaching skywards. That would be the garden around the house. He remembered those trees, but they had been a lot smaller back then.

Katie's car was still sitting outside the workshop. The bonnet was up, but he could see no sign of either its driver or the man who was fixing it. She would be all right, he thought. The old man was honest and would easily repair her radiator. And he'd charge a fair price for the work. No-one had ever accused the old man of doing wrong by a customer. His family though …

Scott went back to his car. At some point he was going to have to enquire about a room at the pub, but not right now. Since he had driven past the town sign, memories had been flooding back. Among those memories was the publican's wife – a garrulous woman with a real taste for gossip. If he checked into the hotel now, the whole town would know he was here in just five minutes.

He wasn't ready for that yet.

He slid back behind the wheel of his car and pulled away from the pub. He'd drive around for a while, just to have a look at the town.

It didn't take long. The town might have grown a lot in eight years, but it still wasn't very big. The houses on the north side all looked fairly new. They must have come with the mine, he thought. The old police station was still there, but it was now part of some kind of town square. The school was bigger than in his day. And it had a swimming pool! Now that was an improvement. Curious, he drove towards the southern side of town where he knew the mine must be. He wouldn't mind taking a look at it. A couple of miles out of town, a good quality bitumen road led off to the left. He turned down it and sure enough, there were the gates to the mine. He drove straight past, following the chain link fence until he came to … an airport? Things certainly had changed.

But now he had run out of excuses. Reluctantly he executed a three point turn on the narrow road and drove back in the direction of town.

There she was again. Standing in the middle of the road. What was with this girl?

Scott pulled up next to her.

'Katie? Is everything all right?' Surely nothing had happened at the garage to send her running away?

'Oh, hello Scott.' The girl seemed pleased to see him. 'I'm heading for the hospital, which I'm told is just down this road.'

'The hospital?' Scott's first thought was since when had Coorah Creek boasted a hospital? His second was – why was she looking for a doctor? Surely the old man …

'Are you all right?' he asked.

'Yes,' she said. A small frown creased her forehead, and then faded as she suddenly grinned. 'No. No. I'm fine. I'm going to work there.'

'Of course, you said you were a nurse.'

'That's right. One who should have known enough about heat stroke and dehydration to carry water.' As she spoke, she raised her hand. There was a new, large and almost full bottle of water in it. 'Anyway Ed, I think that was his name … the man at the garage … said it was a short walk down here to the hospital. I'm expected. So I thought I would walk.'

Scott felt a small surge of relief. If she couldn't remember the mechanic's name, then she had definitely not made the connection between them. But no doubt she would in the not-too-distant future.

'I passed what I think may be the hospital just back there a bit,' Scott said. 'I'll give you a lift. It's far too hot to walk.'

He felt her hesitation. She was feeling a bit lost. A long way from home. He understood how that felt.

'Get in,' he said. 'I've already towed you in from the highway, what does another half a mile matter?'

Her smile was very appealing. Slightly crooked, but it lit her blue eyes as well.

'Thank you,' she said as she slid into the passenger's seat. 'You're right. It is far too hot to walk. I've had more than enough sun for one day.'

He cast a sideways glance at her. Her fair skin was already looking far too pink. He hoped she would be careful. The outback sun would be tough on her. And maybe just not the sun …

'So why Coorah Creek?' he asked as he turned the car again.

'I came to Australia for a working holiday,' she said. 'I was so sick of the cold weather and the rain. This was the first job I found.'

'You won't have any problem with cold wet weather here,' Scott said as he slipped the car back into gear.

Katie had to agree with him. She had never been so hot in all her life. Not even on that holiday in Spain. She was drenched with sweat just from walking a short distance from the garage where her car was being worked on by the shabby mechanic. Her feet hurt, because open-toed sandals were just not the right footwear for a place like this. Her skin felt flushed and burnt, and she was about to meet her new boss. Or at least, that was what she was expecting to do. She had e-mailed him to let him know to expect her this afternoon. But so far very little of this trip had turned out the way she planned it.

She hadn't seen much of Coorah Creek, but what she had seen wasn't quite what she'd had in mind. It was so small! And very quiet. Dry as well as hot. Most of the houses she'd seen were very old and shabby and rather than the red brick of her homeland, they were made of wood. The centre of the town, if that was what it could be called, was tiny, with just a handful of shops. It was such a long long way from Oxford Street and there were certainly no Christmas lights to be seen. The shops did look a bit more prosperous than the garage. That made her hope that her first impressions might be wrong.

Scott, however, had been a pleasant surprise. She cast a quick sideways glance at him. He looked to be in his mid-twenties. About the same age as her. He had a kind face. Not exactly handsome, but not unattractive. His hair was nondescript brown. His eyes were nondescript brown. His skin was tanned, and the hands gripping the steering wheel looked strong and competent. She liked that. The way he had dashed off after dropping her at the garage was a bit disconcerting. He must have had a reason. Some secret perhaps that he didn't want to share. There was nothing wrong with that, of course. Everyone had secrets. She certainly did.

Scott had been there when she needed help and he seemed really nice. She wasn't entirely comfortable alone in the car with a stranger, but she did feel a little bad about lying to him just now. Adventure had very little to do with her reasons for being here. But two accidental meetings weren't enough to encourage the exchange of her secrets either.

Katie's heart shrank a little when Scott turned into a driveway next to a painted wooden sign that identified the Coorah Creek Hospital. The building ahead of them didn't look like any hospital she had ever seen. For a start, it was built of wood. No brick or stone edifice of the type she was used to back in England, this hospital was a long low building built on wooden stumps and surrounded by a deep veranda. She had expected it to be small – but it looked barely big enough to accommodate a handful of patients.

As Scott pulled up near the broad front stairs, a young couple emerged. The girl was carrying a baby in her arms. She looked far too young to be its mother. Katie smiled at them as she got out of the car.

'Hello,' the young mother said. 'I bet you're the new nurse. Doctor Adam told us you were coming today. We've been waiting for you. I'm Nikki and this is my boyfriend Steve.'

'Oh,' Katie tried not to seem surprised by this. 'Is the doctor here?'

'He was,' the young man replied. 'He and Jess had to go. They've flown up to the Isa with an injured miner.'

Katie struggled with this latest information. She knew there was an air ambulance operating out of Coorah Creek. Her new job would include flying in that air ambulance as they tended to patients on outlying stations. Perhaps Jess was the pilot. As for 'the Isa' … she had no idea. There were times she felt as if the Australians didn't speak English at all, but rather some entirely different language.

'Doctor Adam asked us to meet you and show you to your place,' Nikki said.

'All right.' Katie wasn't entirely sure that it was all right, but it appeared that once again she didn't have a lot of choice.

'Right. This way.' Steve turned back into the hospital. Katie paused for a moment and turned back towards the car, where Scott was standing next to the open driver's side door. Obviously he was eager to leave. She didn't blame him. He probably had better things to do with his time than act as her chauffeur.

'Scott. Thanks for rescuing me … again.'

'You are very welcome.' He mimed tipping his hat in her direction and slid back behind the wheel.

As he drove away, Katie felt suddenly bereft. He was the closest thing she had to a friend for several thousand miles, and he was leaving her. She shook her head. Jet lag, she thought. And exhaustion. And the heat. She'd soon find her feet.

She followed the young couple into the hospital. The moment she stepped into the shade of the veranda, she felt the temperature drop. The building was surprisingly cool, despite the lack of air conditioning.

'You don't have any bags,' Steve said.

'They're in the back of my car,' Katie told him. 'It broke down just out of town. It's at the garage getting fixed.'

'I'm sure someone will run them over for you.'

This town must be full of good Samaritans and knights in shining armour, she thought.

'These used to be Doctor Adam's rooms. Before he and Jess got married,' Nikki said as she led the way down a hallway and opened the very last door.

The rooms in question were near the rear of the hospital. Katie stepped into a big living room. There was a small dining table and a big armchair. Empty bookshelves lined one wall. She assumed the doors opposite led to a bedroom and bathroom — at least, she hoped that's where they led. She could see a small kitchen through an open doorway to her left.

'We have to go now,' Nikki said. 'Doctor Adam and Jess will be back in a couple of hours. You'll like them. They delivered Anna together.' She kissed her child's head, and the young man beside her almost glowed with pleasure as she did.

Katie watched them leave, her head in a spin. She closed the door behind them and leaned back against it. The sheer emptiness of her new living quarters suddenly crashed down on her like a ton of rocks. She was a million miles from home, hot and dirty and exhausted. She was about to spend Christmas without her family for the very first time and she doubted there was so much as a kettle and cup in the kitchen for making a cup of tea. To top it all off, she was a nurse in a place where — the girl's words suddenly sank in — a pilot helped to deliver a baby.

She had gambled her whole future on this job. Had she made a terrible mistake?

Chapter 5

Pub or garage? Scott was pretty certain he didn't want to go into either. He'd really rather go back to the hospital and spend some more time with Katie. At least she had seemed happy to see him. And her smile was a far more pleasant prospect than what awaited him.

Garage or pub?

He pulled his car up in front of the pub. Through the windows, he could see someone moving around in the bar. In his rear-view mirror, he could see the garage. No sign of movement there.

There really wasn't any choice. He'd been an angry teenager when he'd stormed out of Coorah Creek, but there were people who would remember him. The publican's wife was one of them. She had good reason to remember him. He winced slightly at the memory. If he walked into the pub, news of his return would fly through Coorah Creek like a storm.

He had to go to the garage and face what was waiting for him there before word of his return made matters a whole lot worse.

It took a lot of willpower to reach for the door handle.

He crossed the street, but instead of walking into the garage, his steps took him a little further to a side gate that led directly to the house next door. Between the scrubby bushes, he could see that his old home had changed; become poorer and more ill kept, with its peeling paint and rusty tin roof. The gate was rusty too. He did not move to open it.

A dog barked.

Scott searched the unkempt garden as the animal barked again. It was a rough, weak sound. Surely not …

The Labrador came into view. She was moving slowly and limping a little, pausing every few seconds to bark in Scott's general direction. She was old. So very old. Finally she arrived at the gate and stared up at him through rheumy eyes.

'Candy, old friend. Do you remember me?' Scott dropped to a crouch and reached his hand through the bars of the gate. The dog lifted her head as if to bark, and then hesitated. She lowered her nose to sniff Scott's outstretched fingers. Slowly her tail began to wag and she licked his hand.

Scott felt tears prick his eyes. His few good memories of Coorah Creek all seemed to involve his dog. Abandoned as a boisterous half-grown pup by some passing vehicle, she had come into a lonely boy's life and made it just that little bit less lonely. She had loved him – unconditionally as dogs too. And he had loved her back because there was no-one else to love. Leaving her behind when he left had almost broken him. But taking her had been impossible.

He'd never expected Candy to still be here. To still be alive after all these years. Her eyes were foggy and her muzzle was almost completely grey, but for such an old dog, she looked quite well. She'd obviously been cared for.

And she remembered him.

'So, are you just here to see the dog, or were you planning to come to the house?'

Scott closed his eyes for a few seconds, as if by doing so he could still avoid this confrontation. The familiar voice was not as strong as it had once been. But the anger was still there. And he felt an answering echo of anger in his own heart. Some things that he had hoped might change obviously had not. Slowly he got to his feet.

The man standing in front of him had aged too. His hair was grey and his skin dry and wrinkled after years of exposure to the harsh outback sun. Ed Collins was fifty, but he looked like more sixty. His eyes, though, had not changed. Not one bit. They were still hard.

'Hello, Dad.' It seemed such a banal thing to say, but he could think of nothing else.

'So, you're back then?'

Not for long, Scott thought. In fact, right now he wanted nothing more than to just get in his car and drive away. But he'd come all this way with a purpose. He couldn't leave without at least trying.

'It's been a long time,' he said.

His father said nothing. The old man was staring at him, his face fixed and unreadable. Scott knew that look. He also knew that his father's hands would be clenched into fists. He had strong hands, permanently stained with grease and oil. Large strong hands and powerful fists.

This was so much harder than Scott had thought. The memories were tumbling around in his mind. Memories that time had faded to black and white were flaring in brilliant colour, and the pain was as real as it had been all those years ago. He felt seventeen again.

Sitting between them Candy whined. Maybe the old dog remembered this too … father and son facing each other down. The air full of anger.

'Did you ever find her?'

After more than eight years, this was all his father had to ask him. Not how are you son? Or what have you done with your life? Not even if he was married or had a family. The bitterness was so strong Scott could taste it.

He shook his head as he turned away.

'No.' He didn't care if his father heard the answer or not.

He was walking away again. This time he didn't have the excuse of youth and anger, but that didn't matter. The desire to get away from that house and his father was equally as strong. And now, as then, he really didn't have any place to go, so once again he walked across the road and into the pub.

The first thing he saw was the tree. He could hardly miss it – covered as it was with flashing lights and tinsel and shining balls of red and silver. Christmas. He'd forgotten all about it. Not that Christmas had meant much to him for a very long time. Not since the day his mother walked out of the house behind the garage. He'd been just eleven years old. The next few years had been dark and unhappy – until the day a seventeen-year-old boy and his father had traded blows – and he'd walked away.

His fists still tingled with the memory.

The holiday meant nothing to him except a chance to earn double time at the various jobs he'd held. He'd never planned to come back at Christmas. He'd never planned to come back ... ever. But plans change.

'G'day. What can I get you?' The man behind the bar was a few years older than Scott. He was unfamiliar. Perhaps the elderly couple he remembered had sold the pub and moved on.

'Beer thanks.'

Scott sat down on a bar stool. He was the only patron in the pub – not surprising as it was barely five o'clock. If someone had asked him to describe this place yesterday, he would have said he didn't really remember. But now that he was here, he remembered it all. The long polished wooden bar. The big windows open to catch any hint of breeze. The fans turning slowly overhead because there never was any breeze. The glasses neatly lined up on shelves behind the bar were also there in his memory.

'Well, look who we have here. Scott Collins. I wasn't expecting to ever see you sitting at my bar again.'

He remembered the woman who had just entered the bar. Her face was a little more lined and her hair a lot more grey. But her eyes were alive with interest.

'Hello Mrs Warren.'

'It's been what – seven or eight years?' Her smile was tentative. 'Hopefully this visit will be a better one than last time you were here.'

'Well, better for me. I got my beer this time.'

'This time you're not seventeen.'

Or fighting mad, he wanted to add. Mrs Warren had refused to serve him that day when he'd stormed in here nursing bruised knuckles and looking for a ride out of town.

'It's a bit late, but I'd like to apologise for the window, Mrs Warren.'

'Apology accepted,' Mrs Warren moved behind the bar. 'Just don't do it again. Your father covered the damage last time. I don't imagine he'd do it a second time.'

His father had paid for the broken window? That was unexpected.

'So, you're back for Christmas then?'

The woman he remembered was always on the lookout for some juicy gossip, and he was afraid he was going to be the subject of that gossip whatever he said or did.

'I need a room,' he said, avoiding the question.

'We have rooms,' Mrs Warren replied. 'The pub is pretty much empty now. Not many people come out here at Christmas. More likely to head east to the coast. I've never been one for the coast, mind. I don't like swimming in the sea. And I'm too old now to be a beach bunny.'

Trish Warren had always talked a lot. That certainly hadn't changed.

'I can pay up front if you like,' Scott said. 'As I have a bad record with you.'

There was no answer. Scott found himself being scrutinised by a pair of very sharp eyes. Mrs Warren gave him a very thorough once over before looking him straight in the face. He held her gaze for a few seconds, then she nodded, as if making up her mind about something.

'That's all right,' she said as the phone at the end of the bar suddenly rang. 'I guess I can trust you.'

'Thanks Mrs Warren.'

'You'd better start calling me Trish.'

While Trish answered the phone, Scott looked down at the beer in his hands. He could still see the small scar on his forearm from the last time he'd entered this bar. Mrs Warren – he would never have called her Trish back then – had refused to serve him a beer because he was underage. He'd just stormed out of his father's house, laden down with a rucksack with all his possessions and a whole heap of anger. He stormed out of the pub too, but on the way he had put his fist through a window. Only some remarkably good luck had saved him from doing permanent damage to himself.

And his father had paid for the window. Scott wasn't quite sure what to make of that.

Trish's voice dragged him out of his reverie. She had hung up the phone and was now talking to the barman he'd seen earlier.

'... at the hospital by herself. Adam needs someone to go over there.'

'It that Katie you're talking about?' he asked.

'Yes. The new nurse.' Trish's eyes narrowed. 'I hear she got towed into town by a stranger today after her car broke down. I guess that was you, wasn't it?'

'I guess so.' He would be a stranger to most of the residents. 'I dropped her at the hospital to wait for the doctor.'

'That was him on the phone. He's not going to get back tonight. He wanted someone to tell her and make sure she was all right. Jack can run over ...'

'I'll do it,' Scott interrupted her.

Trish turned and raised an eyebrow. He knew why. The kid he'd once been hadn't been one for offering a helping hand.

'It'll be better if I do it. She knows me,' he explained. 'Or at least, she's met me. A familiar face might help. She's probably feeling a little lost and maybe a little scared.'

He knew only too well how that felt.

To his surprise, Trish nodded.

'You're probably right. But just stay there and finish your beer. I'll give you some food to take over for her. I know Jess – that's the doctor's wife – stocked the fridge in the flat, but it'll be easier if I send something over she can just re-heat. There'll be enough for two, if she wants you to keep her company.'

'All right. Thanks.'

'Don't get too carried away.' Trish smiled. 'I never got you to pay for that broken window, but you will be paying for dinner for two tonight.'

Chapter 6

It was too quiet. The silence was almost a physical thing. Katie stood on the steps of the hospital and gazed out into the deepening twilight. In the west, the sun was very low on the horizon, a ball of molten gold beneath a sky totally devoid of any clouds. The brilliant blue sky of the afternoon was slowly turning a deep royal blue as the first stars began to appear — like diamonds on soft velvet. It was quite beautiful and unlike any sunset she had ever seen before.

But it was so very very quiet.

She was a girl from London. The city was always full of sound. The rumble of cars, or buses or trains. At any hour of the night or day, you could hear people. The voices of late night travellers. Televisions in living rooms or music floating through an open window. There were dogs barking and street lights. In London you were never alone. There were thousands — millions — of people close by, and at times it felt as if it was a battle just to have enough space to breathe.

But out here, she was terrifyingly alone.

From where she stood, she couldn't see any other houses with lights. In fact, she couldn't see any other houses at all. She might have been the only person left on the planet. She knew the road was just a short distance away, but there were no cars. There were no voices ... just ... she stopped and listened. Suddenly the night was not as silent as she'd thought. There were noises. Creaks and groans from the building behind her. A sudden rustling of leaves in the big gum tree by the car park. The screech of some sort of bird. It was all so alien. How she longed for the comforting rumble of an Underground train.

Casting a nervous glance over her shoulder, Katie walked back into the hospital. That was no better. The hospital was as empty and as strange as the rest of Coorah Creek. There were no patients in the rooms. No other staff. No nurses hurrying about their work, or doctors doing their rounds. There was just her.

A few weeks ago, she would have welcomed the peace. All her life, the only thing she had ever wanted was to be a nurse. To help people. But the reality of her job was not what she expected. She loved the work and caring for her patients brought her enormous satisfaction. Helping someone through a difficult time was a source of joy, and her recent move into A&E nursing had been a reward for a lot of very hard work. Day after day, the long hours left her teetering on the edge of exhaustion, but that wasn't the part that had so nearly destroyed her calling.

As a student nurse, it had not occurred to her that a hospital would be a seething bed of rivalries and politics and unspoken rules. She had withered under restrictions, both official and unwritten, that had sometimes prevented her doing what her heart told her she should. She hated the doctors who seemed to consider the nurses as some sort of private harem. And equally she hated the doctors who treated the nurses as if they were nothing more than servants. This wasn't the medicine she wanted to practice, but in the great overstretched bureaucracy that was the National Health Service, it was the only medicine she seemed likely to ever know.

After one particularly long and fraught shift that lasted almost twenty-four hours, she had looked around and realised her heart was no longer in her job. She was dragging her feet each day as she made her way to work on the Underground. She had to make a change.

This job at a small outback hospital had seemed the answer to a prayer – a chance to get away from the daily grind of a big London hospital. It was a chance to get away from the long hours and the exhaustion and be able to give get more than a few moments to help each person. She wanted to answer a call for assistance as soon as she heard it, and not to have to put one person ahead of another. In a smaller community, she could really make a difference. She hoped that here in this small town, she could recapture her love of her job. She would be working with an air ambulance too. That sounded amazing. Not to mention the excitement and adventure of living in the Australian outback. It hadn't taken her long to get her paperwork in order and book a flight.

It had all sounded perfect – but looking around her now – Katie was starting to wonder if she'd been terribly wrong to come here.

The only lights were in the hallway and in her flat at the rear of the building. The glass doors swung shut behind her. Should she lock them? It didn't seem right to lock the door to a hospital, but if she was the only one there, what was to stop anyone just walking in and stealing something? Or … worse. She examined the door. There didn't seem to be any sort of lock. That settled that, but she would be sure to lock the door to her flat.

She couldn't do that either. When she walked back into her quarters, she discovered her door had no lock either. Did no-one in this town ever lock their doors?

Feeling bewildered and a little bit anxious, Katie walked over to the television and turned it on. The sound of voices filled the empty space around her. That helped, but it did not completely chase away her restlessness.

It was probably jet lag, she decided. She suddenly realised she was hungry. She hadn't eaten since that sandwich in her car several hours and many many miles ago. She had already discovered that her small kitchen was well stocked with essentials – tea, milk and even some home baked biscuits. But she needed something a bit more substantial than that. She took another look in the fridge and the cupboards. She could probably manage some scrambled eggs. Not quite what her rumbling stomach was after, but she didn't have a lot of choice. Her car was still at the garage and she wasn't going to walk out into the night in search of a grocery store. She wasn't a coward, but neither was she stupid. She had no idea who or what might be out there in the darkness here on the edge of nowhere.

Just as she was about to sink into a bottomless chasm of self-pity, she saw a flash of light through her window. A car had just pulled into the hospital car park.

As Katie walked down the corridor towards the hospital's front door, she was beginning to wish she had something in her hands. Something like a cricket bat. But, she chided herself, this was a hospital and she was a nurse. This was more likely to be someone in need of medical help than a murderer.

The glass doors opened and the only familiar face for a thousand miles … or kilometres … smiled at her.

'Hi Katie. We have got to stop meeting like this.'

'Scott!' Her heart slowed its nervous pounding, but not completely. 'I am beginning to wonder if you are the only other person in Coorah Creek,' she joked, hiding her relief.

'Actually, I don't live here,' the laughter in his voice faded. 'I'm just … visiting for a while.'

Katie wondered how long 'a while' might be. Scott was the closest thing she had to a friend, and she wasn't ready to lose him yet.

He was also, she suddenly thought, a very attractive man. Her first impressions earlier that day had been so very wrong. His brown eyes were deep and dark – with a dash of gold. She could get lost in those eyes. His brown hair curled in a way designed to make a girl just want to run her fingers through it. He was tall, with a lean, hard body and his skin was tanned a lovely golden colour. How had she thought him nondescript? His arms looked very strong. Looked like they would feel good wrapped around her. When his eyes met hers, she felt as if she was the only person in the world he was thinking about.

Katie felt her face starting to colour. What was she thinking? It must be the jet lag. Or exhaustion. Or loneliness. She didn't normally get all lustful on the third date – except, it wasn't their third date. Their meetings had been accidents, not dates, even though each time Scott appeared, her heart had given an excited little thump. And besides, a girl couldn't be blamed for feeling … kindly … towards the man who had rescued her twice.

'So, why have you come to the hospital?' Katie reached deep inside herself and found the nurse. 'Have you hurt yourself?'

'No. I come bearing messages and food.'

For the first time, Katie noticed the carrier bag. It was bulging. And there was the faintest smell of food in the air. Her stomach rumbled very loudly.

'Well, I guess that means I came at the right time,' Scott laughed.

Katie blushed and tried to cover her embarrassment by leading Scott down the hallway towards her flat. Once inside, he placed the bag on the table.

'Trish Warren over at the pub sent this over. There's some sort of lamb and potato stew. I hope you're not vegetarian.'

'No, I'm not. Lamb stew sounds good,' Katie said. 'What was the message?'

'The doctor apparently flew to the Isa today with a patient and they are not going to make it back tonight. He rang the pub and asked Trish to make sure you were all right. That you were settled in and had food and stuff. Oh, he sends his apologies too and says he will see you tomorrow morning.'

The news didn't come as much of a surprise to Katie. She had no real idea where 'the Isa' might be, but after hearing the news of the evacuation flight earlier, she had already begun to suspect the doctor wasn't returning today.

'Why didn't he ring me here?' she wondered out loud.

'Apparently your phone was disconnected when the doctor moved out and hasn't been fixed yet. He rang the pub because that's pretty much the centre of the town. He knew someone there would be able to get a message to you.'

'This is the first time I have made it to a job interview and the boss hasn't,' Katie joked.

'But haven't you already got the job? Surely you didn't come all this way just for an interview?'

'I've got the job. But it's sort of a provisional thing. Three months' probation. If I don't like it – or they don't like me ...'

'I'm sure they'll love you.' His words seemed genuine as did the smile that curved his lips.

'Well, thanks for telling me. And bringing the food,' she said, trying to hide the fact that she was blushing again.

'You are welcome.'

He showed no sign of leaving. Not that Katie wanted him to leave. It felt good not to be alone. But there was the matter of dinner. Her stomach rumbled again.

'You need to eat,' Scott said. He hesitated a moment before adding, 'Trish has put enough in there to feed a small army. And I put in a couple of beers. Just in case you felt like company. It doesn't seem right that you should spend your first night in town all alone. But if you'd rather I left, that's okay too. I can easily go back …'

'No,' Katie broke in before he'd finished speaking. 'Stay. Please. I'd enjoy some company.'

A few minutes later, they were seated around her small table, steaming food dished out on plates, and beer bottles dripping condensation onto the wood.

'So,' Scott said between mouthfuls, 'tell me more about what brought you all the way from England to Coorah Creek.'

'I was looking for adventure,' she told him. 'But this job also sounded pretty amazing. I'll be working with an Air Ambulance. Doesn't that sound great?'

The conversation flowed freely, but neither of them allowed it to become too personal. Instead, she and Scott spent the evening sharing anecdotes, talking about books and films and music.

And laughing.

And keeping a promise Katie had made to herself as her plane had risen through the grey clouds above London's Heathrow Airport. She had stared out the glass window of the jet and vowed that as soon as she arrived in her new home, she would have dinner with a handsome man to drive away any homesickness and doubt.

On this first night in Coorah Creek – she did just that.

And Scott did his part too.

Chapter 7

In the early morning light, Coorah Creek looked almost … nice. The gentle wash of dawn colour softened the harsh red of the dry earth to mellow amber. The dusty blue-grey gum trees appeared fresh and green. And as the stars faded, the arc above him was a pleasing royal blue – not the blinding hard blue of midday.

Ed was always up early. This morning, though, he had been awake much earlier than usual. To be honest, he hadn't slept a great deal. After the girl left yesterday, he'd hoped against hope he would see the silver-grey hybrid heading back towards the garage. That hadn't happened. Later, during the evening, he'd considered going to the pub. If Scott was still in town, that's where he'd stay. There was nowhere else.

Convincing himself that he was taking the dog for a walk, he'd crossed the road and strolled past the pub. Slowly, because Candy was an old dog and couldn't walk too fast. There had been no sign of Scott's car. Ed occasionally visited the pub, when he felt the need for human company. Trish was always willing to talk, even if he rarely answered. She served a good steak too. But Ed was in no mood for her gossip. He did not want to learn about his son from her. He'd returned to the quiet dark house behind the garage, and spent the evening with the dog at his side, trying not to listen for the sound of a car pulling up outside his home.

This morning, he'd given up the pretence. Letting Candy out to do her business, Ed had then walked through the rusty gate and stared across at the pub. Mentally, he checked off each of the half dozen cars he could see parked nearby. There was no hybrid.

Ed's heart sank just a little. Had Scott left? Their encounter yesterday had been as harsh as it had been brief. Maybe too harsh, but he was still struggling to come to terms with seeing his son again. Ed was suddenly afraid that he had driven Scott away for the second time.

He felt a gentle nudge against his leg, and bent slightly to pat Candy's head. The old dog waved her tail slowly.

'You want to see him again too, don't you girl?'

Candy barked softly.

'I know.' Ed turned back towards the house. As he was up, he might as well get a cup of coffee and get to work. He had a couple of cars in the shop right now as well as that girl's radiator to replace. He might as well open the garage early, just in case Scott was still in town and wanted to see him.

'Come on Candy. Time for breakfast old girl.'

The dog barked again, but didn't leave the gate.

'Candy. Come on.'

Still the dog didn't move. The road outside was deserted. There was nothing to be barking at. Shaking his head, Ed climbed the stairs into the house. The dog was getting old and senile. She would come when she was ready.

As Scott drove slowly back towards the pub, he glanced over at the house but saw no movement. It was still very early. He assumed the old man wasn't awake yet. He was glad. He just wasn't ready to talk to his father again. He'd spent such an enjoyable time with Katie last night, he didn't want anything to spoil his mood. He had not intended to stay the night at the hospital, but he and Katie had talked over dinner and on into the small hours of this morning. Talked easily and enjoyably about so many things. He couldn't for the life of him remember everything they talked about. But the sound of her laugh – that he could remember. They had drunk his two cans of beer and many cups of coffee until finally, Katie had yawned her way to bed. Scott had spent the few remaining hours of darkness sleeping on the couch, explaining to Katie that the pub was likely to be locked, and he might not get in to his room.

What he didn't explain to her was the other reason he'd stayed. He'd seen the nervousness and loneliness in her eyes and her relief when she realised it was him at the hospital doors. No-one knew better than he how hard it could be leaving home for the first time and being all alone in a new place. He'd been a teenager when he left … ran away … and knew just how scary the wide world could be if there was no one standing beside you. He was a grown man now, yet there were times, and this was one of them, when he didn't want to be alone either. And if he could help ease Katie's way at the same time, he would. Just out of kindness that was in no way related to her blue eyes, or the way she had smiled up at him from under her long blonde fringe.

But oh, she *was* pretty. And not a little bit sexy under that sweet face. Not that it mattered. He was just passing through. It wouldn't be fair to take advantage of her vulnerability. He would never do anything to hurt a woman. He was a very different man to his father. He'd just help Katie through these first few days, if she needed help.

He had left before she woke, starting the car as quietly as he could, fearful of waking her. His errant mind composed a picture of her asleep; her hair falling over her face, her body curled in such a way that a man could wrap his body around her and hold her while she slept. Or wake her ...

Scott shook his head. He was not going to go there! This was the wrong time to be giving any woman a second thought, even if such second thoughts were very very appealing.

He parked the car outside the pub and looked across at his father's garage. The sun was a little higher in the sky now, any residual softness burned away by the rising heat and glare. The light was not flattering. There was nothing about the garage that looked in any way welcoming or homely. The pub seemed so much better right now.

'Good morning!'

Trish Warren was standing by the pub's open door.

'Good morning,' he said. His mind raced trying to think of how to explain his absence the night before. Not that he had to answer to anyone, but he would not want Mrs Warren – Trish – to start gossiping about Katie. That wouldn't be fair. 'By the time I had delivered Katie's dinner ... Well... We talked and it got late. I wasn't sure if your door would be locked, so I slept on her couch.' He put a little extra emphasis on the last word.

'Careful there.' Trish's husband Syd appeared at her side. 'Trish will have you married off before you know what's going on.' The older man smiled at his wife with obvious affection, and much to Scott's surprise Trish almost blushed. She slapped her husband's arm gently.

'Get out of it,' she said. 'I'm just cooking breakfast, Scott. You'd best come and get some. There's nothing more important than a good breakfast to start a busy day. And I'm sure yours will be busy, as you've just come home after so many years.'

'Yes, Ma'am.'

Scott lingered over the well-cooked bacon and eggs and coffee Trish served. He lingered even longer over a hot shower. He even tidied his room before stepping out onto the wide veranda that enclosed the top floor of the hotel. From there, he could see across the street to the garage, which was now open. Somewhere in the shadowy recess of the workshop, his father would probably be bent over Katie's car. He felt a twinge of guilt that he hadn't told Katie that the grim old man at the garage was his father. She'd find out soon enough on the flourishing grapevine of Coorah Creek gossip.

In the meantime, he had come back to the Creek with a purpose. Standing here was not going to get that accomplished.

He found his father removing the radiator from Katie's car.

'Is it bad?' he asked.

At the sound of Scott's voice, his father's hands stilled for a few seconds, but he didn't look up. Then he continued his work. 'It needs a new radiator. I've got one coming on the train on Wednesday.'

'Okay.'

The dimly lit workshop was silent except for the sound of Ed Collins working.

Scott looked around him. Nothing had changed here in the past eight years. The workshop was still littered with tools and engine parts and spare car wheels in a sort of semi-controlled chaos that only his father understood.

'She'll need her things.'

'What?'

'I said she'll need her things. That girl. The new nurse. You seem friendly with her. You could take them over to the hospital.'

His father was asking for his help? Well, not exactly asking; but it was something.

'All right. I'll get my car.'

Scott stepped back into the sunshine, feeling as if he had just taken a first very small step in achieving his goal. And the thought of seeing Katie again was icing on the cake. It was the work of just a few minutes to return to the pub and collect his car. When he returned, there was another car parked at the garage and a tall, dark-haired man was talking to his father. They both turned as he walked into the workshop.

'Adam, this is my son, Scott. Scott, this is Adam Gilmore. The doctor.'

Scott took the man's outstretched hand, trying not to show his shock at hearing the words 'my son' for the first time in so many years. Instead, he tried to focus on the man who must be Katie's boss. He had a firm grip and was as casually dressed as you would expect in a place like Coorah Creek. Scott guessed he'd be considered handsome by some women. Would Katie think that?

'Thanks for helping out yesterday,' Adam said. 'I had planned to be here to meet Katie, but ... well ... the life of a doctor. You know how it is.'

'Glad to help,' Scott said.

'Anyway, we just flew back into town. I thought I would pick up her things and take them over to her by way of apology.'

There was nothing to say to that. Scott helped him load Katie's things into his car and watched him drive away. His father had returned to the workshop, his head once again buried under the bonnet of Katie's car. Scott really wasn't sure what to do. Maybe he'd taken a step in the right direction, but there was still a long way to go. He decided to head back to the pub and make use of the Wi-Fi there. He had a feeling he was going to stay in Coorah Creek longer than just a few days. There were some travel plans he needed to change.

Chapter 8

There was no choice. She was going to have to walk back to the garage and collect her things. Katie rinsed her mouth out with water and looked down at her rumpled clothing. She looked like she had been dragged through a hedge backwards. Sometime today she was probably going to meet her new boss and this was not how she wanted to look when that happened. When she'd left her car at the garage yesterday, she had been too exhausted to think straight. And she had expected to be able to return for her things. It hadn't worked out quite like that. She wanted a change of clothes, some face cream and most of all, she wanted her toothbrush!

Katie avoided even glancing at the couch where Scott had spent the night. He'd been gone before she woke. She certainly didn't want him to see her looking like this, but if he'd still been here, she could have asked him to drive her back to the garage to pick her things up. That would have been a lot easier than walking.

She wasn't entirely sure how she felt about last night.

Scott being there had certainly eased her first night and driven away any fear or loneliness. The food and beer had been good. Not only that, Scott had actually listened to her when she talked and treated her like a real person. She hadn't had a man do that for a very long time. The only men in her recent past were the doctors at her hospital, who seemed to think that the nurses were simply there to serve them ... in more ways than one.

Scott was different. When he looked at her he saw *her*, not just a nurse. And when she looked at him, she felt the occasional flutter in her stomach. She didn't believe in love at first sight, of course, but was there such a thing as like at first sight? Like a lot ...

She left the flat and walked through the hospital, hearing her footsteps echo in the empty hallway. It was a sound she had never before heard in a hospital. She stopped when she reached the hospital veranda. There was no lock on the door ... should she just leave it? And was it right to leave the hospital totally unattended? What if someone needed help? Or broke in trying to steal drugs?

Even as the thought formed, a car appeared at the hospital gates. A small cloud of dust followed behind as it drove up and parked just a few yards away. A man got out and approached her.

'You must be Katie. Sorry about all this. I'm Adam Gilmore.'

On no! She took her boss's outstretched hand, mentally listing all the ways in which this was NOT going to be the best job interview she'd ever had.

'Dr Gilmore. I ... I ... Um ...'

'Call me Adam. We're all very casual out here.'

'Um. Thank you Dr ... Adam.'

'I'm sorry you were stranded last night, but we had to fly to the Isa. And I hear you had car trouble too. Ed Collins will soon get that fixed. But still, I guess it wasn't the best welcome to town. But if it helps, I've brought your things from the car.'

If it helps? How could it not help?

'Oh, that's really good of you ... Adam. Thank you.'

The doctor turned back to the car and began pulling her bags from the back seat. Too late Katie realised that he'd brought everything from her car, including the empty water bottle and the loose shoes she had strewn across the back seat.

'Perhaps you'd better take these.' Adam was holding up a couple of shopping bags containing a swimming costume and some flip-flops that she'd bought the day she'd left Brisbane and headed for the outback.

She almost snatched them from his hand.

'I hope you're comfortable in the flat,' Adam said as, oblivious to her discomfort, he began carrying her two large suitcases up the stairs. 'I used to live there. I liked it, but if you don't, we can maybe come up with somewhere else.'

'No. No. It's fine.' She scurried after him, trying not to think that she was sleeping in her boss's bed.

'Good. Well, here we go.' He pushed open the door to her living quarters and strode in for all the world as if he owned the place. Which, Katie thought, he did, in a way.

The doctor carried her things through to the bedroom and unceremoniously dropped them on the bed. He returned, running his hands through his dark wavy hair.

'Were you all right last night? I asked Trish at the pub to look after you.'

'I didn't meet her,' Katie said. 'Scott brought some food over though, which I think she had cooked.'

'Scott?' Adam frowned. 'Oh yes. Ed Collins's son. I just met him.'

His words caused Katie to do a double take. Ed? Wasn't that the name of the old man at the garage? But that meant Scott ...

'Adam, give the poor girl some space.'

Before Katie could sort out the thoughts spinning in her head, a beautiful woman with short dark hair joined them.

'Hi. I'm Jess Gilmore. I fly the air ambulance and have the utter misfortune to be married to this crazy man here.'

The look the two shared put a lie to the latter part of that statement.

'Nice to meet you, Jess.'

'I'm just going to drag Adam out of here, to give you a chance to settle in a bit,' Jess said. 'When you are ready, drop in to the office. I'll show you around and we can get the paperwork done.'

Jess ushered Adam out and began to pull the door closed behind her, then paused. 'Adam,' she called, 'we need to get Jack around to put a lock on this door.' She raised a hand and disappeared.

Katie stood in the middle of the room, still holding her bag of recent purchases, wondering if Coorah Creek was always like this. People coming and going, without due regard for … well for anything really. It appeared the people here were as foreign as her surroundings. And there were obviously things she had yet to find out; relationships and where Scott fitted in to the picture.

She shook her head. She'd feel better after a bath – or rather, a shower. There was no bath in her tiny bathroom. She took a couple of steps towards the bedroom and paused. Turning, she placed a chair under the knob of her door. She had no idea who this Jack was. If he was going to put a lock on her door, that was all to the good, but she didn't want him wandering in to do it while she was in the shower.

About an hour later, feeling much refreshed with clean skirt and shirt and teeth, she set out in search of the hospital office. It wasn't that hard to find. The hospital wasn't very big, and she could hear voices.

'Katie, come in,' Jess said when she spotted her loitering outside the office door.

'We were just chatting. Ken Travers, this is our new nurse, Katie.'

The middle-aged man was tall and thin, with receding hair and the slightly haunted air that Katie instantly recognised. This was a patient.

'Hello,' she said.

'Ken and I are just setting up his next appointment,' Jess said. 'He'll no doubt be pleased to have a real nurse here again, instead of putting up with my inexpert help.'

'Jess, you've been great,' the patient said with a smile. 'And welcome Katie. We are very glad to have you.'

With that he left.

Jess closed the appointment book as she watched him leave. Then she turned her attention to Katie. 'It is so good to have you here. I help Adam when I can – but I'm a pilot and he needs a real nurse.'

Katie remembered the young mother's words the night before. Jess had helped deliver her baby. They certainly did need a real nurse.

'What happened to your last nurse?'

To Katie's discomfort, a shadow of grief fell over Jess's face. Her eyes dimmed for a minute and she appeared lost in memory. Then she spoke in a voice that was infinitely sad. 'Sister Luke was our nurse for a long time. She was a medical nun. She and Adam were very close and when she died, Adam refused to look for a new nurse for a long time. Then he hired a couple, but they didn't work out. It takes a special kind of person to work all the way out here. But,' Jess took a deep breath and the sadness left her face, 'I'm sure you'll be great. Adam was up all night with a patient, and he's sleeping now, but I'll show you around.'

The hospital was small, but very well equipped. Jess explained that the money came from the Goongalla Uranium Mine – the town's main employer. There was a small and immaculate theatre where minor surgery was performed. Anything major and the patient was flown to the nearest big hospital at Mt Isa. The half-unpacked box of Christmas decorations sitting in the reception area was testament to the fact that the patients' needs came first. At least, that's how Katie chose to interpret it.

'You'll encounter all sorts of things here,' Jess warned. 'I could hardly believe it myself when I first arrived. You'll have to be ready to turn your hand to almost anything. We can't just call for extra help if the going gets tough. There is no-one else, just this community.'

'Do you like it here?'

'I love it,' Jess said warmly. 'It's a unique place ... full of interesting people. In fact, why don't you come and meet some of them this evening? We can grab a counter meal at the pub and introduce you around.'

'Okay.' Katie wasn't sure exactly what a 'counter meal' was, but she knew about eating in pubs. She had often eaten at the centuries old London pub near her home. She imagined Coorah Creek's pub would be very different, but she was willing to give it a go.

'But first things first,' Jess added. 'I need to get you introduced to the paperwork.'

Chapter 9

Scott sat alone at one end of the long, polished wood bar, staring morosely at the glistening tinsel on the Christmas tree. The cheerful decorations seemed almost to mock him as he lost himself in memories of Christmases past. He should have happy Christmas memories, but any he did have were overshadowed by the darkness of those later years when he and his father had lived alone, barely speaking to each other. Times when the holidays had been barely acknowledged in the house behind the garage. Dark times.

There was movement in the corner of his vision as his father walked into the pub.

A flash of surprise crossed Trish Warren's face as she looked up from pouring a beer and saw who her new customer was. Scott guessed his father didn't make a habit of going to the pub. Ed had never been the sociable type. Scott turned his attention back to the cold beer in front of him, running a finger through the wet droplets of condensation running down the glass onto the beer mat beneath.

'I guess I could join you for a drink.'

'I guess you could.'

Ed parked himself on the next bar stool. Not too close, but close enough for a conversation that would be as private as any conversation could be with Trish in the same room.

Scott took a pull on his beer, and watched out of hooded eyes as his father did the same with the glass of Fosters that Trish placed in front of him.

A palpable silence settled over them.

Where did you start, Scott wondered. After so many years, where did you start trying to reconnect? There wasn't going to be an apology on either side. Eight years was far too long for that. But there had to be some way to start rebuilding some sort of relationship. Ed was the only family he had and this was the only chance they were going to get to put the past behind them. But what could he say that wouldn't seem banal, or critical or at the very least draw attention to the huge gap between them?

'So. You're staying at the pub.'

It wasn't a question.

'Yes. I ...' Scott let his voice trail off. He didn't want to say that he thought he might not be welcome in his father's home. He also didn't want to say that he wasn't sure if he ever wanted to set foot inside that house again. Neither comment was going to help the two of them cross the enormous gulf that lay between them.

Silence settled again.

'That your Prius outside?'

'Yes.'

'Hybrid?'

'Yes.'

'Any good?'

'Yes.'

Maybe it was genetic. This thing about cars. In those dark years after his mother left, the only real conversations he and his father had shared had been about cars. The arguments had been about everything else. So Scott guessed it wasn't really surprising that this, the closest thing to a conversation they'd had in so many years, would be about a car.

The silence was back.

Scott was very conscious that his father was making some sort of effort. He was the one who had sought Scott out. And if his conversation has been stilted, at least he'd said more than just one word. But what could he say that wouldn't bring back the past?

The bar door swung open and some people walked in. Even before he looked up, Scott knew that Katie was one of them. He heard her laugh. She was with the doctor and an attractive dark-haired woman. As the three of them greeted Trish and found seats at the bar, the dark-haired woman and the doctor seemed to be always touching each other. A casual brush of fingers together, a hand on an arm. That spoke volumes, and Scott found he was secretly a little relieved. He didn't like the idea of Katie being around that doctor too much, but if he was already spoken for—

She saw him and her face lit up. His heart did a little skip when that happened. It dropped into a different rhythm as he watched her excuse herself from the doctor and start towards him. He was very conscious of his father's eyes moving from Scott, to Katie, and back again.

'Hi Scott!' She sounded pleased to see him.

'Hi Katie. Are you starting to feel a little more settled?'

She nodded, her blonde fringe bouncing in a most beguiling way. 'I wanted to say thanks for last night. For the dinner; and for staying. It really did help.'

'You're welcome,' Scott said, wondering what the rest of the people in the room would make of that exchange. They were so obviously all listening. This was the Coorah Creek he remembered, where everybody knew everybody else's business, especially if it involved who was sleeping with whom.

Katie hesitated for a moment. She looked from Scott to Ed and back again. Scott could see the question in her eyes. He wanted to say something, but he wasn't ready for that just yet.

A few moments passed in tense silence before Katie spoke again.

'Anyway, I'd like to return the favour sometime soon. Cook you dinner. If you'd like to?'

Of course he would. Those lovely blue eyes peeping out from under that fringe would entice any man. 'That sounds great,' he said.

Katie looked extremely pleased. A touch of colour lit her cheeks. 'Well, I guess I had better get back. I'm having dinner with the boss.'

'You'll be fine,' Scott said reassuringly. 'I only met him today for a few minutes, but he seems like a good bloke.' An even better bloke if he was safely married.

Katie nodded. As she turned to go, she spoke to Ed for the first time.

'I'm sorry. I hope I didn't interrupt anything.'

'No.'

She hesitated. 'I hope my car's—'

'It'll be ready Wednesday afternoon,' Ed said with a brusqueness that was all too familiar to Scott.

'All right.' Katie sounded very uncertain. She looked quickly from Scott to Ed and then back again, before smiling at both and turning away to re-join Doctor Adam.

'Ashamed of me, are you?' Ed said as she walked away. 'Didn't want to acknowledge me in front of the girl?'

Scott wanted to say yes, he was ashamed. He didn't want Katie to know he was the son of a man who cheated on his wife and hit his son. He didn't want her to know the blood that ran in his veins. But he'd come back to Coorah Creek to make some sort of rapprochement, so he remained silent.

'I see. Well, you've got no grounds for moral superiority. Not if you spent the night with that girl when you barely knew her name.'

'It wasn't like that.' Scott got to his feet. He wasn't defending himself. After all these years, he didn't expect his father to have a very high opinion of him. And he didn't care either way. But he didn't want Katie's reputation damaged before she'd had a chance to establish herself in her new home. 'I was just helping someone who needed a friend. It's called kindness, but I don't expect you would know much about that.'

He walked away.

Leaving the pub by the back residents' entrance allowed Scott to avoid everyone – his father, Katie, Trish. All of them. Because right now he was in no fit state to talk to anyone. It was partly anger at his father. And partly anger at himself.

He cut through the back yard of the pub and leaped the low fence. Years ago, the land around the pub had all been empty. Now there were houses facing the road, but he was still able to skirt the back fences. That left him facing another low fence. He leaned on it and looked over into the school grounds. The school was a lot bigger now than in his day. There were new blocks of classrooms, a small swimming pool and what looked like a big hall. So much had changed. But not him.

That's why he was angry with himself. He'd come all this way seeking to heal the rift with his father. If not heal it, at least build some sort of bridge over it. While he still could. Because in a few weeks, he'd be travelling to the other side of the world. And he might never come back.

He wasn't an angry teenager any more. He was a grown man who should be able to put old hurts aside and at least have a civil conversation with his father. But every time he looked at the old man, he felt that angry boy rise back to the surface.

He closed his eyes, picturing the town as it had been. The school ground as it had been. He tried to remember the last time his mother had come to watch him play cricket on the dry cracked pitch just in front of where he was now standing.

His mother had been beautiful. He still remembered the pretty white dress she'd worn on that last hot day. He still remembered the long brown hair that she pulled back into a ponytail. He still remembered; but he didn't. The hardest thing he had to do, even harder than talking to his father, was admit to himself that he no longer remembered his mother's face. Or the sound of her voice.

And for that, he would never forgive his father.

Chapter 10

Something was banging. Hard. Loud. Katie tentatively opened her eyes. It was still dark. She closed her eyes again and groaned. The banging didn't go away. She had barely had anything to drink last night. And she'd come to bed early as the jet lag cut in. So this wasn't a hangover.

Why then was there banging?

She opened her eyes again, and this time acknowledged that a very faint light might just be visible at the edge of the bedroom curtains. Slowly she got out of bed and rubbing her eyes, walked through to the lounge room of her new living quarters.

The banging was even louder here.

'All right. I'm coming!'

She opened the door, blinking against the light that poured in from the well-lit hallway. By the third blink, she registered Adam standing on front of her. She pushed her hair out of her eyes as, at the same moment, she registered that she was in her pyjamas. Oh dear.

'We've got to get to the airport,' Adam said briskly, taking no notice of her attire. 'There's been an accident. We have to fly to Galbarra Station right away.'

'Ah … Okay.' The urgency in Adam's voice helped Katie to gather her scattered wits.

'Jess is already on her way to the airstrip. I'm just going to collect some supplies. Get ready as fast as you can and we'll take my car.'

'All right.'

It didn't take long. Katie threw some water over her face and cleaned her teeth. She hesitated for a moment at the half unpacked suitcase sitting on the bedroom floor. Back in England, the hospital had a uniform code she'd had to abide by. Plain cotton scrubs that were a practical as they were hideous. If there was such a uniform code in Coorah Creek, she had yet to learn it. She hesitated for no more than a moment, remembering the urgency in Adam's voice. Then she threw on a clean denim skirt and a blue top. She didn't bother grabbing a jacket. In this scorching part of the world, she didn't need one. A few moments later she was walking smartly through to the hospital, where Adam was waiting.

Katie had done her fair share of flying. Even before her global journey, there had been trips to Ibiza and Greece. The cut price holiday flights had taken her to some pretty basic airports. But nothing like the one at Coorah Creek. It wasn't an airport. It was a tin shed. The plane that was waiting for them was so small it looked almost like a toy in the dim light of the dawn. It was sitting on what looked more like a short bit of road than any sort of runway. The nearest of the tall gum trees looked far too close for comfort. And she expected a kangaroo to hop past at any moment. Definitely not Katie's idea of an airport.

Adam parked his car next to the shed. As Katie got out, Jess appeared from the depths of the shed, carrying a rucksack.

'I made us coffee,' she said as she led the way to the plane.

The inside of the tiny aircraft was a revelation. There were stretchers bolted to the walls, with belts no doubt to hold the patients in.

Well-designed lockers everywhere would no doubt hold a wealth of medical equipment. It reminded Katie of an ambulance which, she guessed, was exactly what it was. An ambulance with wings.

'Why don't you sit up front this time?' Adam asked as he pulled up the narrow stairs and fastened the door.

'Up front?'

'The co-pilot's seat. I usually sit there. You get a great view.'

'I don't want to take ...'

'It's fine,' Jess was already buckling herself into the pilot's seat. 'It'll be nice to have someone new to keep me company. Adam usually falls asleep as soon as we're in the air.'

With a derisive snort, the doctor lowered himself into one of the very comfortable looking seats. Katie hesitantly moved towards the front of the plane. She heard a low whine followed by a coughing splutter as the propellers began to slowly move. Then the engine roared into life. She slid into her seat, fumbling with the unfamiliar seatbelt.

'Let me help.' Jess leaned over and efficiently snapped the seatbelt into place.

The whole plane was vibrating as Jess increased the power and turned the pointy nose towards the runway. With one hand she reached for a microphone. With a shock Katie realised Jess was alerting any nearby aircraft to her imminent take-off. Didn't they have air traffic control out here?

Katie's thoughts were interrupted by the roar of the twin engines as Jess sent the small plane hurtling down the tarmac stip. Katie grabbed the arms of her seat, her fingernails digging in to the surface as the plane shook and bounced. The trees along the fence line were approaching at terrifying speed, and still they had not left the ground. The end of the runway flashed beneath them, as at the last possible moment, the plane lifted into the air and began to climb into the early morning sky. A few seconds later, when the ground still seemed scarily close, Jess banked the plane heavily. The engine roar was incredibly loud as they continued to climb. Katie glanced down and saw the red earth dropping away. The town was growing rapidly smaller, the buildings shrinking until they seemed like toys.

Katie felt her stomach roil. No. No. She wasn't going to throw up. She shut her eyes, but that only made it worse. Taking a deep breath, she tried to focus her eyes on something inside the aircraft, rather than dropping away below her. She watched Jess's hands on the controls. She seemed to know what she was doing. That should be a comfort.

Suddenly, the world dropped away. Katie felt herself falling for several seconds before the seat rose to kick her in the behind. Terrified, she glanced at Jess, but the pilot seemed unconcerned. Jess played with the array of instruments and dials in front of her, as once more the tiny aircraft lurched.

'Sorry about that,' Jess said turning her way at last. 'It's often a bit bumpy first thing in the morning. We've reached our cruising height now. It's only a short trip. Less than an hour. But that should give you time to enjoy the scenery.'

Enjoy the scenery? She had to be joking.

Katie's fingers remained tightly clenched on the arms of the seat as she took long slow breaths to calm herself.

When the frantic beating of her heart had slowed to something approaching normal, she risked a glance out of the window. The world spun and she closed her eyes again against the image of a wide flat brown plain, with not a single sign of human habitation. Where on earth were they? An overwhelming sense of strangeness and of isolation swept through her. Beside her, Jess was chatting away, seeming not to notice that Katie was frozen with fear.

The plane's nose suddenly dipped, and Katie had to bite back a cry of terror.

'There it is,' Jess indicated with a nod as she reached for the radio handset.

There *what* was? Katie risked another quick glance out of the window. She could see nothing except the never-ending plain. Jess was talking to someone on the radio as the aircraft began a steep and swift descent that had Katie's stomach churning violently. Still clutching the armrest as if her life might depend upon it, Katie stared straight ahead into the wide blue sky. But as the plane banked again, she caught a glimpse of a small cluster of buildings in front and below them. But there was nothing to suggest an airport?

Lower and lower the plane dropped. Katie was trying desperately not to throw up as her stomach rebelled again even more strongly. Then she saw what they were heading for. No! It was just a line in the red earth. No tarmac. No buildings. No … nothing. Just bare dirt. Surely Jess wasn't planning to land there?

She was and she did.

The tiny aircraft touched down then rolled and bounced across the uneven dirt. It seemed to take forever to stop. Katie opened the eyes she had kept tightly shut during the landing and glanced over her shoulder. Adam was shaking his head as if he'd just been woken by the bumps. Beside her, Jess was doing her pilot thing. But all Katie cared about was getting solid earth under her feet again.

By the time Katie was out of her seat, Adam had the door open. He was passing a couple of medical bags to someone outside. That brought home to Katie just what they were doing there. She was a nurse and someone was hurt. Her knees were shaking as she carefully descended the narrow aircraft steps. There were two vehicles waiting, both old and battered and driven by men who looked pretty well-used themselves. Adam gestured to her to take the cab of the small ute, and then he leaped into the back.

The driver gunned his engine and the vehicle lurched forward. Katie looked about for a seatbelt then gave up. She tried to calm her mind. She had a job to do. She would forget all about the flight and concentrate on her patient. The vehicle hit a pot hole and Katie grabbed the dashboard as she was thrown about in her seat.

'Sorry,' the driver said. 'This track needs grading.'

Katie said nothing, her whole being focused on the job she had to do at the end of her journey – if she survived.

Chapter 11

'I need a word with you, Ed.'

Ed jumped slightly, and banged his knuckles on the engine block. Rubbing his hand, he withdrew from under the car's bonnet and straightened. Trish Warren was standing in the doorway of the workshop.

'What can I do for you Trish?'

She came into the workshop. She looked around for somewhere to sit, but obviously rejected all the options. Ed had to admit the place was messy but it *was* a workshop.

'I came to say it's high time you joined in the Waifs and Orphans this year. We could use your help setting up. There's always so much work to do. With the party getting bigger every year, the workload just gets bigger too. And of course you are very welcome at the party.'

Ed sighed. The annual town Christmas party was Trish's special project. Every year she tried to get him involved and every year she failed. Not that she ever stopped trying. Trish was nothing if not determined.

'Now Trish,' he said. 'We've had this conversation before. You know that I don't care for Christmas.'

'Rubbish. Everybody loves Christmas. I remember years ago, your house used to be covered with lights. And you hosted a Christmas barbecue too. So don't tell me you don't care for Christmas.'

'Things changed.' Ed felt the first rumbling of annoyance. Trish knew as well as anyone what had destroyed his Christmas. Perhaps better than anyone, because he was sure her gossiping had only made matters so much worse.

'They did.' Trish's voice softened. 'But they are changing again Ed. Surely you see that. You don't want to miss this chance.'

She was right, of course. He didn't. But he wasn't entirely sure what to do. A chance was a fragile thing. Easily broken and lost.

He absently picked up a rag to wipe his greasy hands.

'The party is going to be great this year,' Trish told him. 'It'll serve as a welcome for that new nurse, Katie. And I think Scott is going to stay for it. He's just extended the booking on his room at the hotel.'

Ed looked up sharply.

'How long is he staying?'

'At least a couple more weeks.'

'He's probably staying because of that nurse. She's very pretty and I think they may have something going on.' His voice betrayed his uncertainty.

'Oh, they definitely have something going on.' Trish was obviously pleased to impart that news. 'But does it really matter why he stays?'

She was right. He studied her face and saw the kindness in her eyes. She was a terrible gossip, but she was smarter than she looked. And she had a heart of gold. Trish and her pub were very much the heart of this community.

'All right.' Ed gave way as gracefully as he could. 'What do you need me to do?'

'There'll be working party over at the hall in a few days. They'll need all the help they can get. And you had better show up at the party too or I'll come and drag you down there myself.'

'All right.'

Trish nodded, obviously pleased with herself. She started to walk back to the pub, but stopped in the doorway. 'By the way, you might want to stroll over when you close up. The beef stew is particularly good tonight.'

Ed watched her retreating back and wondered what that was all about. It was almost closing time so he walked outside to lock the petrol bowsers. As he did, he looked across at the pub. Through the open windows he could see a lone figure sat at the bar. Ah. Now he understood. Trish was meddling again.

He went back inside, locking the workshop behind him. Candy met him as he crossed the yard towards the house. She looked at him and whined softly. He patted her.

Maybe Trish had a point. He turned around but changed his mind. It wouldn't hurt to clean up just a little before he went to the pub.

When should we expect to see you?

The words on Scott's laptop screen glowed in an almost accusing manner. The e-mail had arrived yesterday, but he still hadn't answered it.

We will take delivery of the two cars – the Lancia and the Mercedes in mid-January, and would be keen for you to begin work on them immediately to have at least one of them ready for exhibition in the summer.

They meant the English summer of course. To restore either of those cars would take a good six or seven months of hard work.

He looked at the signature and the distinctive logo. As a teenage rev-head with a passion for classic cars, he'd dreamed about working for a place like that. He could still hardly believe that one of the world's great motor museums wanted him to restore and care for their beautiful machines. When he started his own small restoration workshop in Brisbane five years ago, he'd worked twenty hours a day to build his business. A chance meeting with the owner of that signature had resulted in this dream of a job offer.

He was going, of course. He'd be a fool to pass it up. He'd already sold his workshop. That money would help him establish himself in England and start the new life he'd always wanted. A life far, far away from Coorah Creek. After all, there was nothing to hold him here. No-one to hold him here. Not even many memories. At least, not good memories.

Still his fingers hesitated over the laptop keys.

This trip wasn't going quite the way he had planned.

A few weeks ago, while selling his business and preparing to move to the other side of the world, he had begun thinking about what to take to his new life. And what he was going to leave behind. His few mates had already invited themselves to visit him in England. He'd never really had a serious girlfriend. He was leaving nothing behind — because he had nothing to leave.

His mother was long gone. He didn't know where she was or even, to be brutally honest, if she was still alive. Sitting there in his workshop, packing up his tools, another thought had struck with the force of a cyclone. At that moment, he also hadn't known if his father was dead or alive. For the first time in almost a decade, he was overcome with a desire to go back to Coorah Creek. He had to see his father one more time before he shook the Aussie dust from his feet and headed for greener pastures.

He hadn't expected a rapprochement. There was too much bad blood to be healed. He has just ... What?

Now that he was here, he was even less sure.

He hadn't expected to feel ... anything.

Maybe finding Candy still alive had stirred up too many emotions. Made him vulnerable. Or maybe it was the realisation that his father was now a lonely old man. Whatever it was, he found he didn't hate his father as much as he'd thought. He wasn't ready to forgive him. But maybe he could let go of his anger.

He had some time. Christmas was a couple of weeks away and he'd already talked to Trish about keeping the hotel room until then. He didn't need to be in the UK until the second week in January. He could easily move his flight back to the New Year.

He stared out the window, and caught a flash of sunlight. The air ambulance was coming in for a landing. He wondered if Katie was on board. Probably. He wondered how she had managed on this first flight. Perhaps he could drop by her place this evening. After all, he felt a little responsible for her. He'd rescued her twice already. Maybe she'd need rescuing again. Or maybe she'd just want some company. That wouldn't be a bad thing. Nothing would ever come of it, of course. He didn't do relationships. Not really. Not only that, Katie had come to Coorah Creek to live. He had come to say goodbye. But until then, they could be friends, couldn't they.

There was absolutely no reason to think she had anything to do with his reluctance to send the e-mail that he knew he had to send.

Taking a deep breath, he began to type ...

I expect to arrive in the UK shortly after New Year. I'll be in touch as soon as I arrive. I am very much looking forward to starting work on the cars.

He signed off and hit send.

It was probably too soon to go looking for Katie. While he waited, it wouldn't hurt to do a bit more research on that Lancia. He'd never restored one of those before. He wanted to get it right.

Within minutes he was lost in his favourite place – a world of rare and beautiful classic cars. He was so engrossed in what he was doing, he didn't hear the heavy footsteps crossing the bar's polished wooden floor.

'Now that's a nice car.'

Ed pulled up a stool next to Scott.

'It sure is.'

'Ever since you were a kid, you wanted one of those. You had an old owner's manual. The '75 model. Always had your nose in it.'

Neither of them mentioned that the Lancia owner's manual was one of the things Scott had taken with him the day he turned his back on his father and the town of Coorah Creek. It was now sitting in a box in the boot of his car.

'I'm surprised you remember.' Scott had trouble keeping the bitterness out of his voice.

'I remember a lot more than you think.'

There seemed to be nothing he could say to that.

Scott closed that internet window, leaving another displayed. It was the home page for the UK's National Museum of Motoring. The place he would soon be working.

'Now, there's a place I always wanted to visit,' Ed said slowly. 'All those wonderful European cars. I've never even seen a Rolls Royce out here – far less something like an old Aston Martin or a Lotus. I'd love to look under the bonnet of something like that. Just once in my life.'

Scott was startled by the emotion in his father's voice. A profound sadness. It had never occurred to him that the old man might have such strong regrets.

'Why didn't you go there? A holiday or something.'

'I didn't want to be gone from here ...'

The words fell into the space between them. Surely his father wasn't still hoping his mother would come back? Or ... had his father stayed here all those years hoping Scott would come back?

The silence was becoming a little hard to take. Scott finished closing down his computer. The click as he shut the lid seemed very loud.

'That car's done.' Once again, it was his father taking the lead.

'Car?'

'The girl's.'

'Oh. I thought you weren't going to have it ready until tomorrow.'

'The parts arrived this morning. It didn't take long then. I thought you might take it back to her.'

That was a surprise. Scott looked at his father and raised an eyebrow.

'Well,' Ed said. 'The two of you seemed ... friendly.'

Scott wanted to laugh. After all this time, his father was matchmaking? Maybe he was hoping Scott might hang around if he was involved with Katie. It wasn't a bad prospect – but he had a job waiting.

'Don't you want her to pay for it before she picks it up?'

Ed shook his head slowly. 'Son, you sure have forgotten a lot about this town. This isn't the city. We do things differently. She needs the damn car. Take it to her. She can pay me next time she's passing.'

Scott took the keys his father held out, thinking as he did that his father was right. There were many, many things he had forgotten. And maybe not all of them were bad.

Chapter 12

Katie's knees were shaking so much, she almost fell to the ground as she came down the steps of the aircraft. As her feet touched good solid earth, she heaved a sigh of relief, then heaved again as her stomach lurched. She covered her mouth with her hand, and stepped away from the plane. Just in case. When she had her stomach under control, she turned to see Adam coming out of the plane, a brown bag in his hands. Her humiliation was complete as her boss carried the air sick bag over to the tin shed and deposited it in a big metal drum of rubbish.

'Don't feel too bad.' Jess joined Katie on the tarmac and placed a comforting hand on her shoulder. 'Everybody does that at least once in their lives.'

'Did you?' Katie asked.

'Well, no. But I'm a pilot. We're not allowed to get air sick.'

And she was a nurse. She wasn't supposed to get air sick either. Thank goodness there hadn't been a patient on board. The injured stockman had been treated and left at the station in his wife's care.

'Don't worry about it,' Adam offered as he joined them again. 'We'll leave Jess to take care of the plane, and I can take you home. You'll feel better when you freshen up and have a nice cup of tea.'

The mere thought of putting anything into her stomach almost made her ill again. But the doctor was right. By the time she had returned to her flat, had a shower and donned some fresh clothes, she was feeling better. She boiled the kettle and made some mint tea. Someone had once told her mint tea was good for an upset stomach. It was, but not good enough to give her back her energy, or take away the ache in her back.

She lay back on her sofa and closed her eyes.

She tried to empty her mind, but she couldn't. Her mind was churning as badly as her stomach had earlier in the day. One thought was pounding into her brain over and over again.

She had made a terrible mistake coming to Coorah Creek. She felt tears welling up in her eyes, and squeezed her lids even more tightly to stop them overflowing down her cheeks. She had only been here a few days, but already she hated Coorah Creek! Hated it!

She hated the heat. And the isolation. At night, the silence was so overwhelming it kept her awake. She hated the fact that there were no coffee shops or shops of any sort. And she hated working somewhere without structure or uniforms or rules or all the things that made up a proper hospital.

But most of all she hated flying in the air ambulance!

Her stomach twisted again at the mere thought.

It wasn't that she was afraid of flying. She was quite happy in a big jet with hundreds of other passengers. But that little plane… She could open a window and put her hand out - into nothingness. The plane was totally vulnerable to the wind and the clouds. The mere thought of running into a storm made her shudder. She never NEVER wanted to go up in that plane again.

But she had to. It was part of her job, and she loved her job. At least, she had loved her job. Once. She loved being able to help people – watching someone regain their health and strength. But working in a large hospital had taken that away from her. She had hated the overwhelming workload that left her exhausted. Hated being too busy to really connect with any one patient. It was so impersonal. And there was also the mad scramble for advancement. The politics of the place had involved a much greater degree of back stabbing and bitchiness than she had ever expected.

And there were the doctors. She shuddered as she remembered a couple of confrontations. One in particular. A senior consultant. She's seen him miss something and had tried to bring it to his attention. She'd been tactful and done it by asking a question. He'd simply dismissed her. Only when she'd been insistent had he realised his mistake. Katie had saved the patient some unnecessary discomfort, but that doctor had never forgiven her for finding his flaw. Nor had the doctor whose advances she had refused. They weren't all like that, of course. There were good doctors as well as bad. It just seemed to her, in the pressure cooker of a large hospital, the bad seemed to surface more often.

Katie had no illusions. She understood the need for rules and regulations and order in a big hospital. She didn't mind the hard work and she could even cope with the doctors who stepped over the line. But that wasn't the sort of nursing she wanted to do. That's why she'd left and come here. As far from that London medical machine as she could get. Here she had hoped to find a more personal approach to medicine. And she was right. This was more personal, more rewarding. Except for the flying. That was a nightmare. She hated herself for the fear that had left her either paralysed – or being violently sick. But hating herself was not going to make it any better.

And now look at her, lying on a couch wallowing in self-pity! What sort of behaviour was that? It was time she pulled herself together.

She opened her eyes, brushed away the moisture and stared up at the ceiling. Above her, the big fan was going round and round, in long slow sweeps. And round. And …

Katie sat up quickly, her hand on her stomach. She stood up and made a beeline for the bathroom. She opened the door and her eyes fell upon a monstrous spider, all black and hairy, poised on the edge of the toilet seat. It seemed to be watching her. Its beady eyes glinted as it raised its front legs in a menacing fashion.

Katie screamed.

Almost instantly there was a pounding on her door.

'Katie! Katie! Are you all right?'

She spun away from the bathroom and its fearsome denizen and flung herself across the room to her door. She struggled for a few seconds with her newly installed lock, before reefing the door open and literally falling into Scott's open arms.

'Hey. What's wrong? Are you all right?'

She nodded wordlessly into the front of his shirt.

'Come on. Sit down and tell me what's going on.'

She shook her head, digging her toes in and refusing to be led back to the flat. She struggled to get control of her breathing and finally pulled herself together enough to speak.

'That giant spider from Lord of The Rings is in my bathroom.'

'Oh. Well, I guess I had better deal with it, then.'

'Please!' To her own ears she sounded pathetic.

Totally unconcerned, not to mention unarmed, Scott headed for her bathroom. He vanished through the doorway. She heard some scuffling noises, and then what sounded like the window being opened and closed.

'There you are,' Scott emerged smiling. 'Just like Frodo. I did the hero thing.'

'Frodo didn't fight Shelob. Sam did.' Katie automatically corrected him. 'And he didn't kill her.'

'That's all right. I didn't kill this one either. I just put it outside.'

'But it might come back!'

'It's just a huntsman. Totally harmless you know.'

'It didn't look harmless.' Katie's breathing was starting to return to normal. 'Sorry I overreacted. I've had a rough day.'

'Sorry to hear it. Well, I have good news for you. Your car is fixed. I brought it round for you in case you needed it.'

So – you've rescued me again. This is becoming a habit.'

'Always glad to help.'

He smiled and Katie's heart did a little flip that had nothing to do with the spider.

'I'll tell you what,' Scott said, 'if you're up to it, there's a place I'd like to show you. It's one of my favourite places. It might help cheer you up.'

Katie looked into his handsome and eager face. She had no idea where he was taking her, but one thing she did know. Spending a bit of time with Scott would certainly put a little bit of joy back in her day.

'Okay,' she said.

'Great.' He handed over the keys to her car. 'You can drive this time.'

Chapter 13

The track to the creek looked just the same to Scott. It was just two tyre ruts in the rough ground. It may have become a little deeper over the years, but nothing else had changed.

'Are you sure?' Katie had pulled up just off the main road, and was staring down the dusty track, her brow wrinkled in a frown.

'You'll be fine,' he assured her. 'Good Aussie cars are built for roads like this. Just keep your wheels in the tracks and take it easy.'

Katie's response was a dubious sigh, but she put the car in gear and edged forward. 'If I do any damage, it'll be on you,' she said.

Despite her misgivings, Katie handled the rough going well. The car travelled smoothly, if slowly, down the track towards the line of gum trees that marked the creek bank. Scott suppressed a smile as he watched the concentration on her face and the careful way her hands gripped the steering wheel. Katie might be out of her depth here in the outback, but she wasn't about to let it beat her. She had strengths and abilities that maybe she hadn't even found yet. He liked that about her.

He liked watching her. He liked the way she bit her lower lip as she concentrated. He liked the way she could laugh at herself and he really liked the way her blue eyes sparkled when she did.

Finally, they reached the creek. Katie didn't need his guidance as she instinctively parked the car under the trees, out of the hot sun. The bare dirt and a few bits of litter indicated this place was more frequently used now than when young Scott Collins used to come here. Before he was old enough to drive, he'd ridden a pushbike. Once or twice he'd used his father's car, hoping not to be caught. Now the town had grown, he imagined many more kids would be seeking this place out.

As Scott opened the door and got out of the car, he saw movement in the long dry grass as a snake slithered away. It was just a carpet snake. Harmless. But he decided not to mention it to Katie. She'd seen enough of the local wildlife already today.

They moved to the front of the car and looked down the sloping bank to the creek.

'There's not a lot of water.' Katie sounded disappointed.

'Not at this time of the year,' Scott said. He took a couple of steps down the bank then turned to offer her a hand down. It wasn't that he thought she needed his help. In fact, he was sure she didn't. He just wanted an excuse to hold her hand.

Katie started to shake her head, then her eyes met and held his. Understanding passed between them and she placed her hand in his. It felt good to curl his fingers around her small hand and offer her whatever strength he had.

They made their way down the slope. She sat down on an old tree trunk that had washed down the river in some flood many years before. It was hard and bleached to a pale grey by the sun, but was a convenient place to sit overlooking the slow-moving shallow waterway that was Coorah Creek.

He sat next to her. Close enough that he could hear her breathing.

'I had imagined a deep river, with a tyre on a rope that local teenagers use as a swing to jump out into the water,' Katie said.

'There's never enough water for that,' Scott said. 'And when I was growing up here, there weren't that many teenagers either.'

'But the school looks quite large,' Katie said.

'It's grown since the mine came. Back then, there was one building and one teacher. The teacher dealt with the little kids. In a separate room, the older kids did School of The Air.'

'What's that?'

'We did our lessons via radio with a teacher somewhere else.'

'That's very cool!'

'I suppose so. There were only five or six of us. Not enough to justify another teacher. And we were the kids whose parents were too poor to send us off to boarding school. I guess some places still do it now ... although I imagine the internet has changed things a bit.'

'I guess a lot has changed since then.'

Yes, Scott thought. A lot has changed. But a lot has stayed exactly the same. He cast a sideways glance at Katie. She was swinging her feet above the ground. She looked so young. And sweet. For an instant he could imagine she was one of the teenagers who so obviously came here now. He could imagine that he was younger too. The boy he'd been before circumstances, and his father's fists, made him grow up so very very fast.

That sat in silence for a while. Scott had expected Katie to ask about his past. But she didn't. She seemed content with the person he was now. And to let him tell her what he wanted at his own speed. Somehow that made him more willing to tell her.

'You know Ed? Who fixed your car. He's my father.'

'I know.' Katie turned to look at him, her blue eyes shadowed. 'Adam told me.'

'I should have realised. Nothing stays private for long in this town.'

'I did wonder why you didn't say anything. Particularly when we were in the pub together.'

'It's a long story. And not a good one.'

Katie frowned. 'Something happened between you?'

'Yeah … Before this week, I hadn't seen or spoken to him since my seventeenth birthday.'

'That's a long time.'

He knew that. That day seemed an eternity ago. It seemed like yesterday.

'My mum was gone.' The words came of their own volition. 'She left when I was about twelve. I didn't understand it. I loved her so much and I just couldn't believe that she would go away without me. My father has never really been a cheerful or demonstrative person. After she left, he become positively sullen and withdrawn. He put away everything in the house that reminded him of her. He wouldn't talk about her, even though I really needed to. I managed to keep just one photo. I guess that was the advantage of those old photo prints. I hid one where he couldn't find it. I used to look at it and wonder where she was. I vowed that one day, when I was old enough, I would go and find her.'

'Did your father ever tell you why she left?'

'For a very long time I thought it was me. I thought I'd done something wrong to chase her away.'

'No!' The exclamation wasn't loud – but it was passionate. Katie's hand reached out to cover his. 'It wasn't that. I am sure of it.'

His fingers and hers intertwined and he held her tightly.

'I know that now. Just a few days after my seventeenth birthday, I was at the shop, buying some food for my dog, Candy. I thought

Candy was the only one who loved me. I heard someone talking. About my father. He'd had an affair. That was why my mother left.'

'Oh, Scott.' The compassion in her voice seemed to envelope him and warm him, even as the flood of words continued.

'I went back to the house. I was just a kid and I was so angry. I demanded to know why he did it. As I confronted him I realised for the first time that I was as big as he was. I yelled at him. I blamed him for everything. He just stood there and said nothing. Then I hit him.'

'What did he do?'

'He hit me back. Knocked me down. I got right back up and hit him again.'

'And ...'

'He knocked me down again. There was something on his face. A blankness. When I got back up the second time, I just walked away. I grabbed a few things and walked out that door.'

'Where did you go?'

'I went across the road to the pub. My head was spinning and my hand hurt like hell. My knuckles were bleeding. I tried to buy a beer. I figured I was a man now and could handle it. When Trish Warren wouldn't serve me, I put my fist through her window. Guess that shows how much of a man I really wasn't. And it left my hand hurting even more.'

She smiled. It was a slow sad smile, but to Scott it felt as warm as the sun.

'And ...'

'I left Coorah Creek that night. Hitched a ride on a passing truck. I was determined to find my mother. I haven't been back since – until you and I drove into town together.'

'And you never found her?'

'No. I eventually got a job and started working. With cars. That's irony for you. Then I went to night school to finish my education.'

'And now you're back.'

Scott hesitated. He didn't want to say that he was leaving. Going to England. That seemed some sort of betrayal of this moment. Of this strange intimacy that had suddenly come to pass with Katie. He closed his hand even more tightly around hers. 'I just felt it was time to see if— Well, maybe we could make amends.'

'And are you?'

That was a very good question. 'We haven't hit each other,' he said with a wry grin. 'I guess that's something.'

'It's a start.'

'Yeah. There's a lot to make up for. The years between Mum leaving and me leaving were not good. Dad was in a bad place. I can see that now. He took me there too. There was no joy in the house. And none for me anywhere else either. Dad made sure I was fed and clothed, but that was it.'

'That must have been horrible. But a lot of time has passed. You have to at least try to mend the bridges. If you don't, and you lose him too, you will come to regret it.'

He sighed. 'How did you get to be so wise?'

'I come from a pretty close family. I know how much they mean to me. I couldn't imagine how hard it must have been without that.'

'I missed out on a lot of the fun of being a teenager. The other kids always ostracised me because I was Ed Collins's son. When they came here for parties, I was never invited. They came here to make out with their girlfriends, but I always came alone. I should have had my first kiss here with pretty little Alice Lake from school. It never happened.'

A gentle silence seemed to settle around them. The breeze in the trees faded. The ripples on the water seemed to sigh into stillness. The world around them held its breath as the silence grew.

'It could happen now.' Katie's voice was soft and inviting.

Scott didn't need to be told twice. Feeling not unlike a nervous teenager, he leaned forward and his lips touched Katie's. Gently. Softly. With great tenderness. There was an innocence to the kiss that seemed to wash away all the ugliness of his memories. His heart jumped and, in that heartbeat, some of his lost youth returned to him. After a few seconds, they moved apart, just enough to breathe. Scott looked down into Katie's lovely face. This was not Alice – the girl of his teenage fantasies. The girl who shunned him. This was Katie. A warm and beautiful woman, whose shining eyes were all the invitation he needed.

When he kissed her the second time, it was as a man kisses a woman.

Chapter 14

Maybe Coorah Creek wasn't really such a bad place. Katie pulled some dressings from the storage cupboard and headed back towards the treatment room. The past few days had been good days. With both feet firmly planted on solid ground, she'd been working at the hospital with Adam.

It still seemed strange to be calling the doctor by his first name. That wasn't how they did things back home. There were a lot of things about this hospital and this job that weren't like they were back home. She wasn't wearing a uniform. There were no rules and regulations. Patients came in without appointments. And they brought things. The young couple she'd met on her first day here had brought flowers with them this morning when they brought their daughter for a check-up. An Aboriginal man from one of the outlying cattle properties had come by – not for treatment, but to drop off a painting for Adam as a belated wedding gift. The painting was beautiful. It was just a brown canvas covered with brown dots, but somehow it seemed to evoke a wonderful sense of this place that was literally out the back of nowhere.

Everything was a bit strange.

But she had to admit Adam was a very good doctor. She enjoyed working with him. His focus on his patients was total, and she enjoyed being there to assist. To hand him the things he needed before he asked for them. That was what she had trained for. She had started taking over the office paperwork from Jess too. There was a lot to learn. Australia's health system was very different to the British one. But she'd figure it out.

And then there was Scott.

Since that first kiss down by the creek, they had seen each other every day. They had met twice in the pub for dinner. And there had been another trip to the creek bank. This time with some beer and a picnic basket. But tonight, Scott was coming to her place for dinner. And she was as eager as a teenager on her first date.

Which was ridiculous when you thought that Scott had spent the night on her couch the day they met. They hadn't spent the night together since. That kiss down by the creek had changed everything. But tonight, maybe ...

'Katie?'

Adam's voice dragged her back to reality. She was standing in the open doorway of the treatment room, her arms full of the dressings that Adam needed for the injured mine worker whose arm was currently swathed in slightly bloody cloth.

'Sorry.' She darted forward to do her job, all thoughts of Scott pushed hurriedly to the back of her mind.

He didn't stay there though. As soon as she was no longer needed at the hospital, Katie drove to the town's store to get what she needed. She had already discovered that the store's supplies were generous in number but not very broad in content. Obviously artichoke hearts and anchovies were not popular items on home menus in Coorah Creek. Still, she wasn't a bad cook and was sure she'd come up with something.

Behind the serving counter, Ken Travers raised a hand in greeting as she entered the store. He'd been back for another appointment just yesterday. She'd seen the test results and they weren't good. That, she knew, was the disadvantage of this more personal style of nursing. It was harder to accept the bad news when your patient was more than just a number and a chart.

The store was looking festive with tinsel along the shelves, shiny globes glinting in the afternoon sunlight and cotton wool pretending to be snow along the window ledge. Katie had almost forgotten about Christmas. Back home, the shops started getting all dressed for the season in October. But here it was, just a couple of weeks to go, and the store had only just placed a huge box of Christmas decorations by the front counter to attract shoppers. She walked over and picked up some shiny gold tinsel. Christmas. That didn't seem right when she was standing there in a tank top and shorts. It wasn't supposed to be forty degrees at Christmas. And there was no point in crossing her fingers and hoping for snow. A white Christmas was never going to happen out here.

A wave of homesickness hit her so hard, she felt tears prick the back of her eyes. She had wanted this adventure. This chance to rethink her life and her career choices ... but now that she was alone, she missed them all terribly. E-mail and Facebook helped, but Katie knew in her heart that this Christmas would not bring her the joy she always felt at home, around the fireplace with her family.

She allowed herself only a moment of self-pity then shook it off. This Christmas was going to be exciting. A new place. New friends. Scott ...

Would he be spending Christmas with his father? And then what? He hadn't talked about leaving, but she remembered his words on the day they met. Just visiting for a while. That's what he'd said.

He'd come back to try to mend his relationship with his father. But then what? Would he just drive away and not look back?

She didn't want to examine that thought too closely. Instead, she began to rummage around in the box of decorations. There was some tinsel that wasn't too tatty. Some nice shiny glass baubles. Even a star for the top of the tree she didn't have. Surely she could get one though? She didn't think for one minute she could buy one – but someone around here must own an axe. There were plenty of trees about. It might be fun to have a gum tree instead of a pine tree in her flat.

As for snow – well, there was plenty of cotton wool at the hospital. She'd make do.

She assembled her decorations, and started collecting the ingredients for the evening's dinner. Scott was bringing the wine. Maybe he could help her acquire a tree of some sort and they could decorate it together. Her spirits lifted even more. That would be fun! She vaguely heard a telephone ringing, but was too caught up with her plans to pay any attention, until Ken called her to his counter.

'That was Adam on the phone,' he told her in a low urgent voice. 'He needs you at the airstrip right now.'

'Now?' her heart sank.

'Yep. Leave that stuff. I'll get it over to the hospital for you later. Adam sounded like it was urgent.'

Katie wanted to swear. Having no mobile phone service should have made her harder to find. But not when everyone in town knew everybody else in town and where they were at any given moment. Still … whoever needed medical care would be grateful she was that easy to find.

She left the store and drove straight to the airport. Jess already had the plane on the runway. Adam reached down through the open door and helped her on board. The plane was taxiing before she was even strapped in. Katie clenched her hands around the arm-rests of her chair. She was in the back this time. She wouldn't be so scared. Would she?

Her heart lurched as the plane raced down the runway and leaped gracefully into the air. She forced herself to let go of the armrest long enough to remove an airsick bag from the seat pocket. She might need it. As her stomach lurched again, she suddenly remembered her date with Scott. She hadn't called … or even had time to leave a note. Still, this was Coorah Creek. She was sure someone would tell him what was happening.

The plane bounced as it hit an air pocket and all thoughts of Scott left Katie's head. Her only concern now was trying not to throw up.

Chapter 15

This wasn't how he'd planned to spend his evening. Scott took another swig on his beer and glared along the bar at the Christmas tree, shining and sparkling away with no regard for his mood. Bah Humbug!

For a few minutes he contemplated going and getting his laptop. He could answer some e-mails, or even hunt for a place to live in England. There were plenty of things he should be doing. But what he really wanted was to be in Katie's tiny flat, watching her as she cooked, waiting for the smile that lit not just her face, but the whole room. He wanted to listen to her voice. They never seemed to run out of things to talk about, but what he loved most of all was just the sound of her voice. That cute accent had somehow worked its way into his heart and lodged there. A day without Katie in it was not a good day.

And there it was – his real problem.

He was going to leave Coorah Creek very soon.

His aim in coming here was to see his father. If he'd hoped for some sort of reconciliation – it hadn't happened. But at least some contact had been made. All he had to do now was tell his father about his job in England, and leave.

But that also meant leaving Katie – and in his heart of hearts, he didn't want to do that. Just his luck to meet someone like her in the one place on Earth where he would never live again. And just as she was starting to make a home and a life here.

The lights on the Christmas tree twinkled at him, and he scowled again.

Bah humbug indeed!

'So, are you planning to sit here glaring at that inoffensive tree all night, or do you want to make yourself useful?'

Scott turned to look at Trish. She was at her usual place behind the bar doing her usual thing – getting involved in everyone else's business. He grunted in a noncommittal sort of way, but she was totally unaffected.

'Excellent. Some of the men are down at the church hall, getting ready for the Waifs and Orphans on Christmas day. They could use an extra hand.'

'Waifs and Orphans?'

'It started a few years ago, when the mine was just opening. All the people without families got together on Christmas day. It started here in the pub – but it's grown bigger and now half the town comes. We moved it to the hall a couple of years ago.'

'So am I a waif or an orphan?' he asked, his mood not improved one whit.

'That's entirely up to you,' Trish said, her smile never faltering. 'You don't have to be either, unless you want to be.'

Her eyes were far too knowing as she stared him down.

Admitting defeat, Scott tossed back the last of his beer and slid off his stool. At least it would stop him thinking about Katie off somewhere on a rescue mission. 'So, where do I go?'

Scott remembered the Church. As a kid, he'd been there once or twice, but there hadn't been enough people for a permanent minister

of any denomination. Services had been held at odd intervals whenever a churchman was passing through. Times had changed now.
He had spotted at least one other church in the town, and both had
looked prosperous. The hall was a recent addition. A long wooden
building with a corrugated iron roof that was already showing signs
of rust. The weather out here was quick to take its toll.

There were several cars parked outside. Scott slipped his into line
beside them and headed for the open doors of the hall, his mood
starting to lift at the thought of doing something useful. The hall
was surprisingly large and bright. At one end of the hall, dark red
curtains had been pushed back to reveal a small wooden stage. No
doubt the local school kids had performed many a play there. The
place was buzzing with activity. He wasn't the only one Trish had
bullied into helping. He saw Jack North, her sometime barman,
struggling to drag a heavy cast iron bathtub out from under the
stage. That bathtub would no doubt be filled with ice on Christmas
morning to keep the beer cold.

In one corner of the room, a couple of women were pulling
decorations out of a couple of big cardboard boxes. The boxes were
dusty, the tinsel glinting in the strong overhead lights as they sorted
the red, green and gold into separate piles. He could see other
women through a door to his left. They were in what appeared
to be a kitchen doing whatever mysterious things were done in
kitchens before large parties. Further towards the back of the hall,
another door was open. As Scott watched, one of the working party
emerged holding one end of a long broad piece of wood; the mak-
ings of a table no doubt.

This was not Christmas as Scott had ever known it. Christmas
had never been a time of laughter and sharing. Not for many many
years. He started to cross the pale wooden floor. Then another
sound stopped him dead.

A man was laughing. It was a sound he hadn't heard in a very long time – but he knew it in an instant.

He turned slowly to see Ed carrying an empty oil drum from the back room. The drum still bore the hint of last year's festive decorations. Ed was obviously sharing a joke with the man working with him. He looked younger. He looked happy. He looked … not at all like the Ed Collins who Scott hated.

Ed put the drum down in front of the stage. At some point in the next few days, a tree would be placed in there – with sand to hold it firm. Then would come the decorations. For the first time in many years, Ed decided he was looking forward to Christmas day. Especially if Trish was right about Scott.

He turned around and looked down the hall, straight into his son's face.

'It's looking good,' Scott said to the room in general, but his eyes never left his father's face.

Ed didn't hesitate. Still smiling, he walked towards his son. This was an opportunity. It might be the last and he wasn't going to waste it.

'I think it'll be all right come Christmas day,' Ed said. 'But there's still a lot of work to do.'

'I came to help. What do you need me to do?'

'Ellen is giving the orders,' Ed said, motioning towards a small blonde woman who was sorting decorations. 'Let's see what she needs.'

'Decorations have to go on the beams,' Ellen told them. 'There's a ladder in the back room.'

'Yes, Ma'am,' Ed bowed slightly. 'And exactly how to you want them arranged?'

'You are two big strong men,' Ellen slapped Ed's arm gently and smiled at Scott. 'I'm sure the two of you can figure it out.'

'Yes, Ma'am,' Scott aped his father's bow. Father and son exchanged a glance, and hesitantly they both smiled.

They worked together for about an hour. Ed held the ladder while Scott climbed to the rafters to drape tinsel over and along the beams. There were colourful paper lanterns to be added, and spinning paper balls. Any tension between them slowly faded. They didn't talk much, but Ed didn't mind. He was more than content with what they had. Around them, other workers were laying out the trestle tables and wiping away the dust that had gathered since they were last used.

'All right – who needs a beer and a burger?'

Trish and Syd Warren walked through the door clutching boxes. Ed moved to take Trish's load and she gave him a knowing smile as she handed the box over. The beer and burgers were good. Ed enjoyed the camaraderie and for the first time found himself think-ing that he had spent far too much time alone with his bitterness and regrets. He realised now that his isolation from the townsfolk has been his own fault. Most of the newer townsfolk didn't know about his past. Most of the long-time residents didn't care. It had taken the return of his son to show him what had always been in front of him.

The working party disposed of the burgers and beer on no time at all and began to break up. Ed walked out into the night and stretched his back. As he did, he looked up into a sky glittering with stars.

'I missed those stars when I moved to the city,' Scott said as he came to stand beside his father. 'There's nowhere on earth with stars like these.'

'There must have been stars back east,' Ed said.

'Yes. But they weren't like this.'

They stood in silence for a few minutes more.

'I'm heading back,' Scott said. 'Do you need a lift?'

'Well, I kinda like walking at night.'

'Do you want some company?'

'Yeah.'

Scott put his car keys back in his pocket and the two of them set out. It wasn't going to take long to walk back. After two or three minutes, Scott broke the silence.

'I opened a workshop, you know.'

'Did you?'

'Yeah. I restore old classic cars. I'm pretty good at it too.'

Ed smiled in the darkness, a feeling of pride growing inside him. Despite everything, his son had become a good man. 'Well, as a boy you always loved those old cars. You had dozens of books about them.'

'I sure did.'

'There're all still there you know. In your old room. You should come and get them.'

There was a long silence. Ed knew what Scott didn't say. That he didn't want to return to the house where he had experienced so much unhappiness. Ed couldn't blame him for that.

'I've been offered a job,' Scott said at last, 'restoring, among other things, a Lancia Aurelia and a 1956 Mercedes Gullwing.'

Ed let out a low whistle. 'There aren't many of those around.'

'There aren't.'

Scott hesitated and Ed knew there was something important about to be said.

'Not in this country. The job is in England. At the National Museum of Motoring.'

Ed's long stride faltered just a fraction, but he kept walking without looking at his son. 'Ah. That explains why you were looking at their website the other night. That's quite something. You'll enjoy that. When do you leave?'

'I was supposed to go this week, but I thought I might stay a bit longer. Trish has invited me to join the party and as I've put in the work ...' His voice trailed off.

'It will be good to have you here for Christmas.'

They were almost back at the pub. Ed was about to suggest that Scott and he stop for a last beer, when movement up ahead caught his eye.

'Candy?'

The old Labrador was limping slowly towards them, her tail wagging.

'Hey, what are you doing out?' Ed dropped to one knee to pat the dog. Candy's tail waved happily, and she included Scott in the adoring gaze she cast at Ed. 'That old gate doesn't shut properly any more,' Ed said as he stood. 'I'll get on that in the morning. She shouldn't be out on the road.'

Scott nodded his agreement.

'I'd better take her back.' Ed rose to his feet. After a moment's hesitation, he held out his hand. 'Goodnight, son.'

Scott took it. 'Goodnight, Dad.'

As they shook, Ed realised this was the first time he had touched his son since that last night. The night he had lifted his fist to a heartbroken and angry boy. The sense of shame he now felt was overpowering. He wanted to say something. To apologise and ask for Scott's forgiveness. But instead, he turned and, with his dog at his side, crossed the road back to his dark and empty house.

Chapter 16

'It's all right you know. There's nothing to be ashamed off.'

Katie splashed some more water over her face.

'Some people just don't like small planes,' Jess's voice continued from the other side of the bathroom door. 'Really. I have a pilot friend who throws up if he gets into anything smaller than a 747.'

Katie appreciated Jess's good intentions, but right now, nothing was going to make her feel any better. She rinsed her mouth out again, then wiped her face on the towel. From the mirror, a white-faced woman looked back at her, her eyes rimmed with red. It wasn't a very flattering image. She turned away.

Jess was waiting outside. The hangar doors were wide open. So was the door to the air ambulance. Jess was carrying a bucket.

'I'll clean it up,' Katie said, her cheeks burning at the thought of what Jess was about to do.

'Don't worry. I'll do it.' Jess put a comforting hand on her shoulder. 'It's an air ambulance remember. I've had to clean up far worse.'

Katie wanted to insist. Perhaps salvage just a little bit of self-respect. But the thought of climbing back inside that plane was almost enough to make her retch again.

'Thank you,' she said in a whisper.

'It's not a problem.' Jess hesitated. 'You know, some people just aren't cut out for… this.' She waved an arm that seemed to encompass everything from the tin shed that was her hanger, to the aircraft and the whole of the outback. 'I'm not trying to get rid of you or anything. And Adam says you're a good nurse. But maybe … just maybe this isn't the right place for you.'

That thought had already occurred to Katie. And she had trouble shaking it as she drove back towards the hospital and her small flat. It would be so easy to simply go home. Jess and Adam would understand why. And her family would too, when she arrived back in London. No-one would blame her. Well, no-one but herself. To leave now would be to admit that she had failed. Failed to prove to herself that nursing was the right place for her. Failed to recapture her passion for the only career she had ever wanted. And if she gave up now, what would she do? Get a job stacking shelves in a supermarket? Maybe she could get a job at a school. That wasn't what she wanted.

Feeling pretty despondent she turned into the hospital driveway – and saw Scott. He was sitting on the hospital veranda, obviously waiting for her. Her heart did a little somersault.

There was another reason not to pack up and go home. Scott. As a nurse she'd been chatted up by more than a few doctors. She'd been taken out to dinner in fancy restaurants with fine wine. And not one of them had ever made her heart leap like that.

What was it about this man sitting on her doorstep with a bag that no doubt contained beer? In just a few days he had come to mean more to her than any of those smart doctors with their fancy restaurants and expensive wine.

Realisation crashed down on her like a block of concrete. She didn't want to leave Coorah Creek because she didn't want to leave Scott. Yet Scott was going to leave too.

She didn't believe in love at first sight. Attraction – yes. Lust – of course. And there was certainly a fair measure of both between her and Scott. Not love. Not yet. But maybe if they gave themselves a chance, this could become something special.

But Scott was leaving. All she would have is a job she didn't really enjoy. Jess was right. Coorah Creek was not the place for her.

She parked the car, and almost before she was out, Scott was at her side.

'How are you feeling?'

She frowned. 'I'm fine.'

'Trish said you'd been sick on the plane.'

'How does that woman know these things?' Katie shook her head. 'Is she psychic? Does she have CCTV cameras all over town? How does she do it?'

Scott chuckled, and wrapped his arms around her in a mighty bear hug.

He doesn't care, she thought, *that I have been sick on the plane. I hate to think what I smell like. And god knows I look awful. But he doesn't care about that. He cares about me. Me.*

And suddenly she really did feel fine. Even better than fine.

By the time she had showered and changed, Scott had a cup of tea waiting for her. They settled on her couch and Katie felt herself begin to relax. She told Scott about the flight to help a stockman who had fallen from a windmill while fixing it, and broken his arm.

'It was a nasty break. But Adam fixed it,' she said. 'He's a good doctor. He does things on site that would require transport to a hospital back home.' She sighed heavily.

'I hope that sigh wasn't caused by our handsome doctor,' Scott joked.

'No,' Katie grinned. 'I was just thinking—'

'What?'

'When I was younger I wanted to be a doctor. I imagined myself being some sort of hero and saving lives. Doing the sort of thing Adam does almost every day.'

'Why didn't you?'

'I don't come from an affluent family. They wouldn't have been able to afford to put me through medical school. None of the kids at my school ever aimed that high. I was lucky to be able to study nursing.'

'Any regrets?'

'Sometimes. Nursing in a big London hospital isn't really for me. It's too impersonal. The patients all run together into a blur. There are times I felt I wasn't really helping anyone.'

'So it's better for you here?'

'The work is better. But the flying terrifies me. I doubt I will ever be able to do the air ambulance thing properly.'

'You'll get used to it,' Scott said.

'Either that or I'll have to get some better travel sickness pills. The ones Adam gave me today didn't help at all.'

Scott lifted her hand and gently kissed the back of it. 'You'll figure it out. I have faith in you.'

At that moment, as she looked into his smiling eyes and waited for him to kiss her lips, she believed him.

It was quite a few minutes before Scott was able to stop kissing Katie. He just loved the softness of her lips. He could go on kissing her for hours. He could do a lot more too, but he wasn't going to. It was going to be hard enough to leave her now. If this thing between them went any further, he would never want to walk away.

'I spent some time with my dad last night,' he said.

Her face lit up. 'That's great. What did you do?'

'It was that woman again.' He grinned. 'Trish roped me into helping them to set up for the town Christmas party. Dad was there. We worked together for a bit.'

'Are you starting to mend the bridges?'

'I think so. We walked back together afterwards and we talked.'

'What did you talk about?'

It had come. He'd told his father. Now it was time to tell Katie.

'I have a job offer. Restoring classic cars for a motor museum.'

'Wonderful! That sounds just right for you. Tell me all about it.'

She was looking at him, her eyes shining with joy for him. But what would happen if he told her that the job was in England? He couldn't do it. It was wrong, he knew that, but he wanted to postpone that moment as long as possible. He wouldn't lie to her, but at this moment, he just couldn't tell her the truth.

'I met the manager when he came into my shop. He liked the work I was doing. They have two amazing new cars arriving soon. Really rare and valuable. He offered me the job restoring them. It's an honour really.'

'That's great! We should celebrate. I can make that dinner I promised you last night before I got called away.' Katie was getting to her feet. He reached out to pull her back to the couch.

'Wait. Katie. I ... I'm thinking of saying no.'

'Oh.'

She sat beside him, looking at his face. He could see the question in her eyes.

'The job would mean leaving Coorah Creek. There are a lot of things holding me here,' he said. 'I think I am starting to make some connection with Dad ...'

'That's great,' she said softly. 'I'm happy for you.'

'And there's you, Katie. I don't want to leave just yet. I want to spend more time with you. I've never felt this close to anyone before. And so quickly. I don't know what it is ... or what it might become. But I'm not ready to walk away. Not yet.'

He saw the tears in her eyes, adding to their luminous shine. Gently he reached out to run his thumb along her cheekbone. It came back damp.

'I don't want you to.'

He kissed her. Her tears added a spicy saltiness to the softness of her lips. He took her face between the palms of his hands, and kissed those tears away. Then they kissed some more, long deep slow kisses that drove the sadness away.

'You know,' Katie said with a smile when at last they could both speak again. 'You are my oldest friend in this whole country. Not by much,' she added hastily. 'I only met you half an hour before I met some of the other people here. But that half hour; it means a lot when you're a long way from home at Christmas.'

He heard the pain underneath the words. She was homesick. He understood that. He would do everything he could to drive that away. He wrapped his arms around her and pulled her close and as he did he realised something strange. If she was his oldest friend – her second oldest friend – the second person she had met in The Creek – was his father. Maybe there was a lesson there ... but he had no idea what it was.

Chapter 17

The rain on the roof sounded as if all the dwarves from Middle Earth were up there pounding away with their hammers, and had brought their friends from Snow White along for the ride. The ceaseless pounding on the corrugated iron roof was deafening. Katie put her hands over her ears. After a couple of weeks of rising temperatures and brilliant blue skies, the wet season had arrived with a vengeance.

She turned over and covered her head with her pillow.

What sort of a country only had two seasons? Back in England, the changing of the seasons was accompanied by soft changes in light, by leaf-kicking and pristine white snow. There were brilliant summer days, punctuated by bird song, and cold wet winter nights to spend huddled in front of a roaring fire. You knew where you were weather-wise in England.

But not here. Oh no!

There were no leaves to kick – because those scrubby gum trees never lost their leaves. There was no winter … only a wet season and a dry season – differentiated, thusly by one wit at the pub: during the dry season it's hot all the time and doesn't rain and in the wet season it's hot all the time and rains almost every day. Call that seasons? She certainly didn't.

She sat up in bed and glared at the ceiling – as if by doing so she could stop the rain. The drumming continued.

Katie slid out of bed and padded barefoot into the living room. She walked over to the window and stared out at the rain. There wasn't much to see. Without street lights or a light from another building, it was too dark. Sighing, she made her way to the kitchen and flicked the kettle on. Tea would help. It always did.

As she waited for the water to boil, she glanced at the clock. It was just after 11 o'clock. Almost Christmas day. And she felt about as Christmassy as a cold cheese and tomato sandwich.

She poured the tea and walked back into her lounge room. The steam rising from her cup served to highlight the temperature as she went to switch on the overhead fan. Christmas shouldn't be in mid-summer. It just didn't feel right to have Christmas with not even the faintest hope of a snowball.

She blew across the top of her cup to cool the liquid, and took a small sip. Her mum always said a good cup of tea made every situation better. She was probably right … she was about most things. Oh, but Katie missed her family. Especially now. If she was back in England, she would be at her parents' house, with her brother and sister. They'd be drinking tea too – but doing it together. And talking.

A fierce crack of lightning caused her to jump. Damn this storm. Not only was it keeping her awake, her somewhat fragile internet connection had given up the ghost. She'd only managed about two minutes of conversation with her family earlier this evening, before the connection dropped out. God only knew when it would come back.

She sipped her tea again and admitted that really, she was just in a bad mood. Totally homesick. And lonely.

It wasn't just that her family weren't here. She was missing the whole Christmas experience. She hadn't even wrapped a present. Sure, she'd sent some small souvenirs home to her family – but that wasn't the same as piling brightly wrapped gifts covered in ribbons and bows under a tree. She didn't have anyone to wrap a present for.

Except Scott.

She so wanted to give Scott a gift. Somehow, in all the strangeness of this new life, he was the one thing that felt familiar and comforting. That felt like home. She'd taken some time off work and scoured every shop in Coorah Creek for a present. There were not many shops, and nothing that that she wanted to give to Scott. Sure, she could buy him a bottle of wine, or a new hat. But she wanted something a bit more personal than that. Something that would let him know she would miss him when he was gone back to the city for his new job. She wanted a gift that would tell him how wonderful it was to have him in a place that was so strange there were times she wasn't even sure she spoke the same language. Language! That was it.

She leaped to her feet. At her going away party, her friends had given her gifts. The usual joke gifts that suited such occasions. She found what she was looking for in a drawer in her bedroom. It was a book – The English-Australian Dictionary. She flicked through the pages as she carried it back to the couch. There were the usual entries – Sheila as Australian for girl. Bonza meaning good – although she'd not heard any Australian actually say that. There were some interesting words too. She didn't know that a wild horse was called a brumby in Australia. And that the peppers she ate in the UK were called capsicums in the southern hemisphere.

She found a pen and notebook and started scribbling down words … ridgy-didge (genuine), cobber (friend) Pommy (English person) … there was a lot of material. She chewed the end of the pen and tried a few phrases on the notebook. She was getting there. At last she had it figured out. She turned to the front page of the phrase book and began to write. The last word caused her to pause. She flicked through the book one more time, but some words are the same in every language.

When she was done, she pulled out a map of Queensland she had bought on her first day in the country. Coorah Creek was circled in black felt pen. That would make great wrapping paper.

At last the gift was ready. It wasn't anything like any Christmas gift she had wrapped before. There were no ribbons and bows. No red and green and gold fancy paper. It wasn't the most expensive she'd ever given either. But this gift was as personal to her as a gift could be.

She sat back and yawned. The blinking clock on her TV showed that it was ten minutes past midnight. Christmas Day! Not only that, the room was silent. She hadn't noticed that the rain had stopped. A good thing too, she thought, or else Santa and his reindeer would get wet. Or did kangaroos pull Santa's sleigh in this part of the world.

Smiling, she made her way back to bed. Her last thought as she fell asleep was that maybe this wasn't going to be such a bad "Chrissy" after all.

Chapter 18

Christmas morning dawned bright and sunny at Coorah Creek. The trees still shone with the last drops of the overnight rain and the air had that crisp clean taste that only comes after a thunderstorm. The kookaburras fluffed their feathers and chortled as the sun rose. A lone kangaroo hopped across the road on the outskirts of town, and disappeared in the direction of the national park to the north. The huge machinery of the mine was silent on this one day of the year when no work was done.

In her bedroom, Katie slept on, her curtains shut to preserve the cool darkness for as long as possible. The map-wrapped package lay on the coffee table, next to the mug she had failed to wash the night before.

In their nearby house, Adam and Jess were still in bed, but not asleep. Their Christmas had started early with an exchange of gifts and a champagne breakfast in bed.

As always, Ed Collins was out of bed with the sun. His first task this Christmas morning, as it was every day, was to pat the dog, and let her out. Candy wagged her tail as she began her slow and careful descent of the stairs from the back door to the garden.

Watching her struggle, Ed felt sadness steal over him. She was so very old. According to the vet, she wasn't in any pain, but Ed knew he wouldn't have her company for much longer. He looked across the road to the pub, where his son was sleeping. He wouldn't have Scott for very much longer either.

Inside the pub, Trish and Syd were also up and about. As the prime movers behind the Waifs and Orphans party, there was a lot for them to do. Trish and Syd didn't exchange Christmas gifts any more. Their Christmas was all about other people. Deep down, Trish knew this was their way of dealing with the fact that they had never been blessed with children. But she had long since come to terms with that. As long as there were people in the world she could help, she was content.

And speaking of helping … She heard movement in the room just above her kitchen. If Scott and his father didn't sort themselves out soon, she'd do more than give them a gentle nudge in the right direction. In fact, she could probably start today. But, to be fair, she would cook the boy a good breakfast first. He deserved that much.

The smell of cooking greeted Scott as he came down the stairs. And not just the normal breakfast smells of coffee and bacon. He walked into the kitchen to find Trish hard at work.

'Merry Christmas.' He risked giving her a quick peck on the cheek and was rewarded with a smile. She wasn't such a bad sort, he thought, as he helped himself to coffee.

'Tuck into this,' Trish said as she slid a plate onto the table. 'There's a lot of work to do to get ready for the Waifs and Orphans.'

'Yes, Ma'am.'

'Are you planning to go over the road this morning?'

'I'll see my father at the party.' Scott kept his voice casual. He had thought about going to visit his father … but had decided against it. He had no gift to give him. He had no idea what he could even say.

They had barely acknowledged Christmas when Scott was a boy …
it would seem strange to make a fuss now.

Trish said nothing, but the way she did it spoke volumes.

By the time Scott had finished his breakfast, Trish was starting to
pack food and ice into several huge coolers.

'If you're ready,' Trish said in a voice that brooked no denial, 'I
need you to take a load of chairs to the hall. After that, there's ice
in the freezer in the bar. And all this food is just about ready to go
too. You'd better use our ute. You can take bigger loads in that.'

'I'm on it.'

He wasn't the only one. By the time he had driven to the hall,
the back of the ute piled high with chairs and stools, there were
already several cars there. He grabbed the first load and walked up
the stairs. He took one step inside the hall and stopped, feeling his
mouth drop open.

The scene in front of him was all the Christmas dreams he'd
ever had a child. It was his first memories of Christmas, when his
mother was still with him and the house was filled with colour and
life and love. It was everything he had lost when she left. Everything his father had never allowed in those long dark years.

The hall was dripping with decorations. Although Scott had
helped with some of the work, this was the first time he's seen them
in their full glory.

Someone had installed a tree at one end of the hall and it glittered with colour and light. Lights had also been strung along the
timber beams above his head, adding an extra layer of sparkle to the
already dazzling room. The tables he had helped to arrange were
now covered with cloth – the wide range of size and colour and
pattern was testament to the fact that they had come from many
different homes. So too had the assortment of plates and glasses
stacked ready for the start of the party. On some of the tables, there

were vases of flowers; a rare sight in this dry and dusty place. There still weren't many chairs, but he was about to change that.

'Hey, the chairs are here,' a voice called from the back of the room. Several men came forward to help unload the back of his vehicle, wishing him a merry Christmas as they did. The back of the ute was empty in no time at all, and Scott returned to the pub for the next load. Once again many hands helped make light of the unloading. The crowd was growing now. Families walked through the door, calling greetings to their neighbours. Kids were showing off their presents to anyone who might listen. It seemed every family brought something to add to the party. A home baked cake. A bowl of potato salad or a ham. Beer and soft drink were pushed into the ice in the bathtubs along one wall. Then someone turned on the music. As the first Christmas carol filled the air, Scott glanced at the doorway to see his father walk in.

Ed looked like a different person. His greasy overalls had been exchanged for blue jeans and a crisp white cotton shirt. It wasn't just that he looked clean – he looked less worn down by care. Younger too. He crossed the room to where Scott was standing. For a few moments, the two of them just stood there, both not sure what to say or do.

'Merry Christmas, Dad.'

This was what he had come back to Coorah Creek to do. Scott held out his hand. This time if felt almost natural.

All around them, people were hugging and laughing and exchanging gifts.

Ed reached out and took Scott's hand. 'Merry Christmas, son.'

Chapter 19

Katie was running late for the party. Her morning had been thrown out by the arrival of a couple of patients at the hospital. She'd helped Adam set the broken arm of a child who had become too adventurous on the swing set he'd been given for Christmas. And she'd dressed a burn on a woman's hand which was good argument against too much champagne at breakfast before lighting the barbecue for Christmas lunch. She would call her family back in England when the time differences allowed, so she had set off to the Waifs and Orphans party – where she had already arranged to meet Scott.

The hall was humming when she arrived. Music was wafting through the open doors and windows, as was the sound of talk and laughter. When she entered the hall, Katie stopped and looked around her. The old wooden hall had been changed into a wonderland. It was Christmas in all its glory … but so different as to be almost unrecognisable.

The tree that glowed so brightly at the end of the hall was like no other Christmas tree she had ever seen. No tall stately pine, this tree was as broad as it was high. A profusion of branches spread from multiple trunks, the long broad dark green leaves dropping towards the floor. The tree sported as much tinsel and as many lights as anyone could hope for – but the snow in its branches was just cotton wool.

In England, her Christmas had always been marked by a roaring log fire, the flickering firelight adding to the warmth of the room. Not so in Coorah Creek. The room was already hot. There were no woolly scarves or bright Christmas knits. Shorts and T-shirts seemed to be the dress code for most of the partygoers. However there was, she was pleased to see, a smattering of Santa hats.

The room was brilliantly decorated with tinsel and shining glass balls. There were hand-made cut out stars, no doubt produced at the school. There were brightly wrapped boxes under the tree.

The tables were almost groaning under the weight of the food that was laid out. But Katie would not call it a proper Christmas lunch. There were huge bowls of salad and fruit. She spied buckets of fresh prawns – although how they came to be so far from the ocean, she wasn't sure. There were legs of ham cooked on the bone, the thick skin peeled back to reveal the succulent meat beneath. There was ice-cream stored, like the beer, in tubs of ice. There was turkey – or perhaps it was chicken – but it was cold and laid out alongside other cold meats.

Where was the steaming roast and stuffing? The rich dark pudding and the mince pies? Not to mention the roast potatoes and the bread sauce? And where oh where was the gravy? The thick tasty gravy that her mother always made with white wine and just a touch of mustard to give it extra bite.

This wasn't Christmas as she knew it, but the room did exude the gaiety and joy she was looking for. Many of the faces were unknown to her – but even this far from her home, the smiles were the same. And in the midst of it all, totally recognisable and drawing her to him like a homing pigeon to its nest, was Scott.

He was laughing at something someone had just said. He was dressed simply in blue jeans and a T-shirt, but she had never seen any man look so good, as he tossed his head back and laughed again. Even amid the hubbub of noise around her, she could hear his laugh as clearly as if he was standing next to her. He looked so at ease here in the midst of this very summery Christmas, with these people from whom he had run all those years ago. He stopped laughing and turned around, almost as if he could feel her eyes on him. When he saw her, his face lit up. He excused himself and hurried towards her.

'Katie. Merry Christmas.'

'Merry —'

Before she could finish the greeting, Scott had taken her in his arms and kissed her. For a few seconds, all she was aware of was how good it felt in his arms. With his lips on hers. How right it felt. And suddenly, the strangeness of this Christmas day was gone. In some deep and unexplained way, here in a place she had seen for the first time such a short time ago, she had come home.

When Scott finally released her, she was astounded to hear whistles and cheering and catcalls. She looked around at the smiling faces of the townsfolk, and blushed to the very tip of her toes.

'Come on,' Scott said. 'I'll get you a drink.'

By mid-afternoon, the party was in full swing. People came and went as they wished. The food and drink flowed in what seemed a never-ending abundance. Katie smiled to see Trish and Syd Warren moving through the crowds, playing the role of hosts although, in truth, the town itself was the host on this occasion. Adam and Jess were there, as was Ken Travers, the storeowner and her patient. His wife was with him and a teenage girl she assumed was their daughter. Jack North was playing Santa for a group of kids — a couple of whom she believed were his. There were people she didn't know, but she guessed that by the end of the day, no-one in that room would be a stranger any more.

Katie felt a warm glow, and she wasn't certain if it was caused by the soaring temperature, the delicious if somewhat alcoholic fruit punch being served from a huge bowl, or Scott, who was never far from her side, his voice and honest laughter punctuating her day. Whenever possible his hand found hers, although that wasn't too often given their need to distribute food and drink and to constantly embrace both children and adults.

Scott was off collecting another load of ice from the pub freezer, when his father sought Katie out.

'Merry Christmas,' he said.

'And to you too,' she said, meaning it.

'Having Scott here has made this the best Christmas in a very long time,' Ed said. 'I know you have helped too.'

'I haven't done anything.'

'Yes, you have. You've been a friend to him. Given him someone to talk to. And I know you have been encouraging him to try to overcome the bad feeling that's been between us all these years.'

'He set out to do that long before he met me,' Katie said.

'I know. But you've helped him … us. I wanted to thank you for that.'

Katie felt herself blushing again.

'My son cares for you,' Ed said matter-of-factly.

'I care for him too.'

At that moment, Scott re-entered the building carrying a huge bag of crushed ice. To the cheers of the crowd, he upended the ice into the big bathtub full of beer, sending water splashing over the sides. Amid much backslapping, he accepted another beer from one of the men.

'So, are you having a good time?' he asked Katie as he rejoined her.

'Yes. I was feeling really homesick this morning, but I'm not any more.' She gave his hand a squeeze to let him know how much he was responsible for the improvement in her day.

'Scott,' Ed spoke hesitantly. 'I have a couple of things at the house that … That I thought you might like to have. If you could come over.'

'What things?'

'It's better that you come and take a look. It could be now. Or later if you would prefer.'

Scott glanced at Katie, a question in his eyes. She could feel his hesitation. He had declared his intention never to set foot in his father's house again. But things were changing and she knew this was something he had to do.

'Go,' she said without hesitation.

'Will you …'

'I'll be fine. I promised Trish I would take care of the next round of washing up. Then I need to head back anyway. The time will be right to call my family back home.'

'Can I come over to your place later?'

'You'd better. I have something for you too.'

Chapter 20

They walked back towards the garage in silence. Ed found it a little hard to believe that after all these years, Scott was coming back to the house they had once both called home. This was a chance for a new start, but Ed didn't know how to make it work. There were some things he should give to Scott, but that wasn't his only reason for inviting his son back to the house. He still harboured a hope that if Scott could walk back through that front door, some of the pain of the past few years might wash away.

As they approached the darkened buildings on the corner of the town's main street, Ed found he was looking at his home and business with new eyes. Through Scott's eyes. Both buildings were shabby and in need of new paint. The garden, if you could call it that, was overgrown and wild. The grime that went with his business had slowly spread to cover his whole life. And this was how Scott had lived as a boy. He hadn't been a very good father to his son. It was a wonder that Scott had grown into the man he was.

They reached the rusty side gate. Ed automatically looked for movement in the overgrown garden; the flash of gold and accompanying bark that would tell them Candy had noticed their arrival.

For a long time now, she had been the only one to greet his return at the end of each day. Without her the loneliness would have been even harder to bear.

There was no movement in the garden. Ed opened the gate, a frown starting to form on his forehead.

'Candy. Where are you, girl?'

There was no answer. Ed walked towards the house, pushing aside the branches of an overgrowing bush. Then he saw her.

'Oh, no. Candy.' The softly spoken words were torn from the depth of Ed's soul.

The Labrador was lying on her side near the steps leading to his back door. Her legs were caught under her body as if she had fallen while trying to climb the stairs. Her eyes were closed and her tongue lolled from her open mouth. She was still breathing, but every slow laboured breath seemed as if it would be her last. Ed knelt by her head and ran his hand over her muzzle. When she stirred slightly and licked his fingers, his heart almost broke.

He heard Scott come up behind him.

'Help me get her inside.'

Scott hurried up the steps. The door wasn't locked. He opened it and stepped aside to allow Ed to carry the dog through. Ed carried his old friend through to the living room, and lowered her very gently onto a much-used dog bed that sat beside his old armchair.

Ed crouched beside her, stroking her head gently. Scott joined him. Candy opened her eyes and stared up at the two men. Slowly the very tip of her tail began to wag. Just a little. She licked Scott's fingers as he reached out to stroke her, then her eyes closed again.

'Should I go and find the vet?' Scott asked.

Ed shook his head. 'We knew this was coming. She's just old. Too old.' His voice broke. The hands that reached out to stroke the old dog's head were shaking.

The three of them stayed like that for what seemed a very long time. After each breath Candy took, Scott and Ed waited an eternity until she took the next. When, at last she didn't, the room seemed very very silent.

Grief crashed down on Ed like a physical thing. His only friend was gone. He felt so terribly alone. For the first time in many long years, tears began to stream down his face. He looked at Scott and saw the same grief in his eyes. It was as if time had shifted and Scott was a boy again, looking to him for comfort when his mother left. Ed had failed his son then. And he was terribly afraid he would fail again.

Both men rose to their feet. For the first time since they'd entered, Scott looked around him. Ed knew the room hadn't changed much in the last eight years. The furniture was older. Shabbier. But Scott would recognise his home.

He knew the moment Scott saw the photograph. His body stiffened. He walked over to the bookshelf and lifted the silver frame from its place. Inside that frame was a photo of a beautiful young woman and a small boy.

'I thought you threw everything away,' Scott said slowly.

'No. I just put them away. After you left, I wanted something ...' Ed couldn't continue.

Scott turned around. His face, still wet tears, was contorted with grief and anger.

'Why? Why did you do it?'

Ed didn't answer.

'She was beautiful. She was a wonderful wife and mother. And you had an affair! Why did you do that? Why did you drive her away?'

Ed struggled to find the words he needed, but they wouldn't come. He saw the disgust spread over Scott's face. He put the photo back on the bookshelf and turned to walk out of the room, away from this house and his father. Ed knew that if his son left, he would never see him again.

His throat contracted. The words were too hard to speak.

'It wasn't me.'

The words stopped Scott in his tracks, but he didn't turn around. 'What do you mean it wasn't you?'

'I didn't have the affair. She did.'

At first, Scott thought he'd misheard. But he hadn't. His father's voice had never been clearer or more firm.

'You're lying.'

'No. For the first time, I am telling the truth.'

Slowly Scott turned to face his father, still unwilling to believe what he'd heard.

'Why should I believe you?' Ed had given him no reason to trust him, and every reason to walk away.

'After everything that has happened, why would I lie now?'

Scott studied his father's face. The pain in his eyes told Scott that this time he was hearing the truth. He felt as if his whole world was shaking beneath him.

'Why didn't you tell me? All those years ago. Why did you lie then?'

'I needed it to be a secret. I wanted to believe ...' Ed blinked back the tears. 'I wanted to believe she'd come back. I had to believe she'd come back. And when she did, I didn't want her to be the subject of town gossip. If they had to blame someone – if you had to blame someone – I wanted it to be me.'

'And that last day, you let me fight you, and then walk away without knowing the truth.'

'You said you were going to look for her. I wanted you to find her. And if you did, the two of you had to be all right together. It would be better if you both blamed me. And, I guess I still hoped there was a chance for me.'

'That she would come back to you?'

'That you both would.'

Scott shook his head, trying to make sense of what he was hearing. Years of anger and bitterness and hate had been based on a lie.

'I know better now,' Ed said in a very quiet voice. 'She was never going to come back to me. She had the affair, but it was as much my fault as hers. I am not an easy man to live with.'

'No. You're not.'

'Scott, I am so sorry.' Ed's voice cracked with the weight of years of loneliness and regret. 'You are so very like her, you know. Every time I looked at you, I saw her in your eyes. I couldn't stand the pain, so I guess I stopped looking at you. Stopped seeing you. It was the only way I could survive.'

A long moment passed, broken only by the sound of their breathing. Scott looked into his father's face and saw love there. There was fear, too. He was afraid that Scott would walk away again.

Scott reached deep inside his own heart. He'd come back to Coorah Creek looking for answers. Tonight, he'd found them.

They both moved at the same time. In the middle of the room, Ed threw his arms around his son and pulled him into his chest. They held each other for a long moment. When they broke apart, there were tears in both their eyes.

'I have some of her things still,' Ed said. 'I thought you might like something to remember her by. She left me – but she always loved you.'

'And you have always loved her?'

'Son, I fell in love with your mother the day I met her. I'm not entirely sure I have ever stopped loving her.'

'I loved her so much when I was a boy. I tried to find her. I really did. I checked electoral rolls. I posted messages all over the internet and took out ads in newspapers. I used to wonder if she saw them and just didn't want to see me. I can hardly remember her now. Would it hurt you to talk about her?'

'No. I'd welcome the chance to talk. I thought you'd never come back either. I did try to find you ... but I didn't think you would want to see me.'

'I didn't then, but things change. People change.'

'They do.' Ed took a deep breath and pulled himself together. 'But before anything else, I have to bury Candy.'

Scott nodded. 'We can do that together.'

Chapter 21

Katie continued to wave even after the picture on her computer shrank to nothing.

'Merry Christmas. I love you all,' she whispered again to the family who could no longer see or hear her.

She cancelled the call and set the computer to playing music. It had been lovely to talk to her family. They didn't seem quite so far away now. She had laughed at the reindeer face on the Christmas jumper her mum had knitted for her big brother. Her dad had loved the Australian stubby holder she had sent him in the post. It was just a cylinder of foam, designed to keep a beer cold. Not a big issue back home right now, where London was looking pretty under a light dusting of snow.

She sighed. She did miss her family, but today had proven one thing to her. She could manage on her own. Her family would always be there for her whenever she needed them. Their love was steadfast and unconditional. The decision to come to Coorah Creek had not been about her family. It was about a career that was broken and needed fixing. There was no doubt she was feeling better about her chosen path now than she had been the day she walked out of that soulless hospital. There were things she enjoyed about small town nursing. But flying in that air ambulance was not one of them! She shuddered. It didn't matter how long she stayed, she would never get used to that.

But stay she would!

Katie got up and walked to the window to look out across the open spaces that surrounded the hospital. Despite last night's rain, a full day of blazing sun had left the scraggy gum trees looking dusty still. They always looked dusty. Much as she missed England's green and pleasant land, going back now would be a mark of failure. She would stay in Coorah Creek until she had regained her love of nursing. Until she was ready to put her career back on track.

And she would stay because Scott was here. Not in Coorah Creek, but here in Australia. She didn't know where the motor museum was. She guessed it would be in Canberra. That was a long way from Coorah Creek, but not impossible to manage.

She had given up telling herself that it was too soon for her to fall in love with a man who had literally found her on the side of the road. Time didn't matter. Scott had worked his way into her heart and lodged there. The connection between them was stronger than anything she had felt before – and she knew it was not caused by her loneliness or his sadness. Wherever and whenever they had met, they would feel the same.

His stay in Coorah Creek had already been longer than his original plan. He'd stayed because he wanted to make amends with his father. And he'd stayed because of her – she knew that as surely as she knew anything.

Neither of them had said it in so many words – but both of them wanted to give this relationship a chance.

She looked down at her watch. Where was Scott?

It was almost seven o'clock. Scott had been with his father for a couple of hours. She hoped they had finally managed a reconciliation. Feeling restless, she stood up and crossed the room to turn on the overhead fan. The day was still incredibly hot and there wasn't even a breath of wind. Katie glanced out the window to the sinking sun, the light glinting on the tinsel on her small tree. It was really just a branch pulled from what looked almost like a pine tree in the hospital car park, but it was her way of marking the day. Scott's gift was sitting under the tree. She forced herself to sit down again and pick up a book. Scott would come when he could.

Scott was sweating freely as he walked towards the hospital. It wasn't a long walk from his old home, but the night was hot. Christmas always involved a lot of sweat. He tried to imagine what it would be like having Christmas in England. Instead of prawns, a steaming roast turkey would be on the menu. Instead of cold beer, maybe hot mulled wine. Instead of blazing sunshine and the chance of a swim in the creek there could be snow. He'd never seen snow. That might be fun.

Just ahead was the sign pointing to the hospital. And a little way off the road, he saw a light gleaming. Katie's light, welcoming him. His steps hastened.

When she opened the door, it seemed all the emotions of the past few hours just erupted inside him. He gathered her into his arms and held her as if he would never let her go. He felt as if his body was shaking, and Katie was the only thing keeping him firmly on the ground. The emotional roller-coaster of the past few hours had exhausted him. He held her for a long time, before he found the strength to step away.

'Are you all right?' her voice was full on concern as she raised
one hand to gently wipe away the hint of a tear on his cheek. 'What
happened?'

'Candy, my old dog. The one I left behind. She's been with Dad
all these years. She died tonight.'

'Oh Scott, I am so sorry.'

'We … we buried her at the back of the garden. It was so strange
to be doing something like that together.'

'How's your dad?'

'He's going to be okay. We both are.' He ran his hand over his
face. 'I have been wrong about my father for all these years.'

Without a word she took his hand and led him inside. Thankfully he collapsed on her couch – all the while holding her hand
like a lifeline.

'I don't know where to start.' He took a deep breath.

She sat quietly while he told her. Tears shone in her eyes at times,
but she never took her blue eyes from his face. He felt her concern
and her empathy – dare he say her love – curl around him like a
blanket, helping to ease the shock and pain and grief. And slowly,
ever so slowly, a strange kind of joy replaced them.

'I guess all these years, subconsciously I thought it was my fault.
My mother left me. My father hated me. I thought there was something wrong with me. That I was unlovable.'

'No!' The intensity and certainty of her statement was a balm to
his shattered emotions.

'It never occurred to me that my father was struggling to cope
with losing the woman he loved. He says that every time he looked at
me, he saw her in my eyes. That explains why he was so withdrawn
and hard. He was fighting every day to keep himself together.'

'He must have loved her very much.'

'You know, I think maybe he still does. After all these years.' Scott squeezed her hand gently. 'We Collinses are a stubborn lot.'

'That I already knew.'

They both smiled.

'So what happens now?' Katie asked, her voice very soft.

He knew what she was thinking. Would he stay in Coorah Creek or would he leave and take his dream job? She still didn't know quite what 'leaving' meant. It was time he told her.

'I'm going to stay another week or two. Dad wants to do some work around the house and garage. Clean out a lot of old stuff. Smarten it up a bit. I'll help him with that. I think working together will be a good chance to get to know each other again.'

'And then?'

'I'm going to take the job. At the National Motor Museum. It is the fulfilment of a dream for me. Dad understands. He says I have to be true to myself or I'm no good to anyone. He's right. And he says he'll come and visit. It will be fun showing him the cars I'm working on.'

He didn't miss the flash of disappointment in her eyes. But she hid it well. 'Can I come and visit too? Is it in Canberra? It would be exciting to play tourist there too.'

'Of course you can visit, but—' He hesitated. He should have told her this a long time ago. 'The thing is, Katie, the job is at the National Motor Museum. In England.'

Her face froze for a second. Then she let go of his hand. He felt bereft as she walked to the window to stare out into the darkness. The silence stretched on for a long time before she finally spoke.

'I've been there. It's wonderful. You'll love it.'

'Katie—' He stood and moved towards her, but not too close. The set of her shoulders told him she needed a little space. 'Come with me. You've always said you would go home to England. Do it now. We can go there together.'

She shook her head. 'I can't leave yet. I have to do this job properly. I need to understand just what I want to do with the rest of my life.'

His heart sank, but he understood. 'You have to be true to yourself too. And when you're ready, I'll still be in England. I'll wait for you.'

She nodded. Her shoulders heaved as she sighed. When she turned back towards him, she had a smile on her face, but he could tell it was forced.

'This makes my present even more appropriate,' she said as she reached for something under her tree. 'I meant this as a joke against my accent. But—'

Her voice trailed away as she handed it to him. He unwrapped the book and read the message inside – carefully crafted out of Australian slang.

> *To a ridgy-didge Aussie,*
> *You're a bonzer bloke.*
> *With love from your Pommy Sheila.*

He wasn't sure whether to laugh or cry.

'I have something for you too.' He reached into his pocket. 'This was my mother's. Dad gave it to me tonight. I'd like you to have it.'

The silver chain glistened in the light as Katie took it. She looked at the small heart nestled in the palm of her hand.

'I'm going to miss you,' she said in a very tiny voice.

'We have two weeks,' Scott said as he gathered her into his arms again. 'We'll figure something out.'

Chapter 22

Katie couldn't get Scott's words out of her mind. She was supposed to be working, sorting out supplies and making a list for reordering, while at the same time being the only on-call person at the hospital. Adam and Jess had left early that morning on a flight to Birdsville, to pick up a suspected heart attack patient and fly them to Mt Isa. She had felt relieved when Adam told her there was no need for her to come.

She was trying to focus on the job, but her mind was racing. Her feelings toward Scott hadn't changed. If anything, his revelations on Christmas Day had only drawn them closer together. She was so glad he had found what he was searching for, but the thought of being left behind when he went to the UK was devastating. But, at the same time, she couldn't walk away from this job before she'd found what she was looking for.

If you can't be true to yourself—

Her thoughts were interrupted by a screech of tyres as a car entered the car park at high speed. She was on her feet in a second, knowing immediately that there was trouble. Leaving the office she saw Jack North dart through the hospital's front door and hurry down the hallway towards her. She had been in Coorah Creek long enough to know that Jack was the man everyone called on in an emergency. The look on his face left her in no doubt there was something very wrong somewhere.

'Katie, there's been an accident. On the highway. You're needed.' There was no panic in his voice, but a sense of urgency that did not bode well.

'What happened?'

'A car hit a roo. Rolled and hit a tree.'

'How many people?'

'Just the driver.'

'Is he on his way here?'

Jack shook his head. 'He's trapped in the car. Max Delany – the sergeant – called me. Told me to bring you out there.'

For a few seconds, Katie just froze. Go to the scene of the accident? That wasn't how A&E worked. Ambulances brought the injured to the hospital. And there was always a doctor close by to treat them. She couldn't do this on her own. She wasn't qualified. And then there were the legal issues. What would happen if—

She forced herself to stop. She was needed. Someone was hurt and if there was any chance she could help, she had to go.

'Can you tell me anything about his injures?'

'Max said there's a lot of blood. And there's something wrong with his shoulder.'

'Is he conscious?'

'Yes. Max says he's in a lot of pain.'

Katie nodded. She reached for the emergency travel bag that Adam always kept ready to go. She opened it and quickly checked the contents. She had no real idea of what she would need out there, but the essentials were in the bag.

'Let's go,' she said.

It took just over twenty minutes to get there. Twenty minutes of high-speed driving. Katie tried not to think about their speed – or what would happen if they too hit a kangaroo in the road. Jack seemed a good driver. She put a lid on her uncertainty and fears and just let herself trust him.

The accident scene was strangely still. The police car was parked on the side of the road, its lights flashing. There were two other vehicles there – passers-by who had stopped to help. It seemed strange that there was no ambulance. No fire engines. No tow trucks. Just ordinary people ready to help if they were needed.

Katie grabbed the bag from the back of the car and hurried towards a white station wagon that lay against a big gum tree a few yards off the road. The car would have rolled onto its roof, had the tree not stopped it. Instead it rested at a crazy angle – not quite upside down, but not on its side either. She knew in an instant that getting the driver out was going to be difficult and possibly dangerous. As she approached, she noticed a bloody shape lying in the long brown grass not too far away. The kangaroo. She barely had time to hope the poor creature hadn't suffered, when the police sergeant hurried to her.

'The driver's still in the car,' Delany said.

'Is he conscious?' she asked.

'Yes. He's in a lot of pain. And he's bleeding from multiple cuts.'

Katie started to move, but Max grabbed her arm.

'Be careful. The car is resting against the tree. It's not safe. We need to get him out of there before you can treat him.'

'I understand. But I need to see him before you try to move him.'

Max hesitated and then nodded.

Swiftly but carefully, Katie approached the car. All she could see was the underside of the vehicle. One wheel was missing and parts of the exhaust were hanging off.

A man screamed in agony.

In a trice, Katie was crouched beside the vehicle, broken glass crunching beneath her feet as she spoke to the injured driver who was still strapped in his seat, his body trapped and twisted inside the mangled metal.

'It's going to be all right. My name is Katie and I'm here to help.'

A bloodstained face slowly turned towards her, and Katie was shocked to see how very young the man was.

'What's your name?'

'Tom,' the voice was harsh with agony, but he seemed to have his wits about him.

'Hi Tom.' Katie quickly scanned the young man's body. There was a lot of blood, but the wounds seemed mostly superficial. It was his shoulder that worried her. 'Can you move your hands?'

He grunted with effort. Or with pain.

'The ... one hand yes. The other one ... left arm...' His voice trailed off.

'Don't worry, Tom. We'll have you out of there in a minute.'

Katie stood and backed away from the injured man. Max and Jack were waiting. They were holding what looked like welding gear.

'We can cut him out now, if it's safe to move him,' Max said.

'I'll put a neck brace on him before you start. I think his back is okay, but you've got to be gentle.'

'Are you going to give him something?'

The young man groaned again, and Katie's heart sank. 'He needs pain medication, but I'm not qualified ... not allowed to give him morphine ... or anything that will do much good.'

'But we're going to have to lift him out ...' Max said.

'I know,' she almost yelled. 'But I can't. Only a doctor can prescribe—'

She was interrupted by a sound from behind her. The radio on the police car crackled and she heard indistinct voices.

'You have radio contact?' she asked Max.

'Yes. With regional base.'

'Could they get in touch with a Doctor. Maybe call Adam in the plane. He can authorise ...' Max turned before she finished speaking. While he returned to his car, Katie pulled a neck brace from the emergency bag. She tried to avoid causing Tom any more pain as she fitted it, telling him all the while that it would help protect him and that the men would have him out very soon. Her heart shrank every time he cried out in pain.

Just as she finished, Max called her back to the police car and placed his radio in her hand.

'It's Adam. He's on the plane on his way back.'

Relief surged through her. 'How far out are you?' she said into the handset.

'Forty minutes until we land. Then we'd have to get to you.' Adam's voice was distorted by the radio. 'How is he?'

'Not good. He's in a lot of pain and looks like a dislocated shoulder. I've got a neck brace on him, but he's going to need pain meds if they are going to drag him out of there.'

'You're right. In the bag. Everything you need is there.'

Max quickly fetched the bag. Following Adam's instructions, she found the small vials of morphine. And the syringe. She checked the dose with him twice while Max listened.

'All right. Do it. Then get him out of the car. You can call me back then if you need to. Good luck.'

She didn't allow herself to hesitate. She administered the morphine and with a final reassuring word to the injured youth, she stepped back and let Jack and Max do what they had to. Sparks flew as they cut away the car door and the front pillar. The car seemed even more fragile now, and more dangerous.

'Watch his shoulder,' she said. The two men followed her instructions carefully and pulled her patient from the car. The morphine had taken effect, but still he screamed.

Katie was beside him in an instant. His eyes were unfocused with a combination of drugs and the pain. She carefully touched the hand that hung uselessly from his dislocated shoulder. It was cold. That wasn't good.

She drew Jack and Max aside.

'I'm worried about that shoulder. It's pinching the main blood vessel. If we don't fix it, he could lose the hand.'

'What do you need us to do?' Jack asked.

'Brace him. I have to put that shoulder back in. I need to you to hold him down and still. I have to apply a lot of pressure to do it.'

Both men nodded and dropped to their knees beside Tom. Katie didn't stop to think. She'd been taught about this. Seen it done a dozen times before, but never done it herself. This young man needed her to get it right the first time.

She made sure Jack and Max had a firm hold on her patient, then she lifted his arm. Despite the drugs, he whimpered in pain as she slowly began to pull and twist the arm. It seemed an eternity. Just as she began to think she was doing something wrong, the shoulder slipped back into place.

After that, things moved quickly.

Katie strapped Tom's arm and shoulder to prevent too much movement as they loaded him into the police Land Rover to take him back to Coorah Creek. She rode with him, dressing his cuts and talking to him as they went. In the front of the car, Max was attempting to contact Adam.

Just as they approached the road leading to the airstrip outside town, Adam's car emerged. It turned towards them and accelerated for a few seconds before the driver recognised the police car. As they flashed past, Katie saw Adam's face. He flung the car into a high-speed U-turn and followed them back to the hospital.

'Let's get him inside,' he ordered the moment the cars pulled up in front of the building. 'I'll get him stabilised while Jess refuels the plane, and then we'll get him to the Isa for a CAT scan.'

As Jack half carried their patient up the steps to the hospital, Adam paused next to Katie for just a second.

'Well done,' he said.

Chapter 23

'I was scared, you know. Really scared!'

'Climbing inside that damaged car should have scared you. You could have been hurt.'

'No. Not scared for me. Scared for him. That I wouldn't be able to help him. But I did.'

The smile on Katie's face grew even bigger; if that was possible. She was almost bursting with pleasure as she sat opposite Scott in the pub, waiting for their dinner to be served. This was what had been missing from her life. This feeling of achievement. That she had helped someone using her own skill and wits.

'Oh Scott,' she grabbed his hand. 'This is why I became a nurse. I was able to help someone. Adam said I saved his arm. Me!'

Scott's face told her everything she needed to know. He was both impressed and proud. Come to think of it, she felt exactly the same way.

'Here you go,' Ed appeared, three glasses clutched in his hand. He placed the drinks on the table and sat down with them.

'Here's to you,' Scott raised his glass. 'Well done.'

'Yes, well done indeed.' Ed smiled and for a moment Katie put aside her excitement at her own achievement. Here was another reason to celebrate. Scott and his father were beginning to act like they were not just a family, but friends too. She was so happy for him. For all of them. Right now, life was good. Her joy clouded for a moment as she thought of the parting that was ahead of them, in just a few days when Scott headed for his new job. But she shook it off. Nothing was going to spoil this moment for her.

'Hey, Katie!' Max appeared, still wearing his police uniform. 'I've just heard from Adam. The patient is doing fine. He and Jess will be flying back tomorrow after they check in one last time at the hospital. They should be back shortly after lunch. They asked you to hold the fort at the hospital for them.'

'That's good news. As for holding the fort, I'll do my best. But please,' Katie grinned, 'no more adventures like today.'

'And if there were, I'm sure you'd do fine,' Trish appeared carrying plates loaded down with food. She placed them on the table, grinning at the three of them as if she were in some way responsible for the aura of happiness that surrounded them. 'If you keep this up girl, we'll be calling you Doctor Katie.'

They all laughed, but as Trish moved away, Scott suddenly fell silent.

'What's wrong?' Katie asked.

He didn't answer. His mouth curved into a knowing smile and he raised his eyebrows.

'What!'

Still he didn't answer. Realisation dawned suddenly.

'No,' she said. 'It's a nice idea, but it will never happen.'

'Why not?' Scott asked.

'Just because.'

'Do you want to let me in on this conversation?' Ed asked.

'Katie's going to become a doctor,' Scott said.

Katie shook her head. 'Don't be silly. I'm a nurse, not a doctor.'

Scott leaned forward, his eyes shining with excitement. 'But you could be a doctor. You told me that's what you wanted to be. You said nursing wasn't as fulfilling as you wanted. That's because you should be a doctor. You were born for it!'

'It's a nice thought, Scott,' Katie said. 'And a compliment. Thank you. But it's not going to happen. So come on. Eat that burger before it gets cold.'

She followed her own advice, and began eating. During the rest of the evening, Scott's words hovered in the back of her mind. Quite a few townsfolk dropped by to hear the story of the rescue, which by now had grown to epic proportions. Any minute, Katie was expecting someone to ask her about single-handedly pulling the victim from a burning wreck. Obviously the Trish Warren gossip grapevine was flourishing.

It was quite late when they finally made their escape. The three of them walked across the road to Ed's house. After just a couple of days, it was already showing the results of Ed and Scott's work. The garden had been cut back and there was fresh paint appearing on the outside of the house.

'I'll say goodnight,' Ed said. Almost shyly he leaned forward to kiss Katie's cheek softly. 'You did a good thing today, Katie. We are all very proud of you.'

'Thanks,' she said, deeply moved.

'Goodnight son. And take good care of this girl. She's special.' Ed placed a hand on his son's shoulder for a few seconds and then turned away.

'I think he's a nice man,' Katie said as she took Scott's hand and turned their steps towards the hospital. 'He just hasn't had much of a chance to show it.'

'I know.'

They walked in silence for a while. Katie looked up at the stars shining so brilliantly above her. She never saw stars like that in London.

'Do you really think I could do it?' she said.

Scott squeezed her hand. 'Of course you could.'

'But … a doctor?'

'Why not?'

'For a start, there's the question of money,' Katie said. 'It'll be expensive to go back to college.'

'Are there grants or scholarships or something you can apply for?' Scott asked.

'I guess so. But—'

'No buts,' he said firmly. 'We'll make it work. I can help you.'

'I'm just—'

Scott stopped and turned her to face him. His handsome face looked very intense in the bright starlight. 'You are not "just" anything Katie Brooks. You are a smart and determined woman. You can be or do whatever you want.'

'I don't know.'

'But I do.' Then he kissed her.

It was several minutes before they resumed their walk. Katie's mind was racing.

'You know, a couple of the nurses I trained with went on to study medicine,' she said. 'It's not totally impossible.'

'There you go.'

'Of course,' she felt a smile spreading across her face as the doubt began to fade, 'I would have to go back to the UK to do this.'

'I thought that might be the case. You'll have to resign from this job.'

'I'm sure Adam can find someone else. And Jess will be pleased that I'm not being ill in her aeroplane any more.'

'She's not the only one who'll be pleased to see you heading back to England.'

'But Scott, it won't be easy to BE us. I'll be in London. You'll be at the Museum. And I'll be working ridiculous hours. Studying. I won't have time ...'

'It doesn't matter,' Scott said. 'Don't look for the barriers. That's what I have done for the past few years with Dad, and it was wrong. Whatever you need to do, you do it. I'll be there when I can and I will give you space when you need it. I'll support you every step of the way and no-one will be happier than me to see you in a black robe on your graduation day.'

They had reached the steps to the hospital. An outside light was on and Katie could see the sincerity in Scott's face as he spoke.

'You're a nice man too,' she said and kissed him.

Chapter 24

Katie's old car had polished up pretty well. Ed flicked a cleaning rag at a bit of imaginary dust, proud of his handiwork. The grey Prius was parked nearby. Scott squeezed the last box into the boot and shut the lid. He leaned over to rub at the thin scratch on his rear bumper, smiling as he remembered the day that happened.

'Thanks for offering to sell Katie's car,' he said as he joined Ed. 'It would have been a pain to have to take two cars back east.'

'No problems. I've got a buyer in mind. And you can trust me to get the best price I can.'

'I know. She's going to need the money. Medical school will be expensive.'

'On that note,' Ed hesitated. His son was a proud man and he didn't want to offend him. 'I've been living here, alone, for a long time. I don't make a lot of money, but I don't spend much either. I have some savings. If you or Katie need money ...'

Scott shook his head. 'Thanks for the offer Dad. But no. We can do this. Why don't you spend that money on coming over to England for a visit? I'd love to show you the cars.'

'I'll be there,' Ed said. 'But if you change your mind, don't hesitate to ask.'

Scott nodded.

'And I've come to a decision about my own life,' Ed continued. 'I've been waiting all these years for something that is never going to happen and it's time to stop.'

'What are you going to do?'

'I'm going to hire a lawyer. Maybe he can find your mother. Maybe not. But either way it's time I started living my life again. I'm not that old. Maybe there's someone else out there for me after all.'

On the other side of the main road, Katie appeared in the doorway of the town store. She was carrying a couple of plastic bags; supplies for their journey. She darted across to the front of the pub, where Trish Warren was waiting. The two women hugged.

A slow smile across Scott's face as he watched them.

'You take good care of that girl,' Ed said. 'She's worth hanging on to.'

'I know. I think I finally understand what you said about falling in love with Mum right from the moment you met. It must run in the family.'

'Scott. Catch.'

He responded by instinct and neatly caught the bottle of water Katie had tossed at him as she approached. Laughing, she held up a six pack of the clear liquid she had just purchased at the store.

'Well – you've gained something from this whole experience,' Scott joked.

'Yes, I have,' Katie paused long enough to plant a gentle kiss on his cheek before opening the door to stash the water on the back seat of the Prius.

'All set?' Ed asked.

'Yes.' Katie came around the car and enveloped Ed in a bear hug. 'Thanks for everything.'

'No. I have a lot to thank you for.' Ed spoke softly as he returned her hug. 'I'll miss you both.' He said something else too, but Scott couldn't hear him.

Katie rubbed a damp eye and nodded as she stepped back.

'Dad.' There was a lump in Scott's throat. He had never wanted to return to Coorah Creek – but now he was finding it hard to leave.

Ed stepped forward to hug his son.

'I love you Dad,' Scott whispered.

'I love you too, son.' The two men hugged for a few seconds more, and then stepped away from each other.

'All right you two, time you were on your way.' Ed ran a hand roughly over his face.

'You know, just now Trish told me she knew of some puppies that were available,' Katie said, trying to hide a sniff. 'You should think about getting a new dog.'

'No. I'm not really a dog person. That was all Scott's fault.' Ed smiled slowly. 'I was thinking I might get a cat. Just don't let Trish know. Okay?'

They both nodded and with a last long look around, Scott slid behind the wheel of his car. A few moments later, he turned the key and slowly drew away from the garage.

He kept their speed down as they moved through the town. Scott looked at the place he'd grown up through new eyes.

'You're going to miss this place, you know,' Katie said. 'And your Dad.'

'I know. Dad says he might come and visit in the English summer. After we've had time to settle down.'

'Great. He whispered something to you … what?'

Scott cast a sideways glance at the beautiful woman beside him. 'He told me to look after you.'

Katie smiled. 'He told me the same thing.'

The town was starting to recede in the background. 'It was good of Adam to let you go like this,' Scott said. 'I was expecting you'd have to wait longer.'

'I think Jess convinced him it was for the best. They've already advertised for someone new.'

A road sign flashed past. Looking in his rear-view mirror, Scott saw it was the town sign. Even in mirror image, he could read the words. Coming back to Coorah Creek had changed his life for the better. He was setting out on a new adventure, but he would be back. Maybe one day Katie and he would bring their kids here. He'd like to show them the outback.

They drove for a little while, each of them lost in their own thoughts. Then Scott let his speed drop and eased towards the side of the road.

'What's wrong?' Katie asked.

'Nothing.' The car stopped. Scott got out and walked round to open Katie's door. Looking confused, she got out.

'Do you remember this spot?' he asked.

She looked around. 'Was this where I broke down?'

'More or less.'

'Wow. She reached out to take his hand. 'It wasn't all that long ago.'

'Officially it was last year.'

'True, but a lot has changed in a very short time. I can hardly believe I'm going home.'

'That we are going home.'

'It's a little scary,' Katie said in a small voice. 'This medical school thing. I'm still a little afraid of that.'

'Don't be. Ambition is a good thing. Reach for the stars. I am.'

'What stars are you reaching for?'

He took her hand and kissed it. 'I think you know. I know I found something special on the side of this road that day. We haven't known each other very long, but I think this is just a beginning for us. We can take this as fast or a slow as you like ... but I think I already know where our road is leading.'

Katie's heart skipped a beat. 'Be careful what you wish for,' she said with a smile. 'You might get it.'

Laughing, they got back into the car, and before he started the engine, Scott kissed her.

'I love you,' he said.

He started the engine and the car leaped forward. It quickly gathered speed and vanished into the silver heat haze shimmering across the thin strip of grey road.

Acknowledgements

Writing is a funny way to spend your time – sitting alone at a computer talking to imaginary people in your head. But I love it. I also love the many friends and fellow writers (you know who you are) who have always supported me on this journey, and still do. Thanks to everyone at Escape Publishing and Harlequin/HarperCollins Australia for turning my stories into such beautiful books. Thanks also to my agent Julia Silk for always being there when I need her. As always, my thanks go to my husband John, for his unswerving support. I love you. And last, but by no means least, thank YOU, dear reader. Without you, the people on these pages would never become real.

The Christmas Wish

JACQUIE UNDERDOWN

For Brad

Chapter 1

Brielle was too flustered to take in the schoolyard and buildings as she approached. She was late, as always, so she half-walked, half-skipped across the basketball court to the administration office where she was scheduled to meet with the principal five minutes ago.

Her surroundings faded to a blur as she focused on the quaint orange-brick building ahead with a clock tower stretching upwards from the roof. Her breathing quickened the faster she trod.

You'd think after being late to most appointments for a huge portion of her life, Brielle would be used to it. But she wasn't. Her heart was racing and her mind was already trying to come up with an adequate excuse.

It was one thing to be routinely late and know it, but to reveal to others that it was a usual occurrence was another thing altogether. Especially when starting a new job in a new school.

Sure, Alpine Ridge Primary School was actually an old school, opened 1898, in an old town. Her hometown for many years. A school she had attended for two years herself back in the day. But, to date, she hadn't taught here, so to her, it was new.

But that was okay. Brielle was used to new because she hadn't managed to stay at one school for longer than twelve months since her first teaching assignment five years ago. Not that she was bad at her job. No, she was bad at staying in the one spot for too long. It made her antsy.

And antsy didn't feel … safe.

Brielle raced up steps, pushed through doors, and marched into the administration office.

The secretary lifted his head. 'Morning, Brielle. Samantha is expecting you.' He pushed his thick-rimmed glasses onto his nose and frowned. 'Head straight through to her office.'

Brielle managed a tight smile and attempted to slow her puffed breathing as she strode up the hall. This building smelled of must, dust and, as she went by the toilets, the unfortunate scent of boys' urinals.

Samantha, principal of Alpine Ridge Primary School for the last thirteen years, turned to face Brielle as she entered. A phone was pressed to her ear.

'Oh, she's here,' she said into the handpiece. 'Thanks for your time, Paul.'

Brielle clenched her jaw and resisted an eye roll as she stood awkwardly in the doorway, not really knowing what to do with her hands.

She was only five minutes late—okay, maybe more like fifteen— and already Samantha had rung her parents.

That was the problem with small towns—there was always some kind of familiarity between the residents. In this case, Samantha had known Brielle's parents for fifteen years.

But what caused the bubbles of resentment to form inside Brielle was that she was twenty-six years old. A teacher for five years now. Out of home and living away from Alpine Ridge for eight years if you didn't count the fact that she had recently, albeit temporarily, moved back in with her parents.

But that wasn't the point. She was an independent woman and didn't need her parents called because she was five minutes late to her first day of work.

Most importantly, she didn't need her parents stressing about this all day long and giving her an earful this afternoon when she arrived home.

Yes, believe it or not, adult or not, this was the relationship she had with them.

Why did she decide to move back here again? All the reasoning she had last week when she was offered the temporary maternity-leave position, where she convinced herself that coming home might remedy the aimlessness and loneliness she had been feeling for a long time, flew right out her ear.

'I was just talking to your father to check you hadn't been involved in some terrible accident on the way here,' Samantha said.

Talk about an overreaction.

Brielle smiled. 'I'm fine.' *Quite obviously.* 'And I apologise for being late.' *It was the traffic?* No, there was no traffic in a town with a population of seven hundred. *I slept in?* No, that would make her look flimsy. 'I got caught behind a tractor that didn't have the courtesy to move over to the side and let me pass.'

Samantha nodded and gestured to the seat across from her desk.

Brielle sat and smoothed the material of her skirt.

'As we discussed briefly last week on the phone, you will be taking over a grade two-three composite classroom for the last eight weeks of term. The regular teacher, who had planned to make it through to the end of the year, had her baby come earlier than anticipated. So, I thank you for accepting the position at such short notice. However, I expect you to actually be on time from here on out.'

Brielle swallowed hard. 'Of course.'

'Our main priority is to have as little disruption to the students as possible.' Samantha stood. 'Come, I'll take you to your classroom. I believe Jenny, who you are replacing, has prepped all her class plans to the end of the year, so they will be available for you to use if you wish. But you can prepare your own as long as they are consistent with the curriculum.'

Brielle stood and followed Samantha. 'Of course.'

Their walk through the school grounds was brisk. Alpine Ridge Primary was a shady school with lots of leafy trees, now that Brielle had time to take it in. They weaved around small demountable buildings connected by cement pathways until arriving at her room.

Samantha unlocked the door and headed inside, flicking the lights on. That familiar classroom smell greeted Brielle as she headed in—crayons, white board markers and the faint sour scent of spoiled fruit left uneaten in lunch boxes.

'Here we are,' Samantha said. 'I already emailed you all the information on bell times, lunch duty schedules, internal policies and expectations. Your students should start arriving in twenty minutes or so. It's only a small class of fourteen. We haven't had any real behavioural issues with anyone.'

Brielle glanced around at all the colourful pictures covering the walls. A blank whiteboard sat at the head of the room ready for the new day. Her desk, littered with stationery, trays and folders, was set in the top corner of the room.

'As you know, we are heading into the Christmas season. Each year we hold a Christmas fete on the school oval and have parents participate with stalls. We are looking for volunteers to organise it. Jenny is usually in charge of it and does a fantastic job every year, so she's left some big boots to fill.'

Desperate to prove herself after the belittling phone call to her parents and her lack of punctuality, Brielle said, 'I love Christmas. I'd be more than happy to help out.'

Samantha smiled; the first of the morning. 'Excellent. I'll email you with all the particulars, so you can get started on that right away. It's only seven weeks away.'

'Sure. That shouldn't be a problem.' This year Brielle would be on her own for Christmas anyway. Her parents and little sisters were fulfilling a lifelong dream of cruising along the Danube through Europe for six weeks, so a Christmas fete to organise would be a welcome distraction.

After running through some general housekeeping rules, Samantha left Brielle to her own devices. Within five minutes, her first student arrived: a seven-year-old boy named Brock Peters. Of course the father wanted to meet the new teacher and chat for a while, as did most parents after that.

Before Brielle knew it, it was nine thirty, the class was restless, excitedly chattering with one another at their desks like caged budgies, and she had nothing planned.

She clapped loudly three times and all the children's heads spun to face her. 'Good morning. My name is Miss Lane and I will be your teacher for the rest of the year.'

'Good morning, Miss Lane,' the class chorused.

She wrote her name on the whiteboard, then clasped her hands together and looked out over the small class of unfamiliar faces. 'Can you please tell me, one by one, your full name and what you like to do for fun when you're not at school?' She pointed to a little girl with long black hair and big blue eyes who was seated in the front row. 'You can go first.'

In a soft voice, she said, 'My name is Poppy. And I like to help Daddy feed the baby animals on the farm because they're so cute.'

Brielle stared for a moment, then finally blinked. She certainly didn't get responses like that in the city. 'That does sound cute. Lovely to meet you, Poppy.' She pointed to the child next to her.

'My name is Melissa. I like to ride my bike on the big jumps my brother made in the backyard. I jump real high. But sometimes I fall off and it hurts.'

Brielle smiled. 'Sounds like fun. Not the falling off part, though. Good to meet you, Melissa.'

Around the room they went until she'd heard from each and every student.

'Okay, so who can tell me what big day is coming up soon?'

Most of the class thrust their hand high into the air as though they'd burst if they weren't able to give their answer. She pointed to a boy called Fletcher. 'My birthday is in five days.'

'That *is* a big day. But I'm thinking of something else. Something that many of us celebrate.' The hands flew up again and she pointed to Poppy.

'Christmas Day?'

Brielle grinned. 'Absolutely. I want to start making some beautiful drawings of Christmas that we can hang up around the classroom.'

Sure, she felt like a supermarket selling hot cross buns in January, considering Christmas was still ten weeks away, but what child didn't love Christmas? Heck, she still adored Christmas. And besides, it was a distraction for the children, leaving her a good half hour to catch her breath, read through the lesson plans, and work out what they would do for the rest of the day.

After the Christmas pictures, she arranged for the class to make name cards that they would wear until she could match each of their faces to names by memory. Fourteen names wasn't a big stretch, but she needed all the help she could get.

For the rest of the afternoon, they played a rotation of maths games, followed by spelling activities, and ended with a small story written about space, which was a required curriculum subject this semester.

When the final bell for the day rang, Brielle was exhausted. After the haste to finish up at her substitute position in Melbourne, pack up her small apartment and rush to get back here in time, not to mention the weighty anticipation of starting at a new school, it had only caught up with her now.

She dismissed the class to their parents waiting on the front veranda and stretched her neck from side to side, attempting to ease the tension from her muscles.

Poppy came running back in once everyone had left, holding the hand of a very large man. Large in height and breadth. Such shoulders. She eagerly met his gaze.

Familiar blue eyes stared back and she flinched.

Luke Reynolds.

Luke Reynolds is Poppy's dad?

In all her urgency to catch up throughout the day, she had completely forgotten that her best friend, Macie, had said during a quick phone call last week that her niece would be in her class.

'Luke,' she said. 'It's been a long time.'

His focus on her was intense, like he was studying her as a jewellery maker might study the facets of a diamond.

She stroked loose strands of hair behind her ear and shifted her feet, feeling a little wobbly to be on the receiving end of that gaze.

'Brielle Lane. I hadn't realised you were Poppy's new teacher.'

She giggled nervously. Luke had always had that effect on her. 'Here I am.'

'Yes. Here you are. Until the end of term?'

His voice was so much deeper than she remembered. It was as though his vocal cords had been rolled across gravel.

She cleared her throat, nodded. 'Yep.' Her heart was beating faster. Luke always had that effect on her too, though the reasons for it now were not the same as the reasons for it when she was a shy teenager.

Now it was because her blood was running hotter and rushing in a different direction. He was delicious, every last part of him, from his dark hair, big blue eyes, a strong square jaw that all by itself epitomised strength, right down his long hard body to his shoes.

But this couldn't be right. Did she really just use *delicious* to describe her teenage foe? Her adversary from hell? The one man who used to make her blood boil for different reasons altogether?

No matter which way she looked at it, his broad shoulders, the dark, rough growth on his chin, and those eyes—okay, she had already mentioned the eyes, nothing had changed there—he was delicious.

And her fast-beating heart obviously found that revelation shocking because it was completely out of sync with her mind and memories. This shock had the strange effect of muddling her thoughts and disconnecting her brain from her mouth.

Snap out of it, Brielle. You're his daughter's teacher. Bloody well act like a professional. Besides, he's horrible, remember?

She drew herself up straighter.

'Good to run into you again,' he said. 'I guess I'll be seeing more of you for the next couple of months.'

She nodded. 'Good to see you too.'

He took Poppy's hand. Such a big, protective paw when held against Poppy's much smaller and paler fingers. A pang went through her.

'See you later, Miss Lane.'

She managed a tense smile. 'Bye, Luke. See you tomorrow, Poppy.'

By the time Luke had left, her cheeks were flushed with heat. Her insides were all tangled, and she wasn't exactly certain what to make of it. It was like a war was raging inside her between her body and mind.

Her body had very much enjoyed every little bit of that interaction with Luke while her mind wanted to tear it from the pages of her memory and never look at it again.

Stupid body. Why did grown-up Luke have to look so incredible? In the eight years since she had last seen him, he had matured, filled out.

But it didn't matter what he looked like, he was in the no-go zone for a number of reasons.

For one, he was her best friend's older brother. That on its own meant he was off limits. Seriously, how awkward would that be?

And two, she loathed him. He had made her life hell when she was a teenager. At this moment, she couldn't remember exactly why, but there were bound to be many examples if she thought about it hard enough.

But thinking about Luke was something she was not going to do on account of point two above.

No, she was going to focus her thoughts on more worthwhile subjects like settling back into her hometown, getting through the rest of the term with her new, wonderful bunch of schoolkids, and the upcoming Christmas fete.

Chapter 2

Luke gripped the steering wheel and drew his focus briefly off the road ahead of him to meet the eye of his daughter sitting in the back seat.

'How do you like your new teacher?' he asked.

Poppy smiled wide as she nodded. She had a couple of gaps in her mouth where some baby teeth had recently fallen out. Luke found it adorable every time she grinned. 'She is very nice. She didn't yell at us like Mrs P.'

No, Luke couldn't imagine Brielle yelling at anyone, let alone a group of seven-year-olds. 'That's positive. Might be a good thing then getting a new teacher this late in the year?'

Poppy nodded and turned to look out the window at the countryside speeding by in a blur of green. Far off mountains, hazy in the late spring afternoon, pushed up to meet the endless blue sky.

Luke hadn't anticipated a change of teacher would faze his daughter. Not much did. But he was surprised to note that this new teacher had fazed him.

It had been many years since he had seen Brielle—the last time was just before he graduated from university with an agricultural management degree.

To see her back in Alpine Ridge had surprised him. To feel the tug of desire in his stomach the moment he looked into her light brown eyes had surprised him too.

When he was a younger man he'd had an attraction to her, and quite obviously after seven or so years that hadn't diminished in the slightest.

Last he'd heard from his sister, Brielle was teaching in Melbourne. Speaking of his sister ... He pressed his car's touch screen. 'Call Macie,' he commanded.

A few rings sounded over the speakers before his sister answered. 'Hey, Luke. What's up?'

'You didn't tell me Brielle was back in town and is Poppy's new teacher.'

'Completely slipped my mind. It was all so sudden. She only told me about it herself last week. Why, is there a problem?'

Luke cleared his throat. 'No. It was just a shock, that's all. Some forewarning would have been nice.'

'No big deal, right?'

'Of course not.'

'How is she?' Macie asked. 'I can't wait to catch up with her. We're meeting for a drink Friday arvo after work.'

'She seemed fine. We didn't say much.'

'It's kinda cool that she's Poppy's teacher. Funny how things work out.'

'I guess.'

'What's the matter? You sound upset.' Macie always had a keen intuition when it came to him.

Am I upset?

Yeah, he was in a small way. But why in the hell would he be upset about this? 'It was just a shock to see her, that's all.'

'Was she standoffish? I know you two used to have that adversarial thing happening way back when.'

His forehead furrowed as he fought to find memories but came up blank. 'Adversarial? We've never been adversarial.'

'Maybe from her point of view you were.'

'I can't imagine why.' His hands gripped tighter to the steering wheel as a defensiveness shifted within, which was ridiculous. He hadn't even spoken to Brielle for nearly a decade. He had barely given her a thought in all that time unless she was brought up in general conversation. But he certainly didn't want to be seen as an opponent.

'I don't know. I can barely remember myself, it's been so long,' Macie said. 'But I'm sure she'll be a great teacher for Poppy.'

'Poppy likes her, don't you?' he asked, meeting Poppy's blue eyes in the rear-view mirror.

'Yep.'

'Anyway, I'll let you go,' Luke said.

'Sure. Talk soon.'

Luke hung up and sighed. He was feeling a tad ridiculous right about now. What did it really matter that Brielle was Poppy's teacher? Or that Macie hadn't given him any forewarning? Or that his desire for Brielle had clenched deep when he saw her?

He rubbed a hand down his face. He knew why it mattered, he just didn't want to admit it to himself yet.

For the time being, he'd maintain his busy work schedule, stick to his commitment to giving Poppy a stable home environment, and adhere to his self-made policy to avoid romance—even if that romance came in a stunning Brielle-shaped package.

Before long, he pulled into the long dirt road that was his driveway. A tall timber sign with a beautiful script read *Alpine Ridge Dairy.*

He started on the kilometre-long track that cut through myriad grassy paddocks. As he neared the milking shed, to his right a herd

of healthy-looking black and white Holstein cattle were saunter-
ing into a fresh paddock. The second milking for the day was
finished.

Dennis, his second-in-charge, was walking behind the large
herd, corralling them over the fence line so they could graze on
lush pasture for the afternoon.

Luke's goal on the farm from the very beginning was to create
a comfortable and relaxed environment for his girls, so he didn't
allow noisy motorbikes or biting dogs to herd his cattle. Sure, it
took longer, but he wouldn't get milk from stressed cows and it
meant he slept better at night.

During his university days, he worked at all kinds of dairy
farms—from small operations that used robot milkers to big farms
that milked upwards of fifteen hundred cows twice a day every day.

He dreamed of something different to that. So he didn't run
an enormous operation here but kept the profit margins up by
making higher-end dairy products—creamy custard, a variety of
award-winning cheeses, grass-fed butter, and both fresh and sour
cream. Thankfully in a region like this that supported local indus-
tries, he had a good number of wholesalers and direct-to-customer
supply chains.

Dairy farming had a brutal schedule, but with enough hired
help, his farming was made to fit in between being a father, not the
other way around.

His daughter's happiness took priority. He would be there for
Poppy no matter what, especially as her mother wasn't a steady
presence in her life.

Luke continued to his homestead—a small single-storey brick
home that had existed on this property since the early 1900s. It
was his grandparents' farm, and they bequeathed it to him and his
sister when he was twenty-one, a few months after he finished his

degree. Macie built a new home for herself on the opposite end of the land, whereas he was happy to renovate the existing house.

Luke led Poppy inside for an afternoon snack. They sat together at the dining table while they each finished a cheese and Vegemite sandwich and a glass of milk.

'Any homework today?' His whole body tightened in anticipation of her answer, hoping for a no. Homework was not on the list of his most enjoyable activities. In fact, he dreaded it.

Poppy shook her head and grinned. 'Nuh-uh.'

'Good,' he said, rubbing his hands together. 'That means you and I have the whole afternoon together.'

Poppy's grin grew wider. 'Are the calves hungry?'

He rolled his head back and laughed. 'They're *so* hungry. They've been waiting for you to finish school and feed them.'

She was besotted with the calves, a new interest this year. Maybe because she was older and could appreciate them more. And it was a fun chore for her to help out with.

He ruffled Poppy's hair. 'Come on. Go get your gumboots on and let's go.'

They headed out to the nursery—a designated section of the farm where the calves were kept in pens in small groups of three or four. They each had their own hutch to protect them from the weather and a decent area to roam.

This afternoon, the sky was big and blue overhead. Puffs of white clouds drifted across the expanse. Around them was green grass in all directions—the nutritional value of the grasses, the very food his milking stock relied upon, was as important as the herd themselves, so he did his best to maintain the healthfulness of the soil.

Poppy poured canisters of fresh milk into buckets attached to the fences of the pens. The calves took to the attached teats and noisily sucked at the milk.

Poppy giggled and patted a boisterous calf on the head. Luke inspected the calves, their waste, ensuring there were no signs of illness while their immune systems were still developing.

'Are they all okay?' Poppy asked him when they were done.

He nodded and took her hand in his. 'All fit and healthy.'

A toothy grin spilled across her face. 'Phew. That makes me happy.'

'You and me both.'

On the car ride back to the homestead, his phone rang. He looked at his screen and his stomach sank when he saw the name. Renee. Poppy's mum.

He'd been anticipating a call, especially as Christmas was drawing closer. This was Renee's usual routine. She would go off and do her own thing for most of the year, ringing Poppy occasionally for a chat. Then she would announce unexpectedly that she was coming to visit around Christmas time and either stick to her commitment or not.

It was the 'or not' part of the equation that boiled Luke's blood. Poppy would get so excited to be seeing her mother only to be let down, all the old feelings of abandonment rising to the surface.

He answered the call. 'Hi, Renee. I've got you on speakerphone. Poppy's in the car with me.' It was a warning. He didn't want her saying something that would hurt her.

'Mummy,' Poppy squealed.

'Hello, darling. Your voice has become very grown up.'

'I didn't notice,' Poppy said.

'I bet you've grown up so much too?'

'Dad marked my height from last year and I've grown two metres.'

Luke smiled. 'Centimetres.'

'Two centimetres,' Poppy corrected.

'Wow. What a big girl you must be. I can't wait to see you and give you a big cuddle.'

'When will you see me?'

Luke held his breath. All the skin on his body tightened in anticipation.

'I was thinking about dropping by in a few weeks. We could spend a couple of days together. Just you and me. How does that sound?'

'Yesss!' Poppy said.

Luke's heart beat faster—his protective instincts kicking into overdrive. He wanted to hijack the conversation and tell his ex to stop making promises she couldn't keep.

But he didn't. Renee was Poppy's mother after all. He would die if something ever prevented him from seeing his own daughter. Who was he to deny Renee that privilege?

'I'll get all the plans in motion soon and give you a call closer to the date. I'm just a little busy right now.'

'Okay. I can't wait.'

Luke parked the car in the big six-bay shed beside his house.

'I'll talk to you soon, Poppy. I love you.'

'I love you too,' Poppy said.

'Just stay on the line for a moment, Renee,' Luke said. He faced Poppy and smiled warmly. 'Hey, baby, can you go inside and get ready for a shower? I'm just going to talk to Mum. Don't forget to take your gumboots off at the door.'

Poppy nodded and climbed from the car.

When the door was closed and Poppy was a distance away, he spoke. 'I think it's great that you want to come and spend some time with Poppy. But, Renee, don't let her down. That's all I ask.'

'I'm not going to let her down. Geez, give me some bloody credit, will you?'

He squeezed his eyes shut, gritted down on the words burning up his throat. He had given her more than enough credit over the years to the point that he now was ashamed of how naive he had been. 'Just don't let her down. You've made the commitment, so stick to it. Especially so close to Christmas. She doesn't need the disappointment if you don't show up.'

'I will show.'

'And where will you be staying while you're here?'

'With you. Unless that's too much of an inconvenience.'

Too right it was an inconvenience. Their relationship had been over for four years if he didn't account for the on-again off-again years before that as Renee tried to sort her life out. How long was he expected to drop everything to accommodate her?

He lowered his head and rubbed the bridge of his nose. 'No. It's fine.' He'd do anything to make his daughter happy, even if that meant enduring Renee for a few days.

A muffled male voice sounded in the background followed by a giggle from Renee. 'I've gotta go. I'll give you a call soon to arrange specifics.'

'Sure—'

She hung up.

He climbed out of his ute. His legs were heavy as he trudged up to the house. Tension was tightening his body. But, then again, he always felt heavier after dealing with Renee.

As he opened the door, he recognised the emotion blasting through him—resentment. He resented that he had to take measures to counteract the instability Renee brought to his life. But mostly he hated how this push and pull between Renee and Poppy created so much unhappiness.

Chapter 3

Brielle's mother joined her in the kitchen Friday morning while she was preparing a flask of coffee to drink on the drive to school. Better that than showing up late again.

She didn't admit to her parents that the reason she was late for her first day was because she had stopped by a local cupcake shop for a latte. She did not need that hanging over her head, so she stuck with the tractor excuse.

Brielle faced her mum as she lingered in the doorway. Brielle had received her lack of height from her. Unlike her younger sisters, who were fortunate to have inherited some stature from their father, Brielle's stepdad.

Brielle didn't know her biological father—just knew he and her mum were only seventeen when she was born, and he now lived somewhere in Western Australia with a new family. But he must have been who she got her eye and hair colour from because she was the only one in the family with sandy-blonde hair and light brown eyes.

'Now, I just want to quickly remind you before you head off that you need to turn the lights off at night,' Mum said.

'I did—'

'You left the hallway and kitchen light on all night. Paul just rang me from work to let me know. If you want to stay here, you've got to abide by his rules. You know how he feels about conserving power.'

Despite Paul being the only dad she had ever known, it had never felt right to call him *Dad*.

Brielle swallowed her frustrated sigh. She definitely recalled turning every light off before heading to bed because she knew this kind of confrontation would be the consequence otherwise. But she might be wrong. 'Of course. I'm sorry. I'll make sure I turn them off from now on.'

'And please do not let this happen while we're away. The last thing we need is to come home from an expensive holiday to an astronomical electricity bill.'

She had only been home a week and was already regretting moving back in. Macie had offered her a room at her house, but it was pre-arranged earlier in the year that Brielle would housesit while her family were overseas. It seemed silly to move in with Macie only to move out again a short time later. 'It's fine, Mum. I better go or I'll be late.'

'Yes, we certainly don't want more phone calls about your lack of punctuality again. Paul was so embarrassed.'

Brielle didn't acknowledge the barb; she'd received enough of them to last her a lifetime. Instead, she kissed her mother on the cheek. 'I won't be home until later this evening. I'm meeting Macie for a drink.'

'Okay, good. That will work out well. We were planning to take the girls to the movies.'

Brielle bit her tongue to stop from asking why it was the better option to go to the movies without her—she would have liked a night out with her family—but experience had told her not to even bother. 'Have fun.'

She strode out the front door and down to her car. Heading into summer, the weather was marginally warmer at this time of year. Though it never got too hot up here in the highlands of Victoria, and the mornings almost always possessed a slight chill. As she passed over the mountain ranges last week on her way from Melbourne, she was not surprised to see gleaming pale patches of snow on the uppermost peaks.

Brielle clung tightly to her hot flask of coffee for warmth as she climbed into her car. She placed it in her cup holder then stared through the windscreen at the long residential street. Her hands gripped tightly to the steering wheel. Small brick homes built well before the fifties bordered the road on both sides. Big leafy trees ran parallel.

The seasons were beautiful here, each quarterly change delineated not so much by the calendar but by the flora. Autumnal hues of red, brown and yellow were her favourite. But there was something cleansing about spring's greens and the vibrancy of colour in the flowers at this time of year.

This street and the house she had lived in since she was ten years old was so familiar. Time hadn't changed much of anything. On the inside too, she had noticed.

Brielle had believed that living away from her family for eight years might have healed the old wounds she had carried throughout her late childhood. She thought that independently creating a life of her own would have helped her close the doors of her past.

But as the days bled into new mornings, she was starting to see that living away from Alpine Ridge may have exacerbated the problem.

All the while she resided in the city, she never quite belonged. A country girl at heart, she could never tolerate the rush of people, the traffic, and the unceasing ebb from day to night without pausing for a single breath.

And now, because she had been away for years, it didn't feel like she belonged here in Alpine Ridge either.

Perhaps she never really had. Not since her mum met Paul when Brielle was only ten. As much as she hated to admit it, her mother had stopped being her parent from that moment on.

Sure, her physical needs were taken care of, but emotionally, not so much. Especially once her twin sisters came along. Brielle was always in the way. A burden. Someone to endure because there was no other choice.

She was made to feel as though she should be grateful to be taken on by a man who wasn't her biological father.

Not much had changed.

When she was old enough, Brielle was passed off to a boarding school three hours away on the opposite side of the mountains in Gippsland. She came home on the school holidays to a family that she was always on the outside of, nose pressed to the glass, looking in on a life she could have had.

Brielle loved her sisters so much, but there were more than ten years between their ages. And she missed out on most of their childhood while attending boarding school, then heading to Melbourne to study at uni when she turned eighteen.

Maybe that's why she had spent every moment she could with Macie and her family. There, she was never anyone but a welcomed guest and, to Macie, almost a sister.

Brielle started the engine. She hated to dwell on such things. This was meant to be a fresh start, a good opportunity, a little bit of fun, but being back here had triggered all those old feelings of exclusion.

She shook her head, tossing the thoughts aside. She was a grown woman. And wasn't that what life was all about—making it on your own? Well, maybe that wasn't everyone's path, but it was hers.

At the end of the day, Brielle arranged the class to tidy their desks and pack the workbooks they had been using in trays so she could mark them over the weekend.

All the parents lined up on the veranda, chatting with each other, awaiting the release of their children. Her stomach twisted when she saw Luke from the corner of her eye. He had his arms crossed over his chest, a smile on his face, as he chatted with a mother. He hadn't come in to talk since that first day. Instead, he would simply nod or offer a short wave from outside.

'Okay, class. Thank you so much for a fantastic week. Now, don't forget the reading homework I've set. I hope you all have a great weekend, and I'll see you on Monday morning.'

'Good afternoon, Miss Lane,' the children chorused, then, in an orderly fashion, like they'd practised the previous afternoons, filed out to meet their parents.

Brielle went to her desk and started on next week's lesson plans.

After an hour or so, though, she was falling behind as she struggled to concentrate, knowing that soon she would be meeting up with Macie. Six months had rushed by in a blur since she had last seen her good friend.

Her phone buzzed with a message.

Hi Brie, we still on for drinks at 5?

Brielle grinned as she typed back a reply.

Absolutely. I need this. I'll see you soon.

By the time Brielle finished her lesson plans and made it to the local pub—a big square two-storey building on Main Street surrounded by an enormous deck—it was twenty minutes after five. Professionals and tradies had already begun to fill the place.

Macie was waiting at a small table when Brielle strode inside. The scent of stale beer and the low hum of chatter rushed to meet her. Macie stood and Brielle squealed as she raced over to her, throwing her arms around her friend.

'I missed you.'

Macie released her from her hug and grinned. 'I can't believe you're home. I thought you were joking when you rang to tell me the news.'

Macie was tall like her brother. They both got that from their father along with thick black hair and blue eyes.

'I know. My head is still reeling. It all happened so fast.'

They went to the bar for drinks, then took a seat across from each other at a table. Familiar faces filled the room. Some smiled. Some waved. Some pretended not to see her. Eight years wasn't enough to notice any real change to appearances.

'So, how are you finding the local school?'

Brielle sipped her drink before answering. 'Honestly, I'm really enjoying the more intimate size.'

'And how's my gorgeous little niece going?'

'Oh my gosh, Poppy is absolutely adorable. At the beginning she was shy, but over the week her character has really begun to show. I'd completely forgotten that you said Luke's daughter would be in my class. It caught me off guard when he stopped in to pick her up.'

Macie grinned. 'You weren't the only one caught off guard. I got a phone call from Luke asking why I hadn't told him you were Poppy's new teacher.'

Brielle didn't hide her eye roll. 'Poor Luke would have taken that as a personal insult not to be given prior notice about all matters big and small, I'm sure.' Her words came out with a little more salt than she had intended.

Macie tilted her head to the side. 'Play nice. He's my brother after all.' Her tone was light, but Brielle's cheeks flushed with heat and she had to look away.

'I'm sorry. I just don't understand what it is about Luke that rubs me up the wrong way.'

Macie nearly spat out her drink. 'Please, the wrong choice of phrasing there. The last thing I need are images of Luke rubbing anyone up … wrong way or not.'

Brielle tossed her head back and laughed. 'Great. Thank you. Now I have that image in my head.' And for some reason, picturing that wasn't as bad as she would have thought as a teenager.

'I had forgotten you were old foes.'

'Not exactly foes.'

She arched a brow. 'Then what would you call it?'

Brielle shrugged. 'I don't know. I think I've always had this feeling he doesn't like me. I guess that made me defensive.'

'He actually couldn't believe that you ever thought him adversarial.'

'Really? You talked to him about this?'

'It came up during his phone call.'

A rush of curiosity surged under Brielle's flesh and it stunned her to feel it—why should she care about what Luke thought or said? 'He was surprised? Like, he never picked up on the fact that I bristled every time he came near us?'

'Men are clueless. Luke especially. His ex is evidence of that.'

Brielle leant back in her chair. 'She's still out of the picture?'

Macie nodded. 'She likes to pop back up whenever she wants for a few days to see Poppy. But, most of the time, she barely even calls.'

As much as Luke wasn't on Brielle's list of most liked people, she was empathetic to his situation. Raising a child on his own couldn't be easy. And poor Poppy having such a wayward mother. This had to be affecting her.

'He's grown up so much, Brie. And he's a great father. Honestly, I think if you gave him a chance, you'd be able to see that. And who knows, maybe you two could be friends. Believe me, the more friends you have in this town, the easier it will be for you to slide back in.'

Brielle frowned. 'Maybe.'

Macie laughed. 'Okay. I get it. This will take time.' She lifted her glass in the air. 'Luke aside, I'm just so glad you're back in Alpine Ridge.'

Brielle didn't lift her glass, but frowned instead. Her next exhalation was a long sigh.

'Oh no,' Macie said. 'What? You're not happy to be home?'

Macie had been her best friend since they were ten and met at primary school. She was the first person on the first nerve-racking day to take Brielle under her wing and show her around the small school.

And here they were, sixteen years later, still friends and Brielle working as a teacher at that very school.

Brielle shook her head. 'I guess I've been away too long. Don't get me wrong, my job is great, but it's only until the end of term. I don't even know what's happening next year or where I'll be.'

Macie nodded, her expression showing she understood the deeper roots of the issue. 'Give it time. Alpine Ridge will start to feel like home.'

Brielle didn't miss that Macie had left the 'again' off the end of her statement. She knew as much as Brielle did that Alpine Ridge had never felt like home—not really.

'I'll work it out,' Brielle said, then lifted her glass in the air.

Macie mirrored her action, a sympathetic smile flittering on her lips. 'Here's to friendship and long-awaited homecomings.'

Brielle grinned as she clinked her glass against Macie's. 'To friendship and homecomings.'

Chapter 4

Luke rummaged through Poppy's bag before school most mornings. School notices, half-eaten pieces of fruit, even lizards randomly captured during playtime would dwell inside for eternity otherwise.

He pulled out a scrunched notice from the dark depths and unfolded it, ironing out the creases with his fingers so it was at least readable.

'Remember you're to give me notices the afternoon you get them,' he reminded Poppy as she ate her breakfast of boiled eggs and toast soldiers.

Poppy winced. 'Oops. I forgot.'

'Just try to remember next time.' He was never too hard on her about it; she was only seven after all. He was sure school notices were the last thing on his mind when he was her age.

He read the notice to himself as he stood at the bench, Poppy's half-made lunch beside him. It was a Christmas fete notice. He had been wondering when this was going to be sent out. Most years he participated by conducting a cheese stall.

The notice contained all the usual information and a request for families to volunteer their time and services to help fundraise for the school.

His heart thudded a little when he read Brielle's name at the bottom. So, she had volunteered to organise the fete this year? Quite a commitment considering the small amount of time she had been at the school.

After breakfast, he and Poppy drove to school early. He wanted to meet with Brielle for a few minutes. He could have simply signed the notice and given it to Poppy to return, but a small part of him was curious to see if what Macie had said was right. Did Brielle see him as an adversary?

The school grounds were relatively empty bar for a trickle of students. He held Poppy's hand all the way up to her classroom. He had studied grade two himself in this very building and shuddered at the memory.

His teacher, Miss Belmont, was not quite as endearing as Brielle. She was horrible and used to scream like a banshee at them. The number of times he had to stand at the back of the classroom, humiliated, was innumerable. No wonder he learned to hate school.

Brielle was at her desk when he strode through, Poppy leading the charge. 'My daddy will have a cheese shop at the Christmas fete,' she announced, her voice an octave higher than usual.

Brielle's head popped up, eyes wide.

He gently pulled Poppy back to him and squatted in front of her so they were at eye height. 'Honey, it's polite to say good morning first instead of barging in.'

'Oh,' Poppy said. 'Oops.' She looked at Brielle who was now standing, a smile on her face. 'Good morning, Miss Lane.'

'Good morning, Poppy.'

Luke's body warmed with a rush of attraction. He had always found Brielle so gorgeous—particularly her shining brown eyes, feline almost with the way they slanted upwards.

But he was three years older than her and Macie, and when she was over at his family's house nearly the entirety of every school holidays, it felt *inappropriate* to crush on her.

It felt far from inappropriate now. A three-year age gap was nothing.

'My daddy said he will have a cheese shop at the fete,' Poppy said.

Brielle's smile grew, though there was an obvious strain around the edges. 'That's great news.'

So far, she hadn't even looked at him.

'I'm so excited,' Poppy screeched.

Luke stepped closer. 'I participate most years. I thought I'd drop in and let you know. I'll sell the stock at wholesale prices and donate two dollars from every sale to the school.'

Finally, she had to look at him. Her smile faltered and his heart sank to see that it was true—she thought him an enemy. An uneasiness started in his stomach and worked up his body.

'That sounds great. I'll just take a note,' she said, turning away to her desk and picking up a pen. She jotted something down while he waited.

He was going to ask outright why she didn't like him, opened his mouth to do so, but Poppy pulled her hand from his and screeched, 'Livvy!'

He turned to see Sam Mathews and his daughter walking into the classroom. Poppy threw her arms around Livvy and they both giggled.

'G'day, Luke. Good morning, Poppy,' Sam said.

'Morning, mate.'

Poppy and Olivia had become fast friends since Livvy started at the school earlier that year.

'You'd think they hadn't seen each other for a year instead of just a weekend,' Sam said with a chuckle.

Luke smiled and shook his head. 'Kids.'

It still confounded him how fast time passed. It seemed like a year or two ago that Luke was at high school with Sam, and now their girls were best friends.

Luke blew out a long breath, relieved now for the well-timed distraction, and that he hadn't made whatever this was between him and Brielle any bigger than it had to be.

What concern was it of his if Brielle had an issue with him? As long as he remained pleasant, like he would with any other teacher, it would be enough to see him through to the end of the school year. 'I'll leave you to it. Nice to catch up, Miss Lane.'

When outside, he kissed Poppy on the forehead. 'I'll see you this afternoon, honey. Have a good day. I love you.'

'I love you too.' Then she sprinted off to the playground with Livvy.

As much as Luke wanted to pretend it didn't bother him that Brielle obviously had an issue with him, the fact that he prickled the entire way home in the car was a fairly solid indication that it did.

Thank goodness for the multitude of tasks ahead of him back at the farm, so he could keep his mind off Brielle Lane.

When he collected Poppy that afternoon, he stood on the veranda with the other parents and chatted, attempting not to look inside the classroom.

At three o'clock when Poppy came racing out, they collected her bag and he gave Brielle a short nod before they headed to the car.

See, not a problem. Brielle Lane didn't bother him in the slightest.

With Poppy in her seat, they started home.

'How was your day?' he asked, glancing at Poppy through the rear-view mirror.

'Good. We're making a special Christmas surprise for the fete. But Miss Lane said we're not allowed to tell anyone. But I really, really want to tell you because it's so exciting.'

Luke laughed. 'Best not be the person who gives the secret away. I'm happy to wait until the fete to find out.'

Poppy frowned and crossed her arms over her chest. 'Fine.' After a small space of silence, she said, 'It's really beautiful, though.'

'I'm sure if you're involved it will be. But it's a secret, right?'

She frowned again. 'Yes.'

He laughed. This would torture Poppy for weeks now. Did Brielle not realise little kids loved to tell exciting secrets, especially those that revolved around Christmas?

Or maybe she did know and this was her way of punishing parents.

The sign to Alpine Ridge Dairy gleamed on the left when he pulled in to his driveway. Rocks and dirt crunched under his tyres as he drove towards his homestead.

Nearing the big shed, he spotted a blur of colour from the corner of his eye. His gaze flickered to the house and his heart sank when he saw it was his ex sitting on the front doorstep.

'Mummy,' squealed Poppy. 'Mummy's here. She didn't tell me she would be here today. Was it a secret?'

He suppressed a sigh and instead looked into the rear-view with a false smile. 'I didn't know either.'

After parking in the shed, Poppy climbed out and sprinted across the grass towards Renee. Luke followed after her more slowly. He was in no rush to see Renee again. For her to turn up like this meant there was some catastrophe in her life and Luke, as always, was the soft place she crashed.

The only problem was, he didn't want to be that for her anymore.

That tight aching resentment he always felt when face to face with Renee flooded him when he saw her bloodshot and swollen eyes. His assumption—the new boyfriend had left her.

'Hi, Renee. What a pleasant surprise.' He couldn't hide his sarcasm. After the third time she'd come running back with promises that she missed them and wanted to make it work, then bolted the moment something or someone better came along, he'd run out of energy to be polite.

'Hi, Luke.'

Poppy had her arms wrapped around Renee's waist, her head pressed against her hip. She beamed up at Luke. 'Mummy said she has come to stay.'

Luke grinned as convincingly as he could. 'That's great, honey. Lucky us.'

Poppy nodded emphatically.

'Come on in. No use standing on the doorstep all afternoon.'

He fixed Poppy and Renee some afternoon tea but didn't partake himself, suddenly short of appetite. He went out to feed the calves, to give Poppy some time alone with her mother. But, mostly, he couldn't be bothered with whatever sob story Renee had to share.

And that was the saddest part in all of this, that he had been reduced to a seemingly apathetic, uncaring person when that was far from who he was.

He spent a little longer than usual in the yards. He ran soil tests in the paddocks to check moisture content, despite the fact he'd already done it less than a week ago.

Eventually, his appetite returned with a vengeance, and he finally went home.

'Where's Mum?' he asked Poppy, finding her on her own in the living room watching television.

'She wanted time alone.'

His jaw clamped tightly as he bit down on his anger. 'What does that mean?'

'She's having a bath.'

He nodded, exhaling his frustration. 'What do you feel like for dinner? Tacos?'

She jumped off the couch. 'Yes!'

'Want to help me make them?'

She nodded and followed him to the kitchen.

Dinner was cooked and on the table when Renee made an appearance. Her eyes were still bloodshot and glassy. 'Smells good.'

He gestured to a seat.

'I helped make them,' Poppy boasted.

Renee sat next to Poppy and bumped her shoulder against hers. 'Clever girl.'

During dinner, Luke didn't ask why Renee was here or how long she was staying. Those questions would wait until Poppy was asleep and out of earshot.

At eight, Renee tucked Poppy into bed. This was Luke's usual bedtime too. Waking so early in the morning meant it was near impossible to have late nights. It worked well with Poppy's schedule, so it wasn't usually a problem.

He made a cup of tea for himself and Renee and met her in the living room.

She frowned as she sat in the lounge next to him and held her mug of tea between her palms. Renee was a beautiful woman— long brown hair and big brown eyes. She was kind for the most part.

Unfortunately, she too easily felt caged. That's what motherhood was to her—a prison. That's what her relationship with Luke was. No matter how much freedom he allowed, to her it was a claustrophobic nightmare.

'So, what's the story, Renee?' Not that he really wanted to know. The excuses always grated on him because he couldn't see how anything was more important than their daughter.

'William cheated on me.'

'He's the current boyfriend?'

'Of course, Luke. I've been with him for a year now, remember?'

He nodded. Many men had come and gone; he honestly couldn't keep track. 'So what does that mean for you?'

She sipped her tea. Tears pooled in her eyes. 'I was talking to him this afternoon while you were out—'

His body tightened. He didn't want Poppy exposed to the uncensored maturity level of her phone calls. Mostly, he didn't want Poppy to think that Renee's irrational, messy relationships were what love was like for everyone.

He wanted Poppy to know the beauty of love. The goodness. The happiness. Because it existed—his parents were proof of that. He also had many mates who were content in their marriages.

'—and he apologised and said it wouldn't happen again.'

He wanted to roll his eyes and tell her she was worth more than that, but it always fell on deaf ears. He could say it until he was blue in the face, but she had to believe it herself.

'So, you're getting back with him?'

She smiled bashfully. 'He's a good guy. I love him. He's going to come pick me up tomorrow morning.'

Luke closed his eyes and rubbed the bridge of his nose as he sighed. When he looked at her again, he said, 'This is the last time, Renee. Mother or not, this isn't good for Poppy. I work so hard to give her some stability between the moments you come in and shake it all up. Running in and out of her life is hurting her.'

'Oh, don't give me that, Luke. She's perfectly fine.'

His jaw ached from clenching it. 'Because you're not here to see the aftermath. Can you even understand what it must be like for her to have her own mother reject her time and time again?'

'I'm not bloody rejecting her. I've got a life to live too. The earlier she learns that, the better.'

'All I'm saying is that this is the last time. You will not turn up on my doorstep unannounced again. If you want to come and see Poppy, you book a hotel, you set a date and you stick to it. If I have to pay for the hotel just so you actually make the effort, then fine. But no more of this bullshit.'

'Don't patronise me with all your rules. I'm her mother and I have rights too.'

He shook his head and hissed, 'You're far from what I would call a mother and maybe it's time you realised that.' Harsh, but he had reached his limits on this. He was sick of glossing over the truth.

Renee's eyes bulged and a flash of hurt crossed her features, but it was soon replaced by anger. He was past caring.

Tomorrow he would wake up to a distraught little girl wondering why her mother had left so soon … yet again. 'All you do is cause hurt and turmoil and I've had enough. I won't be the stupid fool you use to pick up your pieces anymore. I need a life too and you running in and out whenever you choose doesn't allow for that.'

'Oh, so that's what this is about. What, have you got a girlfriend or something who doesn't approve of me?'

He placed his tea on the coffee table and got to his feet. He was so weary. Weary of Renee. Weary of this life. 'You know where the spare pillows and blankets are. I'm going to bed.'

Despite the buzzing rigidity all through his body, fatigue won out in the end and he fell asleep.

When he woke to his four am alarm, Renee was gone.

Chapter 5

The children were restless, fidgeting and chattering. Brielle stood at the front of the classroom. 'All right, class. For the remainder of the afternoon, we are going to continue on our special Christmas card project.'

The class cheered and clapped, excited smiles spreading across their faces.

At the beginning of the week, in moments of spare time or when the children's focus waned, she got them busy on the special project.

She had prepared some templates for the kids to construct Christmas cards for their parents, guardians, grandparents, or anyone who meant a lot to them.

The students went to the trays located at the side of the classroom and collected their half-constructed cards. They pulled out their coloured pencils and set about creating three cards each along with three different handmade Christmas tree decorations as an accompaniment.

Poppy was back after a day off yesterday. No note was provided, though the office said they had received a phone call from Luke regarding her absence.

Luke had walked her up to the classroom this morning, said his goodbyes to Poppy and left. He didn't even glance through the windows, let alone come inside. That had stung her until she saw his face. His eyes were bloodshot as though he hadn't slept all night. Lines of tension were grooved into his forehead.

That might have been why she wasn't too surprised when forty-five minutes into the project, Poppy stood up and burst out sobbing before running outside.

Brielle's heart raced. What could have upset her like this?

'Class, remain in your seats and continue with this project. If anyone is out of their seats when I get back, you will be sent to the office to explain to the principal.'

She raced out the door after Poppy.

Poppy was rushing down the covered pathway towards the car-park when she finally spotted her. 'Hey, Poppy. Hold up.'

Poppy picked up the pace until she was running.

Brielle raced after her. 'Poppy. Stop there, right now!' She hated to use her severe voice, but the last thing she needed was this little girl making it to the carpark and putting herself in danger.

Poppy finally stopped and swung around to meet Brielle's gaze. Her shoulders were rolled inwards. Tears were streaming down her face.

Brielle jogged to her and squatted down so she was at eye height. 'Hey,' she said with a soothing voice. 'What's the matter?'

Poppy crossed her arms over her chest. 'Mummy won't want my Christmas card.'

'I'm sure she will. She'll love it because you made it.'

Poppy shook her head hard, more tears rolling down her cheeks. Her nose was running. Her words were choked with the strain of pushing them past her cries. 'No. She doesn't want me.'

'Of course she does.'

Again the head shake. 'I heard Daddy talking to her and he told her not to come back home.'

All the air rushed from Brielle's lungs. 'Oh, sweetheart, come here,' she said, pulling Poppy in for a cuddle. Poppy cried against her shoulder.

'I don't think my mummy loves me,' Poppy howled.

Brielle's own eyes glossed then. If there was one thing she understood, it was the pain of that realisation. 'I'm sure your mum loves you very much.'

She allowed Poppy to cry against her until all the tears were out. 'Come on, let's go back inside.' Brielle stood up taller and took Poppy's hand. 'For the time being, just leave Mum's card to the side and get back to it when you feel a little better, okay?'

Poppy nodded as she glanced up at her with watery blue eyes so full of sorrow it broke Brielle's heart.

The students were rumbling with chatter when they got back to the classroom. Livvy jumped out of her seat and ran to her friend. 'You okay?'

Poppy nodded, but a frown was still marring her face.

Livvy cuddled her friend and warmth filled Brielle's chest. 'Okay, let's all go back to our seats and keep going with our projects.'

With the class in a semi-state of order again, Brielle looked up Luke's phone number on the database and went out onto the veranda to call him.

He answered within five rings. 'Luke speaking.'

'Luke, hi. It's Brielle Lane.'

'Is everything okay?' His voice held a hint of alarm.

'Everything is fine. But Poppy got a little upset in class just now and she ran out towards the road. I assume she was going to run home.'

'She did what?'

'It's okay. I caught her and we had a chat. Would you mind dropping in for a talk this afternoon when you come to pick Poppy up?'

A long sigh sounded. 'Sure. Of course. Is she okay? Should I come get her now?'

'It's probably best to let her finish out the day and not create a big show in front of the class.'

'You're probably right.'

'I'll see you soon,' she said.

'Thanks for ringing.'

Brielle ended the call and stared out over the school grounds. Already her stomach was twisting. This was the hardest part of the job—dealing with parents.

It should be easier because she knew Luke, but for some reason this had her more nervous than usual. Maybe because she could empathise with Poppy so much. Seeing the pain on her little face had rekindled all the old emotions Brielle experienced as a child.

The afternoon flew by without any more outbreaks. Poppy was laughing again by the end of the school day with Livvy, who Brielle had asked to sit next to Poppy for the remainder of the day.

When Luke arrived on the veranda waiting for the bell to ring, she couldn't bring herself to look at him. If she wanted the courage and composure to talk to him about such a personal matter, she had to keep a level head.

At three, she dismissed the class. As she waited for the crowd to clear out, she drew a few deep breaths for courage.

Luke strode through with Poppy in his arms. Poppy's head was on Luke's shoulder. She was a tiny thing in comparison to his big frame and looked so fragile.

'Hey,' Luke said, face expressionless, yet there was a hint of despondency in his gaze. Unmissable weariness shaped his expression.

'Hi, Luke. Thanks for stopping by.' She stood before Poppy and smiled. 'Now, Poppy, I really need a hand with something very important, and I think you're the perfect person for the job.'

She lifted her head from Luke's shoulder, eyes a little brighter.

'I need fifteen copies of tomorrow's homework sheet. Can you head down to the office and wait for them while they make the copies, then bring them back here, please? I've called ahead, so they know you're coming.'

Her smile was full of pride. Luke let her down and Brielle gave her the homework sheet that she had placed in a folder.

'See you when you get back,' Luke said as Poppy skipped out the door, folder under her arm.

'Take a seat,' Brielle said, gesturing to the chair opposite her desk. The nerves were raging now.

He sat, hands rubbing at his thighs. His leg was bouncing.

'So, as I mentioned on the phone, Poppy ran out of class crying today. I thought I should tell you what happened, so you can manage it knowing all the facts when you get home.'

She explained how they were making Christmas cards when the incident occurred. 'Poppy said that she overheard a conversation between you and her mother and from that inferred that her mother no longer loves her.'

Luke's head dropped into his hands and he groaned. He rubbed his face for a moment before he lifted his head again. His frown was deep. 'I thought I was doing the right thing. I didn't realise Poppy was listening.'

Sympathy rocketed through her; his eyes were pained with genuine weariness and confusion.

'I don't need to know the particulars, Luke. I understand it's personal. But I guess I just need to know how to proceed with the cards so Poppy doesn't get upset again. I told her to put her mother's card aside until she was feeling better. But I'm happy to stop the project completely if that helps.'

He shook his head. 'No. It's fine. I'll have a good talk with her tonight. Poppy's mother turned up out of the blue a couple of days ago. She does that. She was gone the next morning without even a goodbye. Poppy takes it hard and sees it as a personal rejection.' He sighed. 'I can't blame her for feeling that way.'

Brielle nodded, starting to get the full picture.

'I thought I was doing the right thing and told Renee that she wasn't to drop in unannounced anymore. I said that she couldn't'—he glanced at Brielle, his face flushing with colour—'always expect me to pick up the pieces every damn time she falls.'

'I see.'

'I know that sounds harsh, but my history with Renee is long. I was at my wit's end, but Poppy wouldn't see it that way. God, I can't believe she heard all of that.' His lips wavered with emotion and it hit Brielle right in the heart.

Her next breath in was thin, rushed. 'I'm sorry this is happening, Luke. I'll try to be as sensitive as I can to Poppy here in class and weigh the impact certain activities might have on her.'

'Thanks. I appreciate you dealing with Poppy the way you did today. I'll definitely have a talk with her tonight and explain the circumstances so she can understand them a little better.'

Poppy came back in. 'All done, Miss Lane.'

Brielle stood and smiled warmly at Poppy. She was an adorable little girl—so much like Luke and Macie in appearance. She could admit to being a little bit of a kindred spirit with her now that she knew her real circumstances.

Macie had given her the social version of the story in the past, but to hear and see the impact Poppy's mum was having on Luke and his daughter cemented the sad realities of it.

Poppy handed her the folder filled with the photocopied home-work sheets.

Luke stood, his size dwarfing the already smaller-sized furniture in the room. 'We best get home then, hey, Pop?'

Poppy nodded.

'Thanks again,' Luke said, then took Poppy's small hand. The glow of affection as he gazed at his daughter, the way he stroked her hair down to her back, all showed how protective and devoted he was. It seemed such a contrast to his big stature.

This was a side to Luke Reynolds Brielle had never known. And she had to admit, it stirred her compassion.

Brielle waved at Poppy as they strode out of the classroom. There was no way she could concentrate after an afternoon like that—it had evoked too many of her own memories.

She remembered so many nights at boarding school as she tried to fall asleep, filled with such angst as she tossed around her own mind the reasons for her mother sending her away.

So clearly, she recalled having the same thought Poppy had today: that her own mother didn't love her.

She shook her head to toss the memories aside and grabbed her handbag. Within moments, she was in her car heading home but very much not wanting to.

Where else could she go? She decided to grab a cupcake and a coffee, then look at all the little tourist gift shops located on Main Street until she had regained some equilibrium.

A little later, as she was looking at some local artists' paintings, her mobile rang. Macie's name flashed on the screen.

'Hi, Macie.'

'Hi, Brie. Luke just rang me. He's really upset about what happened with Poppy today. So am I, to tell you the truth.'

Brielle sighed. 'It's shaken me up too. I really feel for them. It's such a tricky situation.'

'Yeah, it is. He said he opened up to you about what was going on.'

'He gave some detail.'

'Thanks for being there for Poppy.' She didn't miss the waver in Macie's voice. This was an issue that obviously affected the entire family.

'That's fine. I really hope they can sort it out.'

'Yeah, me too.' Macie cleared her throat. 'So what are you up to?'

'I'm just wandering around the shops.'

'Don't want to go home?'

Brielle's heart stuttered. 'Not really.'

A small silence. 'Come over for breakfast on Sunday. We do it every week. Mum and Dad have been wanting to see you again.'

'Really? I've been meaning to catch up with them, but just haven't had the chance. What time should I be there?'

'Around nine?'

'Great. I'll see you then.'

Brielle lingered around the stores until they closed their doors for the night, then finally, reluctantly, she headed home.

Chapter 6

Luke rushed through his Sunday morning milking and additional duties so he could make it to Macie's on time for the family breakfast. Macie came at seven to pick Poppy up so she wasn't in the house by herself while Luke was out on the farm.

With all the drama and emotion the week had thrown at him, he wouldn't miss this chance to relax with his family. Mostly, though, he kept this routine so his daughter would know that despite her mother not showing her love as well or as often as was ideal, Poppy had an extended family who loved her to the moon and back and wasn't afraid to express it.

He arrived at Macie's house a little after nine. Boisterous chatter sounded from the kitchen-dining space—the room they all hung out in drinking coffee, cooking, and eating their spoil of bacon and eggs.

Poppy was sitting on Dad's lap while Macie and Mum were making espressos or mixing pancake batter.

'He made it,' Dad said. 'Good to see you, mate.'

Luke smiled.

'Hi, darling. Come here,' Mum said, holding out her arms. 'Give me a hug and a kiss.'

He kissed Mum's cheek as she drew him in for a cuddle. 'How are you?' She was a good two heads shorter than him but was definitely the family leader.

'I'm good.' They had all been told about what happened with Renee and Poppy's subsequent outburst at school. Luke had tried his hardest to reassure Poppy that her mum loved her dearly and that any problem or worry she had was for him and Renee to work through.

But it was so hard trying to express one thing to his daughter only to have Renee negate it time and time again. Saying you loved someone and showing you loved someone were two very different things.

A knock came at the front door. Luke glanced at Macie, eyes widening in question.

'Brielle. I asked her to pop in.' She rushed out of the kitchen and down the hall to the front door.

His stomach clenched in anticipation. After their meeting during the week, he had opened up quite a bit to her, more so than he had expected himself to. He wasn't sure how her knowing so much about him might change their already strained friendship, if he could even call it a friendship.

But she had been so easy to talk to. Her empathy was obvious in the gloss of her eyes as they had spoken. Whatever the issue was between him and Brielle, he was thankful Poppy had a teacher who obviously cared for her wellbeing.

Brielle strode into the room alongside Macie. She was wearing short denim shorts and a white, sleeveless blouse that tied at the waist. Her legs were toned and pale. His breath rushed in as he took in her appearance. *Absolutely stunning.*

'Miss Lane,' Poppy said, eyes wide. 'Dad, look, it's my teacher.' Her words were full of wonderment as though it was incredible to be seeing her teacher outside of school hours.

He remembered when he was younger it was always such a shock to see his teachers in the supermarket or around town as though before that moment he hadn't realised they existed outside of the schoolyard.

'Yes, it is,' he said.

Brielle smiled and his heart accelerated a fraction. Maybe he was suffering from a little shock himself to be seeing her in casual clothes and a relaxed environment.

'Hi, Poppy. You can call me Brielle outside of school if you like.'

She nodded, her grin wide.

Brielle hugged and kissed his parents as they welcomed her back to Alpine Ridge. She then moved towards him, which he was not at all expecting, as he stood near the bench in the kitchen.

'Hi, Luke. Good to see you again,' she said, lifting onto tiptoes and drawing her face closer to his. His stomach tightened when he caught her scent of subtle vanilla. As she kissed his cheek, his lips met her soft skin.

He went a little dizzy as a moment he had imagined over and over again as a teenager was realised.

'Good morning,' he said, then cleared his throat to undo some of the tension there.

His thoughts were somewhat tangled because, after the standoff-ish way she had been during their previous encounters, this was unusual. But then again, she may have thought it impolite to have kissed his parents and then leave him out.

As breakfast was prepared, they all chatted from their various positions around the room, sitting on stools or standing at the stove.

Mum asked Brielle, 'So when are your parents heading off overseas?'

'In a few weeks.'

Mum frowned. 'You'll be having Christmas by yourself this year?'

Brielle nodded.

'Well, that's not on. You'll be spending the day with us. We're having the usual family lunch. Nothing fussy. But we would love for you to join us.'

Brielle smiled. 'Thank you. I'd really like that.'

Mum narrowed her gaze as she turned to Macie, who was flipping pancakes in a pan on the stove. 'I can't believe you didn't ask Brielle already.'

Macie shrugged. 'Honestly, it hadn't even crossed my mind. It's still seven weeks away.'

'And that seven weeks will fly by before you know it.'

'So are you staying in Alpine Ridge for good now?' Dad asked.

Brielle shook her head. 'I'm not sure yet. I've applied for a few positions, but I haven't heard anything back.'

Luke couldn't handle that uncertainty. He always liked to know what was ahead of him and how he was getting there. Perhaps it was something his father, a sheep farmer, had instilled in him. Farmers ran very much on an unwavering schedule and worked their hardest to reduce risk and uncertainty, though it was inevitable.

'Positions here in Alpine Ridge?' Dad asked.

'No. A couple in Melbourne.'

An aching tightness filled Luke's chest to hear that her stay was only temporary. Then he wanted to thump his own forehead for worrying about something like that; it wasn't like they even had a chance at romance. Because one: she barely tolerated him. Two: with his current personal life, the last thing he wanted was to drag in the uncertainty of a relationship and impact Poppy's life even further.

For a long while now, he had liked Brielle, more than he was willing to admit. He couldn't lie to himself that a relationship with her, if his circumstances were different, was something he would definitely consider.

But then the third reason filled his mind, the one that had restrained him since he was a teenager.

Three: Brielle was his sister's best friend.

To pursue her made him feel like he was overstepping some boundary or taking a risk that would affect more than himself if things turned sour.

Breakfast was dished up and they ate it together around the large dining table. A big table was one item they all had in their houses— extra-large eating facilities for those inevitable occasions when the family and extended family got together.

The food was delicious and, as always, way too much was prepared. That's the way it had been his entire life. There were always leftovers for days.

'I missed this,' Brielle said as they finished their meal.

Mum smiled. 'What's that?'

'You guys. Breakfasts together. I missed being here with you all.'

'We missed you too,' Mum said and there was a definite punch of sincerity in her tone.

Dad and Macie nodded in agreement.

'Thank you for inviting me over.'

'It was our pleasure,' Dad said.

With breakfast over, they started clearing away the dishes from the table and wrapping up the leftovers.

Luke carried uneaten bacon to the kitchen at the same time Brielle was walking out to grab more dishes and talking over her shoulder to Macie. She didn't see him coming and ran directly into him, face first.

She pressed a hand to his chest and this simple action sucked all the air from his lungs, made his skin tingle. 'Woah, Luke.' Her forehead furrowed as she pressed harder against him. 'Holy hell, your chest is like a bloody brick.'

He threw his head back and laughed. 'I'm sorry?'

She rubbed her forehead and giggled. 'Yes, you should be. That hurt.' She drew her hand away and he went to step around her, but she shifted in the same direction and they collided again.

'Sorry again?' he asked with a deep chuckle.

'Yes. This is all your fault. You're so big I can't see around you.' She grinned.

'I'll step to my right, okay?' he said.

She nodded and they managed to move out of each other's way. His eyes met Macie's and the grin fell from his face.

Was it obvious he had been flirting a little just then?

He cleared his throat and set about wrapping the bacon before placing it in the fridge. When Brielle returned with more dirty cups and cutlery, he ignored her. He didn't miss her confused frown.

On his way out of the kitchen, the skin on the back of his neck and all his scalp tingled as realisation dawned. He understood now why Brielle had seen him as an opponent. Over time, as his feelings for her had become more romantic in nature, he had done his best not to make it obvious to his family. And for much of the time that meant hiding his emotions, not looking at her, and sometimes even ignoring her.

No wonder she was uncomfortable around him.

He felt like such an arse. He had to tell her.

But how did he explain this without admitting that he was once attracted to her? That he was still attracted to her?

This realisation sent shivers of warning all through him. His heart was speeding ahead in a direction he didn't want it to go. He swore he wouldn't get involved with another woman unless it was for love. That was how it had to be. He had a daughter to consider. A daughter who was still reeling from her tumultuous relationship with her mother.

So that meant one-night-stands, brief affairs and casual dating were off the table.

He needed stability for Poppy and for himself. A parade of women traipsing in and out of his life would send the absolute wrong message to a curious young girl.

But, really, he was kidding himself. It wasn't like Brielle was interested in him anyway. Though, he did notice the blush on her cheeks as they danced in the doorway.

Even so, she wasn't sticking around in Alpine Ridge, so that meant that there was no point exploring this attraction.

Chapter 7

The final weeks of the school year rushed by in a blur. It was as though Christmas had a special force that propelled the days towards it at lightning speed.

Saturday was the day of the big Christmas fete. Brielle would be glad to see the back of it. Sure, small town, small fete and all, but she had underestimated the amount of work that was required to organise such an event.

If there was one silver lining, though, it was that her parents had taken off on their holiday at the beginning of the week. That eased up some of the added tension at home at least.

Six weeks on her own was a blissful outlook after the last couple of months. Once independence had been tasted, it was hard to fit back into the family groove, especially for her.

When parked, she grabbed her thick folder and rushed to meet the carnival ride operators who were already waiting by their trucks hauling the swing-chair ride, a big slippery dip and a mirror maze.

She gave them the map of the layout and where each ride needed to be positioned around the huge athletic fields located at the back of Alpine Ridge Primary, then left them to set up.

Already waiting for her was a handful of teachers and volunteers who would be erecting the stalls and makeshift eateries. She directed a couple of teachers to start bringing out all the required plastic chairs and foldout tables that were stored in the gym.

Over the last few weeks, the grade five-six composite class had been in charge of hand-sewing Christmas-themed tablecloths for each stall. The grade four class made posters.

Brielle's students had crafted a big papier-mâché wishing well where visitors could throw in money and make a wish, while the grade one and prep classes made decorations to be hung up around the stalls. Christmas overload, but that's what it was all about. Each teacher was put in charge of setting up their own class's creations.

Soon enough, the fete was starting to take shape and resemble the rough outline on Brielle's map. And with summer now here in Alpine Ridge, the weather had made for a hot and sweaty time of it.

Nearing opening time, the parents who were holding stalls began to arrive. Brielle showed them to their designated space all decked out with the children's signs, decorations and merry tablecloths.

The local cupcake shop owner had nominated to hold a stall, along with her sister-in-law who would be peddling flowers from beautiful red and green carts.

There would be fairy floss for sale and face painting. One mother had organised a lucky dip, and there was the obligatory cake stall for which many of the parents had prepared slices, biscuits and tarts.

From across the fields, as she helped haul food items that had been kept cold in the school's canteen, she noticed Luke had arrived. She dropped off the plate in her hands at the cake stall and dashed over to direct him where to go.

'Hi,' she said, unable to hide her fluster. So far, despite most of the day running smoothly, she had been putting out many little fires thanks to her lack of foresight.

His eyes widened a fraction. 'Hello.'

Her brow furrowed in reaction to his alarmed expression. 'What?' she asked self-consciously. 'Is something the matter?'

He shook his head and gestured to her face and chest. 'You're really sunburned.'

She placed both hands on her cheeks. 'Oh, God, really? I put sunscreen on.' She checked her watch. 'But that was almost four hours ago. Is it bad?'

He nodded. 'Pretty bad. Especially pale skin like yours.' He jogged back to his ute, reached in through the open window to the glove box and pulled out a tube of sunscreen. He handed it to her.

'You're a lifesaver. Thank you.' She quickly applied some to her face and the exposed skin on her chest and arms.

'Probably should put some on your legs too,' he said, gazing down.

She leant over, checking them. They were pale pink. 'I am going to be in so much pain tonight.' She coated her legs with a thick layer and handed the tube back.

He shook his head. 'Please keep it. And apply some more later on.'

'Thank you. I'll repay you, I promise.'

'No need. Now, where do you want me?'

She balked. There was one place that came to mind when he said that and it wasn't found here but rather the bedroom.

What the hell is wrong with me? The sun was obviously affecting her brain. She swallowed hard and pointed ahead of them where his empty stall had been set up.

'I'll get to it then,' he said.

She opened her mouth to reply but caught Samantha rushing towards them from the corner of her eyes. She turned just as Samantha called her name.

'Hi, Samantha.'

'Yes, hi. The stage?' Samantha's gaze was flittering around the place. Two deep lines formed between her brows. 'I can't see where you've put it and it needs to be decorated with the Christmas tree before the guests start arriving.'

Brielle's stomach sank like a giant weight had dropped. She thumped her forehead, which hurt more than she would have liked thanks to the sunburn. How could she have completely forgotten to organise the stage, let alone designate a space for it?

Each grade was performing Christmas carols throughout the afternoon—it was the highlight of the fete for all the parents. The stage was six metres long, made up of big heavy parts and would require lots of muscle and a trailer.

See, this was what happened when a disorganised person pretended to be capable of organising anything.

Luke stepped forward and held out his hand to shake the principal's. 'Hi, Samantha. Luke Reynolds.'

'Luke. Yes, I know your parents well.'

'Brielle was just chatting with me about the stage. I've got some friends arriving any minute and we're going to set it up. Give us about half an hour and I'll have it sorted.'

Samantha nodded. Obvious relief showed in the lowered set of her shoulders. 'Thank goodness. Half an hour should be fine.' She turned to Brielle. 'Come and find me when the day is over, please, I'd like to have a chat.'

Brielle nodded.

When Samantha was out of earshot, Brielle sighed as relief flooded over her. 'Please tell me you weren't just saying that to get her off my back.'

Luke was already pulling his phone from his shorts pocket. 'Nope. I'll see what I can arrange.'

'Oh my God.' Her hand rested over her heart. 'Thank you so much.' For a second time today, he had saved her butt.

She was starting to see that perhaps she'd had it completely wrong about this guy. Not only was he deliciously tall and muscular, and those blue eyes, my gosh, the way they glinted under this sunlight left her panting, but underneath all that, he was actually a pretty decent human being.

'No worries. Now let me make a few phone calls so I don't get caught in a lie here.'

She smiled, gesturing for him to proceed. 'Go ahead. If you get this done, I will owe you forever.'

He arched a brow at the same time a cheeky grin curled his lips. And if she was reading that eyebrow correctly, it all by itself possessed innuendo.

Within fifteen minutes, three big guys had climbed out of a ute towing a massive trailer. One she recognised as Sam, Livvy's father. The other two were obviously his brothers judging by the similar brown hair, eyes and massive stature.

Brielle directed them to the gym for the stage parts. They muscled the large pieces onto the trailer, tied it down and whisked it to the fields. Stalls were lifted to new locations and the stage was squeezed in.

By the opening time of two pm, everything was ready and children along with their parents were trickling through the gates. Though it was a small school with few students, many of Alpine Ridge's and bordering towns' residents attended.

As she watched the smiling faces and heard the laughs and excited shrieks, she allowed her first breath of relief. It still confounded her that amidst all the turmoil the morning had thrown at her, combined with her weary muscles, her stinging sunburned skin and scattered brain, she had somehow managed to pull this off.

The late afternoon brought in a cooler breeze just in time for the children's performances. Her own class had been rehearsing with the school's music teacher 'Silent Night' and 'All I Want for Christmas Is My Two Front Teeth' for many weeks.

Once the prep and grade one classes were finished, her kids took the stage. They were all dressed in black shorts and red T-shirts with a sparkly Christmas tree on the front. As she watched them perform, not perfectly, but that was to be expected, pride filled her up.

With the hectic craziness the last couple of months had thrown at her leading up to this event, she hadn't had time to feel anything. But now as she watched the smiling faces of the parents and the delight in their eyes seeing their child on the stage, she felt the deep bond formed with their children. Her throat ached and her eyes blurred with tears. She quickly blinked, not wanting anyone to see her sudden case of wistfulness.

Poppy was watching her dad in the crowd. Macie and her parents had joined him to see the performance. Big smiles filled their faces. Such love emanated from their gazes. What a lucky little girl Poppy was to have a family that loved her so much.

All Brielle's life, she had ached to see that exact expression on her own mother's face. But it never came.

That's why she was drawn to the Reynolds household. Their closeness resonated with her own deep desire to experience that for herself.

Watching them now amplified her own loneliness. Never was it more apparent that no matter where she lived, what she did, she didn't really belong anywhere. She had no one to truly rely on.

Brielle was a burden to her family, and so spent all her time ensuring she was never that for anyone else. That's why she didn't stay at a school for more than a year. Her relationships never lasted longer than six months. She always bailed before anyone realised that they didn't really want her around.

Her parents saw that as Brielle being flighty. But Brielle saw it as an insurance policy defending her against feeling rejection ever again.

The only exception was the Reynolds family—she stuck with them like they were her lifeblood. And, in a way, that's what they had been—the only place she was accepted with open arms no matter how long she stayed.

As the fete came to a close and the visitors ebbed away, Brielle went to find Samantha. She wasn't sure what she wanted to chat with her about. Surely she couldn't have anything negative to say about the fete, and yet Brielle couldn't make her shoulders relax or her mind stop turning over the day's events.

Yes, there was the hiccup with the stage, and a few other small dramas, but, overall, the fete was a success.

She spotted Samantha near the slippery dip and headed over.

Brielle strained a smile as she stood face to face with her boss. 'You wanted to have a talk before I left?'

Samantha nodded and crossed her arms over her chest. 'About today ...'

Brielle held her breath.

'You did a great job. I'm impressed.'

Only when a broad and genuine smile curled Samantha's lips did Brielle exhale, her newfound relief loosening the muscles of her neck and shoulders. 'I'm so glad.'

'To organise an event of this nature at such short notice is no small feat.'

She shook her head. 'Not at all.'

'You've shown me that you're dedicated and can be counted on, which are highly valued traits. For that reason, it's my pleasure to offer you a full-time position here next year.'

Brielle's lips parted, her eyes wide. 'A … full-time position?'

Samantha smiled. 'The teacher you replaced handed in her resignation last week. She wants to stay at home with her baby for a while longer. So that left an opening that I think you are well suited to fill.'

She shook her head. 'Wow. I don't know what to say.'

'You don't have to say anything yet. I'll email you through the particulars this evening. Have a read and let me know what you decide.' Samantha placed a hand on Brielle's shoulder. 'I think this would be a great opportunity for you and for us.'

'Thank you for the offer. I'll let you know as soon as I come to a decision.'

'Great. And thanks again for today.'

'My pleasure.'

As Samantha strode away, Brielle couldn't move for a long moment as a storm of conflicting thoughts filled her mind. She turned and peered out over the school grounds, littered with the fete's remnants.

A full-time position here would be a great opportunity. Deep down, she knew that. But the part of herself that feared pain and loneliness resisted.

If she had been given this position a few months ago, she would have jumped at it. But since she had been home, she wasn't convinced that Alpine Ridge was where she belonged. And if she did choose to stay, she wasn't sure there was enough to keep her here for long.

Brielle took a five dollar note from her purse and went to the wishing well her class had made. It was painted red and green and covered with holly, bells and Christmas baubles. She waited until there was no one around to step up to it and push her note into the small slot.

Before she let the money drop, she closed her eyes and contacted that aching part of herself. That raw wound left over from her childhood.

She whispered, 'All I want for Christmas is to be shown where I belong. I want to feel a part of something bigger than myself. Please, lead me in the right direction.'

The note slipped from her fingers and joined the other coins and notes sitting in the bottom of the well.

She smiled bashfully as she rolled her eyes at her own absurdity and looked from left to right to make sure no one had seen her. Seriously, how desperate must she be that she resorted to wishes to help her make big life decisions?

With a deep sigh, she turned around to rush away before anyone noticed her but ran directly into what felt very much akin to a brick wall.

'Ouch!' She rubbed her forehead, then wished she hadn't because her sunburn stung more as the day progressed. She must look like a rosy-cheeked Santa herself.

When she glanced up, she peered directly into familiar blue eyes. And instead of prickling like she usually did when she saw those eyes, a lust-fuelled awkwardness came over her.

'We've got to stop meeting like this,' Luke said with a grin.

'Seriously, I get it. My face colliding with your chest does not bode well for me.'

He laughed. 'Poppy wanted to come over and say goodnight before we head home.'

Poppy was standing beside her father, grinning. 'Thank you, Miss Lane.'

'My pleasure. Did you have a good afternoon?'

'Yep.' She held up a green piece of card. 'I won the cupcake voucher in the raffle.'

Brielle's eyes widened. 'Wow. Aren't you a lucky girl?'

She received a nod and an adorable toothy grin in reply.

She met Luke's gaze again. 'Thank you so much for today. For volunteering your time, for the sunscreen and for organising the stage.'

'It was no drama. And we all had a great time. You did a bloody brilliant job.'

Her cheeks flushed with heat. 'Thanks.'

'Anyway, we're going to head off.'

'Good night, Miss Lane,' Poppy said.

'Good night, Poppy. Have a good weekend, and I'll see you Monday. Only one more week left of school.'

Poppy jumped up and down. 'Yes!'

Luke took Poppy's hand and together they walked away towards the parking lot.

As she watched them leave, despite her usual rationality, Brielle couldn't banish the thought that barely twenty seconds after making her wish she had run into Luke.

She chuckled at her own ridiculousness. As if a wish thrown into a well made by her students could have any bearing on real life.

Although, in some small way, she had definitely felt the tug of fate right before she face-planted into Luke's chest.

Chapter 8

Poppy lined up before the counter at the local cupcake store, Love and Cupcakes. Luke stood beside her, watching his daughter's eyes widen with amazement as she took in the myriad flavours of cupcakes, each coated with buttercream icing, chocolate or sticky drizzles. Since winning the voucher at the fete last weekend, she hadn't stopped asking when she could come here.

'How many cupcakes can I buy with this?' Poppy asked the lady at the counter and handed over her gift card.

'You can buy twelve. But you don't have to use it all at once if you don't want to.'

Poppy nodded, finger in her mouth as she thought. Then she looked up at Luke. 'I want to buy six, so I can share them with you, Nan, Pop and Aunty Macie.'

Luke smiled. 'I think that sounds like a great idea.'

She chose a combination of different flavoured cupcakes and the attendant boxed them up for her.

When they turned to leave, Luke jolted to see Brielle pushing through the door with her back, carrying a big serving platter in her arms. He raced to hold the door open for her.

'Miss Lane!' Poppy squealed.

Brielle turned and smiled at them. 'Hello to you both. Didn't I just see you at school, Poppy?'

Poppy nodded and grinned. 'Yes, but Daddy said I could use my voucher to get some cupcakes. Are you getting cupcakes too?'

'No, I'm returning a platter.' She peered at the attendant and smiled. 'You forgot this after the fete.' She handed the platter over. 'Thank you so much for helping fundraise this year. The cupcakes were a huge hit.'

'Glad I could help.'

'I'll catch you later,' Brielle said and started towards the door.

Luke and Poppy followed beside her.

'We're going to see the Christmas tree lights,' Poppy said.

They walked outside into the warm evening air. 'Me too. I'm meeting up with your Aunty Macie.'

'So am I!' Poppy squealed excitedly again.

Tonight was the Christmas tree lighting event. The entire town attended each year. Since the beginning of December, colourful blinking lights were strung up above Main Street. Power poles were wrapped in tinsel, and shop windows were filled with wonderful displays of gumnuts and eucalyptus leaves, Santas dressed in shorts and singlets, and kangaroos leading sleighs. Just walking past them this afternoon had left Poppy gasping with excitement.

Tonight's ceremony would be a lovely treat for Poppy to mark the end of a long school year. And since Renee had dashed off, perhaps Luke was still trying hard to compensate for it.

'Leave your car here,' he said to Brielle. 'There'll be no parking spots left closer to the park. We're going to walk down. You can join us if you like?'

She glanced at her car, parked a little way up the road, then back at him. 'Sure. That'll be fun.'

They started along the footpath towards the centre of town, past the pastel-coloured stores.

'So the fete was a success?' Luke asked.

'A huge success. Thank goodness. Remind me never to volunteer to organise it again.'

'I won't have to. You're heading back to Melbourne now, aren't you?'

'I've actually been offered a full-time position at Alpine Ridge Primary. The teacher who I took over from has decided not to come back.'

Luke beamed at her. 'That's great news. So you would be Poppy's teacher again?' he asked.

Poppy's eyes widened. 'Will you?'

Brielle looked down at the footpath. 'I've not accepted the position yet. On Monday I was also offered a placement in Geelong as a substitute again, but it's only part-time. I'm not sure what direction I should head in.'

His smile disappeared. He cleared his throat, an attempt to hide his rising disappointment. The intensity of this reaction surprised him.

Surely she wouldn't be considering anything other than the full-time job. A no brainer, really. It offered more stability. And she would get to stay here, close to her family. Close to Macie.

Steadying his voice, he said, 'So, after all your excellent work organising the fete, Samantha must have been impressed to offer you a full-time position.'

She met his eyes and smiled. 'Yeah, I think she actually was a little impressed because it was the evening of the fete when she approached me with the offer. Which is a compliment, considering the not-so-great start I had.'

'How so?'

'I was late for my first day.'

His shoulders shook as he laughed. 'Why does that not surprise me? I think in the entire time I've known you, you have not shown up on time for anything.' Despite his own obsessiveness about schedules and punctuality, he had to admit that he had always found this lackadaisical side to Brielle endearing.

She shot him a sidelong glance, a smile curving her lips. 'Oh really? I thought I was always so good at hiding my lateness.'

He laughed again. 'Not one bit.'

'Lucky I got an extra cupcake,' Poppy piped up between them. 'Because now Miss Lane will be able to have one too.'

Brielle ran a hand down the back of Poppy's head. There was such genuine affection in that simple gesture, Luke's chest flooded with warmth.

'Thank you, Poppy. That's really thoughtful of you.'

He glanced away and squeezed his eyes shut for a moment so he could gather himself. The more time he spent with Brielle, the more he noticed how well she fit into his life and he into hers, and the more he wanted her. Wanting her meant those reasons for steering clear were fading more and more into the background.

He glanced at her beautiful smile. Her bottom lip was like a ripe apricot with a crease down the centre. He wanted to lean in and kiss those lips so badly he ached. Those few freckles on her nose were like sweet flecks of cinnamon and her hair—well, he could thread his fingers through the strands and gently pull her closer to his face …

This surge of desire was like a storm. For so many years, he had managed to ignore his physical needs and focus on his bigger priorities—his farm and his daughter.

But now, as much as he was resisting, he couldn't stop his attraction to Brielle from flourishing.

He glanced at her again and this time their eyes met for a heartbeat, two, and then she grinned and gave a coy half-shrug before she looked away.

He was in big trouble. Here was this beautiful woman, flighty and directionless and everything he didn't need right now. And here he was wanting, aching, for every inch of her. It didn't make sense. But he was one to know that affairs of the heart often didn't.

Chapter 9

Brielle wasn't a firm believer in the credence of Christmas wishes actually coming true, no matter how thoughtfully and earnestly she wanted her wish to be granted. She was old enough and wise enough to know that there was no magical Santa sitting in the North Pole beholden to the whims of people across the globe.

Yet, as she walked beside Luke and Poppy down to the park, she had a strange sensation that fate might be giving her a big shove towards Luke, of all people.

Completely bizarre.

Running into Luke at the cupcake shop seemed like a small twist of fate because minutes before, on her way to Main Street Park to meet Macie, she'd had to circle the street three times in an effort to find a carpark. In the end, the only spot available was outside Love and Cupcakes.

She didn't think much of it until she remembered a platter on her back seat she had been meaning to return to the shop, and when she went inside, Luke and Poppy were there.

As she had met Luke's blue gaze, tingles had fanned along her arms and up to the back of her neck—that strange sensation that occurs when fate meets reality.

'Do you believe in Santa, Miss Lane?' Poppy asked, jolting Brielle out of her reflection.

'Absolutely,' she lied. But it was a good lie—one young kids loved. She had believed in Santa as a child. The fantasy that he existed was so exhilarating. And then her stepdad decided when she wasn't quite eleven that she was old enough to know better. When she had her own children, she swore to keep the belief alive as long as she could.

'Why do you ask?' Luke asked, his brows lowering.

'A boy in class said that he isn't real. And I told him to shut up and stop being a liar.'

Luke squeezed his lips together, holding back a smile as he nodded. 'Fair enough.'

Brielle's lips twitched. 'I must have missed that conversation.' She glanced at Luke and couldn't stop her full-blown grin when she saw his.

'What did you ask Santa for?' Poppy asked.

She waved her hand dismissively. 'Oh, nothing much. Did you end up making a wish in the well?'

Poppy nodded. 'Yep. But I'm not going to tell because then it won't come true.'

Brielle tapped the side of her nose. 'Exactly right.'

Luke chuckled. 'You two are as bad as each other.'

They soon arrived at the Main Street Park. The large grounds were swelling with people. A real Christmas tree sat front and centre—an enormous green pine, thrusting high into the evening sky. Oversized decorations and ribbons adorned the branches.

As they approached, Brielle waved to Macie and Mr and Mrs Reynolds who were waiting near the tree. Brielle didn't miss Macie's slightly narrowed gaze, as though she was studying this arrival with interest.

'We met up at the cupcake shop up by accident and decided to walk down together,' Luke said in answer to the questioning looks.

'Lovely,' Mrs Reynolds said.

Macie's eyes narrowed even further as she looked at Brielle. 'Yes, lovely.'

Poppy rushed to greet her grandparents and show them the cupcakes. 'I've got one for each of us. I must have known that Miss Lane was going to come too because I got six.'

'Wonderful foresight,' Mrs Reynolds said.

'I can't wait to eat them,' Poppy announced excitedly.

'Well, go ahead and dish them out,' Luke said.

Poppy beamed like it was Christmas morning already and handed a cupcake to each of them. Brielle received a pretty cake with red icing and a big love heart on top. She bit into it and groaned as the rich chocolate taste filled her mouth.

'Oh my goodness, these are amazing.' When she glanced at Luke, she found him already watching her. Something hot and unfamiliar burned in his gaze.

She looked away.

Luke stood close all evening, not at all the distant man she remembered. He listened attentively, got involved in conversation and was generally kind.

Something had changed between them. But what?

At six pm, even though the long summer twilight hadn't yet brought darkness to Alpine Ridge, the Christmas tree lights were turned on to the applause and cheers from the thick crowd.

Pink, red and yellow lights sparkled like glitter against the deep green spindles of each branch. Poppy jumped up and down, clapping and giggling. Luke held a supporting hand to her back.

They bought sausages in bread with tomato sauce for dinner from one of the few food vendors set up around the border of the park, then they headed to the stretch of grass in front of the stage to secure a good position.

Mrs Reynolds unfolded a blanket for them all to sit on. The local orchestra was tuning their instruments—trumpets and flutes and violins. Luke sat down and Poppy sat on his lap, her back against his chest. He wrapped his arms around her and kissed her head.

Brielle's heart was melting to see the way this big strong man was so tender with his daughter. Afraid if she sat too close to Luke she'd drift towards his enticing heat, she opted for a seat next to Macie.

All through the concert as the band played popular Christmas carols, she couldn't concentrate. Luke filled her every thought. As she inconspicuously watched him clap hands and sing with Poppy and attend to her every need, she warmed from the inside.

Every now and then he would glance her way and throw her a devastating smile. Now that who he was on the inside was shining through more brightly, he was becoming even more attractive to her. It was hard to improve something that was already pretty damn perfect, but Luke had managed to do it.

Brielle jumped to her feet. 'Um, I'm going to grab a drink.' She needed space to breathe and consider what was happening to her body and heart.

'I'll come with you,' Macie said.

Brielle and Macie headed to the drink stall. While waiting at the counter, after Brielle hadn't uttered a single word, too consumed by the confusing thoughts in her head, Macie said, very matter of fact, 'I know you like him.'

Brielle's heart thumped hard. She looked around her, feigning that she had no idea who Macie was referring to. 'Who?'

'My brother.'

'No.' She shook her head. 'Not at all. He's a ... friend.'

Macie arched a brow. 'I'm your best friend, Brie. I know you better than you think. And I know my brother. You like him.'

Brielle sighed. 'I don't. I mean … I don't know. I don't know how to feel. Only a couple of weeks ago, I thought I really didn't like him one bit. And now … now I have these weird feelings.' She groaned. 'He's your brother and that makes this conversation so awkward.'

Macie shook her head. 'I think it's a good thing.'

Her forehead creased. 'You what?'

'Even if you haven't realised it yourself, you've crushed on him since forever. Why else would you care so much if you thought he didn't like you?'

Brielle's mouth opened and closed a couple of times, yet she still couldn't find the right words. She hadn't thought of it that way and maybe Macie had a point.

'I just wanted to say that if you think you shouldn't go there because of me, then that's ridiculous because it really doesn't bother me,' Macie said. 'If you like him and if he feels the same, then don't let me stop you.'

Brielle shook her head. 'It's not like that. Truly. Maybe I've just realised he's cute'—she winced as she reminded herself that she was talking to Luke's sister here—'kind of. But there's no chance of a romance. At all. I don't even know if I'm staying in Alpine Ridge. I don't even know if he—'

'Likes you?'

Brielle shrugged, nodded. 'Yeah. I mean … I don't know.'

'He does. Believe me,' she said, pointing to her chest. 'I know.'

'It doesn't matter anyway. There will never be anything between us.' But even she could hear the lack of conviction in her words.

Did she want him?

No. He was Luke. And she was ... still lost, obviously.

Again Macie's brow arched. *Damn eyebrows knowing everything.* 'I think you just need to make up your mind once and for all.'

'She says to the least decisive person on the planet.'

Macie smiled. 'Exactly my point.'

The stars were twinkling overhead in the night sky by the time the last carol was sung.

Brielle, Luke and Poppy said their goodbyes to Macie and her parents near the park's entrance. Then she walked back up to her car with Luke. Poppy was unusually quiet. Luke was a little quiet too for that matter.

'Tired?' she asked, looking up at the slice of moon in the sky.

He chuckled. 'Always. This is past my bedtime, believe it or not.'

'I'd believe it. You'd have to get up early, wouldn't you?'

He nodded, a weariness expressed even in that action.

An image of Luke waking up in bed popped into her head, which, in turn, made her think of crawling in beside him and pressing herself against his big, hard chest ...

Gee, Brielle, you're getting carried away here.

She licked her lips and changed the subject—anything but Luke in bed. 'What a great night.'

'I've looked forward to it every year, ever since I was a kid.'

'Me too,' said Poppy.

'Christmas is the best time to be home in Alpine Ridge,' she said, and truly meant it.

Too soon they arrived at Luke's car. 'Here I am,' he said.

A deep pang of regret went through her—regret that the night was over and that Luke was going home without her.

Poppy opened the car door and climbed into the back seat, her eyelids already drooping.

'You have one sleepy little girl there,' Brielle said.

Luke ducked to look through the window at his daughter. 'She'll be out of it by the time we get home.'

'Lucky you're strong enough to carry her into bed.'

His smile grew. 'Is that an attack of my body again? I know you have an issue with my chest.'

Brielle didn't miss the flirtatious lilt to his words. 'No problem with your chest. Or body. Not at all ...' Her words trailed off as the heat she noticed earlier in his gaze returned. The intensity in his look made her body throb with desire.

His smile faltered on his lips, replaced by something much stronger—lust.

Her breath hitched and she cleared her throat. She needed words to fill the space and distract her from these sensations. 'What's changed, Luke?' She blurted out the question before she could stop herself.

His head cocked to the side. 'What do you mean?'

'When we were younger, even recently, I always got this feeling that you didn't like me. And that you didn't want me anywhere near you.'

His eyes dipped and his shoulders hunched on his long exhale. When he looked at her again, apology was present in his gaze. And something else. Reluctance?

She crossed her arms over her chest as all her old defences kicked in. Maybe she wasn't reading him right, and he was about to confirm everything she once believed was true about him—that he really didn't like her and was simply trying to be polite. Everything inside her urged her to get as far away from him as fast as she could, because to hear that now would be so hurtful.

Gah! Why do I care so much about what he thinks of me?

As the answer to her question stung her on the tongue, goose-bumps spread along her arms. Was Macie right? Did she care about Luke's rejection so much because, deep down, she cared about him?

She peered into his blue eyes, his handsome face, and realisation dawned. Yes. Macie was right. She did care about Luke. A lot.

'I'm sorry you ever felt that way,' he said, words soft and sincere, unaware of her inner turmoil. 'I hadn't even realised I was making you feel like that until recently.' He glanced up at the flickering streetlights and ran a hand down his face.

Brielle was barely breathing.

'You see, Brie,' he said, taking a step closer so she had to tilt her head back a little farther to see his face, 'I've had a crush on you for a while now.'

Her lips parted in surprise as her gaze flickered between his eyes and she interpreted all the earnestness within them.

'But when we were younger, the age difference seemed a big deal. In a way, it was. And I did everything to not let you or anyone else know how I felt because it didn't feel right. And, I guess that's what you perceived as me being a jerk.'

She let out a long breath, and with it went all the angst she had ever felt about Luke. 'I didn't realise,' she whispered, unable to find volume in her voice.

'I'm embarrassed. And I regret it so much. And I'm deeply sorry. I didn't have the skills back then to deal with this crush more appropriately.'

'You had a crush on me,' she whispered.

A bashful smile curled his lips. 'Yeah.'

Well, that changed her perspective completely. A burst of heat found her cheeks.

'Can you forgive me?' he asked.

It took her a moment to find her voice. 'Of course.' But she didn't know how to process this. She had to go back through all her old memories and now reference everything with this new insight.

'Thanks.'

Silence fell upon them. She looked into the back seat at a now sleeping Poppy and smiled. 'I, um, better let you get your daughter home to bed.'

His grin was kind. 'Yes. Her father too.'

Brielle giggled. 'Have a good night.'

'You too.'

As she started for her car a few metres ahead, he called out, 'You're still coming to Macie's on Christmas Day, right?'

She turned back to him. His blue eyes were shining under the dim streetlight. He was so sexy, it stole her breath. 'Sure am.'

He winked and her legs weakened. 'See you then.'

When she climbed into her car, she started the engine but took a moment before driving off. Her mind was awash with thoughts about Luke's admission.

Her veins were electric. Excitement and desire burst from within.

Now that she had some understanding of why their relationship had been 'seemingly' combative, her defences were crumbling. Those old mechanisms she had employed to protect herself against rejection were deactivating where Luke was concerned.

And in their place, a strong and loud thought appeared in her mind.

I like Luke Reynolds. A lot.

Chapter 10

On Saturday after the morning's milking was complete, Luke had to attend a day-long agricultural convention in Wattle Valley.

Macie had offered to look after Poppy for him. They were going to have a girls' day out, starting with a pedicure, then were heading to see a movie together. He appreciated Macie so much—she was a fantastic aunty. Without Poppy's mother around, it was reassuring that she still had good female role models.

The heatwave was sticking around but, hopefully, a cool change would be coming through soon. It made the convention tiring as he checked out the latest in all things farming under the heat of the sun. He inspected tractors, feeding equipment, and the latest in milking cups, sterilisation and soil-testing technology. But all he could see was Brielle.

He still couldn't believe he had confessed his crush, but he had found himself unable to look into her eyes and continue to hurt her by saying nothing. The way her cheeks blushed had made his blood flow faster and to regions he'd rather it didn't in public.

All he had wanted to do was admit that he still felt that way about her, but he held his tongue.

Later that afternoon, he made the trip back home. The entire drive, Brielle filled his thoughts. His heart and his body were telling him to go for her. But his head was saying no.

Something was holding him back and he couldn't quite see or articulate it, could only taste it like a faint drop of flavour on his tongue.

He liked his life with Poppy. He had his routine. That would be enough for now.

When he arrived home, Macie had already bathed Poppy and she was dressed in her pyjamas. She had made lasagne with a golden crunchy top and had it sitting on the bench cooling. The rich meaty aromas filled the house and tickled his hunger.

'Poppy's already eaten,' Macie said, following him into the kitchen.

He nodded. 'Thanks heaps. I appreciate it.' He pointed to the lasagne. 'And for this. I'm bloody starving.'

Macie smiled. 'I thought you might be.'

'So how was your day? No dramas?'

'Not at all. We had a great time.' She wiggled her freshly painted fingernails in front of him. 'And I come off looking better for it.'

'Win-win.'

'Exactly.'

Macie rested her hip against the bench and crossed her arms over her chest. He could sense she was readying herself to open up about something and intuition hinted it involved Brielle.

He busied himself, grabbing a beer from the fridge and uncapping it, not meeting her gaze as he did.

'Did I tell you that Brielle decided to take the position in Geelong?'

His heart wrenched. He lowered his beer from his lips. 'What? Why would she do that? It doesn't make sense.'

A slow smile crept across Macie's mouth. 'I'm joking. I just wanted to see your reaction. And that was the reaction I was expecting if my presumptions are correct.'

He scowled at his sister. 'So, she's not going to Geelong?'

She shook her head, that grin still front and centre on her face. 'She's accepted the position here.'

Relief filled him and it surprised him how strong a sensation it was. Regardless of what he had been telling himself, to have Brielle stay obviously meant a lot to him. 'Good. I think that's the right decision.'

'And why would that be?' Macie asked.

'It's full-time.'

'And?'

'And she knows the students already. It would be less disruptive for them.'

'And?'

He glowered at his sister. 'I know what you're doing and I'm not going to fall for it.'

Macie's smile faded, replaced by a sympathetic frown. 'It was a huge decision for her, Luke. And a lot more difficult than I think you're aware of.'

He took a sip of beer, his forehead furrowing. How difficult could it possibly be? 'Why?'

'You know what it was like for her growing up. Her family. She always felt like the outcast and, if I'm to be honest, was treated like one. She was basically made to feel like nothing more than an inconvenience as soon as her twin sisters came along. Why else do you think she went to boarding school? And then moved away as soon as she could? She's so damn scared of rejection, that's why she keeps chasing her tail and never really getting anywhere. I was surprised she even came back.'

'I ... I didn't realise,' he stammered.

Hearing that explained a lot. Firstly, why she had spent so much time with his family when they were younger. And why she had hightailed it to the city when she finished high school.

Maybe she wasn't the flighty person he had thought she was, or at least not for the reasons he'd assumed.

He recalled the tears in her eyes when he had come to see her that day at school when Poppy was upset. Her kind words. The genuine empathy.

She had known exactly what Poppy was feeling because she had experienced it herself.

His protective instinct bubbled up inside him and he wanted to rush to Brielle and take her in his arms. But alongside that instinct was guilt for ever contributing to her feelings of rejection.

'No, she doesn't shout it from the rooftops,' Macie said. 'But she also hasn't done a great job of hiding it.'

He could see that so clearly now. 'No, she hasn't.'

Macie unfolded her arms and pressed a hand to her hip. 'I'm going to say something and you have to promise to hear me out.'

He kept his eyes locked on his sister's, waiting.

'I know you like her—'

He opened his mouth to object, but found he couldn't do that anymore. Hiding his emotions had only caused Brielle pain.

'—and I know she feels the same way, even if she hasn't quite admitted it to herself just yet.'

'What, are you the romance whisperer or something? You can't say how she feels.'

She rocked her head from side to side and smiled. 'No, I'll admit I'm guessing. But it's a pretty accurate assumption, I believe.'

He placed his beer on the bench and crossed his arms. His neck and jaw were rigid. 'What are you trying to say?'

She shrugged. 'That I don't care. If you like her, you have my blessing. I don't want to be a reason why you don't pursue her.'

He shook his head. 'You're not.' But even as he said it, he knew it wasn't the truth. He had certainly taken his sister's feelings into account because if he did have a relationship with Brielle and it went awry, it would hurt Macie too.

She arched a brow. 'Then why have you done everything you can to try and hide how you feel about her from me?'

A small resigned smile. 'Fine. I admit it. I was worried about how it might affect you.'

Her grin was broad. 'Honestly, as much as it grosses me out thinking about my big brother with my best friend, I think you two would be good for each other.'

'That's your expert opinion?'

'Not expert, just an opinion offered with love. And I told Brielle the same thing.'

'Jesus, Macie. Why?'

'Because, like I said, I sense she's attracted to you too. Especially now you've pulled your head out of your arse and actually talk to her.'

He shook his head. 'A bit harsh.'

She shrugged, grinned. 'The truth can be.'

He picked up his beer and took a long swallow before resting it on the bench again. 'She's so unstable. You know that. With the way Renee is, I need to ensure I don't have girlfriends coming in and out of my life. And I just don't think Brielle could ever stick around in the one place for long.'

'I don't know. Maybe she needs you to help with that.'

'It's not just me, though. Poppy's in this equation too.'

'Brielle adores Poppy and you know it.'

'Yes, but are we enough for her to finally settle down? You have to admit, it's a risk.'

Macie took a step closer and with her voice lowered, said, 'And maybe you need to admit to yourself that she's worth the risk.'

He didn't say anything because he didn't know how to feel about that just yet.

'You've got to take care of your own needs too, Luke. You keep going like this, ignoring what you want and taking yourself out of the equation, you're going to burn out. And you're going to wake up one day, when Poppy is no longer living at home, and you're going to be alone regretting not having acted on your own wishes.'

What a slap in the face. 'Bloody hell. Don't hold back, Macie.'

'I've held back long enough. So have you.' She kissed him on the cheek, finishing with a couple of light slaps on his face for good measure. 'I'm heading home. I'll see you at breakfast tomorrow. You have a good night.'

Chapter 11

Brielle was last to arrive at Macie's on Christmas morning. She was prepared to be on time, only to realise she had no sticky tape when she started wrapping presents. She took off in her car to buy some, but nothing was open on Christmas Day.

If this were Melbourne, there would be countless convenience stores to choose from. But this was regional Victoria, so her expectations were swiftly readjusted. In the end, she had to resort to using staples.

The result wasn't what could be called beautiful, but the gifts were wrapped and that was the main point. The paper was only going to be torn open anyway.

Brielle could hear Christmas carols from inside the house as she arrived at Macie's front door. She knocked, but no one answered, probably unable to hear over the melodious din. She discovered the front door was open anyway, after giving the doorknob a twist.

Big adhesive kangaroo footprints ran a line down the long tiled hall. She giggled when she saw them. These were the joys of having children around at Christmas time. All the childhood jovialness could be played out under the guise of entertaining the kids. That's why it was her favourite time of year as a teacher—and she ensured Christmas was as fun for her students too.

She followed the kangaroo paws to the end of the hall and took a left into the lounge room. At the end of the prints was the Christmas tree, and Luke and Poppy were sitting underneath it on the carpet. Brielle's smile was unending as excitement filled her bones at the sight of them.

The coffee table had a Christmas-themed table runner, with ornaments like globes, little trees and Santa figurines on top. Tinsel was strung from the walls around the room. The stems of the lights were wrapped in ribbon. Pretty holly and ivies were hanging from the ceiling just above head height.

The Christmas tree was blinking with multi-coloured lights. Big, fat baubles of blue and silver dripped from the branches, shimmering as the lights reflected off them. Perfectly wrapped presents with big red bows and bells spilled out from underneath.

Luke and Poppy glanced up when they saw her and their grins mirrored her own.

'Good morning,' she said, placing her bag of gifts down and holding her arms wide as Poppy raced towards her. She wrapped the little girl in her arms. 'Merry Christmas, Poppy.'

'Merry Christmas, Miss Lane.'

When Poppy had unwrapped herself again after a tight hug, Brielle said, 'You can call me Brielle outside of school, remember?'

Poppy nodded with a toothy grin. 'I know. I keep forgetting.'

Luke had stood to turn the carols down and was coming towards her. His presence was enormous, and his warmth and scent sent tingles through her as he leant in and kissed her cheek. 'Merry Christmas.'

She had to force herself to breathe and find words. 'Merry Christmas, Luke.'

He was dressed in a pair of shorts coupled with a black T-shirt with an abstract multi-coloured picture of a Christmas tree on the front. What that black did in contrast to his tanned skin and pale blue eyes left her pulse galloping.

'Poppy has been so excited for you to arrive,' he said.

'I'm sorry I'm late.'

'Would you be upset if I told you that I asked you to come thirty minutes earlier than when I wanted you here, so you wouldn't actually be late?' asked Macie as she strode into the lounge room. She wore a red T-shirt with a glittery red-nosed reindeer on the front, which quite comically matched the green T-shirt with a glittery Christmas tree on the front that Brielle wore.

'Very clever.' She grinned and held out her arms, giving her friend a hug. 'Merry Christmas.'

'Merry Christmas to you too. Mum and Dad are just finishing dotting the ham with cloves, then they'll join us so we can open the presents. Poppy has been bursting with eagerness.'

'So have I,' Brielle admitted. 'It was a little lonely waking up to an empty house this morning.' Despite all the tangled emotions she had about her family, she loved them. And this year was the first year she had spent Christmas without them.

'I know the feeling,' Macie said. 'It's a shame there wasn't a big strapping boyfriend under the tree for me when I woke up.'

Brielle giggled because that statement echoed her own thoughts when she had walked in and found Luke under the tree—like he was a present waiting for her to unwrap.

Her mouth went dry at the thought of unwrapping Luke Reynolds, and this wasn't the right time or company to be having such fantasies. She coughed. 'Maybe you need to remember to ask Santa for a boyfriend next year.'

When Mr and Mrs Reynolds were finished with the ham, they all sat down in the lounge. Brielle had bought the Reynolds a gift basket of various bottles of quality wines from a local vineyard. They politely didn't comment when they noticed the staples on the cellophane wrapped around the wicker basket.

Macie, however, almost toppled over with laughter when she saw the wrapping on her gift was held together with staples.

'Oh my bloody goodness, Brielle,' she managed between bursts of giggles.

'What?' Brielle asked, feigning innocence but unable to stop her own laughter. 'I forgot to buy sticky tape.'

'I would expect nothing less memorable than this,' Macie said, holding up a staple, then bursting into laughter again. When she had managed to calm down and wipe the happy tears away, she pulled the rest of the paper away to reveal her gift— a Spencer & Rutherford handbag Brielle knew Macie had been eyeing.

Macie's eyes widened as she gasped. 'Oh my goodness. Staples or not, this is so perfect.'

Brielle beamed. 'Glad you like it.'

'Like it? I love it.' Macie leant over and wrapped an arm around Brielle. 'Thank you so much.'

'My pleasure.' Brielle reached for the next present. 'Now, what do I have for Poppy?'

Poppy's face lit up. 'Do I have staples too?'

Brielle nodded emphatically. 'Of course. I wouldn't want you missing out on the authentic Brielle gift-giving experience.'

Luke's deep chuckle sounded in the room, along with an unrestrained laugh from Mr and Mrs Reynolds.

Poppy opened a set of My Little Pony figurines, leaving only Luke to get his present. She handed over his gift.

He unwrapped a personalised year planner. Brielle had ordered it from an online store a while back and was able to choose the picture on the front and have his name embossed along the top.

Dotted throughout the pages were beautiful detailed drawings of grassy paddocks and dairy cows.

After he had flicked through it, he met her gaze. He wore an expression she'd not seen on him before—shocked gratitude.

'This is so thoughtful, Brie. Thank you.'

Her grin was wide, if not a little modest. 'You're welcome. I remembered from when you were younger how much you loved to schedule every single part of your day.'

Mr Reynolds guffawed. 'Nothing's changed.'

Brielle had been recalling many memories from those days these last couple of weeks. And despite what she had originally assumed, they weren't all bad. She could remember many small gestures of kindness from Luke.

Like when she was fifteen and the town bus had dropped her and Macie out the front of the Reynolds' farm after a day at the local markets. It was raining so hard, the long dirt road up to the house was a sloppy muddy mess. Luke, without any prompting, had driven the ute down to pick them up and bring them up to the house.

Or the time when she was sixteen and was spending the night at the Reynolds' place. Mr and Mrs Reynolds were in Melbourne for the weekend and Luke was home for his end-of-semester break from his first year at university. Brielle had slipped on the wet tiles getting out of the shower and thumped her head on the corner of the vanity, splitting the skin. Luke had been so calm when she was freaking out, applying first aid, then driving her to the hospital a few towns over where she was given six stitches.

Brielle shook her head to clear the memories. It was her turn to open her presents. Even as she got older, this part of Christmas was still so exciting.

Brielle's presents were all beautifully wrapped, not a staple to be found. Mr and Mrs Reynolds had bought her a collection of stationery for her to use at school. Macie had got her a gorgeous piece of artwork by a local artist along with a key to her house.

Brielle held the key between her fingers and met Macie's gaze.

'You're to move in the moment your parents are back from their holiday,' Macie said.

'Thank you.' Her voice was soft and her smile was warm. 'This means a lot to me.' She focused on the key again as she spun it in her hand. This small object was a representation of the new life she had chosen to make here in Alpine Ridge.

'And to me,' Macie said as she hugged her.

Brielle unwrapped Luke and Poppy's present next. Poppy was straining to say what it was as Brielle tore the paper off.

'Oh wow,' she said, turning the box over in her hand. It was one of those new electronic personal assistants.

'You can set alarms and reminders. I thought it might help with …' Luke trailed off and pressed his lips together.

Brielle grinned. 'My punctuality? Reminders about sticky tape?'

Luke shrugged, his lips twitching. 'Or you could just ask how the weather will be. Stuff like that.'

'Thank you. It's very …'

'Practical?' Macie guessed.

'I was going to say thoughtful.'

Mrs Reynolds stood up and clapped her hands together once. 'How about we get these celebrations started and I open a bottle of champagne?'

With the gift giving over, they retreated out onto the back deck with a tall glass of champagne each. The outlook from the high vantage offered views of Luke's dairy farm. In the distance, cows were grazing in a paddock, their deep mooing heard on the gentle wind every now and then.

Anticipation for when Brielle could move in here with Macie surged from deep inside. Only two weeks left and she could fly the coop ... again.

A little shell-shaped plastic pool was set up for Poppy on the lawn in front of the deck. Luke helped Poppy dress into her swimming togs and rubbed sunscreen on her face and arms.

She had never felt the desire to have children before in her life—maybe because she looked after a classroom full of them most days—but there was something about seeing oversized Luke being so gentle and attentive to his comparatively tiny daughter that stirred Brielle's long dormant maternal instincts.

Poppy squealed as she raced towards the pool, drawing Brielle away from her thoughts. She blinked a couple of times and focused on the conversation around her, only to find Macie already watching her with an eyebrow arched high.

Had I been staring at Luke?

She turned away from her friend's all-knowing gaze.

Sure, Macie had given her the green light as far as Luke was concerned, but though these feelings she had for him weren't new, they were newly acknowledged, and she needed time to get her head around them.

Mostly, she needed to know if she could put away her fears of rejection, her inevitable running before a relationship ever became too deep, and take the leap. With Luke being so entwined with his family, and the fact that he had a daughter who needed to be considered here, she wouldn't have that luxury.

No, if she were to go there with Luke, she had to be sure he was truly what she wanted. She had to know that it would be real and worth it.

She squeezed her eyes shut and shook her head. She didn't even know if Luke would be interested in a relationship anyway. These concerns could all be for nothing.

'Everything okay?' Luke asked.

She opened her eyes to find him watching her with two deep lines of tension sitting between his brows.

She managed a tight smile. 'Absolutely fine. I thought I'd forgotten the dessert I was meant to bring today. But then I remembered I dropped it over last night. See, I can be organised.'

He smiled, though she could tell it was to humour her.

To distract the assessing gazes away from herself, she beamed and lifted her champagne glass in the air. 'Merry Christmas, everyone!'

The table laughed as they raised their glasses and chimed them together. 'Merry Christmas!'

They sipped at the amber bubbles from their glasses.

Mrs Reynolds leant forward and said, 'Welcome home to Alpine Ridge, Brielle. Macie told me you were taking a permanent position at the primary school. It's great to have you home for good.'

Her heart thundered at those three little words—*home for good*. Permanency had always been a frightening prospect for her, yet it was the one thing she wanted more than anything else.

Funny how life worked that way.

Lately, though, all roads were leading her back to Alpine Ridge. Maybe it was time she faced her long-held fears about rejection once and for all or she may never get the life she truly wanted.

By the late afternoon, Brielle felt like all she had done was eat. For lunch, they had delicious honey-baked ham, fresh prawns and oysters, and plenty of different salads. Plum pudding, pavlova and trifle followed for dessert. During the day, she had drunk a variety of different wines, brandy, and now a snifter of locally made port.

In two words she was stuffed and tipsy—not a bad state to be in.

'Let's play cricket,' Mr Reynolds said.

Luke jumped to his feet. 'I'm in.'

Brielle thrust her hand in the air like she was one of her eager students. 'I'm batting first.' When she did lunch duty at school, she often played cricket with the kids on the oval. She wasn't too bad at it and planned to show off her unexpected skills.

They set up a pitch on the long stretch of lawn. Mr Reynolds bowled first while Luke played wicket keeper. Mrs Reynolds, Macie and Poppy took various positions fielding. They stood close to the pitch, anticipating Brielle wouldn't hit the tennis ball far.

But when the ball came down the line from Mr Reynolds, Brielle lined it up and smashed it to the left. It went flying.

With a chuckle at the stunned gazes, she ran as fast as she could, bat in hand, back and forth along the pitch, managing four runs by the time Poppy had raced for the ball and thrown it to Macie, who then tossed it to Luke.

'Don't go easy, Dad,' Luke yelled as Mr Reynolds lined up for his next bowl.

'I underestimated this one,' Mr Reynolds said with a grin.

His next bowl was fast, but she managed to hit it with the tail end of her bat. It didn't go nearly as far but evaded being caught. She sprinted as fast as she could to the end of the pitch, only just getting her bat over the line before Luke received the ball back and slammed it into the wickets.

She managed to make another twenty or so runs when she hit the ball and took a risk on a second run. From the corner of her eye, she could see the ball being fielded quickly, making its way back to

Luke. She sprinted as fast as she could and thrust the bat out in front of her just as the ball was tossed into Luke's hands.

She didn't slow, nearly there as his arms swung the ball towards the wickets. The wickets fell mere centimetres before she made it over the line.

Having run so fast, she couldn't slow down in time and charged into Luke's side with a thud. He went flying backwards, and she toppled over, landing on top of him.

Her face was only inches away from his as he held her waist.

'Woah,' he said. 'You okay?'

Being so close to him, combined with their heavy breathing, conjured all kinds of thoughts she didn't need to be having about Luke with his family watching. But with her chest to his chest, her thighs entwined around his thighs, and certain other areas pressed nice and firmly together, she couldn't help it.

Eventually, she blinked, realising she actually had to answer him. 'I'm fine. You broke my fall. Thank you.'

'Maybe this big body of mine isn't such a bad thing after all,' he said with a laugh.

She shook her head slowly. 'Not bad at all.' In fact, his hands on her hips felt just right. The electricity sparking between them was intense. Arousing.

There was a lot of thick muscle beneath his clothes, and until now, she hadn't realised how strong he was. She quickly moved to climb off him. He helped her, lifting her as though she weighed nothing.

'Thanks for catching me,' she whispered when she was back on her feet and dusting down her shorts.

The smallest of smirks curled the corners of his lips. 'My pleasure.'

'All right, you two,' Mr Reynolds said. 'We've got a game to play here. Who's batting next?'

Chapter 12

A day of rest for a dairy farmer was non-existent. So at four o'clock, a little later than he would normally do the second milking, Luke and his dad took off together to get the milking done and feed the calves.

As he arrived at his property, many of the cows were already restless, eager to get in and have a good feed while he relieved their full udders.

Once the herd was back in a fresh paddock for the night, he showered and headed back up to Macie's.

The women were more than tipsy and Poppy had retreated to the lounge to watch a Christmas cartoon. Already, her eyes were drooping with the need for sleep. He stopped in to kiss her forehead and ask if she needed anything on his way through, but she was content as she was.

'Beer?' his father asked.

'Read my mind.'

Luke continued out to the back patio to meet the women.

'And he's back,' Macie said. 'We were just talking about you.'

He took a seat, rested his elbows on the armrests and clasped his hands in front of his waist. 'I don't even need to ask if it was all good. I couldn't possibly believe it could be anything else.'

They laughed. Mum reached over and slapped his thigh. 'Of course it was all good.'

'We need some music,' Macie said. 'And by music, I mean songs that have no Christmas theme whatsoever. If I hear "Winter Wonderland" again, I'll scream.'

'Agreed,' Brielle called after Macie as she bounded off inside to change the playlist.

'So what do you think, should we start dishing up leftovers for dinner?' Mum asked. 'Everyone hungry again?'

Luke's stomach growled on cue. 'Doesn't matter what time of day you ask me that, the answer is always the same.'

'So that's a yes?' Mum asked with a grin.

'Definitely. Poppy's getting tired in there, so it will be good to have her fed sooner rather than later.'

They all helped bring out the platters of leftovers and spread them out on the table. More bottles of wine were opened and poured.

'So, you don't even get Christmas Day off, Luke?' Brielle asked as they ate their dinner. 'That must be hard.'

'I don't really know anything different. I can still enjoy myself in between.'

'What if you're sick? Or want to go on a holiday?'

He smiled. 'I have employees. They help me out.'

There was relief in her features and it surprised him. Why this curiosity?

'Don't worry,' Macie said. 'He has time for a relationship if that's what you're worried about.'

Brielle's cheeks burned bright red. A little heat flushed his own face too.

'Do not embarrass them,' Mrs Reynolds said as sternly as she could despite the small grin slanting her lips.

He met Brielle's gaze briefly.

Had everyone known about his attraction all along?

'Macie, you've obviously got nothing better to talk about,' he said.

'I wouldn't say that.'

'The ham is really delicious, Mrs Reynolds,' Brielle said, an obvious attempt to change the subject.

'Thank you, Brielle. I'll have to show you the recipe.'

'I'd like that.'

After dinner, Poppy went back into the lounge room to watch a movie. When Luke checked on her fifteen minutes later, she was sound asleep on the couch. She would spend the night here at Macie's, so he didn't have to disrupt her later on to take her home.

He lifted her into his arms and carried her into the spare bedroom, tucking her in nice and tight.

'Goodnight, sweetheart,' he whispered as he stroked the hair from her forehead and kissed her soft cheek. He loved his daughter more than anyone else on the planet, more than he had believed possible, and regardless of the trouble Renee gave them, he would forever be grateful for this most beautiful gift she had given him.

With Poppy tucked up for the night, Luke was able to relax. The cows were content in their paddocks. Poppy was sound asleep. Now he had some time for himself.

He shared another beer with Dad as they all spoke about old times and plans for the future. They laughed as they swapped funny anecdotes.

As the night progressed, the conversation was reduced to hilarious laughter, interspersed with terrible singing when a catchy song came over the speakers.

His attention was drawn to Brielle when her phone dinged with an incoming message. She flicked it open as it rested on the table-top. It was a picture of her mum, dad and sisters with their arms around each other, smiling.

He studied Brielle's reaction to it, the stillness that came over her. He could sense her uneasiness within his own body. She stood, blinking back tears, then rushed inside the house, closing the door behind her. He looked to the others, but they were too busy in conversation to notice.

He lurched to his feet and followed.

He found her in the kitchen, hands against the bench, head dipped between her shaking shoulders.

His heart ached with sympathy as he went to her and placed a hand on her back. 'Hey, Brie, what's the matter?'

She started at his touch, then sank back into it once she realised who it was. It took a few moments before she turned to look at him, wiping the tears from her cheeks as she did.

'I'm fine,' she said.

'You're not fine. You're crying.'

She drew in a shuddering breath and released it as a long sigh. 'I just feel like a bloody third wheel all the time. In my own family. Here they all are overseas having a holiday together and not once did they ever expect me to do anything besides housesit for them while they were gone. I know I'm an adult and have been living out of home for years, but they didn't even think to ask me to join them. I would have loved to have gone too.'

His frown was deep. 'I'm sorry you feel that way. I can't even imagine—'

She shook her head, threw her hands up, and then let them fall against her thighs with a slap. 'What does it matter? It's never going to bloody change.'

He supposed if it hadn't by now, she was probably right. 'I'm sorry,' he said again, unable to think of anything else to help soothe her wounds.

'I just hate that I feel like I don't belong, you know?' More tears fell and she didn't bother to swipe them away this time.

He stepped closer. 'Maybe you're trying to fit in with the wrong people. They might be your family, but sometimes that doesn't guarantee you'll feel like you belong.'

He knew this from how Poppy felt about her mother's comings and goings. Poppy was never going to feel like she belonged to her mother, and why would she? It didn't mean she couldn't have that sense of belonging with him and his extended family.

Perhaps it was the same for Brielle. 'Maybe you just need to find the right crowd who will accept you completely.'

Her eyes darted to his. 'There's only one place I've ever felt comfortable.' Her words were soft, hoarse.

He intuited the answer, but he asked anyway because he wanted to hear it for himself. 'And where is that?'

'Here,' she whispered.

His body screamed for him to take her in his arms, hold her tight and tell her that she always had a place here with his family … with him. He had thought so long and hard about this since his conversation with Macie and regardless of all the reasons for not pursuing a romance with Brielle, he couldn't find a good enough excuse not to.

So strong was his desire, these long-held feelings, that they trumped everything else he thought was more important.

Maybe because he had seen how great she was with his daughter and how understanding she was of Poppy's situation with her mother.

Maybe because he knew how well Brielle fit in with this family from the first moment she stepped through the door.

Maybe because Macie had given him his blessing.

But mostly, he damn well wanted Brielle so much, he was no longer able to resist. If he didn't have her in every way he needed, then he was afraid this deep throbbing desire and restlessness in his soul would never cease.

Yes, Brielle was flighty, but now he understood why. He could be the remedy to that. He could be the person she needed to feel safe, accepted, loved.

'Brielle,' he said and was surprised by how hoarse his voice was. 'I need to tell you something.'

She nodded.

'Remember how I told you I had a crush on you when I was younger?'

Again she nodded, her lips slightly parting as she listened. His body pulsed with the desire to lean over and take those lips between his.

He glanced away to regather his thoughts. It was now or never. If he didn't admit the truth to her, right here, he never would. He peered into her eyes. 'My feelings haven't changed. If anything, they've deepened.'

Her tongue ran over her bottom lip. Her chest rose and fell as her breaths deepened. 'I think I feel the same,' she whispered.

The edges of his lips curled. 'You *think* you feel the same?'

Her small smile mirrored his. 'I *know* I feel the same.'

Bliss worked through his body, into every fissure, every old scar, every vacant space. 'I want to be that safe place for you. I want you to know that I'm who you belong with, and, where I am, you'll always be accepted.'

Tears sprung to her eyes again, and he hoped like crazy they were happy tears. When she smiled, she confirmed his suspicions that they were.

He took another step closer, pushed his hand through her silky hair until his fingertips rested at her nape. His breaths were shallow in his throat as he anticipated kissing her. He burned to feel her lips, to taste her for the first time after so many years of imagining just how good it would be.

So slowly, he drew her face closer to his as he dipped his head. When their lips met, she sighed her appreciation. The sensuality in that sound surged through his body, tightening and tugging the muscles in the deepest pit of his stomach. Blood rushed through him, making his head light.

He opened his mouth and, with only the gentlest of coaxing, hers opened too. When their tongues met, his blood heated until he was fever high. He gripped her waist and she wrapped her arms around him, tugging him closer so that their bodies were warm and flush against each other.

Their kiss deepened, as did their breathing and the magnetism that pulled them together. Never had he felt like this—high, feverish.

And he wanted more, so much more he ached with the need. He pressed his growing erection against her belly and a moan tore from his throat. If he didn't pull away now, he was going to find himself in a very compromising position if any member of his family were to walk in.

With all his willpower, he pulled away from her. Face still close to hers, eyes intense, he said, breathlessly, 'You have no idea how long I've wanted to kiss you.'

She chuckled quietly. 'I think I have a fair idea.'

'Come back to my place tonight,' he said before he could filter his words.

She stared at him for a long moment, saying nothing. His stomach twisted as he awaited her answer. 'I'd like that.' Her cheeks flushed with colour; he'd never seen a more beautiful response in his life.

Just hearing those words from her sweet lips, he was hard as a rock, filled with brilliant anticipation.

She lifted up onto her tiptoes and dragged his head down until his lips met hers again. Their kiss was something different now, a precursor to what lay ahead.

Too soon, she shifted back from him, but just before she did, she whispered across his lips, 'Now.' Not a question, but more like a command. As though if they didn't get the hell out of there now, she would be forced to have sex with him right here.

Luke didn't know if he'd heard anything sexier in his life and because his own body echoed those exact sentiments, he nodded.

Feigning tiredness, Luke told the others he was leaving. Brielle innocently asked if he would mind dropping her home on the way.

Within ten minutes after extended goodbyes and ignoring suspicious looks, they were in his car, driving across the property to his house. Brielle had her hand high on his thigh. The heat from her touch was burning a hole through his flesh.

Before they had even got out of the car, they were kissing again—the sweetest Christmas kiss. And then he was lifting her out, carrying her through the front door and up to his bedroom.

What they then did together on his bed was so hot and sweet and everything he could never have imagined. Sex with Brielle was better than his mind could have conjured. The suppleness of her flesh beneath his palms. The slick warmth between her thighs on his fingers, then his tongue. And the exquisite pleasure as he pushed deep inside her, the writhing, the thrusting of her body as she searched for more and more, was beyond mere fantasy.

Brielle was solid and real in his arms, burning and panting as her legs wrapped around his. Soft and luscious naked skin against naked skin.

And when he took her there and she called his name, he lost himself in her, in them, the moment. His release was blistering. He could barely think, could barely speak, could only groan as he spilled deep inside her.

As she lay in his arms afterwards and they drifted off to sleep, he had the thought that there was no other Christmas present that had ever come close to Brielle.

Chapter 13

A soft buzzing alarm woke Brielle from her sleep. Early morning moonlight snaked through the cracks of the curtains, illuminating the bedroom in silvery light.

She rolled closer to the heat of Luke's naked body and silently willed him not to leave this bed.

He wrapped an arm around her waist, nestled his pelvis against the curve of her behind, and kissed her shoulder. 'Good morning.'

His voice was like rough silk, deep and gravelly. It strummed the strings of desire in her belly. Memories of last night played again and her body awakened with the need to feel Luke inside her.

She pushed back against his waking erection and he groaned. 'If you do that, I won't be able to tend to the cattle.'

She smiled teasingly to herself. 'Surely they could wait a little while longer.'

And wait they did, because she didn't need to hint twice before Luke rolled her onto her back, arched his strong body over hers and kissed her like her lips were life-giving.

Their lovemaking was slower this time, less frenzied than last night, but no less explosive.

Afterwards, as she lay on his chest, he stroked the hair from her forehead.

'I could get used to this,' he said and kissed her head.

She lifted up onto her elbow so she could look at his face. 'You mean that?'

'Absolutely. I want you, Brielle, in my bed, my heart, and in my life.'

When Luke had said to her last night that she belonged with him, any remaining doubts she once held had vanished. As she had looked into his earnest gaze, and heard the honesty in his voice, she knew with all her heart he was right.

She had nothing else, no other excuse, to continue to resist what was obviously so strong between them. To have someone say the exact words she had longed to hear—that she was accepted and would be loved—set the wrongs of her past right.

'I want the same,' she said and pressed her lips to his. When she reluctantly dragged herself away from the kiss, she was smiling.

'What?' he asked.

'I wished for you.'

His grin grew. 'Really? What do you mean?'

'I made a wish in the well at the fete that I would be guided in the right direction. I don't know if I can credit it with what's happened since, but it's like everything in my life was pointing me to you.'

'Either way, you got here in my arms, so I'm glad.'

'Me too.'

He kissed her sweetly, then frowned with apology. 'Now, why don't you try to go back to sleep. I'll come wake you up when I'm finished in the sheds.'

She nodded.

The bed was cold without him, but she managed to fall back to sleep. After what seemed like a single blink of her eyes, he was in her ear, gently calling her name.

The sun was streaming through the curtains. Luke was in fresh clothes, his hair wet, and he smelled like soap.

'Breakfast is nearly ready.'

A lazy smile arched her lips as she stretched. She could definitely get used to this.

After dressing, she met Luke in the kitchen. He was making pancakes. On the table were blueberries, yoghurt, farm fresh butter and maple syrup.

Her stomach rumbled as she went to him, grabbed his hips and planted a kiss on his face. His rough morning stubble was a delightful texture against her kiss-bruised lips. 'You're spoiling me.'

He grinned, twisted her, and before she knew it, her back was against the bench. She giggled as he lifted her, seated her on top, and kissed her hard on the mouth.

Brielle's body ignited in flames. His hands scorched her skin as they roamed over her hips and along her ribs.

'Daddy?' came a small, curious voice from behind them.

Luke jumped back from Brielle, while Brielle spun her head to find Poppy standing in the doorway, eyes wide, and Macie standing behind her, equally stunned.

'Um … should we come back later?' Macie asked.

Luke shook his head, clearing his throat as he went to them. 'Not at all. It's fine.' He was breathless.

Brielle's cheeks were burning. She slipped off the bench and stood on the opposite side, avoiding eye contact with Macie and Poppy.

'I didn't realise … I thought you … Poppy wanted to come home so she could play with her presents …' Macie stumbled.

'It's okay.' Luke crouched in front of Poppy and kissed her cheek. 'Good morning, gorgeous girl. Did you have a good sleep at Aunty Macie's?'

She nodded, but her eyes shifted behind Luke's wide shoulders to meet Brielle's gaze. 'Were you kissing Miss Lane?'

Luke stood, exhaling noisily. He tugged a hand through his dark hair. 'Ah … yes. I was.'

Poppy's eyes bulged again now that her suspicion was confirmed. 'Do you love her?'

Luke's gaze flickered to meet Brielle's. He smiled. 'It's something like that. Yes.'

Poppy jumped up and down on the spot, grinning and laughing. 'I knew Santa was real. Johnny Peterson was wrong. I knew he was.'

Macie gently touched the back of Poppy's hair. 'What's that got to do with Daddy kissing Brie?'

Poppy beamed up at them all, her missing teeth deepening the innocence of her smile. 'I made a wish in the well. I said that what I wanted for Christmas was for Daddy to love Miss Lane. And it came true.'

Brielle's heart thumped hard in her chest. Luke looked between Poppy and Brielle with an expression of wonderment. 'It looks like Santa did his job.'

'Yep. You wait until I tell Johnny at school.'

'Well then,' Macie said. 'Maybe I'll be asking for a boyfriend next Christmas if that's how simple it is.'

Brielle burst into laughter.

'I think there might have been a few other factors at play,' Luke said.

'Don't I know it,' Macie said. 'I've only had to witness this between the two of you for a good portion of my life. All I can say is that it's about bloody time.'

Now that Brielle had finally confronted her fear and gone after what she truly wanted, she had to admit she wished she had realised this many years earlier. But the heart could only love when it was ready and not before.

'Anyway, I'm going to leave you two alone. You sure you don't want me to take Poppy for the day?' Macie asked.

Luke shook his head. 'She's fine here. We're just about to have breakfast. You sure you don't want to stay?'

Macie eyed the pancakes. 'I guess I may as well.'

Luke grinned at his sister.

When they all sat down together, it wasn't strained or awkward. In fact, with the way they chatted and joked like they always had, and the way Luke would lean across and kiss her cheek every now and then, with Poppy laughing and asking her curious questions, it felt a lot like everything Brielle had ever wanted.

Above the Mistletoe

JULIET MADISON

To those I've lost, who will forever remain in my heart.

Chapter 1

'I quit!' Angelette Beaumont flung her handbag strap over her shoulder and stormed from the Manhattan showroom. It may have been silly to get upset by the singing Christmas telegram her boss had organised to generate Christmas cheer among staff, but this was the last straw. The last thread from the twisted cord holding her life together had finally unravelled.

She tightened the cashmere scarf around her neck, hailed a cab, and blurted her address to the driver.

She couldn't get to her apartment block fast enough. The cab stopped and started, caught in slow, heavy traffic, and the sparkly city seemed to be engulfing her from all directions. She kept her gaze fixed on the back of the driver's seat until she arrived home and, once in her apartment, turned on the heating and took off her coat, scarf, and gloves, flinging them onto the dining table.

A long, slow exhalation released from her lungs as she sunk into the couch.

No more.

No more tinsel and flashing lights, no more shiny gifts under over-decorated Christmas trees.

And no more Christmas.

She closed her eyes and willed herself to relax. But the beep of a text message made her jump. She switched her phone to silent, ignoring the message from a work colleague asking why she'd left so suddenly. She'd sort out the logistics of her rash decision later, but for now, she needed a reprieve. Angelette glanced around her plain but stylish apartment, void of any decorations. No, she needed more than that.

She needed to escape.

She went to her laptop on the dining table and opened a browser, tapping a fingernail on the keyboard while she thought of her options.

I need to get as far away from New York as possible.

Angelette found a world map and ran her finger across the screen, hoping the perfect place would jump right out at her.

Florida?

The Bahamas?

Mexico?

No, she needed somewhere completely different.

Her finger travelled across the map and down, to the cute little shape of Australia.

Yes.

Somewhere with sunshine and warmth, peace and quiet. Maybe a hidden tropical rainforest retreat, or a shack in the outback, or a cute cottage in a sleepy, small town. Somewhere it didn't feel like Christmas at all, where she wasn't faced with frantic, shallow consumerism, and where merry holiday travellers didn't bombard her in the streets.

And somewhere where the memory of last Christmas could be forgotten.

'Welcome to Seekers Hill, love.' The cab driver turned to her and smiled as he stopped the vehicle.

'Um, thanks.' Angelette shielded her eyes from the low glare in the sky. 'It's almost eight pm, shouldn't it be dark by now?'

The man chuckled. 'Daylight saving, love. Give it another hour.'

'All day sunshine? Sounds good to me.' She smiled at the thought and paid the driver a small fortune; it had been the only way to get here at this time after her never-ending flight, two hours on a train, and an hour on a hot bus with failing air conditioning until it reached its last stop where the cab had to take over for yet another hour.

She stepped from the car and heat slammed into her skin. She wriggled her toes, her legs aching from sitting for so long.

The driver lifted Angelette's suitcase from the trunk, or 'boot' as he called it.

'There you go. Hope you enjoy your stay, and have a merry—'

'Thank you, thank you, yes, yes, I will,' she interjected, before he could say the forbidden word.

Red dust swirled behind the cab as it took off, and Angelette exhaled slowly before wheeling her suitcase up the slight incline to the reception office of Seekers Hill Inn and Cottages.

A tinkle sounded as she pushed open the door, and she glanced up at a bundle of silver bells attached to a ribbon hanging from behind the door.

'Oh, I was just about to close up. Hi,' said a short woman from behind the desk with hair so tightly curled it looked like it was about to explode.

'Hi,' Angelette responded with an eager smile. She couldn't wait to get to her cottage and collapse on the bed.

'Can I assist you?' The woman gave her a curious look.

'Assist? Yes, I'm checking in, of course.'

The woman's eyebrows rose and her mouth formed an O shape. 'You are? Are you joining a guest who's already checked in?'

'No, I'm on my own.'

'Oh.' She tapped away at the computer and her eyebrows furrowed.

Angelette peered closer. 'Angelette Beaumont. I'm staying for ten nights, booked online recently.'

'Hmm.' The woman continued tapping away. 'That's strange. I don't seem to have anything on record.'

Angelette's heart beat a little faster.

'I'm sorry?' She peered even closer. 'I have my confirmation email. Here. I'll show you.' She got out her phone. 'Oh darn, it's out of charge.' She kicked a heel on the floor. 'Oh, hang on, I printed a copy too, in my travel documents wallet.' She got that out and smiled. 'Yes, here it is!' She handed it over and waited for the woman to say *oh of course, sorry about that! Here's your room key.*

But she didn't.

'That *is* strange,' the woman said, eyeing the paper and then the screen. 'One moment.' She typed something in and then her eyebrows rose and her cheeks flushed. 'Oh dear.'

'Oh dear what?'

The woman, from her seated position, looked up at Angelette with an awkward smile. 'It appears there's been some kind of technical error. A double booking.'

'Double booking?'

'I've found your booking, but unfortunately the guests who first booked your cottage have already checked in.' She folded her hands together on the desk.

Heat crawled up Angelette's face despite the air conditioning and her legs weakened. 'Um, no. It can't be. I booked this cottage. I got the confirmation. I came all the way from America to stay here. Surely your other guests can stay in a different room?'

The bells tinkled again and Angelette spun around. A man entered. 'Oh good, you're still open,' he said. 'Love the cottage, it's wonderful by the way.'

'Are you staying in the garden view cottage?' Angelette interrogated him.

'Yes, we are. Why?'

'Right. Well, the thing is …' Angelette crossed her arms and was about to tell him about her situation when the man interrupted.

'Look, sorry, I'm only popping in quickly as I need something for my wife.' He looked at the woman behind the desk. 'Do you have an ice pack or something cold? Her ankles are so swollen from the heat and the pregnancy, and she's really uncomfortable at the moment. I need to get back to her.'

The words that Angelette had been about to speak dissolved, and she fiddled with the teardrop pendant nestled between her collarbones.

'Sure, let me grab one for you.' The woman went into the back room and returned with a couple of ice packs. 'These should help. And if there are any other concerns, please call our after-hours emergency number.'

'Will do. Thanks so much!' He dashed out.

Angelette's shoulders sunk and she sighed. 'Well, can you put me in a different cottage then? Or even a room at the inn?'

The woman shook her head. 'I'm afraid all our cottages and rooms are booked out until after Christmas.'

'Are you saying there's no room for me at the inn?' The high-pitched inflection at the end of her question accompanied her rising anxiety.

'I am. I'm so sorry. But rest assured we will refund your deposit immediately.'

'Rest assured? How can I rest assured when I don't have anywhere *to* rest!' Angelette planted her hands on the desk.

The woman stood. 'Let me call around and ask if there's anywhere else for you to stay. But there's not much around here, the closest available room could be hours away, and that's if they're not all taken.'

Oh man, this can't be happening.

Angelette tapped a foot impatiently while she waited for the woman to ask around, her chest rising with hope then falling at each, 'Thanks anyway,' that the woman spoke into the phone.

The woman sighed, her cheeks still flushed. 'I really am very sorry.'

'I'm sure you are. But right now, sorry won't cut it. I'm exhausted, I'm jet lagged, I need a good sleep, a shower, some food, and I need to charge my phone!'

Her eyes pinched back tears. Her vacation hadn't even begun and already it was starting to resemble yet another Christmas disaster— just like the past three years.

'Here.' The woman handed her a bag of potato crisps. 'On the house.' Then she handed her a can of soda. 'This too.'

Angelette shrugged and mumbled a thank you.

The woman tapped her chin. 'Hmm. There might be one place you could stay.'

'There *might* be? Just get me something. Anything!'

The woman nodded and picked up the phone again. 'Hello, Mac? Hi, it's Cherie from Seekers Hill Inn. Do you have a vacancy in your room above the pub?'

A pub? That didn't sound too bad. Maybe a bit noisy but at least there'd be food and she could drown her sorrows in red wine until she could find alternative accommodation.

'Yes, yes, I understand, but she is quite desperate.'

Gee, thanks.

'Uh-huh. Uh-huh.' The woman nodded.

Please, please, please! Please don't let anyone else be about to take it!

'Yes, well I'm sure it'll be fine, please book her in. Angelette Beaumont.' The woman straightened up. 'Thanks, Mac. Please bill her first night's accommodation to us and we'll cover it. Thank you, merry Christmas to you too.'

Angelette relaxed her shoulders with an exhalation. This was more like it. And they sure as hell *should* be paying for her after this disastrous mix-up. Once she'd had a wash and a good sleep, she could search online for somewhere else to stay, or maybe even this pub would be a decent enough getaway from the world of Christmas for a while. She could read all the books she'd downloaded to her Kindle and live in another world for the next ten days. Perfect.

The woman, Cherie, handed her a piece of paper with scribbled words on it:

The Mistletoe.

'Mistletoe?'

'Yes. That's the name of the pub, it's only about a twenty-five-minute drive up the hill, and they've reserved the room above it just for you. It's right in the heart of the lovely little town. You'll have a beautiful view of the hills, and there's a general store, an art gallery, an antique shop, a lovely community park, and the local historic cinema is screening Christmas films every day until Christmas! You'll have a wonderful time there.' Cherie smiled in satisfaction.

Angelette narrowed her eyes. She'd definitely avoid the cinema, but the art gallery might be nice, and a shady spot in the park to read some books. But a pub named after a Christmas novelty? How bizarre. Did they even have mistletoe in Australia?

Anyway, it was just a name. And now she had somewhere to stay tonight. It couldn't be that bad.

Chapter 2

'Oh, dear God.' Angelette paid the cab driver for the second time that night with the brightly-coloured cash Cherie had given her as compensation.

'I hope this one works out for you, love. Enjoy, and have a—'

'Thank you, thank you, yes, you too.' She gave the cab driver a quick smile and closed the door before he could say it.

She eyed the monstrosity and took what she hoped would be a calming breath. It didn't work. The pub, although cute and quaint with its mismatched bricks in the outside walls and swirly wrought-iron sign with 'The Mistletoe' painted on it, glowed like a beacon with an oversupply of fairy lights, tinsel, and a bright red and green wreath on the front door.

It's just the outside, she said to herself. *To draw in the customers. Those who* like *Christmas.*

The inside would be a simple country pub, and her room would most likely be a modest but functional space in which to rest one's head.

She lifted her suitcase up the three steps to the ajar front door, light from inside forming a triangle on the doorstep, and stepped into the narrow entryway.

The scent of alcohol reminded her that she could relax with a nice glass of wine soon, and her stomach grumbled with the scent of roast potatoes and lamb.

But when she went to step from the rectangle-shaped entryway into the pub itself, she was met with a strong, bare, muscled arm blocking the way in front of her.

She looked up to its owner, a thirty-something man wearing a Santa hat.

'No one comes in here without following the rules,' he said, a sneaky smile threatening to form on his lips.

'Rules? Um, sure. That's no problem, I'm sober and respectable and I'm wearing appropriate clothing, so I can't see any issues. I'm just here to check in. And then get a meal, and something to drink.'

She glanced inside. Bright, shiny, sparkly crap stung her eyes from every direction. She would have to try her hardest to avoid looking around at all the Christmas decorations, or ask for the meal to be taken up to her room. But despite scoffing the potato chips and soda while waiting for the cab, she was so hungry she was sure all her focus would be on the plate in front of her.

'I mean the *Christmas* rules,' he added.

She raised her eyebrows.

'No one comes in here without wearing a Christmas accessory. Pub policy.'

Oh, dear God. What kind of place was this? And who did he think he was, telling her what she had to wear?

She crossed her arms. 'Oh, I'm sorry, I must have forgotten to bring my Santa hat. Oh well, I'll just come on in and get to my room.' She tried to shove past him.

'Uh-uh.' He stood close and crossed his arms too like a bouncer at a nightclub. 'For situations like these, we have contingency plans.'

Her eyebrows rose even higher, compressing the headache that had begun to form.

He gestured to a basket on the floor in the corner of the entryway. 'A plentiful supply of accessories to choose from. Take your pick.'

Angelette glanced down at the basket she'd failed to notice before and the music from *Jaws* blared in her mind. 'Umm, maybe some other time.' She forced a friendly smile. 'Now if I could just get to my room?' She tugged at her suitcase.

The man softened his stance and unfolded his arms. 'Angelette, I presume? I'm Mac.' He held out his hand and she slid hers into his, its warmth surprising her—most handshakes in New York at this time of year were either cold and icy, or soft and fluffy from wearing gloves and mittens.

'Nice to meet you,' she said. 'Thanks for giving me a room. I've travelled a long way.'

'So I hear. Let me show you to your room.' He picked up her suitcase and stepped onto the nearby staircase with a loud creak. 'Follow me.' She stepped up along with him. 'But if you want dinner, you'll need to abide by our rules. No Christmas accessory, no dinner.' He shrugged.

She held back an insult. 'I'll have dinner in my room then.'

'We don't do room service I'm afraid, have to keep a constant eye on the patrons. If you want to have your dinner in your room, you'll have to come down and get it and then bring back your dirty plate afterwards.'

They reached the top of the stairs. 'So I'll order a pizza.' She huffed.

He laughed. 'Good luck. It might arrive in about three hours. There's no delivery service in this neck of the woods.'

'Then I'll go to the store and buy some supplies and make my own.'

'Store closes at five every day.'

Angelette lowered her head and rubbed her left temple. She didn't know how to handle a crowd of happy holiday-goers right now.

'Here you go.' He gestured to a closed door on the left of the landing. 'That's your room.' He gestured to another next to it. 'And that's the bathroom.'

She eyed the third door.

'And that's someone else's room. You have to share the bathroom facilities, I'm afraid. But there's a lock so just knock on the door and if it's free you're good to go.'

Oh, wonderful.

Mac unlocked the door to her room and pushed it open, a loud squeak sounding. 'Oops, forgot to put some WD-40 on it. I'll do that later.'

Angelette stepped inside the room and when the light flickered on, she gasped. Not exactly the deluxe cottage she'd been looking forward to. The beige walls had peeling paint in the corners, the floral wallpaper borders were more degenerative than decorative, and the weathered wooden bed frame looked like it had spent twenty years in full sunlight.

'It's not that bad,' Mac said, wandering around the stuffy room, and opening the window a little higher. 'Just waiting for some more fresh air to filter in, and I've already cleaned and vacuumed it.'

She glanced at the thin and patchy carpeted floor, the odd stain here and there.

He switched on the ceiling fan which made a clunky sound with every rotation.

Angelette eyed him carefully. 'When was the last time someone stayed in here? Willingly?'

He chuckled. 'Umm, I think it was … ahh, oh, I can't remember. Anyway, you have a drawer full of clean linen here …' He pulled open a drawer. 'Washing machine is in the bathroom. And I almost forgot! I even put chocolates under your pillow.' He shoved the pillow aside and smiled with a satisfied nod.

There lay a chocolate bar that was deformed from being half melted.

Her stomach grumbled, but she ignored it. 'I have to do my own laundry and make up my own bed?'

'If you want clean sheets after a few days, yes.'

Angelette put her hands on her hips and assessed the room. 'I'll probably only be here for one night. First thing tomorrow I'll be searching for alternative accommodation.'

'I thought Cherie had looked into other options for you and failed to find anything close.'

'Well, yes. But there has to be *something*. I'll arrange my own transport to get there if I have to.' She gave a nod and looked around for a power point to charge her phone.

'Good luck. In the meantime, come downstairs and enjoy a delicious dinner before our kitchen closes. Then there's a café across the road that does a decent breakfast, or if you prefer you can buy some supplies from the general store which opens at seven. And if you like, there's …' His voice trailed off as she plugged her charger into a power point near the old closet. 'Hang on, I wouldn't put that in there, it might …'

A spark shot out from the power point when she attached her phone to the cable and switched it on. 'Agh!' She quickly unplugged it. 'Did I use the wrong one?' She examined it. 'No, this is the special one I got for Australia.'

'Um, yeah, it's a bit wonky, that power point. Haven't had a chance to get it fixed yet.' He pointed to the bed. 'There's another under there.'

'Under?'

'Yep. At the head of the bed, underneath. I'd put it in for you, but I can't squeeze my arm down there and can't fit underneath the bed.'

'Oh.'

'I could move the bed for you, but with the state of the frame I'm worried it could, ah …'

'Collapse.' She eyed the lopsided tilt of the frame towards a chipped bed knob. She didn't want to think what could have possibly led to that. He gave a quick nod and scratched his head. 'Don't worry, the mattress is all new and the sheets are clean, but I haven't been in a position to update the furniture yet, sorry.'

She sighed. 'Oh well, it'll have to do.' She sat carefully on the bed and reached her hand between the bedhead and the wall, feeling for the power point. 'Aha.' She stuck the charger in and switched it on, bracing herself for a spark, but luckily the only light was the charging symbol appearing on her phone.

She sat up and exhaled.

'Towels are over there.' He pointed to a chair next to a small desk. 'And I guess I'll see you downstairs shortly.' He slid his hands into his pockets and rose up and down on his toes.

'Guess so. Thanks.'

He smiled and turned, then turned back. 'Oh, your key.' He tossed it her way and she caught it.

'Nice reflexes considering your jet lag.'

With all the upheaval of the last hour or so her nerves were on high alert. Her stomach grumbled. 'Oh, is there a minibar?'

'Nothing mini here. But if you mean a small fridge, then that can be arranged.'

'Yes, please.'

He held up his pointer finger and turned. 'Be right back.'

He returned, his arms bulging from lugging in a small white refrigerator from the room across the hall. He went to plug it into the wonky power point but hesitated. 'Hmm.' He manouvered the closet sideways a little. 'Aha. Forgot this one was here.' He plugged in the refrigerator to a hidden point in the corner.

'Thanks.' She glanced through the doorway to the landing. 'Doesn't the person in the other room need it?'

'Nope. I'm good.' He stood.

'It's your room?'

'Yep.'

Mac smiled and left, and she took a few minutes to acquaint herself with the room, checking every corner and crevice for the deadly bugs the media warned about in Australia, and her stomach grumbled again.

It was inevitable she'd have to go downstairs. Maybe a good meal would distract her from her negative emotions. She only hoped Mac would take pity on her situation and relax his Christmas rules, just for tonight.

Chapter 3

'Nope, rules are rules. The basket is there, knock yourself out.' Mac grinned at Angelette, as she stood at the door to the pub a few minutes later.

'You are kidding, right?'

He shook his head.

'I don't like to celebrate Christmas.'

'Everyone here joins in the fun. It's the rules, passed down by my father,' he pointed his thumb over his shoulder, 'who's inside by the way, and *his* father before that, though he's *not* inside. Family tradition. You can't mess with family tradition.' He crossed his arms.

She sighed in resignation and bent down. 'Well, alright then, I'll just find something discreet and be done with it so I can eat. But don't expect me to be happy about it.'

She rummaged through the items: reindeer antler headband, sparkly clip-on dangly earrings, Rudolf's red nose, a couple of Santa hats, an elf hat, a tinsel garland, and other similar items. 'There's nothing discreet in here.' She turned and looked up, but Mac was in conversation with someone near the door. She rummaged some more.

'Thanks for a great night, Mac, see you again tomorrow!' A woman with a smile wider than the off-the-shoulder neckline of her dress tumbled out through the doorway, laughing as she tripped on the floor-length hem. 'Whoops, knew I should have had this taken up. Oh, I better return this.' She unclipped a thick elastic belt from around her waist, the bells hanging from it jingling a bit too loudly for Angelette's tolerance levels as it landed in the box in front of her.

'Found something suitable?' Mac asked, eyeing the box.

'Nope. Aren't there any understated Christmassy bracelets, or anklets, by any chance?'

'Whatever's in there is all we've got.'

She picked up the belt, each bell connected to the others by a sparkling tinsel-like ribbon. A fake poinsettia adorned the front where the clasp joined.

'Good choice. I was going to wear that last night, but ...' He gestured to his abdomen, which showed no signs of being fond of alcohol or greasy food. 'Didn't fit.'

'I haven't chosen it yet; I was just looking.' She rummaged again to make sure she hadn't missed any less Christmassy options. She looked up at Mac, whose stance hadn't budged and, by the looks of it, his rules wouldn't either. She sighed again. 'Guess it'll have to do.' She clipped it around her waist.

Mac grinned. 'Welcome to The Mistletoe, come on in!' He held open the door, and she lowered her head as she jingled into the pub.

Jolly chatter, laughter, and Christmas music rushed into her ears, and she resisted the urge to cover them. Her skin tingled with the change in temperature from humid heat to refreshing air conditioning, and she felt all eyes on her as she walked through the crowd, most likely all locals by the way they seemed as comfortable as if in their own homes. Her Christmas belt was a minor attraction compared to some of the more exuberant accessories people wore. One woman had Rudolf the reindeer earrings with a flashing red nose, so large and dangly her earlobes practically touched her shoulders, and a man wore elf boots with jingly baubles on the upward-curving pointy toes.

This place was downright silly.

'I'm assuming you'd like somewhere reasonably quiet to sit?' Mac asked, ushering her to one corner of the pub, past the bar and near the entrance to the restrooms.

She gave a curt nod. 'Please.'

He gestured to a table for two and pulled out a chair for her. She sat and he placed a menu in front of her. 'Whatever you like. On the house, courtesy of the Seekers Hill Inn satisfaction guarantee.'

'I didn't know they had a satisfaction guarantee.'

'They do now.'

So they should, she thought to herself.

She eyed the menu and her eyes stung at the green and red shiny Christmas tree ornament in the middle of the table. Bangers and mash? What on earth was that? Rissoles. Schnitzel. Chips. She longed for a pumpkin and spinach risotto with pine nuts like her chef friend served in her cosy NYC restaurant, but they had no such thing. 'I'll have a pizza with the lot, thanks. And fries. And those chicken skewer things for entrée. Oh, and extra cheese on the pizza too, please. And a glass of your best red. Or maybe a bottle, and I'll take it to my room.'

Mac's eyebrows rose and he nodded, jotting it down on a pocket notepad. 'Happy to help if you can't eat or drink it all.'

'No help needed. But thanks.' She would ask for a take-out container and have the leftovers for breakfast.

Before too long she was devouring her meal, and her annoyance at her predicament softened with the comfort of a full stomach of tasty food. She sat still for a few moments after, grateful Mac had the decency to let her eat in peace as he served other customers their drinks. She stood, stretched, and made her way to the bar to thank Mac and ask for a take-out container to bring the leftovers up to her room. As she leant against the bar, he gestured to a partially bald man with leathery tanned skin who sat on a barstool.

'This is my father, Ned.' Ned nodded and smiled, held out his hand, grasping hers with a warm handshake. 'Co-owner of this fine establishment and kitchen all-rounder.'

'Oh, hello, nice to meet you.'

'Likewise. How was your food? I made sure to supervise our chef and ensure your satisfaction, extra cheese and all.'

She smiled. 'It was delicious, thank you. Actually, I was going to ask, could I take the leftovers up to my room?'

Ned sprang to his feet quicker than she expected. 'Onto it.'

He returned moments later with a container. 'Feel free to come by in the morning and we can heat them up, or give you a fresh meal if you prefer.'

'Oh no, that's okay, cold pizza is still good. Mac put a refrigerator in my room.'

'Microwave.' Mac held up a finger. 'I'll have our spare one brought up shortly. No need to have cold food, although in this heat it may be a welcome change.'

'Really, it's no issue, I'll—'

'Not at all, anything we can do to make your stay more comfortable, we'll do,' Ned interjected.

She shrugged and nodded. But with any luck she'd be gone by mid-morning and on her way to somewhere more suitable for her anti-Christmas vacation.

'One more, one more, Mac, me man,' an older man mumbled nearby, holding up a shot glass. 'Nah, make it two.'

Angelette looked away, not wanting to watch someone get stupidly drunk and no doubt try to hit on her as she walked by, like so many in the past.

'Whoa!' the man exclaimed after his glass clunked on the bar. 'I think it's really kicking in now. Another, me man, another.'

Geez. Did they really encourage people to destroy their health with alcohol? Then again, she did have a bottle of wine in her hand. But at least it had antioxidants.

Angelette glanced at the glass as Mac refilled it. She narrowed her eyes.

'Soda water.' Ned gently nudged her. 'But don't let him know. Our beloved Barry. He's, ah, not *all there.*'

'Ah.' Angelette tilted her head back in understanding.

'He's the heart and humour of this place and we like to look out for him. Used to be a drunk. Got sober, but by the time he did, the damage was done and he suffered a stroke,' Ned whispered.

Angelette felt a surge of sympathy. Barry's gaze caught hers just as she was about to say her goodnights. 'Well, hello. Merry Christmas, young lass. Welcome to my pub.'

She raised her eyebrows at Mac, who shook his head, then reached his arm over the bar to pat Barry on the back. 'Baz used to help us out a lot here, didn't you Baz? Anyway, Angelette is staying at the pub tonight, there was a mix-up at Seekers Hill Inn and they didn't have room.'

Barry held up his hands in the air, then they fell with a slap onto the bar.

'Oh! What an apostrophe!' He shook his head in dismay.

Ned chuckled. 'Catastrophe, Barry, *catastrophe.*'

'Yes, that's what I said. Such an apostrophe, this young lady getting kicked out of the inn.' He frowned. 'Don't you worry, me lass, you'll be taken good care of here.'

She offered an amused smile and Mac covered his mouth with his hand, hiding a suppressed laugh.

She said goodnight, dropped her Christmas belt into the accessory basket, and walked up to her room, the heat from the pub entrance following her up the stairs.

She grabbed a towel and knocked on the bathroom door before opening it. She locked it behind her, and within moments she exhaled in relief as refreshing water ran down her back, wishing it would wash away all the memories of her last Christmases.

Chapter 4

'Huh?' Angelette squinted as light invaded her closed eyes. She rubbed her ears as a vaguely familiar clunking sound continued. Disoriented, she glanced up at the wobbly ceiling fan, then scrambled around the bed to find her phone, unplugged it and gasped when she saw it was past twelve pm. She hadn't drifted off till three am and even then sleep had been sporadic.

The fog of jet lag coaxed her head back down on the pillow. She checked her emails, hoping for a 'Yes! We have a room for you, we'll see you tonight for check-in,' but there was nothing except 'All our rooms are booked out, I'm afraid,' and 'Sorry, but we can book you in advance for next Christmas?'

Next Christmas? Were they serious? She needed to sort out accommodation for *this* Christmas and certainly wouldn't be coming back here *next* Christmas. Next year, she'd find an affordable remote island to stay at.

Even the travel agents she'd contacted late last night had said they wouldn't be able to get her anything decent until the twenty-seventh of December, the day she was due to fly back to the States.

Angelette sighed. Unless a miracle occurred, or the pregnant woman in her room at the inn went into labour and the couple relocated to the hospital, she'd be stuck here in the town of mistletoe and crazy Christmas costumes for another nine nights.

She rolled onto her side and yawned, the mattress surprisingly comfortable despite the bed's lopsided tilt. Maybe it wasn't so bad after all, and at least she'd caught up on some sleep, though more would be welcome. Angelette resisted the desire to doze off again and heaved herself up off the bed. She needed to get adjusted to the time zone ASAP. Dragging the curtain aside, more light and heat streamed in.

Might as well go for a wander and find out what this town has to offer in the way of coffee, pampering, shady reading spots, and peace and quiet …

After scoffing the leftover pizza and downing a glass of water from the pitcher Mac had brought up along with the microwave last night, she put on a white slip dress and sandals and went downstairs.

Barry from last night entered the small foyer and picked up a necklace of tinsel and jingly bells, slipping it over his head. 'Ah! Lovely lass, Andrea, was it?'

'Angelette,' she replied. 'Hi, Barry.'

'You joining me for lunch? What a nice treat that would be, if I do say so meself.'

She smiled. 'Sorry, I'm going for a walk to check out the town. Maybe get a massage if I'm lucky. But you enjoy your lunch.'

'Ooh, a massage,' he responded, just as Mac opened the door to the pub, nodding a good morning to her, or good afternoon more like it. 'Nothing like a massage to release all those dolphins.'

'Sorry?'

'A massage, it makes you feel so good, eh?'

'Oh, you mean *endorphins*, Barry,' said Mac.

'Oh yes, sorry! Endolphins, I meant to say.'

Angelette caught Mac's eyes with a subtle smile.

'You go on in, Baz. Sandy will look after you for lunch, I'm off for the afternoon with Tilly.'

'Rightio, me man. Give the lovely lady a big hug for me.'

'Will do.' Mac clapped him on the back, and Barry entered the pub whistling a Christmas tune.

Mac, Ned, Baz, Sandy, Tilly ... did anyone in this town have names that weren't shortened?

'How'd you sleep?' Mac asked, as they both stepped out of the pub. 'Wait. Don't answer.' He held up his palm. 'I know you're jet lagged and the bed probably isn't the most comfortable. Just tell me something positive about your first night stay and I'll be happy with that.'

'Hmm,' she said, 'well, the dinner was lovely, as you know, and the pitcher with a lemon wedge was thoughtful. However, I've had no luck finding somewhere else to have my vacation.'

His blue eyes held a subtle glint in the midday sun. 'In that case, I hope you enjoy your first Christmas at Seekers Hill! It's a great little town, you know.'

She chewed the corner of her lip. 'I'm sure it is. I'm not here to celebrate Christmas though, just have some time away from all the noise and lights and tinsel of New York City.'

'Fair enough.' Mac slipped his hands into his pockets. 'May I ask why you don't like Christmas?'

Angelette's stomach dropped and the ground beneath her feet felt like quicksand. She folded her arms and glanced across the road. 'Oh good, the general store. I'll grab some supplies later.'

'Angelette?'

'Sorry. Ask me anything but that.'

'Sure. Okay, I'll ask the most overused question in the history of questions. What do you do for a living?'

Oh great. The second worst question at this point in time. Warmth rose up her neck and cheeks.

'Um. I just work in a, um, showroom place.'

No need to explain that she'd actually quit and was currently unemployed.

'Oh cool, what do you *show*?'

She shrugged. 'Just bathroom stuff, you know, toilets and things. Toilets. Just toilets, actually.'

Mac raised his eyebrows. 'Oh. Cool.'

'I used to be a designer, but ...' She unfolded her arms to hold up her hands as though in defeat.

'Of toilets?'

'No, an interior designer and decorator. But, well, that's in the past and for now I'm just working in a toilet showroom in Manhattan.'

'Manhattan would be an exciting place to live and work, I bet. Never been there myself.'

'It is ... but is that your way of downplaying the *non-exciting* place I work at?' She tilted her head with a curious gaze at Mac.

'Of course not. Everyone needs them.'

Her face got warmer.

'Oh, no need to get all flushed.'

She flushed even more.

'I mean embarrassed. Sorry! Accidental pun.'

'No offence taken.'

'I mean, you have a job and that's the main thing. I've been working in a pub all my life. I'm sure toilet sales are a bit more exciting sometimes. You gotta work, right? And it's better than following a pipe dream.'

Her eyes widened. 'When I come in for dinner tonight you're probably going to tell all the patrons about my occupation, aren't you?' She crossed her arms again.

He held up his palms to face her. 'No, no, don't worry. I'll keep my lid shut.'

She cast him an *I'm not amused* glance.

'I'll make sure you're not the butt of every joke.' He winked.

She shook her head and turned away.

'Seriously, though, Ange ...'

'Angelette,' she corrected.

'Angelette. I won't, I promise. And that's the end of my jokes, too. Sorry. I couldn't resist. I get it from my father.'

She waved away his apology. 'Nothing wrong with a sense of humour, I guess.'

'It's one of life's greatest gifts. You're welcome to make as many jokes as you like about me and my job too. Go for it. I mean, you're a professional, you're cultured and travelled, and I'm in the same place I've always been, never given anything else a go, really. You're way ahead of me in the ambition department.'

She observed his gentle eyes that really didn't seem to hold any sense of curiosity of life beyond this place. 'You never wanted to venture out into the big wide world?'

She became aware that somehow they had begun walking along the street together.

He shrugged. 'I backpacked a bit in my twenties, but not for long and I always came back. I dunno, it's just ... home, you know?'

She nodded, but she didn't know.

With a life growing up in multiple different locations and five different foster homes before she turned eighteen, *home* was the pipe dream to her.

'You're lucky,' she said. 'Your dad seems nice. Is your whole family here?'

He lowered his head a little and kicked a twig off the sidewalk.

'Mum passed away six years ago, and my ...' He looked far into the distance, squinting. 'And it's just us. Me, Dad, and Tilly.'

'Your wife?'

He laughed. 'I don't think she'll be anyone's wife for at least another couple of decades or so.'

Oh. A daughter.

As they reached the park, a young girl with wavy brown pigtails came skipping up to him, Ned a few paces behind.

'Uncle Mac!' *Wrong again. Niece.* 'Look what I found.' The girl handed Mac a small pebble that was painted with the words *Ho! Ho! Ho!* 'Grandad says one of Santa's elves has been leaving them around town for people to find.'

'How cool is that!' Mac held the pebble up to the sunlight. 'Oh wow, can you see it?'

'See what?' she asked.

He knelt down and held the pebble closer to her eyes. 'A bit of sparkle. Do you think it's ...'

'... magic elf dust?' Her eyes widened and looked directly into her uncle's.

Mac nodded.

Tilly held the pebble close to her chest and grinned widely. 'I'm going to find more! Let's go!' She yanked Mac's hand.

'Hold your horses, missy.' He gently turned Tilly to face Angelette. 'Don't forget your manners.'

'Oh,' the girl said, her sweet little voice a stark contrast to all the masculine ones Angelette had been exposed to up till now. 'Hi. What's your name? I'm Tilly. Matilda, actually.'

Angelette's heart fluttered at such pure childhood innocence. She bent forwards a little, holding out her hand. 'I'm Angelette. It's lovely to meet you, Tilly. I mean, Matilda.'

The girl's soft as silk skin met hers. 'Wow! Is that like an angel's name?'

Angelette smiled.

'Uncle Mac.' She turned and looked up at him. 'Is she an angel? Is she working with the elves?' She turned back and lightly pinched Angelette's hand. 'Are you really an angel?'

Angelette knelt down to her eye level. 'No, it's just my name. But maybe there are some secret angels around here, who knows?' She glanced around as though looking.

'I'll keep my eye out,' Tilly said.

'Me too.' Angelette winked and straightened up.

Angelette ... her name had always attracted compliments, but she hadn't been named by doting parents. Apparently one of the carers had picked it because she was the only child in her care to sleep easily through the night—peaceful like an angel. Angelette wished she could have stayed with her, or someone like her, but by the time she'd found parents who wanted her, she was nearing adulthood and didn't want *them,* deciding instead to forge her own independent life. Though Angelette didn't know where Tilly's parents were, or if either of them were in the picture, she was lucky to have Mac and Ned and looked like a well-cared-for girl.

Mac gave her a thankful smile, then got out his phone. 'Let me give you my number; if you have any problems while you're here, or need anything, call me, okay?'

She nodded, adding him as a contact after he texted his number to her, and waved goodbye as she walked further down the street and Tilly began searching nearby shrubs around the park for more pebbles.

Ho! Ho! No. She couldn't let herself get caught up in any Christmas frivolities, as much as she used to enjoy the fun of the season.

She would have to make the most of her vacation, any way she could manage with the cards she'd been dealt, just like she had done her whole life.

Chapter 5

She'd avoided the cinema with its Christmas screenings, and had enjoyed the air-conditioned comfort of the art gallery momentarily until she'd realised their latest exhibition was a photography showcase entitled 'Christmas Around the World'. But, despite the local antique and second-hand bookstore's tinsel decorated shelves, she had scored a decent copy of a bestselling suspense novel to while away her time under a tree in the park.

She crunched an apple then tossed the core into the shrubs behind the tree. She'd just turned the page on a cliffhanger in the book when two pairs of feet stopped in front of her. She glanced up to meet the gaze of a smiley pair of teenagers as one of them thrust a piece of paper towards her.

'Hi! I hope you'll be at our Christmas Carols in the Park tomorrow night; can we count on you to be there and support underprivileged children?'

'Oh.' She reluctantly took the flyer and her eyes skimmed over it. 'I'm not actually sure that—'

'Every purchase of an LED candle will go towards charity,' one of the girls piped up, 'and we'll have a lemonade stand and a sausage sizzle!'

Angelette nodded. 'Thanks for letting me know.' She offered a smile but stole a glance back at her book. She didn't want to be rude, but she was finally enjoying some time on her own. 'Well, maybe I'll see you there,' Angelette said, if only to satisfy their mission so they could move on to the next potential attendee.

'We'll keep an eye out for you!' one of them chimed, and they bounced off.

Angelette turned the page but had to turn back again to remember what the cliffhanger had been. She yawned. It must be about bedtime in New York. She persevered and read on, hoping to gather momentum, but moments later she gasped after dropping the book having suddenly nodded off to sleep.

Oh, might as well surrender, just for a bit.

She put the flyer between the pages and closed the book, placing it on her lap and leaning her head against the tree trunk behind her.

Fragmented dreams of singing elves and a garden overflowing with painted pebbles intruded into her mind and she woke on and off.

The next thing she knew, she woke to find a pebble at her feet. Or was she still dreaming? 'Huh?'

Her gaze refocused and she looked up. Tilly was standing in front of her.

'Oopsie, I tried to not wake you up!' The girl covered her mouth with her hands and giggled. 'I just wanted to leave a pebble here for you so you could have a special Christmas gift from the elves.'

'Tilly,' Mac called out on his approach. 'Sorry,' he said to Angelette, 'she's quick on her feet this girl.'

'That's okay. I need to adjust my body clock and shouldn't really be sleeping until tonight anyway.' She picked up the pebble, a blue background and a white star painted on it. 'Don't you want to keep it?' She held it out to Tilly.

She shook her head. 'I found *four* others.' She held up four fingers, and Mac patted the heavy pockets on his cargo shorts. 'This one is for you.' She smiled.

Angelette couldn't object to such a gift, so she thanked her and placed it on top of her book. 'Well, it's lovely. Thank you, Tilly.'

The girl twirled happily from side to side. 'Will you be at the carols tomorrow night?'

'Me? No, I think I might be, um, busy with something tomorrow night.'

It wasn't a complete lie. She would be resting in her room with more reading material.

'But it's the bestest most amazing night of the year! Apart from Christmas Eve. And—'

'Tilly, I don't think Angelette can make it, sweetie. Let her enjoy some peace and quiet, hey?' He gestured for her to come to him.

Her smile flattened and she trudged back to her uncle.

A touch of guilt twisted inside. 'Tilly, what were you about to say?' Angelette asked.

The girl turned back to face her.

'That I'm going to be on stage for the first time ever.' She beamed. 'At eighty-fifteen o'clock pm.' She gave a firm nod.

'Eight-fifteen,' Mac corrected.

'On stage? Wow,' Angelette remarked. 'Wait.' She tapped her finger against her temple. 'I think I may have seen you before. Are you …' she leaned forward, '… famous?'

Tilly giggled and covered her mouth again. 'No, silly.'

'Not yet, anyway,' Mac said. 'She's singing. With her kindergarten class, and a solo.'

Angelette stood and placed her hands on her hips. 'A solo? Well you must be famous then. Only famous people do solos.'

Tilly tucked one pigtail behind her ear.

'Angelette is here to relax and have some time out, Tilly.' Mac eyed his niece. 'There'll be plenty of other people to watch you perform. Me included. I'll be in the front row,' he said proudly.

'Oh, but I want the angel to come too. She's pretty. And she reminds me of ...' The girl lowered her head and Angelette's heart sank.

Her mother?

'You know what?' Angelette poised her finger in the air as though remembering something. 'Silly me. I'm not really busy tomorrow night. I must be getting my days confused. I'll be there at eighty-fifteen sharp.'

What am I doing?

'You will? Yay!' Tilly jumped on the spot. 'Uncle Mac, she's coming!'

'So I heard.' Mac glanced her way and mouthed *thank you*.

'What are you singing?'

'It's a surprise,' she said, and skipped off towards the playground equipment.

Mac hung about. 'So are you going to tell me or not?'

'Tell you what?'

'Why you're so against Christmas? It can't be that bad if you're agreeing to come to our most Christmassy event of the year.'

Oh, it was.

'Well, your adorable niece's invitation *was* pretty irresistible.' She smiled, then sighed, leaning back against the tree. Mac sat next to her, waving at Tilly as she slid down the slide. 'The thing is,' she added, 'my last three Christmases, I've had bad stuff happen.'

Mac nodded.

'Three years ago, I'd scored an awesome design job, but then the company went bust due to tax fraud. I lost my holiday pay and my stability. Jobs of my kind at the time were scarce.'

Mac nodded again.

'So, after all my hard work building up to the position, it was gone and I was left unemployed. Did some waitressing in a friend's restaurant while searching for months to find a similar job but nothing came of it. I thought about opening my own business but I needed more experience and more contacts for that to work, not to mention the time to make it work, but I had to pay the bills.'

'I see.' Mac rubbed his chin. 'Well, I guess that *kinda* sucked then.'

'Kinda *definitely*.' She crossed her arms over her chest. 'It's tough in NYC, so many people, so much competition, we're all just rats in the race. Opportunities like that are hard to come by.'

'But you still had a job. You still paid the bills. Wasn't that a positive?'

She clasped her hands under her bent knees.

'Well, yes, but it was such a downer after I'd come so close to my dream job.' Although it *had* been, even to her own ears her reason sounded like a weak excuse. She tried to think of a better way to explain how crushed she'd felt losing the opportunity after working so hard for it, but really she just wished Tilly would skip back to them and put an end to their conversation.

Mac nodded, though she could tell by his plain expression he didn't think she had much to complain about. 'But why the strong objection to Christmas itself?' He eyed her with a curious tilt of his head. 'What happened at Christmas the following year?'

She stood and brushed off imaginary dust from her thighs, avoiding his eye contact. 'Don't worry. It doesn't matter.'

She'd shared enough. She barely knew this man and she was here to get away from everything, not relive it.

'If you say so. But, if you want to share anything, I'm willing to listen.' He stood and gave her forearm a light touch, and she met his gentle gaze. A tiny part of her heart wanted to share; to welcome his kindness and be comforted by it, but she couldn't. It would just be too hard. 'Tilly!' he called out. 'Let the other children have a go on the slippery dip, okay?'

She glanced over to find three children patiently waiting. Tilly skipped over to the swings instead.

'That girl.' He ran a hand through his scruffy short hair. 'More energy than I had as a teenager. God knows what we'll be in for in another few years.'

Angelette nodded and smiled. 'Teenage girls are a handful,' she said, remembering her own wayward years.

Especially when there wasn't a mother around.

'Mac?'

His brows rose. 'Yeah?'

'If you don't mind my asking, where are Tilly's parents?'

She regretted asking as soon as she spoke, but curiosity got the better of her, and he *had* probed for her secrets too.

He scratched his cheek. 'Ah. Well, Tilly's dad, my brother, he—'

'Uncle Mac, look!' Tilly called out. 'I found another one!' She ran over, a colourful small rock in her hand.

'Oh, awesome. A total of how many now?'

'Five.' She held up her free hand, spreading her fingers. 'Can we take them home now? I want to put them in my fairy garden.'

'Sure thing, diddly-ding,' he said in a singsong voice.

'Yessy wessy, Uncle Messy!' Tilly laughed, and a grin formed on Angelette's lips.

Angelette gathered her things and stood as Mac made his exit, his eyes not as bright as they had been before.

Chapter 6

There was no chance of reading quietly in the park the next day either, as the town folk set up for the Christmas carols. The commotion had disturbed her early in the morning, and the park was visible in the distance out the periphery of her window, the noise of musicians practicing and people laughing and calling out reverberating through the air.

Nevertheless, she lifted open the window to let in some fresh air, which blew in with intermittent warm gusts along with the morning sunlight. She began hanging up her laundry that she'd put in the washing machine last night, regretting it thanks to the *thump, thump, thump* and *whir, whir, whir* noises as she'd been trying to sleep. Hopefully she hadn't disturbed Mac in the adjoining room. Then again, living above a pub, he was probably used to noise.

The makeshift clothesline—a heavy-duty rope—was strung across the corner of the room from one wall to the other, where the light through the window could dry it. With this weather, her garments would probably be dry by the time she finished hanging them up. She pegged her white slip dress and it wafted back and forth like a ghost, billowing out suddenly here and there when the gusts burst in. As she hung up her underwear, a buzzing irritated her ear. She flapped her hand around her head as a fly whizzed past.

'Darn.' She noticed the rip in the flyscreen on the window. The pest continued buzzing loudly, as though circling her on purpose. She flicked her hands about, then as it rested near the window frame, she cautiously picked up the book she'd bought and leaned over slowly. She held the book up, then brought it down with a whack, narrowly missing the fly which simply flew up to a higher position on the window.

'Great. So you can find your sneaky way in through that little gap but you can't get back out?' She shook her head at the nuisance as it rested on the inner part of the wooden frame near the flyscreen, and another gust of wind blew in, sadly not blowing the fly away. She'd have to position the book's spine at it to squish it. She eyed her target, held the book at the ready, then—whack!

Not only did she nab the fly, but the entire flyscreen in its frame dislodged from the window and crashed down to the beer garden below, along with the book.

Angelette's hands flew to her mouth. As though as shocked as her, the wind blew in even harder, and her freshly washed knickers escaped their peg and flew out the window too.

She gasped, and quickly put another peg on her bra before it joined in the party. She leaned on the windowsill and peered through the open window to the patio with chairs and tables below. The flyscreen had landed on a table, which thankfully no one was sitting at, the book was on the ground, and her underwear was now stylishly draped on a large pot plant like a Christmas decoration.

Her eyes darted to two people to the left, who were chuckling and looking up. God, she'd have to go down there all red faced and retrieve her items as discreetly as possible, no doubt adorning herself with a Christmas accessory on the way through—though her rosy cheeks would be festive enough. She took a deep breath to steady her nerves and was about to walk away from the window to face the embarrassing predicament that awaited her below, when one of the two people gestured for someone to come outside. The top of someone's head appeared in view, turned to take in the disturbance, and then looked up, Mac's squinting eyes catching hers before his mouth spread into a grin.

'Everything okay up there?' he called to her.

She gave a thumbs up. 'Yep. Um, yep. It's just that the, ah, the window kinda fell out,' she called down to him.

Mac picked up the frame in one hand, the book in the other.

Please don't see them, please don't see them …

He went to turn toward the building but did a double take as he passed the pot plant.

Oh no. Angelette covered her eyes, then peeked through the gaps in her fingers as he placed the book down for a moment to pick up the underwear by the corner, holding them up to the blazing sunlight.

'These yours?'

Oh great, thanks Mac, tell the whole town why don't you?

She gave a reluctant nod.

'I'll be right up,' he said, positioning the book under his arm so he could hold the frame in one hand and the knickers in the other.

Could this *supposed* holiday get any worse?

Old wooden floorboards creaked under the weight of his heavy footsteps, and Angelette opened the door, stepping onto the landing and closing the door halfway so he wouldn't see the rest of her underwear collection. But then she remembered he'd have to come in and fix the window.

'What would you like first?' He glanced at the items he carried.

'I'll just take these, thank you.' She gently snatched the knickers from his grasp and ducked back inside, hanging them on the line as far away from the window as possible, with two pegs. Then she took the book, placed it on the chair and sighed as she let him in to deal with the window. 'I can't believe that actually happened.'

'It's okay, it's old. Things break around here all the time.'

She furrowed her brow, for a moment thinking he meant her underwear was old and broken. 'Oh, the window. Yes.' She rubbed her forehead where a slight headache was forming, then took a swig of water from her water bottle.

Mac looked at her and smiled. His eyes softening. 'Hey, it's no big deal. They're undies. Everyone wears 'em.'

Her face warmed. Yes, but why did hers have to decide to put themselves on display?

She nodded. 'Crazy gust of wind.'

'It happens.' He placed the frame down and surveyed the open window.

'Do you want me to take the clothesline down so you can, ah, get easier access?' she asked.

He shook his head. 'No need.' He ducked under the clothesline and checked the window, then picked up the flyscreen frame, angled it underneath the open window, and slotted it back up into position. 'It should hold, but just in case ...' He dashed into his room and back again, carrying a small tool kit. 'I'll add a couple of reinforcements.'

In a flash he had drilled something into each side at the top and bottom of the flyscreen frame, securing it in position. He then covered the rip in the screen with some clear masking tape. 'It's not perfect, but it'll do.'

'Thanks, Mac. I'll try not to break anything else while I'm here.' She managed a chuckle.

He shrugged. 'No big deal. All part of life. Just enjoy your holiday, okay?' He smiled and went to walk out, then turned. 'You still up for tonight?'

She nibbled the bottom corner of her lip, wondering what else could go wrong if she ventured out to the carols. Then she remembered Tilly's excited face. 'Sure. I look forward to hearing your niece sing.'

'Thanks, she's so excited she couldn't even eat breakfast, my dad said.'

Angelette smiled. She used to feel that way about her design and decorating projects when she was studying. Sometimes she'd get so engrossed in what she was creating and working on she'd forget to eat, or sleep. It had been like fuel in its own right. But since her confidence had been overridden by the difficulty in finding a suitable job and the need to pay her bills, along with everything else that had happened in the last three years, she didn't know if there was any point in taking a leap of faith with her dream career. All the faith she'd had had been quashed. Maybe it was self-doubt stemming from never having had an encouraging parent to help her move forward, or someone to say *great work, kiddo. You're a star.* Tilly was lucky to have Mac and Ned. And despite preferring to be one hundred miles away from anything to do with Christmas, she could suck it up for one night and help support a young rising star.

Mac returned downstairs and Angelette placed her hands on her hips. *What to do now?* She stood there for a while, uncertain or bored she wasn't sure, but something led her to her luggage where she'd tucked a notebook and pencils. She sat on the bed and glanced around the room. Before she realised what she was doing, she had sketched a basic floor plan and a couple of elevations—one of the bed area and the other of the desk by the window—adding improvements such as smart storage, wall art, comfy soft furnishings, lighting, and décor, to turn the room into a better version of itself. She could show Mac, but doubted he'd be interested in taking up time renovating and decorating when he seemed perfectly happy with everything the way it was. If only she could click her fingers and magically change the room. Along with her memories. But life wasn't magical, despite what the holiday season would have people, especially children, believe. She'd have to settle for magic on the page.

Angelette popped the notebook in her shoulder bag, freshened up, and went into town to find something to eat and look for somewhere relatively quiet to draw and escape the world around her, in mental preparation for that night when it would no doubt come closing in on her.

She sat at an outdoor table at a small café adjoining the art gallery, which was across the road from the back end of the park with views to the nature walk and the inclining hills beyond. She declined the waitress's offer to make the most of her vacation and purchase entry into the gallery itself after her brunch. Christmas and History were now her least favourite subjects.

Shade from the table umbrella cooled the sweat that had prickled the back of her neck on the walk through town, though speckles of sunlight scattered themselves on the paved patio area. With the many tall trees surrounding the gallery, it was a slightly cooler part of town, though still stinking hot compared to what she was used to.

She sat still, taking in her surroundings, absorbing colours, textures, shapes, lines, patterns … as her mind often did without thinking. Designing had become ingrained into her, though after working so long in the toilet business, the natural tendency to analyse the aesthetics of her environment had become less prominent. But here, with no bathroom facilities in direct sight, and no work to be done, her mind could roam free. Maybe it wasn't so bad, being here. It wasn't the resort type of stay she'd hoped for, but at least she was far away from home.

A healthy buddha bowl, they called it, arrived at her table, containing a mixture of salmon, poached eggs, kale, quinoa, shredded beetroot, and avocado sprinkled with black sesame seeds. She wriggled in her chair to seat herself more upright, and methodically placed a sliver of each ingredient onto her fork, engulfing it with an eager bite. When she was halfway through, she took a few sips of her banana smoothie and picked up a pencil, her hand poised above the paper of her notebook.

Without thinking she sketched quickly; a round table, two chairs, and a flower centrepiece. Behind it were French doors opening into a café. She added a small potted olive tree in the corner, and another table and chairs. By the time she had finished her meal, she had created a basic illustration of a French inspired café.

'Huh. Not bad,' she whispered to herself.

'Not bad indeed,' the waitress said as she approached to remove her plate.

'Oh. Sorry, talking to myself.' Angelette chuckled as her cheeks warmed.

The waitress smiled. 'I wish our little establishment looked as fancy as that. You're a talented artist. Do you do any bigger pieces?'

Angelette's brows rose. 'Me? Oh no, only sketches.'

'You're really good, you should do something with that.'

'Thank you. I did a long time ago, studied design, but nothing much came of it.'

'Shame. Well, don't give up.' The waitress picked up her empty smoothie glass. 'Can I get you anything else?'

Angelette glanced at the menu propped up into the napkin holder. 'Yes, actually, I'll have a slice of cheesecake and a cappuccino, thanks.'

The waitress smiled. 'Maybe by the time you finish it all, you'll have another masterpiece to show me.'

Angelette shrugged. 'I don't know about that, but thanks.'

But sure enough, when she'd devoured her dessert and coffee, a second drawing had emerged from her subconscious, of a reading corner with a cosy armchair, blanket and cushion, and a tall shelf of books behind it. She added a tall lamp casting gentle light over the chair, and a cat curled up at the feet.

She smiled at the drawing, realising it had been a long time since she'd felt connected to her creative flow. Maybe this vacation *was* working ... helping to smooth out those raw edges of her pain.

She caught the waitress's eye and showed her. 'Your praise must have inspired me,' she said. 'Thank you.'

'Oh, that's gorgeous. You could frame this. I'd love a special corner like that in my house. I only read in bed, there's no room for anywhere special to set up like that.'

She handed the drawing to the waitress. 'Here, you take it. A tip for your hospitality.'

'Really? I can photocopy it if you prefer.'

'No, I don't need it. I'm just randomly sketching to pass time.'

Was she really? Or was her creative muse giving her ideas to help her have a second chance at her dream career? Maybe by the time this holiday was over, she'd be able to move on from the things that had happened and start fresh, make some new plans. Besides, she would have to start thinking seriously about what she was going to do for work now that she'd quit her job. Her savings would eventually run dry if she didn't.

She paid for her meal and wandered around the gallery gardens for a while, birds flitting from one tree to another, butterflies resting on leaves then fluttering off somewhere else, while guitar strings vibrated and feedback interference rang out in the distance through an amplifier as someone tuned and checked their instrument. At the entrance to the gallery steps, she glanced up to her left beyond the tall horizon, the pointed tip of a temple visible in the distance. She remembered reading about it when she'd researched the town before booking her ticket. It's how the town got its name; people would travel from afar to the temple, seeking inner peace and enlightenment. Maybe she should go there and explore, learn how to meditate and discover her own inner peace. But in all honesty, she wanted a simple, do-as-she-pleased vacation from her usual life. Angelette walked back towards town, eventually nearing the Little Treasures shop where she slowed her pace. She stopped when a cute wooden angel statue caught her eye. It was about the size of a book, sitting in the window display among various holiday books and items. It stood out to her, not overly Christmassy, just … nice. Sculpted, subtle, and smooth with a combination of natural and white painted wood. The wings had a subtle glimmer of glitter. Something inside her wanted her to buy it, but then she remembered she was here to relax and forget about life for a while, not get sucked into holiday consumerism.

She walked on quickly before she succumbed. There'd be more than enough Christmassy things to deal with tonight.

Chapter 7

Angelette stood at the entrance to the park at seven-fifteen, or as Tilly would say, seventy-fifteen o'clock pm … one hour before the young star was due to perform. Her heart wanted her feet to turn her around and walk right back to The Mistletoe, but with a preparatory breath, she forced them to step forward.

I can do this. I'm here for Tilly, that's all. It'll be fine.

The townsfolk chatted and laughed, and children with their faces painted as unicorns and reindeers ran around chasing each other with star-shaped LED wands. She tried to stay focused on putting one foot in front of the other.

'Would you like to buy an LED candle and support charity?' a teenager, wearing a bright red 'volunteer' t-shirt and reindeer antlers, asked.

'Um, sure, guess so.' Angelette checked in her purse that she had the correct Australian coins and handed over two dollars. She popped it in her bag for later and, as her mouth salivated at the scent of something tasty and probably unhealthy frying, wandered over to where people were lining up at a large table, smoke wafting up in the air. This must be the sausage sizzle those girls in the park had mentioned. Whatever they were cooking, she wanted it.

Soon after, she had two soft, fluffy pieces of white bread on a paper plate with a sausage placed diagonally across each, and a zig-zag of ketchup, mustard, and mayonnaise. She folded the corners of the bread together and lifted it to her mouth, taking a bite.

Oh my God. Sooo good.

When she was done she approached the old-fashioned looking stand nearby with triangular bunting framing the table edges and bought an icy lemonade with a straw poking through a lemon slice. Also *sooo* good.

She took the opportunity to pause and notice her surround-ings; it was like an explosion of happiness all around. Crowded in a sense, but not in a New York City kind of way where people rushed past you in all directions, tourists stopped mid-sidewalk with cameras positioned high up in the air, and others hung about idly on street corners. For a moment she smiled softly, glad she had escaped her usual world for one so different and somehow … comforting. But when a man with a Santa hat and tinsel gar-land hanging around his neck like a Hawaiian lei came near, she remembered Christmas again and reminded herself not to get too happy. Last time she allowed herself to get too happy at Christ-mastime, everything went wrong. Devastatingly wrong. This way, she could be mentally prepared and protect herself from any more disasters. It was the only way she'd ever learned how to cope with life: be grateful for what you had, yes, but don't get too caught up in those positive feelings, otherwise the downfall would be so much more painful.

'Oh, Mac. Didn't recognise you for a moment.'

'I thought you wouldn't recognise me *without* the Santa hat or some other sparkly accessory.'

'I was caught up in the atmosphere.' She gestured around. 'Good turnout, I didn't know the town's population was this high.'

'People come from further afield too. Always a great night,' he replied. 'Anyway, wanted to make sure I found you before the carols get underway.' He pointed to a spot up near the front of the stage. 'We've got a picnic rug in the VIP lounge,' he joked, 'if you'd like to join us? Though I understand if you'd rather hang about on the sidelines. Whatever you prefer.' He shrugged.

Angelette checked her watch. She could either lay low for forty-five minutes until Tilly came on stage, or she could sit on the rug with Mac and his dad and try not to let her heart rate rise too much with anxiety. She thought of the girl—excited and nervous, unable to eat properly from anticipation—and decided Tilly's feelings were more important right now. If the young girl looked down from the stage and couldn't see Angelette in the crowd like she'd promised, it would be disappointing.

'I'll join you. But first …' She eyed another food stand. 'I might grab some popcorn, it smells delicious. Do you want some?'

'Sure, I'll come with you.'

Mac insisted on paying and carried two large red and white striped cardboard tubs over to the spot where Ned sat on a low-to-the-ground foldout chair.

'If it isn't our special guest! How are you doing this fine evening, Angelette?" Ned held out his hand and she shook it.

'Well, thanks. I hope you don't mind me joining you in prime position here.' She smiled.

'Not at all, we saved you a seat.' He patted a large floor cushion that had an intricate zigzag pattern with every possible colour under the sun.

'Thanks.' She sat, handing him one of the popcorn tubs.

Mac sat on another cushion and they positioned the tub between them, the cinema-like scent wafting up to her nose and bringing back memories of the good ol' days, when as a young adult she'd hang out with friends who'd now long gone, watching movies and leaving reality behind.

Snacking on popcorn would give her something else to focus on apart from the singing on stage, but she'd give her full attention to Tilly's performance. For some strange reason, her stomach jittered with nerves for her. Maybe it also reminded her of the time she'd had to perform with her classmates on stage in elementary school and she'd forgotten the words and had to mime. At least it hadn't been a solo; she didn't have the voice for that.

Mac waved to another parent who sat nearby and gave a fingers-crossed gesture. The crowd quietened as a woman in a red dress took to the stage, tapped on the microphone, then thanked every-one for their attendance and gave a rundown of what was to come. She stepped off the stage, holding out her arm in welcome for the first performer: a man of about fifty who Angelette thought she'd seen coming out of the art gallery in a shirt and tie when she'd had lunch.

The small orchestra to the side of the stage played their instru-ments, and each nostalgic note tugged at her heart, sharpening memories she didn't want to resurface. But as they became clearer, she blinked hard to hold back the emotion that began welling up, and shifted with discomfort on the cushion. Maybe she'd overesti-mated her confidence at being able to be here for Tilly. Was it too late and too rude to back out?

The man's smooth voice began crooning 'It's Beginning to Look a Lot Like Christmas'. To Angelette, it had been looking a lot like Christmas for weeks. When the singer got to the part that mentioned candy canes, he plucked a few red and white canes from his top pocket and tossed one into the front row, then another, then …

Don't throw it to me …

Toss! Mac held up his hand and caught it. He held it to Angelette, but she shook her head. 'I'll save it for Tilly,' he said close to
her ear, his breath warm on her neck.

Tilly. Angelette shook her bad memories from her mind. *Tonight
was for Tilly, the vibrant young girl who still believed in magic, and deserved
to for as long as possible.* She wasn't about to cry for the first time in
ages among a crowd of people, brought down by a cheesy Christmas song and flying candy canes. No. She sat up straight as the song
continued and she ate more popcorn. The crooner was followed by
a girl of about eighteen whose voice sounded twenty years older,
singing 'Hark the Herald Angels Sing'. They were both impressive,
but still, she tried to stay neutral about it all.

As a choir sang 'The Holly and the Ivy', she delved her hand into
the popcorn tub at the same time Mac did, and their hands collided. She quickly withdrew hers and gestured for him to go ahead,
but he did the same. She chuckled and lowered her head, reaching
her hand back in and taking a handful, and when she brought it to
her mouth she realised she'd taken too many and a few popcorn
puffs fell down her chin and under the front of her top. Mac kindly
averted his gaze as she awkwardly covered her chest with her raised
hand and reached in discreetly with the other to pluck them out
and discard them. Luckily Ned hadn't seemed to notice; he had his
eyes locked on the stage, camera at the ready, singing along with the
choir. She shook her head at her embarrassment, and Mac smiled
but didn't comment. Not that they could have much in the way of
conversation anyway with the loud music right in front of them.

She noticed Mac check his watch and adjust his position on the
cushion, pulling his phone from his pocket, clearly getting ready
for his niece's special moment. She leaned towards his ear.

'Would you like me to take photos, so you can focus on watching her?' she suggested, hoping that was okay.

He nodded. 'Sure, thanks.' Handing her the phone, he got his dad's attention. 'Are you filming or taking photos, Dad?'

'Video, so I can watch it again later.'

He gave a thumbs up, and Angelette was pleased she had something extra to focus on. She remembered times in her life when she'd been so lost in a special moment she'd forgotten to take photos, and other times she'd been so focused on taking photos she hadn't really absorbed the moment.

Mac picked up his LED candle as the sun slowly descended behind the hills, though the sky was still bright. She got hers out of her shoulder bag and placed it in front of her on the rug while she held the phone up, the MC welcoming Seekers Hill Primary School kindergarten class to the spotlight.

The students filtered onto the stage in a line, all wearing reindeer antlers, one boy yawning and trudging along slower than the others, another walking a little too eagerly and bumping into the child in front. And then Tilly, the last in line, a wide smile lighting up her face as she entered. Mac clapped, then whistled. The students got into their positions, aided by their teacher who scurried about them, gently grasping a few students' shoulders to shuffle them along a bit further until she seemed satisfied and stood to the side of the stage. Tilly's gaze scanned the audience, then paused as she obviously noticed her uncle, her smile stretching wide. The girl's eyes brightened when she locked eyes with Angelette, and her heart warmed inside. Ned waved and she smiled wider and then, appearing to concentrate on what was to come, raised her chin and looked into the distance.

The boy in the middle stepped forward, his nose painted red. Angelette snapped a photo of the group as they sang 'Rudolph the Red-Nosed Reindeer', the children pointing at the boy whose two pointed fingers were either side of his bright nose, tipping his head side to side with the rhythm to show off his best feature.

When the kids piped up that his nose glowed like a lightbulb, a child behind the boy held up a large cardboard cut-out yellow lightbulb above the boy's head and the crowd laughed. Luckily, she'd managed to snap a picture in time before the lightbulb disappeared.

A man dressed as Santa—probably sweating like mad in the summer heat—came on stage and acted out the part asking Rudolph to guide his sleigh. And then Tilly rushed up to the front for the finale, holding up a newspaper to show that Rudolf had gone down in history. They paused their positions on stage as everyone clapped and took photos, and Mac whistled again. Angelette zoomed in on Tilly and the newspaper to snap another photo. The teacher ushered them off stage one by one, until she got to Tilly, taking the newspaper from her hands and helping the antlers off her head. She took off her makeshift oversized brown reindeer top, revealing a blue cotton sleeveless dress underneath, then walked back to centre stage where the main microphone was. The teacher adjusted it a little for her, tapped it to check it was working fine, then patted her on the back and scurried off, leaving the six-year-old in the spotlight.

Angelette's chest rose in anticipation, and she took a photo before she got caught up in the moment.

The orchestra began playing, and Angelette knew the song instantly. Tilly started singing 'Silent Night' and Angelette had to lower the phone a moment as her hand instinctively went to her chest, this time for the emotion of the moment instead of fallen popcorn. She stole a glance at Ned whose mouth was in a permanent smile, then Mac whose face was still and strong, but his eyes soft and shiny. The girl's sweet voice captured the whole park, everything else quiet. LED candle lights began swaying and she turned around and took a photo of the crowd in awe at this little star's sweet rendition. A beautiful voice for someone so young, she hadn't heard it as distinctly during the class performance.

When Tilly reached the high notes near the end, Angelette's heart fluttered. Her skin tingled as though the notes were tiny stars falling onto her from the sky, and she reminded herself to take slow, deep breaths.

Stay strong, stay strong.

She blinked and squeezed her eyes shut a moment to push back tears that threatened, even though they would be a worthy response to Tilly's performance. But they were also rising up in response to so much more ... Tilly, and the lyrics, so bittersweet.

She took another deep breath and, when the crowd clapped and cheered, she took one last photo then placed the phone down, joining along with the clapping.

She may not have wanted to celebrate Christmas, but these few minutes were worth the pain. At least for now. She didn't know how she would cope when Christmas Day actually came, but she'd try not to think of that yet.

As Tilly left the stage to the congratulatory arms of her teacher, Ned put down his phone and wiped his eyes. 'Oh, that girl, what she does to this old heart of mine!'

Angelette patted his forearm and hoped it wasn't too personal a gesture.

Mac smiled with pride, catching his dad's gaze for a moment. She felt a little in the middle of their special moment, but they didn't seem to mind.

The MC on stage allowed time for the students to find their way back to their families in the audience before speaking again, and Angelette barely registered any of what she said as Tilly came dashing towards them, leaping into Mac's embrace, then Ned's. 'So proud of you, sweetheart,' Mac said.

'We both are,' said Ned, then gazed up at the sky. 'We all are.'

Tilly sat on the rug in front of Angelette and clasped both her hands. 'You came.' She smiled. 'The angel came, Uncle Mac.' She glanced at him.

Angelette nodded. 'And what an amazing performance that was.'

Mac plucked the candy cane from his pocket and handed it to his niece, along with a water bottle.

'Yum, thanks!' She tore open the wrapper and licked the candy, then shushed everyone as the next performers appeared on stage. Instead of leaving soon after the girl's performance as Angelette had first intended, she stayed put for the whole show. Mac and Ned sang along with Tilly to all the songs, but Angelette simply sat there and smiled, glad she was able to be a part of someone's happy memories, even if her own were hard to come by.

When the official carols ended, the MC invited everyone to hang around a little longer and enjoy more of the festivities, while those with babies sleeping in prams and parents' arms left.

'Can I play with my friends at the playground?' Tilly tugged at Ned's shirt.

'Isn't it past your bedtime, missy?' Ned asked.

Tilly shook her head. 'Bedtimes don't count at Christmastime.'

Mac chuckled. 'Off you go, but no more than twenty minutes,' he said, and she dashed off with her friends.

Mac went to walk over too, but Ned said, 'I'll go. You show our guest around a bit more and make the most of the evening. Meet you back here in twenty, or should I say thirty?' He winked.

'Thirty.' Mac held a hand to Angelette's shoulder. 'Thank you for coming. You made a little girl extra happy.'

'My pleasure. She's amazing.'

He nodded. 'I don't know how long she'll last in this small town with that voice. Better make the most of it while she's here.'

Angelette nodded.

'Hey, I don't mind if you're all Christmassed out and would rather head back. I can walk you?'

She was about to say *yes, thanks*, but glanced at the lemonade stand instead. 'Actually, I might have one more drink.'

Mac's eyebrows rose. 'Have we converted you back to Christmas?'

'Not quite. Just thirsty after all the popcorn, that's all.' She smiled.

They both got a lemonade and wandered around, Mac chatting briefly to a few people here and there, eventually stopping underneath a beautiful old tree. She couldn't remember if it was the one she'd sat and dozed under that day after she'd arrived—everything looked so different with fairy lights and decorations, tents and gazebos, and people everywhere.

'You're lucky,' she said softly.

And without her having to say what he was lucky for, he simply said, 'I know.'

She worried that maybe she sounded jealous, but it wasn't like Mac had a perfect life, there were clearly things he didn't like to talk about too.

As though reading her mind, and dispelling her assumption, he cleared his throat. 'My brother died.'

Angelette swallowed a sudden lump in her throat. 'Oh, Mac, I'm so sorry. Tilly's father?'

He gave a weak nod. 'Two years ago. Poor girl, only four and both parents gone suddenly.'

'Both?'

He glanced at her, then looked into the distance. 'My brother, Jimmy, was shocked when his girlfriend Nora became pregnant unexpectedly, was scared of being a father.' He took one last sip of his lemonade then tossed it into the trash can nearby, and she did the same. 'But he became the best dad Tilly could have wished for.

He and Nora got married, and we agreed to take care of Tilly while they went on a honeymoon road trip up north.' He leaned against the tree behind them.

Angelette wanted to ask what happened but thought it best to let him keep speaking at his own pace.

'They didn't even arrive at their first destination.' Mac's voice faltered. 'Head-on collision with a truck. Both died instantly.'

Angelette gasped, her hand covering her mouth. 'Oh my God, Mac, I don't know what to say. That is just … awful.'

'Yep,' he said, grasping firmly at a branch and looking like he was about to snap it in half.

'I'm so sorry. I cannot imagine how hard it must have been. How hard it *is*.'

Mac nodded, his eyes distant. 'Nora was an only child, and her parents are older. Tilly sees them as often as possible, but they agreed that it'd be best for her to live with us and stay in familiar surroundings.'

Her heart ached as he talked about his brother, how he had lived in the room above The Mistletoe with Nora until Tilly was born, then it became too cramped and disruptive, so they'd moved in with Ned. Jimmy, a carpenter and builder, had commenced building a granny flat out the back of their dad's place to eventually use as not only a small home for the three of them, but an office for the small construction company he was going to start up. The basic structure and outdoor painting were complete, but they had planned to paint the interiors, get carpet in the two bedrooms, and finish setting it all up after their honeymoon. They never got the chance.

'We hardly even go in there,' Mac said. 'We *could* finish it up and Dad could rent it out for some extra money, but …' He exhaled loudly.

'Grief takes all our time and energy,' Angelette said knowingly.

He caught her gaze and nodded. 'One day, I guess. For now, the priority has been looking after Tilly. And *that* takes a lot of time and energy.' He managed a chuckle.

Angelette kicked a twig on the ground. She couldn't think of anything else to say. Maybe she should return to the room. She opened her mouth to say so, when Mac spoke first.

'So, I've bared my soul. Tell me ... what happened the Christmas after you lost your job?' He faced her with full attention.

'Oh, it doesn't matter. Just a silly thing. What you've been through is much worse.'

She wished she'd never mentioned the three Christmases to him now. The second Christmas would pale in comparison to his grief, and there was no way she was bringing up the third.

'Hey, there's no competition here. Pain is pain. And if you flew halfway across the world to get away from your memories, I'd say it's not just a silly thing.'

'It's more the cumulative effect of the past three Christmases,' she attempted to clarify.

'I'm all ears.'

She sighed. 'Okay then. Well ...' She fiddled with her bracelet, a stylish, silver bangle. 'It's quite simple. I was dumped right before my first ever real family Christmas.' She flicked her hand in the air. 'See? I told you it was silly.'

'Getting dumped is never fun.' Mac inched closer to her. 'You'd never celebrated a real family Christmas before?'

She shook her head. 'Still haven't. I grew up in an orphanage and then multiple foster homes.'

Mac's eyebrows rose. 'Oh, man, that must have been tough. So you never met your biological parents?'

She shook her head. 'And I didn't want to, I knew they had given me up and I didn't see the point in going on a search only to be heartbroken. I learned to look after myself and not get too close to anyone. Until Darius.'

'The one who ...'

'Spoiled my Christmas, yes.' She nodded.

'Go on.' He slipped his hands in his pockets.

'Oh.' She was surprised he wanted to hear more ... or maybe he was more relieved at the change of subject away from his brother. 'I'd been seeing him for about six months. We were happy. And it seemed to be getting serious. He invited me to spend Christmas Day with him to meet his parents and siblings at the family home.'

'You must have been excited.'

She nodded. 'I'd been looking forward to it for weeks, my first experience of a family Christmas, and finally getting somewhere with a relationship.' Angelette's gaze rose to the night sky, stars blurring as her mind rushed back to that time ... the anticipation of experiencing a sense of belonging, and of what family life might have been like if she'd had one. She'd even baked gingerbread men cookies the day before Christmas Eve to give to his parents as a thank you gesture. 'But on Christmas Eve,' she continued, 'after his office closed and we met for drinks, he was acting strange. Shifty and uncomfortable.'

'What changed?'

She could still remember that look of pity on Darius's face that had said it all.

'He did. His feelings, at least. He said he didn't think it was going to work; not just the family visit, but the relationship.'

She still didn't understand how things had changed so quickly between them, but they had, and though he'd tried to let her down gently, it had stung.

Mac shook his head with a 'tsk'. 'Sounds like an attack of cold feet,' he muttered. 'Anyway, his loss.'

'Thanks, but it was mine too, at the time. I'm fine with it now, but it put another dampener on my Christmas memories. I spent that Christmas Day on my own watching sad movies and eating microwaved pizza and all the cookies I'd baked. I thought of calling some friends but they already had plans with *their* families, and I didn't want to be all like, "hey, my boyfriend dumped me and my dreams of a family Christmas have been shattered, can I gatecrash your Christmas?"'

'Understandable,' Mac responded. 'Family has always been an important part of my life, and Christmas too.' He scratched his head and shifted his stance from one foot to the other. 'Um, if you like, you're welcome to ...'

She hadn't thought of him as a guy who'd be lost for words or fumbling to get a message across. But she had an inkling of what he was going to suggest, and though his compassion warmed her heart, she didn't want him to ask.

'My dreams have changed since then,' she interjected quickly before he could continue. 'Right now, I'm perfectly happy to have a non-Christmas on my own.' She managed a confident smile. That way she wouldn't be let down again. Or worse.

Mac stilled. 'Well, if it means anything, I'm glad you gatecrashed our Christmas, and I really hope you'll enjoy Christmas again one day.' He smiled.

She hoped so too. But right now, it just wasn't possible.

Chapter 8

Mac was right, she was all Christmassed out and it wasn't even Christmas yet. She spent the next few days keeping to herself as much as possible, bar one early dinner in the pub where she had to wear a red and green glittery bow clipped to her hair courtesy of the entry rules. She was onto her fourth book, having binge-read in the park for almost three days straight, and now it was the day before Christmas Eve and her mind was restless. She needed to do something a little less passive. She headed downstairs to walk to the gallery café with plans to do more sketching while enjoying a delicious slice of cake.

She opened the door and stepped outside the pub, her gaze swinging to the left where Mac was watering plants along the side of the building with a large metal watering can.

'These babies are dying in this heat,' he said. 'I don't know how my mum managed to keep them blooming. I've never had any luck keeping them alive for long.' He straightened up and sheltered his eyes from the sun. 'Off to do more reading?'

'Nah, sketching this time.'

'Some designs, like you used to do?'

She shrugged. 'Sorta. Just random, nothing professional.'

'That's good. Maybe you'll find a way to get back into it, so you—'

'Don't have to go back to selling toilets?' she interjected.

'Not at all. So you can do something you love, was what I was going to say.'

'Maybe,' she replied.

'Hey,' he said, 'I know the big day is near and you don't want any fanfare, but you are more than welcome to join us tomorrow night for our Christmas Eve buffet. Lots of great food for a set price, plus half price drinks. We close early at nine though, I have to go help Dad with Santa Claus duties when Tilly goes to sleep.'

'Thanks, but I'll give it a miss.' She forced a thank you smile. It must have looked fake, because he frowned.

'You sure? Maybe you need to make some new, happier Christmas memories.'

She crossed her arms. *No, please don't start.*

'It's just, after losing my mum, then my brother, I've realised how precious time is—how precious spending time with people you care about is. I know you barely know us, but maybe you have an opportunity here to rewrite Christmas.'

She shook her head, her cheeks becoming warm and flustered. 'I'm so sorry for your loss, I truly am, Mac. And I'm grateful you're trying to make me feel welcome. But it's not what I want right now.'

He crossed his arms too. 'Fair enough. But, Angelette, don't waste the time you have being angry at Christmas.'

She didn't know how else to feel towards the season that had broken her heart.

'Maybe just, I dunno ...' he continued. 'Try to move forward.'

Her heartbeat intensified. 'That's why I came to Australia, to move forward and enjoy some time off.'

'Yes, but you also came here to escape. I know you've had some struggles, but if there's anything I've learned in my short life here on earth, it's that we can't escape life. Good or bad, stuff happens.'

Angelette let her arms fall to the side in frustration. 'Well, I'm sick of the bad stuff happening. There's nothing wrong with wanting to escape.'

'But have you really? Escaped it all?'

She twisted her lips to one corner, agitated by the tone of his questioning. What right did he have to talk to her like he knew anything about her life? 'Well, it's a bit hard with all your Christmas decorations and Christmas carols and Christmas rules!'

'We can't just mute Christmas, Angelette. All I'm saying is there comes a time when we have to accept what's been and gone and move on from it.'

Move on? He has no idea! Her nerves rattled, she stepped forward. 'Oh yeah? And what about you? You should take your own advice. Move on. Finish your brother's granny flat, for starters.'

He glared at her. 'Don't tell me how to handle my grief.'

'Then don't tell me how to handle mine!' Furious, she turned away from him.

'Angelette,' he raised his voice slightly, as though his words alone were a firm hand on her arm, urging her to turn back around. She faced him but clamped her jaw tight. 'Seriously, what is it? What else has made you so against Christmas that you'd travel halfway across the world to try and escape it?'

Her heart was about to break apart into a million pieces. 'It doesn't matter.' She turned around.

This time he did place a hand on her arm. 'Angelette. I didn't mean to upset you. Talk to me. Maybe it'll help to get it out.'

'Forget it. Like I said, it doesn't matter.' This time she turned away and kept walking. She couldn't believe he had been so confrontational. It was none of his business. Mac, the life-sucks-sometimes-but-get-over-it guy, wanted her to move on. Well, she would. From this place.

She huffed and marched on with determination.

By the time she took a seat at the café her nerves were still rattled. She kept adjusting her position, moving the cushion on the chair behind her, and rearranging the items on the table.

'Already had a coffee or would you like another one?' the waitress asked.

'I'd love one please.' She also ordered brunch and took a huge swig of water from her glass. She was too shaken up to draw.

Her phone beeped with a text from Mac:

I'm sorry.

So he should be. What kind of landlord tells his tenant what to do when she's trying to enjoy at least some kind of vacation in a place she never even planned to stay at?

She ate her food with gusto, ordered cake and a frappe, and sat and looked around at nothing in particular for what seemed like hours. As much as she tried to forget the argument, it replayed in her mind, and she sighed. Angelette got up and paid for her meal, leaving quickly before the waitress could wish her a happy Christmas.

She walked through the park and came to the tree she'd stood under with Mac last night. The memory of his words about his brother stung her heart, and she considered typing *I'm sorry too* in reply to his text message, but didn't want to get caught up in a text conversation. She would apologise in person. She knew that *he* was grieving, but he didn't know she was too. Just in a different way.

Before the emotions could rise up within her like a tsunami, she sat at the base of the tree and got out her Kindle which she'd brought just in case, opened the book she was reading, and continued with relief. If she couldn't really escape her life, at least she could escape having to think about it for a while by reading a book.

As more shade eased its way across the grass, she checked the time and realised she had been there for ages. Now more at ease, and reconnected to her simple goal of having a relaxing vacation, she stood, stretched her arms above her head, and flung her bag strap over her shoulder. Time for a nap—in a real bed, this time. When reading had done its job, sleep was the next best thing.

She walked out the front of the park, turned left, and came face to face with Ned and Tilly.

'Angel!' the girl exclaimed.

'It's Angelette, love,' her grandfather corrected.

'Angel-ette,' she tried again.

'It's okay,' Angelette responded. 'Nice to see you, Tilly. Ned.' She greeted them both. 'I can still hear your wonderful voice some-times.' Angelette smiled.

'Really? From so far away?'

'Oh,' she chuckled, 'I mean, in *my mind*. The memory of it.'

'Oh!' Tilly giggled. Then she got something bright out of her pocket. 'Look, another painted pebble. From the elves.'

'Wow, it looks like a ladybird.'

'It is, a *magical* one.' She rotated it in the sunlight to show the hint of glitter among the red and black spots.

'We're off to the movies, would you like to join us?' Ned asked.

'Oh, yes, pleeease!' Tilly clasped her hands together with eager-ness. 'The Polar Express is on.'

Her heart lurched. It was the last thing she wanted to do. 'Umm …'

'It's okay if you can't.' Ned must have sensed her apprehension.

'But I want you to,' said Tilly.

Angelette placed a hand on Tilly's shoulder. 'You know when you stay up really late and then you get up early the next day, and it makes you really tired?'

'Like after the Christmas carols?'

Angelette nodded. 'Although I'd love to come, I'm feeling really, really tired, like that. I think I need to have a nap.' She yawned for extra effect. 'But you're going to have a great time with your grandpa. Are you going to have popcorn?'

She nodded. 'And a choc top!'

'Ooh, we better get there quickly before they all sell out!' Ned grasped Tilly's hand. He glanced at Angelette and winked. It was as though he knew. Maybe Mac had said something.

'Have a great time!' Angelette waved them off, a touch of guilt twisting inside, then glanced across the road at Little Treasures. She walked across and stopped at the window display. It was still there. The angel statue. She opened the door with a jingle, and within minutes was walking back to the pub, the angel carefully wrapped and stored in a brown carry bag with the swirly Little Treasures logo on it.

She stepped into the entryway of The Mistletoe. Peering through the door to the pub, she saw Mac, his back to her, talking to Barry. She turned to the stairs and walked up, pausing when she got to her room. A small posy of flowers sat in a small jar at the foot of the doorway. Angelette's heart softened. She bent and picked up the slightly wilted but still pretty blooms. Of course, she knew who had picked them. She unlocked the door and went inside, placing her bags on the chair, and the flowers beside the bed. Footsteps creaked on the stairs.

'Angelette?'

She glanced toward the open door to find Mac peering discreetly in.

'Barry said you scooted past. He may be somewhere else these days but he also doesn't miss a beat, that guy.'

Angelette tucked a strand of loose hair from her ponytail behind her ear. She stepped to meet him at the threshold. 'I'm sorry, too,' she said. 'I shouldn't have said anything about your brother, that was uncalled for.'

Mac shrugged. 'It's okay. I'm the one who's sorry. I shouldn't have pestered you. What you're doing here is none of my business, and you don't have to tell me anything.'

'Apology accepted,' she said.

'I was just feeling a bit raw, I think. I haven't spoken about Jimmy in a while, and then Mum's flowers died ...' He sighed.

'I understand.' She gestured to the jar beside her bed. 'These look good enough to me. Thanks, it was a nice gesture.'

'All good now?' He waved a hand between them.

She nodded. 'I promise I won't give you any advice or decorating tips.'

'And I won't tell you what you should and shouldn't do. It's your life, and I want you to relax while you're here.'

'Thank you. I actually did end up having a relaxing day.'

'I'm glad.'

'Oh.' She glanced at the brown paper bag. 'I bought a gift for Tilly. I hope that's okay. Not really for Christmas or anything, just because. But would you like me to give it to you and you can give it to her on Christmas Day anyway? Tell her it's from *the angel*.' She drew a halo in the air around her head with her fingers and smiled.

'That's so nice of you. Would you like to give it to her yourself though? You can drop it off personally on Christmas Day at my dad's house. I'll text you the address. No need to stay and celebrate, though you're completely welcome, of course. Everything else in town will be closed. But no pressure.' He held his hands out in defence as though yet another Christmas invitation might push her over the edge.

'I'll think about it. But I'm not sure. Just knowing she's getting it is enough for me, even if I don't see her reaction. I know she'll like it.'

'Sure. Let's wait till then in that case, and if you'd rather not come, I'll pop over that arvo and grab it from you. No worries.' He gave a reassuring nod.

'Thanks.' She went to close the door, but stopped. 'Mac?'

'Yes?'

'I'm probably not up for the Christmas Eve buffet tomorrow, but I could do with a decent dinner tonight; what's on the specials menu?'

A smile grew on his lips, and his eyes brightened. 'Whatever your heart desires. Let us know and I'll have the chef, or my dad, whip it up for you.' He gave a thumbs up.

'In that case, let me think on it. I'll let you know after I've had a nap.'

'No probs.' He smiled again, and something else stopped her from closing the door. Whether it was the emotions from the day, the whole vacation, or lack of physical contact, she needed to do something.

She placed her hand on his upper arm, then moved closer to him and let her arms embrace him. He did the same, and comforting warmth from his firm and sculpted torso spread throughout her body. She exhaled and her muscles relaxed. He didn't release her until she released him, and she looked into his eyes and said, 'Thank you.'

Chapter 9

Having had an enjoyable dinner at the pub the previous night with no altercations or embarrassments, no over-questioning from the locals, and not even any human autocorrect moments from Barry, must have given Angelette false confidence.

She stood at the bottom of the stairs, Christmas tinsel garland around her neck, and was about to push open the inner door to the pub for the Christmas Eve buffet she said she wouldn't attend, when a song came on the jukebox: 'O Holy Night'.

She froze, instantly transported back to last Christmas Eve, when the song had come on the radio in the cab she'd had to hail unexpectedly in the late afternoon, just as snow began falling. So far removed from where she was now, but still, the song flung her back. She was surprised, and glad, that they hadn't sung it at the carols in the park.

Her heart throbbed, prickles of sweat tingled on her forehead, and the garland around her neck became as heavy and suffocating as a heat pack. She tore it off and tossed it into the accessory basket and dashed up the stairs.

She thought she could do it, but she couldn't.

Not tonight.

She collapsed onto the bed and fought back tears, focusing on her breathing, and willing her nerves to calm down. She lay there for half an hour or so, took a deep breath, and then made herself heat up a microwave meal she had stored in the fridge. Marginally better with some nourishment, she checked her Facebook messages, replied to a few simple ones, ignored the Merry Christmas chain-letter gifs telling her if she forwarded it to twenty other friends good news would be hers tomorrow, then opened her Kindle.

Reading would help.

Then a shower. A cold one.

Then some more reading.

Then funny cat videos on YouTube.

Then a snack.

She completed each task as though they were part of an important mission, then sat on the bed with a packet of choc chip cookies and munched away, brushing off a few crumbs that had fallen onto her sheets. She took a sip of water and plucked another cookie then put it back again. Her stomach was full. There was nothing left to do, or occupy herself with.

Angelette walked to the window and glanced out at the dark, starry sky. They twinkled and she shivered, remembering how Tilly's performance had touched her heart and brought some emotions to the surface. She sighed. Mac was right. She couldn't escape her life. Distract herself sometimes, yes, but not escape. She'd travelled all the way to Australia but her problems had still come along for the ride.

Angelette closed the curtains and got into bed, slipping under the sheets and laying her head on the pillow. She hadn't noticed till now that the muffled sounds from the pub had quietened. She checked the time; just past ten. Mac was probably playing Santa duty at Ned's house. If she was lucky, maybe sleep would claim her before the tears did.

But as soon as she closed her eyes, her chin trembled.

Memories surfaced, along with the accompanying emotions.

She sniffled, held her jaw as tight as she could, but a moan escaped. An ugly, raw, never-before-heard moan, as though her pain was a prisoner trying to clamber out of her lungs. She let it out, and pain coursed through her muscles and heart with spasmodic sobs. Oh boy, she knew it would hurt, but not this much. She cried and cried, hoping she would tire herself out and fall asleep, but she stayed awake, gripping her pyjama top across her chest as though it might contain the emotions.

As her crying eventually reduced to sporadic sobs and sniffles—more from fatigue than from the emotions having resolved themselves, because they were nowhere near done yet—she gasped a little when she heard footsteps outside her door.

A light tap on the door sounded. 'Angelette? Are you okay?'

Maybe if she ignored him he would go away. She tried to stay quiet but her sobs had so overtaken her body her chest kept spasming automatically, creating sharp intakes of breath she couldn't help but voice.

'Can I come in?'

'I'm okay,' she managed, but her voice was croaky and weak.

'It doesn't sound like it. Please, may I come in? Otherwise, I'm going to have to use my key.'

She got up and went to the door, her legs shaky. She was too tired to argue or worry about what he thought of her.

She opened it slowly, a couple of inches.

'Angelette. Hey, it's okay.' He grasped the door and opened it further, somehow inching his way in. He touched a hand to her cheek. 'Come sit down.' He sat on the bed next to her. 'Whatever it is, I know Christmas is tough for you. You don't have to explain. I just want to make sure you're okay. You shouldn't have to be alone if you're feeling this way.'

She couldn't string any words together, just kept sniffing and wiping her tears.

'Tilly is all tucked up in bed and Santa's been and gone, I don't have to be back there till seven am, I told her not to open any presents till I arrive.'

So he wasn't going anywhere until she either assured him she was feeling better, or told him why she was so upset.

'I'm sorry,' she said.

'What for? Crying? No need to apologise. Just let me know what I can do to help. Even if that's leaving you in peace.'

The thought of him leaving the room now seemed unbearable. She thought she'd wanted to be alone, but she didn't. 'Stay,' she whispered.

'Sure. I'll sit here as long as you need.' He took hold of her hand and sat still next to her, not saying anything, giving her the safe space she so desperately craved.

She turned her wrist and glanced at her watch, but the clock face blurred under her teary vision. 'What's the time?' she asked.

'Ten past eleven,' Mac said.

Angelette sucked in a sharp breath. 'Hold my hand for another five minutes?' she asked.

He gave it a reassuring squeeze. 'I can do that. Whatever helps.'

She sat there silent and still with him apart from her body swaying with her breath, as though she was a tree moving in the wind and he was the roots, strong and steady, supporting her.

She wiped her eyes to clear her vision and fixed her eyes on her watch. One minute to go. She counted it, right down to the last second, then her breath shook, and she feared she might not be able to take another.

Eleven-fifteen pm, Christmas Eve.

One year later, despite the time difference.

A strange sound rose up from inside and she let it out, a half shriek and half gasp, and Mac moved his hand to her back, holding onto her tightly. He rubbed it as she tried to regain her breath, but each inhalation stung, and each exhalation left her unsteady and dizzy.

'Talk to me, Angelette, let it out,' he whispered.

She turned her face towards him and though the room was lit only by the soft orange glow of the bedside lamp, his eyes held an unwavering kindness and authenticity she'd never seen in any man before.

She swallowed a lump before speaking. 'Eve,' she simply said.

He sought out her gaze more deeply. 'It's Christmas Eve, yes.'

'No. *Eve*.' She held her hand to her heart. '*My* Eve,' she said. 'My daughter. Oh, my beautiful daughter!' Sobs exploded and she lurched forward, pins and needles overtaking her, afraid she'd pass out.

'You have a daughter?' He rubbed her back, and her cries intensified. 'Try to slow your breaths. That's it, you're doing great.'

His comfort helped, at least to stop her from somehow dissolving into herself from the pain she'd held inside for so long. She forced her breath to slow, took a sip of water. She needed to get this out or it would forever eat her up inside. She looked at him again. 'I *had* a daughter.'

'Oh.' His shoulders sunk.

'She was born at eleven-fifteen on Christmas Eve. Except, she was already … She wasn't … She'd already gone. Stillborn.' She held a hand to her mouth as she realised she had never said that word out loud before now. An unexpected pregnancy, and then, unexpectedly, it was all over. Between breaths and sobs she explained. 'Darius and I had a brief reunion a few months after we broke up, but the result of that—our little surprise—was not a welcome change in his life. I should have known better than to have a stupid fling with my ex, but hey, it happened.' She held up her hands. 'He gave me enough money to get some things I needed and take six months off work to look after her, but turns out I didn't need it.' She drew in a deep breath in preparation for the next part. 'I was thirty-four weeks pregnant when I noticed she wasn't moving around or kicking as much anymore. I planned to get it checked out at my next prenatal appointment the day after Boxing Day, but on the afternoon of Christmas Eve, the movements stopped completely, and I felt some cramps and twinges. Maybe I should have called an ambulance, but I called a cab. I wasn't too far from the hospital.'

Mac nodded for her to go on, a solemn look on his face.

'They did an ultrasound, and ...' Angelette gulped down a hard lump in her throat. The memory of seeing the image always took her breath away. 'I could see that she was gone. She was completely still, and ... it felt like a part of me died too when they told me there was no heartbeat.'

'Angelette. My God, I'm so sorry,' he said softly, stroking her back with one hand and her hand with the other.

'They said I could have a c-section or deliver her naturally. I opted for natural, as I could feel it already starting to happen, and I *wanted* to feel her, experience it fully. Maybe I thought that somehow she'd wake up in the process, or that the physical pain would overtake the emotional. But it only made it worse.'

'Oh, Angelette.'

'In a few hours she was out, and I held her to my heart until Christmas morning. She was so beautiful, so tiny, so perfect.'

Angelette picked up her phone, aching to see her daughter's face again, though she knew it would be painful. 'Can I show you a photo? I'm sorry if that's weird. But, it helps, you know, to acknowledge her, to know she was here, however briefly.'

'Sure, I understand. I'd love to see her.'

She opened the album and found one of the photos, holding it up for both of them to see. Eve's beautiful, soft, grey skin, her blackened lips like a thin ribbon tied into a sweet bow. So still, so peaceful. But ... gone.

Mac shook his head and his eyes became glossy. 'Oh, my. How precious.' He didn't flinch, or look away, he just looked at her. A wave of relief rolled through Angelette's body at having revealed this tender part of her history to someone trustworthy, and who she felt safe with, even though she'd only known him a week.

'Do they know what caused it?' he asked.

'A stroke from unknown cause,' she replied. 'Just one of those crazy, inexplicable, unexpected things.'

'I'm so very sorry. I completely understand now,' he said, drawing her into an embrace. 'I'm sorry.'

She found herself falling back onto the bed and, wishing the bed would swallow her up, she nestled into her pillow, Mac by her side, arms still around her, not letting her go.

Chapter 10

The buzz of an alarm dissolved the dream Angelette was having of trying to push a cab by hand along a road covered with snow. The ache in her body she'd felt in her dream lingered, or maybe it was from all the crying. 'Huh?' She shifted onto her back, blinking to get her bearings.

'It's okay, no need to get up.' Mac's voice made her realise he had stayed with her all night. She watched him as he sat up, stretched, and stood, running a hand over his head. 'I'm going to jump in the shower and head over to Dad's. Do you need anything?'

She shook her head. 'Just sleep.'

'Okay,' he said. 'Did you want me to bring Tilly's present over to her? Where is it?'

Angelette rose up onto her elbows, suddenly alert. 'I'll do it. I'll give it to her.'

'You'll come?'

She nodded. 'But not now. Lunchtime?'

Mac smiled. 'Twelve pm on the dot. I texted you the address before, there's a pink cubby house out the front, can't miss it.' He rubbed his hands together as though he was the one about to receive a gift.

She lay back down again. 'Thank you, Mac. For last night.'

'Don't mention it.' He bent down and squeezed her hand gently. 'Will you be okay?'

'Yep. I think so.'

'Good.' He smiled softly and planted a quick kiss on her forehead. 'Call me if you need anything. Otherwise, I'll see you at lunch. It *will* be Christmassy, but, if there's anything I can do to make it easier, I'll try.'

'No, no need. It's important for Tilly, and yourselves, to have Christmas the way you like it. I'll be okay. I'm okay with it.'

'If you're sure. She's going to be thrilled, will I keep it a surprise?'

Angelette managed a tiny smile, imagining the surprise on Tilly's face. 'Okay. But let your dad know to make sure it's okay.'

'Of course it's okay. There's always enough food on the table to feed us for a week.'

Angelette sighed and relaxed back onto her side, her forehead still warm and tingly from his lips. Mac left the room, and the sound of the shower running soothed her back to sleep.

The ache in her muscles had finally eased when Angelette awoke. Her heart was cracked open, raw, vulnerable, but soothed. At least for now. She knew her grief would be an up and down battle, but she also knew now that she could and would deal with it. Not by escaping, but by moving through it, step by step. She slowly eased herself up off the bed, remembering the strange feeling of putting her feet back on the floor in the hospital that day; weak, shaky, and dizzy. A nurse had helped her to the bathroom and had told her what to expect on returning home: the bleeding, the cramps, and pressure from the milk coming in with no baby to nourish with it.

They'd given her a brochure for a therapist who dealt with perinatal loss. She'd had one session, but kept rescheduling her follow-up until she eventually cancelled it. It hurt to talk about it, so she focused on her work at the bathroom and toilet showroom which, although not what she wanted, was a way to get on with life, pass the time, and pay the bills. Angelette hadn't wanted to use the money Darius had given her to take six months off without a baby to look after. After she'd told him about Eve's death he refused to take his money back, had told her to keep it, so she'd saved it. It had come in handy to get her to Australia.

After last Christmas, Angelette hadn't had much of an urge to design and decorate again or look for a job in that field—it required motivation and inspiration, and her grief had drowned all of that. But now, the creative urge was starting to breathe again, gradually getting its oxygen back. She walked to the window and opened it, breathing in the summer morning air, remembering that she'd be giving her gift to Tilly at twelve. But with Mac and Ned extending their hospitality above and beyond, she wanted to give them something too. All the shops were closed, but she had an idea.

She grabbed her towel and headed to the door so she could take a shower first, and stepped on a piece of paper that looked like it had been slid under the door. She picked it up.

Left your breakfast outside the door, don't trip on it. Hopefully the bugs don't get to it. Mac.

She smiled, opened the door, and to the side of it was a plate with a lid covering it. She brought it inside and lifted the lid. Moisture steamed up from the omelette, surprisingly still slightly warm even though it had been a couple of hours since he'd left. She could heat it in the microwave but decided to enjoy it as it was, quickly checking for any signs of bugs first. When she was done, she revelled in the refreshing stream of water that ran over her like a waterfall, washing away the residual pain from last night and giving her a clean slate for now.

And soon she was outside, standing across the road from the pub, taking photos. She walked back over to it and took some close-up photos of the flower beds Mac's mother had nurtured. Then she found a shady picnic table in the park and sat with her drawing supplies, sketching the front view of The Mistletoe, followed by one at a different angle, starting from the flowers and looking up at the grand old building. She did her best but worked quickly, conscious that she wanted to be on time. When she was satisfied, she signed the pictures and slid each into a plastic sleeve, one for Mac, one for Ned.

Angelette took her supplies back to her room, put the drawings into the bag with the angel statue, checked her reflection in the bathroom mirror and, despite puffiness around her eyes, she felt comfortable enough to go. Here she was, having tried to avoid Christmas, about to have a Christmas Day lunch with the owners of the most Christmassy pub around. She'd thought her first experience of a family Christmas would be with Darius, but it was now to be with people she'd only known for a week. Yet somehow, they felt closer to her than Darius had ever been. Mac was giving her the gift she'd always wanted but had never received, until now.

Chapter 11

A modest red-brick home stood proudly at number 2 Percival Street, a rusted metal letterbox perched slightly lopsided at the front of a concrete driveway that was cracked from years of use and the harsh Australian climate. The hot pink plastic cubby house also stood proudly to the side of the large, level backyard. And the granny flat Mac had mentioned was in the far-left corner, a simple but stylish rectangular structure with a smaller square section at the front with double glass doors as a separate entrance, probably the proposed home office. It was painted a cream colour with an earthy red corrugated gable roof that nicely complemented the red of the main house.

Angelette smiled. This looked like what a happy family home should look like. Her inner child was getting her long overdue Christmas Day celebration.

She walked up the (also cracked concrete) steps to the front door, a Christmas wreath hanging in the centre of the stained-glass window. She took a deep breath and knocked.

Here we go. I can do this.

'Who could that be?' Mac said from inside, presumably to Tilly, whose little footsteps became louder. The door opened and the girl looked up at her, breaking into a smile.

'Angel! Ette!' she exclaimed, opening the screen door.

Angelette bent forward and tightly hugged Tilly, who smelled of candy and had glitter on her hands. For a moment she thought she would burst into tears again. Here she was, having lost her daughter, while this girl had lost her parents. Life seemed so unfair and random.

'I got a sparkle craft kit, look,' Tilly said, tugging on Angelette's dress and leading her to the coffee table where she was creating an artwork with stickers, markers, and glitter glue. Angelette managed a quick smile and wave to Ned and Mac on the way.

'That looks so fun!'

'Welcome, love,' said Ned. 'So glad you decided to join us.'

She shook his hand and thanked him for letting her come along.

'Thanks for the breakfast,' she added to Mac.

'I hope you're still hungry though.' He ducked into the adjoining kitchen and the scent of garlic and roast meat wafted into the air as he opened the oven. 'All done, but I'll let this rest a little before carving.'

He came back out and Angelette held up the brown paper gift bag, eyeing Mac as if to ask if she should give Tilly her gift now. He gave an eager nod.

'Tilly?' Angelette approached, kneeling down at the coffee table next to her. 'I have something for you.'

The girl's eyes widened. 'I thought all my presents were finished!' She gestured to the colourful Christmas tree with wrapping paper strewn all around with a variety of toys, books, and ribbons.

'This one is from me.'

'But I didn't get one for you because I didn't know you were coming.' She looked worried.

'That's okay, I don't need a gift. Just being here is enough.' She pulled out the present wrapped in red tissue paper and handed it to Tilly, who studied it first, shook it a little, then tore off the paper.

She held it up. 'Wowww!' She turned and held it up to show her uncle and grandfather. 'It's an angel.' She turned back to face Angelette. 'Just like you!'

Angelette smiled. 'I thought you might like it. A special angel to always watch over you and keep you safe.'

Tilly hugged it to her chest as though it was a soft, cuddly teddy bear and squeezed her eyes shut for a moment. 'Thanks!' She stood and dashed off down the hallway, then came back. 'I put it on my windowsill, it's my most beautifulest gift ever.'

'I'm glad.' She glanced at Mac and Ned who also thanked her. 'Oh, I have something for both of you, too. It's not much, and all the shops were closed so I couldn't pick up a bottle of drink or chocolates or anything, sorry.'

Ned waved her apologies away. 'We have everything covered.'

She handed each of them one of the drawings of The Mistletoe.

All was silent for a moment as they took it in. Ned looked at her with glistening eyes. 'Angelette, this is absolutely beautiful. You've captured all the little details so well.' He traced the lines with his finger. 'What a special gift, thank you.' He brought her into an embrace.

Mac smiled. 'I love how you've shown it from the perspective of the flowers, as though they're looking up at the building.' He shook his head. 'You must get back into design. In fact, by next Christmas promise me you'll try?'

Angelette pondered his encouragement, then nodded, and shook his hand, which turned into an embrace too. She did want to give her new business idea a go. What did she have to lose now, when she'd already lost everything else that mattered?

Tilly stood on tiptoes to look at the pictures too, mouthing another *wow*, then as though a lightbulb appeared above her head, she grabbed her art supplies and dashed back to her bedroom.

'Did you tell Angelette how the pub name came to be?' Ned asked his son. Mac shook his head. Ned took a seat on the couch and patted the spot next to him for her to sit, while Mac perched on the armrest.

'My father—Tilly's great grandfather, Anthony—had bought the pub from another family who had run it for three generations, since it was first built in the eighteen-hundreds.' Ned settled back to get comfortable on the couch, as though getting ready for a long story. 'He'd done some renovations, but hadn't decided on a new name yet, since the previous name was The Patterson Family Inn.'

Angelette nodded with interest.

'Anthony was engaged to my mother, Lillian, or Lil as everyone called her, and they got married before the pub was officially reopened. Their ceremony was in the community park on Christmas Eve, under a huge arch decorated with mistletoe.' Ned smiled. 'Oh, let me show you an old photo.' He went into the hallway then returned, a black and white framed picture in his hands of his parents standing under the mistletoe arch, happy smiling faces with the promise of more to come.

'How lovely,' Angelette said with a smile.

'They had their reception in the pub that night with close family and friends, which began our traditional Christmas Eve buffet we've had ever since.'

Ahh. Angelette now felt bad that she hadn't attended after Mac's invitation, and hoped her breakdown that night hadn't interfered with Mac's happy memories.

'At the end of the reception, the happy couple were chatting to each other and then they made an announcement. In honour of their special day and the special time of year, the inn was now to be called The Mistletoe so they could carry on their happy memories for years to come and always remember how it came to be.' Ned ran a hand over the photo protected under the glass.

'And,' Mac added, 'that's how the Christmas Rules came to be, too. It was my grandma's idea—that each Christmas season, anyone who entered the premises would need to honour the Christmas tradition and wear a special accessory.'

It all made sense now. How insistent Mac had been that she wear a Christmas accessory, and how extra important Christmas was to him. It was his family's legacy, founded in love and tradition.

Angelette's heart softened and warmed. 'That is really special. Like something you'd read about in a book, or watch in a movie. I've never known any traditions, didn't grow up with any, but I can tell how much it means to you,' she said. 'Thanks for sharing your family history with me.' She smiled. 'I can see some of you, Mac, in your grandparents. Your grandma's smile, and your grandfather's eyes.'

'That's what I always said,' Ned responded. 'He has my mum's smile, for sure.' He gave his son seated next to him on the armrest a firm clap on his knee, and Mac smiled. 'And *his* mum's dedication,' Ned added, a bit more solemnly. 'To family, to the business, to … doing what's right.'

'Aw, shucks Dad, stop or you'll have me getting all sentimental too.' He chuckled and lowered his head.

'We were so glad Miriam, Mac's mum, survived long enough to meet her first grandchild,' Ned said. 'Tilly doesn't really remember her as Miriam died six months later, but we have some precious photos.' Ned found some and shared them with her, along with pictures of Miriam when she'd been well. Angelette had to bite her bottom lip at the emotion of seeing the obvious decline in the woman's state of health, and yet, such love and pride at having her baby granddaughter in her arms, as though she'd been waiting for that all along. 'We really wished she was here when Jimmy and Nora passed. She was so strong and would have helped us keep it together. But somehow, we had to, for Tilly. And I honestly feel she *was* helping us somehow, from beyond. Still *is*.'

'I'm sure she is,' Angelette said softly, placing her hand on Ned's arm. Just like she knew grief, Ned and Mac sure did too. Differently, and yet the same. That gaping hole in the heart that never closes, no matter how much time passes.

'Ta-da!' Tilly appeared suddenly.

'Oh!' Mac said, standing, wiping the corner of his eye. 'What do we have here?' He bent to her level and kissed her forehead.

Tilly held up a piece of paper. 'I made a present for Angelette.' She said her name correctly for the first time.

'For me?' Angelette held a hand to her heart, then accepted the drawing.

'It's you,' Tilly said, pointing to the face of the woman, then tracing the wings with her finger. 'An angel. Just like the one you gave me.'

Now Angelette had to wipe the corner of her eye. 'Oh, sweetie, that is so nice of you. Not only can you sing, but you're a great artist too.' She held the drawing up and studied it some more. There was glitter on the wings, like in the statue she'd given her, and beyond the horizon was a rainbow. Little did Tilly know how much that sign of hope meant to her; having lost her baby she hoped one day there'd be a rainbow after the storm she'd experienced. 'I'll treasure it forever.'

'Will you be here for my birthday in June?' the girl asked eagerly.

Her heart sunk. She would miss this wonderful human. 'Oh, Tilly, unfortunately I'll be back home in America. But, I promise, I will send you a surprise in the mail, how about that?'

Tilly's smile faded at first, but then it returned and she nodded. 'I can't wait!'

She made a mental note to check the date with Mac before she left town, so she could fulfil her promise. It looked like even though she wouldn't be here physically, she'd keep in touch with these special souls. 'Now,' Angelette said, looking towards the kitchen, 'how can I help?'

They all went in and shared the load, carrying trays and dishes filled with food. Mac tossed some dressing onto a salad and brought that out, and Ned used oven mitts to carry the dish of roasted vegetables. Tilly carefully adjusted the table decorations and added three small candles. 'Don't forget our special lights, Grandad,' she said.

'Oh yes, of course.' Angelette eyed the candles as Ned explained. 'We light one candle for each person we miss.'

'That's a lovely idea.'

Before they sat at the table, Ned picked up a box of matches. He lit one and held it to one candle. 'For Miriam, my love.'

Mac held a hand to his dad's back. 'For Mum.'

'For Grandma,' Tilly added.

Mac lit one and then said, 'For Jimmy, the best brother I could have asked for.' His voice faltered.

'My second born son. Miss you, buddy,' Ned said.

'Daddy,' Tilly whispered.

Angelette's chin quivered.

Mac lit a match and got Tilly to help hold his hand as he held it towards the third candle.

'For Mummy,' Tilly said.

'Nora,' Mac and Ned said together.

'I love you all,' the little girl said. 'And we miss you. Don't we, Uncle Mac and Grandpa.'

'We sure do,' Ned said. 'We sure do.'

'Tilly,' Mac asked. 'Do you have an extra candle?'

'Um, I think so,' she said, going to the sideboard and rummaging in a drawer. 'How about this one?' She held up a half-melted candle in a glass jar.

Mac nodded. 'Angelette?' He held it to her. 'Would you like to light one?'

Her heart beat quickly and she gulped. She wasn't sure, but it was such a nice gesture that she nodded. Maybe it would help her, too, somehow, as lighting the candles had obviously helped them.

She took a deep breath and placed the candle jar in the centre of the dining table.

'Who's yours for?' Tilly asked.

Angelette lit a match and held it to the candle. 'For my own little angel I miss every day. Eve.' Her eyes stung with fresh tears.

'For Eve,' Tilly said, lightly touching Angelette's hand.

'For Eve,' Mac and Ned said in support.

Hearing her daughter's name sent shockwaves through her body, but she held steady, determined to get through this. She breathed deeply, and watched the flame flicker about; bright, warm, and glowing with life.

It was one of the most beautiful, bittersweet moments she'd ever experienced. She'd never felt more connected—to Mac, Tilly, Ned, and to this town, that although not what she'd expected, had turned out to be a much-needed part of her healing journey.

The crescent moon glowed gently in the clear night sky, stars twinkling around it, and silhouettes of tall trees created tangled patterns as Angelette looked up in awe. This country town skyline was so different to the city one she knew.

'Amazing, isn't it?' Mac said, walking slowly alongside her as they headed back to The Mistletoe.

'Totally.'

'So,' he said, 'you did it. You got through your first family Christmas.' He held up his hand and she high-fived it.

'Guess so. I thought I'd be holed up in my room waiting anxiously for the day to pass.'

'This was much better, wasn't it? Tough at times, I know. But better?'

She nodded. 'You were right. Christmas should be a time to celebrate what we have.'

After the emotional candle-lighting ceremony, they'd enjoyed a delicious lunch of roast turkey with cranberry sauce, honey-glazed ham, roasted vegetables and crispy potatoes, refreshing salads, and more. Dessert was pudding with ice cream, followed by tea and coffee with cookies and chocolates. She was officially completely full and couldn't imagine needing to eat again for another week. But Ned had given her a plate of leftovers anyway, which Mac carried in a plastic bag.

After lunch, Mac had helped his niece make paper planes with bright colours and glitter. Then they'd played board games, a few easier ones at first so Tilly could play along, then when Tilly was happily playing with her new toys outside, they'd sat on the back deck playing Scrabble while sharing their tea and chocolates. Ned had won, thanks to a triple word score right at the end. Tilly was hungry again before any of them, so they plated up some leftovers for an early dinner, and Tilly put on one of her favourite movies before Mac helped her have a bath and get into bed. By request, Angelette had read her a bedtime story, something she never thought she'd get to do. And the girl had gone off peacefully to sleep. Despite her family's tragedy, she was lucky too, to have these two men providing so much love, care, and stability. Angelette had learned to read from a young age as a way of soothing herself when there was nobody to read her a bedtime story.

'So, one full day left, eh?' Mac reminded her.

'Yep. I was thinking I might head up to that lookout near the waterfall. I haven't walked that far yet. Better make some use of the trainers I packed.'

'Sounds like a plan. And what time do you have to leave the following day?'

'If my calculations are correct, I'll need a cab by eleven am to get me to the bus stop.'

'Consider me your taxi driver, then.'

'Really? It's a long round trip for you. Can the pub handle you being gone if Tilly's with your dad?'

'Of course. We have backup options, and Sandy who works at the bar also helps with babysitting sometimes.'

'Thanks, Mac. If you're sure, that'd be a huge help. I can pay for gas, of course.'

'No need, consider it compensation for the less than five-star status you had to endure during your stay.' He caught her gaze and winked.

She chuckled. 'Five stars is not all it's cracked up to be sometimes. And I've been getting used to the flies and occasional spiders. I'm practically an Aussie now.'

'True blue,' he said, giving her a pat on the back as they arrived at the front door to the pub. He unlocked the door and they walked into the darkened entryway. 'Let me know if you need anything tomorrow, otherwise I hope you have a bloody awesome last day here,' he said, accentuating his Aussie accent.

'Haha, I will.'

'And how about a special farewell breakfast in the pub the day after tomorrow, before we leave for the bus stop?' he said. 'No Christmas accessories required this time.'

'Oh yeah, Christmas is almost over. I'm going to miss seeing you in your Santa hat and tinsel necklaces.'

Mac smiled and bent over the accessory basket. 'One last time then, eh?' He placed the hat on his head and she playfully flicked the white fluffy pompom.

They walked up the stairs, the pub strangely silent, and when they reached the landing, Angelette turned to face her door while Mac faced his. But then they turned back to each other, and he placed the bag of leftovers on the small side table outside the bathroom.

The faint moonlight shone through the skylight above, illuminating the perfect angles of his sculpted physique. Her heart beat a little faster, this time not from anxiety or pain. 'Thank you, for today,' she said. 'And last night. And everything.'

He smiled and nodded. 'Thank *you*. For being with us, for being brave, and choosing this random little place on earth to have your vacation.'

She held up her hands in a show of surrender. 'It looks like the universe had other plans for me this year.'

'Indeed,' he replied, taking a step closer.

'And I'm glad,' she whispered, matching his step closer with one of her own.

'I'm glad too.' He was right in front of her, his breath warm on her face.

Somehow, their fingers twirled softly together and with his gentle grasp he pulled her in even closer, his lips hovering near hers, as though waiting for her to initiate. It was probably a bad idea considering she was leaving soon, but … the universe had other plans. She softly touched her lips to his, his warmth spreading throughout her entire body in an instant. In response, he ran his hands up her arms and around the backs of her shoulders, his palms sending shots of bliss across her skin, and enveloped her in his strong arms, their kiss intensifying. She held onto his waist, then brought a hand up to his cheek, stroking the stubble under his cheekbone and tracing his lips with her finger in between kisses. His hands went to her hair, tingles running like wildfire across her scalp, and she didn't want him to stop, didn't know if *she* could stop.

But she had to. Before it went too far. Complicated was not what she needed after everything she'd been through.

She savoured one last, slow kiss, then gently pulled away, smiling. His mouth was still slightly open, as though eager for more, his chest rising and falling quickly, but then he sought out the truth in her eyes and smiled too, moving his hands down to hers again, and stepping back slightly.

She bit her lip, stifling a giggle as though she was a schoolgirl who'd been busted kissing in a secluded corner.

Mac's smile widened. 'That was yet another unexpected surprise,' he said.

'I've been attracting a lot of those,' she replied.

He touched her cheek with his palm. 'You're a strong, special person, Angelette. Don't ever forget that.'

She nodded. 'And I'll never forget you,' she added.

Mac let out a heavy exhale. 'We should probably save our goodbyes for when you're actually leaving, huh? There's still more of your vacation to enjoy.'

Angelette straightened up. 'That's a much better idea. I don't think I can handle a goodbye yet.'

Or at all.

'How about a goodnight, instead?' he offered.

'That, I can handle.' She picked up her bag of leftovers. 'Goodnight, Mac,' she said softly.

'Goodnight, Angelette.' He offered a little wave.

They turned to their respective doors.

'Sleep tight,' he added.

'I will.'

'Oh, and Angelette?'

She turned to face him. 'Yes?'

'Don't let the bed bugs bite.' He winked, unlocked his door, and smiled through the gap until he was inside his own room.

She chuckled, went inside, and just to be sure, checked under the bed sheets before getting into her pyjamas and snuggling under the covers.

Chapter 12

Angelette's footsteps had both an ease and a determination to them as she walked the winding pathway through the park the next day, past the war memorial, and past her 'reading tree'. She stopped momentarily as she noticed another tree nearby with a sign that said 'Wishing Tree'. She thought she had noticed it before but hadn't paid any attention to it until now, as though her brain's anti-Christmas filter had blocked it out. She walked closer. There was a stand with pens and tags for people to write on and hang their wish from the tree. Many tags had fallen off and become enmeshed in the ground around the tree, some had the ink washed away by rain, and others were freshly written on. Her hand hovered near the pens and she wondered if wishes came true what she would wish for. Right now, she didn't know. She removed her hand and walked away from the tree, continuing on with her original plan.

She found Drifters Lane, which was just beyond Ned's house, where the land began its incline to meet the mountain further up. A sign with a map of the walking track, the length and duration of the walk and emergency advice stood near the drinking fountain where she took a few quick sips. She powered up the track, lifting her sunglasses onto the top of her head when the trees and native plants around her closed in and the track narrowed.

She smiled at a couple of people who passed her on their way down the hill, rosy-cheeked and shiny from their walk. With each step, she imagined moving forward metaphorically, choosing to believe that although her past had been difficult, her future could still be different, better … she just had to keep stepping towards it.

She paused here and there to catch her breath and read the signs about the native flora and fauna species one might come across on the walk, but she was really only interested in what was at the top.

When it came into view, she quickened her pace and arrived with a loud exhalation. To her right was a lookout with a railing that separated the mountain from the valley below. And as the cliff face curved around to the left, a small but stunning waterfall cascaded to the rugged land below where it joined a stream leading down the hills until it disappeared from view.

She inhaled the beauty and exhaled her tension from the walk, and her mind, and took a photo. Was that the first photo she'd taken on this vacation? She checked her phone and realised that apart from the photos she'd taken at the Christmas carols with Mac's phone, and those she'd taken of The Mistletoe in order to sketch it, it was. The first photo purely for her. After all, she hadn't been here to make memories, but to escape them. She took a couple more from different angles, and walked further around the curved area, closer to the waterfall itself. Surprisingly, she had this view all to herself. And before anyone else came up the track, she knew she had to take the opportunity.

She took the piece of sketching paper from her bag, holding it tight as a firm breeze pushed and pulled at it, the edges flickering back and forth.

She held it up and re-read what she'd written, her breath quickening and her fingers trembling. She clamped her lips together and closed her eyes a moment, then opened them and said the words out loud.

'My beautiful Eve … Our time shared was brief, but precious. Thank you for visiting my world. I wish you could have stayed. But I know wherever you are, you are lighting up that part of the world. I love you and will never forget you.'

She folded the paper into a plane like Mac had showed Tilly, pressing the creases firmly with her fingers. Then she held it poised in the air, pointing towards the waterfall, and propelled it forward with a quick toss.

'Fly high, my angel.'

The paper plane arced forward and downwards, joining the stream of water and merging with the white froth below; her words sent out to the universe, cleansed by water and home with mother nature. She sucked in a deep breath and held her hand to her heart, absorbing the moment. She didn't want to say goodbye to Eve, but she had to. But like her letter had stated, she would never forget her, *could* never forget her. And she knew that even if she did move on successfully with her life, she would always have that pocket of grief inside her heart, and that was okay. Life didn't have to be perfect. She didn't have to have it all healed and figured out. She just had to find a way to make the most of where she was at, and cherish the gift of life that *she* had.

She stood there a while as the wind caressed her skin, tousled her hair, and refreshed her spirit. Then she turned away and walked down the hill, not stopping until she was back in the park and standing in front of the Wishing Tree.

She plucked a tag and wrote her wish on it, snapped a photo, then hung it from a tall branch with a smile, knowing that it would come true, because it was within her power to make it happen.

'Here she is, our VIP!' Barry exclaimed, as Angelette entered the pub the next morning for her farewell breakfast buffet. 'And I thought *I* was the only Very Impotent Person around here,' he added.

A laugh burst from Angelette's throat and she coughed and had to catch her breath. Mac, who was behind the counter, laughed heartily, as did several others, and he handed Baz a plate. 'Don't worry, Baz, you'll always be *important* to us.'

'Ah, love you guys to the moon and back,' he said, touching a hand to his heart. He looked at Angelette. 'Hey, no Christmas accessory?'

'Baz, Christmas is over,' she said. 'It's the twenty-seventh of December today.'

He tipped his head back in realisation. 'Ah … I forgot. What a shame, I love it when everyone's in the Christmas spirit.'

'I'm sure you'll keep everyone's Christmas spirit alive until next year.' She smiled, patting his back.

He nodded. 'Speaking of spirits,' he said, lifting his shot glass up high, 'fill 'er up, Mac, me man!'

'But Baz, it's only morning.' Mac made a show of shaking his head.

'No better way to start the day I say.' He handed it to Mac, who filled it with soda water.

'You know you don't *really* drink anymore, right, Baz? It's much healthier for you.'

'Ah, Mac, whatever you put in this baby does the trick.' He sculled the water and exhaled with satisfaction.

'In that case, enjoy, my man.' He poured him another, then eyed Angelette. 'Hungry?'

'You bet.' She smiled.

He handed her a plate and she went over to the buffet table.

'You got things from here, Sandy?' Mac said to his assistant behind the bar.

She gave a confident nod and Mac emerged from behind the counter, plate in hand, ready to have breakfast with her and take her to the bus stop.

She piled her plate high with scrambled eggs, smoked salmon, mushrooms, tomato, spinach and toast, while Mac went for the chipolata sausages, hash browns, scrambled eggs and mushrooms.

They sat at a table and chatted to other patrons as they ate, some asking her what New York was like, some asking what she did—or used to do—for a living, others asking why she chose Seekers Hill for her holiday. She answered honestly but without too much detail, and asked the locals about their favourite Seekers Hill memories. It was like chatting to old friends: safe, supported, and comfortable to simply be who she was.

When Angelette had finished her breakfast, she checked her watch. Time had flown by. She stood and stretched. 'Well, it looks like my vacation has come to an end.'

Mac's smile faded. 'Looks like it,' he said. 'Let's go get your bags, shall we? Dad and Tilly should be out front soon.'

She gave a nod. 'Goodbye everyone, it was nice to meet you all!' She waved, hugged a few people she didn't really know, then Barry came up to her with arms outstretched.

'Oh, Angelina,' he said, and she didn't try to correct him. 'I'll miss you! Such a sweet face you have.' He cupped her cheeks with his hands.

She leaned forward to hug him, but he held a hand in front quickly. 'Oh! Make sure you don't kiss me,' he said, 'because I have a coleslaw.'

She grinned, sighting the blister on his top lip, also not correcting him. 'Don't you just hate those things?' she said, and he nodded his enthusiastic agreement. She held him in an embrace. His eyes brightened and he walked her to the door, along with Mac.

'Can you keep an eye on the crowd for me while I'm gone, Baz? Make sure no one misbehaves?' Mac said.

'I'm onto it.' Baz gave a thumbs up, then waved at Angelette again.

She went back upstairs and counted her bags, Mac taking the heavy luggage, and she glanced around the room. 'I'll miss this little room,' she said.

'You're welcome to stay here anytime,' he offered. 'Maybe I'll start fixing it up a little … get a new bed, put up a stronger flyscreen to withstand those crazy gusts of wind.' He winked.

She shook her head at the embarrassing memory and they made their way downstairs and outside, where Tilly rushed into her arms.

'Angelette, don't go!'

'Oh, sweetie, I have to.' She held her at arm's length to look into her eyes. 'But don't forget, there'll be a special package arriving in June for your birthday, remember?'

Her eyes lit up a little.

She held the young girl close and rubbed her back. 'You were the highlight of my vacation.'

When she'd said her goodbyes, Ned gave her a kiss on the cheek and wrapped his arms around her too. 'Thank you for sharing Christmas with us, it was very special.'

'Likewise. Thank *you*.'

'And I'll keep lighting that extra candle for you and Eve on all our special occasions.'

'Oh, Ned ...' She went to say more but no words came out, she simply held a hand over her heart.

Mac stood by the door of his ute, he'd called it, and she fare-welled Ned and Tilly again before hopping in the passenger's seat.

'Ready?' he asked, starting the engine.

She nodded and waved through the window until they turned the corner onto the main road, and out of Seekers Hill; a place she hadn't expected to enjoy, but now held a place in her heart.

On the way, instead of talking, Mac had put on the radio and they'd shared in singing out-of-tune renditions of hits from the 90s, even-tually ending up in hysterics. It was the most fun Angelette could remember having in a long time. But her chest tightened as they arrived at the bus stop with twenty minutes to spare. It was almost time to say a difficult goodbye.

She stood on the dry, red dirt, shading her eyes with her hand from the glare of sunlight reflecting off the metal frame of the bus stop. Somehow her stylish sunglasses weren't cutting it.

Mac wore a wide brimmed hat, and held the tip of it. 'Would you like to borrow this?'

She smiled and shook her head. 'It's okay, I'll take some sunshine now while I can, before the recycled air and artificial light of the airport and plane, followed by the freezing air in New York. I think I'll snap-freeze as soon as I exit the airport.'

Mac chuckled. 'It gets cold here in winter, did you know? Not freezing cold, but enough to, maybe, turn the heater on for a bit.' He smiled and she fake-laughed.

'Geez. Must be so tough!'

He looked down the length of the deserted road, then focused on her eyes. 'This is tougher,' he said, bringing his right hand to her left one and interlacing their fingers.

She swallowed and held his gaze, wanting to absorb those eyes, then got out her phone. 'One photo … to remember you by?'

He nodded and she took a selfie of them both, hat and sunglasses off, wide cheesy smiles and wrinkly, squinting eyes. Perfect.

'Send it to me?'

'Of course.'

'And stay in touch?'

'Of course.'

He stroked her cheek with the back of his hand. 'You blew in with the wind and took my breath away, Ms Beaumont.'

Her heart fluttered and she stood close to him. 'You helped me finally acknowledge my loss. My grief. You gave me a safe space to express it. I'll always be thankful.'

'Me too. And you made my niece's Christmas extra special. She hasn't looked so happy, since … before it all happened.'

'I can't wait to hear all the updates about how she goes. She'll grow so fast!'

Mac nodded. 'Expect lots of photos, texts, and glittery artworks.'

Angelette smiled. 'Thanks for making me so welcome, and sorry I was such a Scrooge.'

'Hey, you had every reason to be. I'm sorry I made you wear those silly accessories.'

'Rules are rules,' she said in an authoritarian tone. 'But really, thank you, Mac. I know I still have a long way to go, but I'll get there. I'm going to return to the therapist I saw once and work through a few things, finally face what happened and get some strategies to cope when those memories come up.' She glanced into the distance.

'That's really brave of you.' He held her shoulders. 'You've got this. Okay?'

She nodded.

The faint hum of an engine muffled the air and they both looked down the long country road where a bus appeared in the distance.

Her heart beat fast. This was it.

She looked into Mac's eyes. 'Bye, Mac.'

'Bye, Angelette.'

Their foreheads rested together and she closed her eyes, his heat radiating through her. She pulled back a little and looked into his eyes. Her lips wanted his, but … she wrapped her arms around him. Tight. Lingering. And that was all. They'd had their one-off kiss and it had been amazing and that memory was enough. There was no need to complicate anything now.

Mac must have thought the same, as he didn't try to kiss her, simply returned her embrace and waited till she was ready to let go.

She pressed her lips together into a smile of surrender and stepped onto the bus as he handed the driver her luggage for the side compartment. She sat at the back, next to the window, and waved through the glass, her breath high in her chest.

He tipped his hat in an old-fashioned gesture and stood there smiling, waving until she could no longer see him. Then she rested her head against the back of the seat, closed her eyes, and exhaled for what felt like forever.

Chapter 13

The Following Christmas

Angelette opened her eyes and looked outside the window of the cab. The sun was long gone and the stars sparkled. She checked the time on her watch.

Almost there.

She straightened up, eager to finally offload her luggage and get some rest ... and of course, make her wish come true. She smiled to herself as she checked the photo on her phone that she'd taken last year of the tag at the Wishing Tree ...

I wish ... to return to Seekers Hill and see Mac, Tilly and Ned again.

It wasn't really a wish, of course, but more of a promise to herself. She had never promised it to Mac or Tilly, because she didn't want to create any uncertain expectations between them. She wanted to get her life, and herself, back together again and then surprise them.

Mac may have moved on, of course, emotionally at least; though in their regular contact over the past year he hadn't mentioned meeting anyone, unless he preferred to keep that private. But it didn't matter. Either way, she wanted to be here. For a visit or indefinitely, she didn't know, but she had to try something new and see where it led. And she couldn't wait to see the girl who had also stolen her heart.

They passed Seekers Hill Inn and Cottages and she chuckled. This time, she wouldn't be walking through their jingly doors.

Twenty minutes later her heart fluttered as the cab drove into the town and she saw it: The Mistletoe, complete with tinsel, sparkling fairy lights, and flashing red and green globes around the front door.

'Here is fine, thanks,' she told the driver. He parked on the side of the road opposite the pub and she paid her fare.

He helped unload her luggage, which was a bit more cumbersome than last year. 'You sure you're right with all this?'

'Yep, I'm sure someone inside can help me.' She gestured to the pub.

'Sure thing. Well, you have a merry Christmas!'

'Thank you, you have a merry Christmas too.' She smiled. She wouldn't be cutting anyone off mid-greeting this year.

Angelette inhaled the warm country air she had missed so much, and wheeled her luggage across the road to the slightly ajar front door. She pushed it fully open and rested her luggage against the wall in the entry foyer.

Then she knocked.

'We've just closed up for the night,' Mac's voice called out.

'I'm here for the room,' she called back.

'Oh yes, almost forgot, Mrs Montlake, was it?' His voice got louder as he neared the door, and she caught a glimpse through the glass of Mac carrying a broom.

He leaned it against the wall and peered through the glass, his eyes disbelieving, then opened the door, his mouth hanging open.

'You're not Mrs Montlake.'

'I was cheeky and booked under a pseudonym.' She grinned.

'Angelette, is it really you?' He stepped towards her. 'Wow, what a surprise!' He grasped her arms and then pulled her into a strong hug.

She held on tight, pushing back tears. This hug had been a long time coming and the thought of it had kept her going through some of the darkest moments of the past year as she'd faced her past and her grief and marched forward in hope.

'I missed you,' she said.

'I missed you too.' He pulled back and studied her face. 'Are you here to escape Christmas or celebrate it?'

She smiled. 'I'm here to make the most of the life I have,' she replied.

'For a week or so like before?'

She tapped her chin. 'Hmm, I was thinking longer. Depends. Maybe even indefinitely.'

'What about New York?'

'I've never felt more at home than I do here, Mac. If things are different with you, I understand, but my heart is telling me to be here and for once I'm going to trust it.' She gave an affirmative nod.

His smile lit up the darkened foyer. 'I've wanted nothing more for the past twelve months than for you to walk through that door again. I didn't think it would happen, yet here you are.' He picked up her luggage and she smiled at the sparkly red and green wristband on his right forearm, complete with a bell on it. 'Let's get these upstairs!' She walked with him up the creaky stairs, stopped at the landing as he rested the luggage against the wall and took her hands in his. 'By the looks of it, I think this Christmas is going to be even better than the last.'

'I know it will,' she replied, leaning close to him and planting a firm kiss on his lips. He enveloped her in his arms and kissed her back with more purpose and passion than a year ago, creating waves of bliss as her nerves tingled and her heart opened to let him in.

'Shouldn't we be kissing *under* the mistletoe?' she said with a giggle as they took a breath.

'Unless you want to dig a ditch outside and lie in the dirt, *above* the mistletoe is fine with me,' Mac replied, and they continued, kissing and smiling at the same time.

When she eventually pulled back, she asked, 'Is my room all fresh and ready?'

'It is,' he said, 'but …' He glanced at his door. 'This time I think I'll upgrade you to the deluxe suite.'

A smile grew slowly onto her lips and she nodded her agreement.

'But first, what can I get you? A cool drink, a hot chocolate, a meal?'

'How about all three?'

'Only because you're a VIP.' He winked, then led her back downstairs.

She noticed the accessory basket on the floor. 'Still following the Christmas rules, huh?'

'Of course. But, I'm happy to let them slide for tonight if you prefer, since we're officially closed.' He pushed open the door to the pub, but she bent over the basket.

'Oh, not at all. Rules are rules,' she said, picking up a sparkly Christmas belt and wrapping it around her waist. 'Passed down by your father,' she added, putting a tinsel garland around her neck. 'And his father before that.' She fed her arms through an elf vest. 'Thanks to your grandma's idea,' she said, sliding a reindeer antler headband onto her head. 'No Christmas accessory, no dinner.' She picked up a Santa hat and popped it onto his head.

'If I must.' He held his hands up in defeat. 'Now, let's see what I can whip up for you.' He rubbed his hands together and again pushed open the door to the pub. Angelette stepped through with her chin raised, smile wide, knowing that this Christmas would indeed be much better than any other she'd had before.

Epilogue

Six Months Later …

'Happy Birthday, Tilly!' Angelette exclaimed, drawing the eight-year-old girl into an eager embrace as soon as she opened the door to Ned's house.

'Thanks Aunty Angelette!' she said. 'Is it all finished now?' She jumped up and down on the spot.

'It sure is. Didn't we promise the cottage would be all ready by your birthday, so you could do the official opening ceremony?'

She nodded rapidly. 'I can't wait!'

Angelette and Mac led Tilly to the backyard, Ned following, and Angelette took a moment to admire the exterior of her and Mac's new home, and her home office. She had convinced Mac and Ned not to call it the granny flat anymore.

The sign, 'AngelEve Designs', was displayed proudly above the door to the office entrance. A small area filled with natural light, where she would run her online decorating consulting business which she'd been doing successfully for the past year; helping people around the globe bring more pleasure and functionality to their home or work environments, at a fraction of the cost of an in-person designer. She'd work to their budgets and source all the items they'd need from their local area to set up, revamp, or decorate their living spaces. Clients would simply submit photos and videos of their spaces, measurements, and she'd do the rest. It was her dream job, and she'd created it herself. And even better, she could work from *anywhere* in the world; even the tiny town of Seekers Hill.

She would have been happy to continue living above the pub, but Mac had decided he wanted to be closer to Tilly as she grew, help Ned out more. He'd invited Angelette to come and live with him in the home that Jimmy had built, honouring it by turning it into something special. They'd also hired a new pub manager to reduce Mac's work hours, who now took residence in the main room above The Mistletoe. The smaller room had been revamped and was rented out as needed to visitors.

All the unfinished threads of their lives were weaving together to create a new one.

'Where are the scissors?' Tilly asked, still jumping around.

'Here, but be careful, okay?' Ned handed them to her.

Angelette had tied ribbon to the two posts on either side of the small steps leading up to the deck outside the office, and also between two potted plants either side of the front door to their home.

Tilly stood by the office ribbons first. Ned got his camera ready.

'I officially welcome Tilly to be our grand opening ambassador,' Angelette said through a pretend microphone made by her fist. 'Would you like to say a few words?' She held her microphone out to Tilly.

'Yes.' She cleared her throat. 'I am very honoured to be part of this momentous occasion.' She giggled. 'I've been rehearsing that!'

she said, through a hand covering her mouth. She cleared her throat again. 'Anyway. As I was saying. This is a very special office, and it's now time, ladies and gentlemen ... I declare AngelEve Designs officially open!' She cut the ribbon with the scissors and everyone clapped.

Angelette's heart soared. Though her business was technically already open, she now had a dedicated space to keep business and home life separate, and she couldn't be happier.

'Now to the next one,' Tilly said, moving to the front door where the other ribbon was. She crouched next to the little memorial garden where a stone plaque sat, which they'd had engraved with Jimmy and Nora's names. 'In honour of my mum and dad,' Tilly said softly. 'We'd like to thank them for this opportunity, and we know they'll always be here with us.' She kissed her fingers and touched them to the plaque. 'May this home bring many happy memories and lots of fun. I now declare the cottage officially open!' She cut the ribbon and they all clapped again. 'Welcome home, Aunty Angelette and Uncle Mac,' Tilly said.

Angelette scooped her up and swung her around, though the girl was getting rather heavy and she wouldn't be able to do that for much longer.

'Welcome home, buddy,' Ned said, giving his son a hug and patting him on the back.

'Thanks, Dad.'

'You too, love.' He kissed Angelette's cheek and grasped her hand.

'Ned, we'd like you to be the first through the front door,' Angelette said.

His eyebrows rose. She held his hand and led him to the door, opened it, and he stepped through, saying, 'Wow,' and, 'Oh I love this'. Tilly followed, saying the same, and then Angelette glanced

at Mac with an excited smile. He held her hand and together
they stepped through the doorway into the small but perfect home
she'd lovingly planned out and decorated to suit both their needs.
She knew, with all of her heart, that she'd finally found her real
family.

Acknowledgements

It's been a long time between books and I'd like to thank my partner and family for always encouraging me and celebrating my progress with me. Also my many writing friends who never fail to provide a quick bit of reassurance late at night, or feedback on my ideas. Thanks for the fun in travelling this creative journey together.

Thanks to all at Escape Publishing and Harlequin/HarperCollins Australia for publishing my stories, and to my editor Johanna Baker for your feedback and help in making the manuscript squeaky clean.

Thanks to my readers for your ongoing support! And if this is the first book you're reading from me, thank you and welcome to my little world. I hope you enjoy the story! This story is short, sweet, and means a lot to me, and I hope you enjoy the journey with these characters I've created.

His Christmas Feast

NORA JAMES

When one door closes, another one opens.

Chapter 1

As Christophe wiped down his outdoor table in preparation for the Christmas party, he caught a glimpse of his neighbour's golden curls above the fence and his heart skipped a beat. Should he say something to her? Would she turn with contempt if he did, or gaze at him with those angelic hazel eyes and offer him a smile that would light up his world better than any shiny decorations? He never knew what to expect with the gorgeous twenty-four-year-old who lived next door. By the time he'd decided to shout out 'Merry Christmas' she'd disappeared.

It was probably just as well.

He had plenty to do and needed to stay focused. Emily was capable of ruining his mood with one word, so staying away from her, especially on a day like today, was highly recommended. He hurried back inside and set out to make the filling for his dessert, a *bûche de Noël* in the tradition of the Christmas logs served in France. He whisked together butter, icing sugar and vanilla, before gently folding in the raspberry purée he'd made. His guests expected nothing less than a fabulous lunch from a French chef and he wouldn't let them down.

Besides, he was determined to spoil all the lonely souls he'd invited, the friends, acquaintances and friends of friends who would otherwise spend the holiday alone. This would be a Christmas to remember, a day without regrets or sadness, he'd make sure of it. For them and for him.

As he spread the sweet-scented mixture on the *génoise* he'd baked, the front flyscreen door banged shut. Someone had let themselves in and Christophe smiled at the ease and freedom of living in Marandowie. There weren't too many places in the world where you could still leave your front door open without a worry.

'Chris? You presentable?'

He recognised Joe's voice immediately. 'In the kitchen. Naked but it doesn't matter.'

'I'll leave the veggies in the entrance, then.'

Christophe chuckled at the embarrassment in the young farmer's voice. There was nothing like a laugh in the morning, and he loved to tease Joe, who had a few preconceived ideas about the French, one of them being that they had a predilection for nudity. 'Just kidding. I'm dressed.' In the most informal way—barefoot, in shorts and a T-shirt— but it was enough, another thing he loved about living in Australia.

Joe appeared carrying a huge box of vegetables as if it were a feather and slid it across the kitchen bench. 'You had me worried there, mate.'

'That was the point. Give me a second.' With the help of the tea towel under his cake, Christophe quickly rolled the dessert into a log. 'I'll decorate it later.'

'Wow! I'd have turned that into chook feed. You're damn good with your hands.'

'Shame it's not a pretty girl telling me so.' He said that, but he didn't really mean it. Women were problems. He placed the dessert in the fridge.

'With that accent of yours, I don't think you'd have any trouble finding one if you wanted to.' Joe winked. 'Brought ya lettuce, tomatoes, cucumber, capsicum, a whole heap of stuff. Even fresher than when I cart it up to the restaurant.'

'Thanks, Joe. If you're not careful with that ocker accent of yours, you, on the other hand, are going to scare away all the women. You don't have to lay it on that thick, you know?' Christophe couldn't understand it. Joe was young, good-looking, educated, charming even, but he always pretended to be nothing like it. Maybe he wanted to sound tough. Or maybe it was his way of saying with every breath he took that he belonged here in the Australian country, the way the Bretons back where Christophe was from celebrated their roots every day with their music and food.

Joe shrugged. 'Me, an accent, mate? I haven't the faintest idea what you mean. You must be thinking about some other drongo.'

Christophe piled up the salad vegetables on the sink, ready to be washed, although they could wait. It was too early to chop them all up. They'd oxidise and turn brown before it was time to eat. And he had other things to do in the meantime: set the table, organise the drinks, make the orange and ginger sauce that would turn the turkey and chestnuts into a sublime main course.

'So who did you invite in the end? Everyone we talked about?' Joe rested his sunburned forearms on the benchtop and leaned forward, such concentration on his face that he seemed ready for state secrets.

'Let's see. My mate Jago. Nico, the new kitchen hand. Both great guys.'

'I'm more interested in the ladies. Zoe? Elizabeth?'

'Yep. And Flick. You know, Felicity.'

'With her stuck-up guy.'

'Nobody's perfect. And he's the man who owns the walls of my restaurant.'

Joe cleared his throat. 'Marta?'

'Yeah.'

Joe rubbed his nose and grinned. 'Okay. What about Emily? Did you invite her?'

At the mention of her name, Christophe automatically glanced at her house through his kitchen window and there she was, probably pottering around under her verandah now, her pretty head of curls shining in the morning light the only thing he could see over the old fence. His stomach tightened—with what? Angst, excitement, he wasn't sure …

Whatever it is, it makes me feel like a teenager.

He quickly turned his attention back to Joe.

'Invite who?' Feigning ignorance seemed to be the best approach. Granted, Emily had assets most men would fight, lie, even kill for, but she'd been nothing but obnoxious to Christophe and it was just as well.

'For goodness sake, Chris, *Emily Brighton*, your neighbour. The optician. If you haven't noticed her maybe you should go get your eyes checked, although she's on holidays at the moment.'

'Oh, that Emily. Why? You interested in her?'

'Nah, course not. Not like that. I've known her way too long. We used to play together as kids. She was still in her nappies and I wasn't long out of mine. Got up to all sorts together a few years later, hiding her mother's groceries, taking the mail out of letter-boxes and putting it into others.' He dropped his gaze to the floor, chuckling at the memory. 'She's a nice girl. And she's on her own. Everyone around here knows that. You do too, right?'

A nice girl? She was as pretty as they come. Sexy as hell, too. But nice? On what planet did Joe live? 'She hasn't exactly warmed to me.'

'Heard you're fighting over fixing the fence.'

'Something like that.' In fact they seemed to fight over anything and everything the minute they opened their mouths. Especially the past few times he'd been in Marandowie.

'It's your party, Chris. I suppose you know what's best. Must be strange listening to a bunch of people having a good time next door on Christmas Day when you're sitting there all alone in her circumstances, though. I'm just saying.'

Christophe sighed. The whole purpose of the party was to make sure no one around him felt left out on Christmas Day. He couldn't take enough time off to fly home to be with his parents and brothers like he had last year. He could barely bring himself to think about them, it pained him so much to be away from them for the festive season. That was the price to pay for living in the Lucky Country. If he'd had to spend his second Christmas here all alone it would have broken his heart, so he understood all too well what Joe meant about Emily.

Still, there had to be a limit. Christophe wasn't the only one involved. Inviting someone as touchy as the young woman next door had the potential to spoil the party not just for him, but for everyone. He'd seen it before: one person with the wrong attitude was capable of ruining the day, and if anyone was capable of the wrong attitude, it certainly was his belligerent neighbour. He wasn't the one to blame. She had made her own bed by being so incredibly difficult, at least around him.

Joe grabbed the empty vegetable box. 'See ya around noon, then?'

'Great. I wonder if anyone will recognise you, all dressed up.'

'Oh, yeah. About that … I'm only comfortable in work boots or these.'

Christophe looked down at the worn thongs that protected the farmer's tanned feet and smiled. 'Do your best, Joe. Whatever that turns out to be will be fine by me.'

He listened to Joe whistle his way through the kitchen, into the lounge room and out of the house. Christophe checked his watch, then opened the oven. The turkey was roasting nicely, an even, crisp brown skin forming all over. He basted it and carefully collected some of the juices, spooning them into a saucepan, to serve as a flavoursome base for the orange and ginger sauce.

Next, he lined up the ingredients for the sauce. He squeezed garlic through a press and fried it with ginger. He added butter and cornstarch and, once absorbed, honey, water and his favourite part: a good cup of Cointreau. He poured the liqueur and held up the bottle to the light. There was hardly any left! It had slipped his mind to stock up on it. Luckily, he had enough for the sauce and plenty of other alcohol in his drinks cabinet for after lunch *digestifs*.

Soon the tangy, mouth-watering scent filled the house. He especially loved this sauce when he added spice. He hesitated. Some people couldn't take the heat. But a small amount would really lift it.

He turned off the cooker—although he'd only be a few seconds, he couldn't risk burning the sauce—and headed down the back to his herb patch in search of a mild red chilli. Nothing spiced things up quite like ... Emily! There she was again, this time down at the back of her garden, where Christophe could see her through the broken fence.

Her perfect curves danced under her thin nightdress as she leaned forward and watered her geraniums in the cool of the day. Suddenly, and somewhat against his will, he imagined himself tearing off the simple black and white strappy nightie in a flash of sweat and sweetness and excitement and ... *Bon Dieu!* He let out a sigh.

She glanced up at him and froze, like a deer surprised in the forest by an unexpected hiker. As she came back to life seconds later, her expression hardened. She mumbled something unintelligible to herself, or perhaps to him, before hurrying inside.

'Excuse me,' he shouted to make sure she heard him, 'but this kind of thing wouldn't happen if you let me replace the fence.' Or if she put on some decent clothes when she was planning on heading out into the garden. Not that he was complaining about the sight of her sun-kissed skin.

As he pulled a small chilli off a bushy plant, Emily reappeared, this time in a loose T-shirt and an old pair of tracksuit pants. Talk about self-sabotage. She couldn't find anything more unflattering if she tried. Perhaps that was the point. She kept the worst of herself just for him. Well, she'd failed if she was trying to make herself look repulsive. She'd at least have to put a paper bag over that pretty face and those loose, golden curls.

She stomped up to Christophe and stopped, tight-lipped, her eyes filled with blame.

'It's not my fault,' he blurted out before she accused him of something. Knowing her, she'd say he was stalking her. 'You're the one who didn't get dressed.'

'You're never in the garden this early.'

'I have things to do today.'

'You crept up on me. Did you know I was watering my plants in my nightie? Thought you'd get an eyeful, is that it? I bet. You men are all alike. If you think my knees are wobbling just because you're called Christophe Duval and are dark and handsome, think again.'

'Get an eyeful? That's ridiculous! I had to pick a chilli in my own garden. Is there a law against that? Am I supposed to fumble my way down to the herb garden wearing a blindfold? Wait a minute, you think I'm handsome? Dark and handsome?' It wasn't how he pictured himself.

'You eat chilli in the morning? Is that what the French do, Christopher?' She insisted on the final 'r', squinting as she watched him attentively. 'You're scowling, monsieur. That will give you premature wrinkles. Oh, dear, I'm getting on your nerves first thing in the morning.'

And not just any morning: Christmas morning, a day for peace and good will. Mind you, Emily was particularly capable when it came to annoying the hell out of him any day of the year—he had to give her that. 'No, I don't eat chilli for breakfast, Emily. It is not what the French do, generally speaking. It's Christophe not Christopher, as I've told you a hundred times and you're …'

He looked into those big almond-shaped eyes of hers and lost the end of his sentence. He had to remind himself how painful she was. 'It has nothing to do with annoying me or not. I frown when I concentrate and I'm concentrating on cooking, that's all. I'm busy preparing a Christmas lunch. *Voilà*.'

'*Oh là là*, a Christmas lunch. You're having people over.'

'Yes, people. I didn't invite any dogs.'

A smile lit up her face. 'That's actually quite funny. You surprise me. The French aren't known for their humour.'

'Thank you. I think.'

Suddenly, the warmth left her expression. 'Wait a minute. You're not calling me a dog or more precisely a bit—'

'No! I wouldn't. I said dogs as opposed to people. I could just as easily have said elephants.'

'And now you're calling me fat.'

'Fat? Excuse me?'

What on earth was she talking about?

'I am not an elephant. I may not be a rake-thin model but I am proud of this body and you are not going to shame me. Women are beautiful in all shapes and sizes.'

'Of course.' Stunned, Christophe watched her stomp back up the garden path. Once again their conversation had turned sour faster than milk in the sun. He couldn't figure it out. He couldn't figure *her* out. All he'd expected was a brief conversation about Christmas, a few polite words, maybe even best wishes for the special day.

He shook his head as he returned inside where the caramelised orange scent wafted through the air. He wouldn't have her believe that he was an arrogant Frenchman who'd called her names on Christmas Day. He'd change her perception one way or another, simply for the pleasure of proving her wrong.

He was too busy right now, but maybe he'd drop by with a box of chocolates or a tin of Christmas tea tomorrow. Boxing Day was for giving boxes of things, wasn't it? He thought so, although he could be wrong about that. There was no such thing as Boxing Day in France. In his country, the day after Christmas was for nursing your stomach and catching up on sleep.

It was probably better to get it over and done with. If he was feeling brave and there was still time, he'd make an effort and call in quickly to see Emily later this morning, once he'd finished the food preparations. Five minutes was all he needed to chit-chat with her and smooth things over.

Actually, that would be four minutes too many.

The table sparkled with silver gumnuts, the turkey felt firm but not hard when pressed, and the mini-quiches and vol-au-vents he'd made from scratch looked inviting on their shiny trays. He had forty minutes to spare, plenty of time to shower and change and even put his feet up and sip a glass of red for a while to relax before the party started.

He clicked his tongue. What about Emily? He really ought to go over and make peace with her. It was Christmas, a time to be pleasant with everyone.

But he wasn't foolish enough to invite her to lunch. He hadn't changed his mind about that. No poison at his table, thank you very much.

He chose a bottle of pinot noir, tied a red bow around it and walked over, through his big front garden and around the corner block to her entrance. No going through a little gate between the two properties like a few people had installed around here, to make it easier for neighbours to visit on these sprawling semi-rural blocks.

That was one thing he was sure of: there was no gate between his and Emily's homes, no bridge between the two of them, no connection at all. It'd be a miracle if she let him replace the horrible, broken fibre-cement fence that separated their houses with the same wooden panels he had on all other three sides of his property, let alone put in a gate.

When he reached her front door, he knocked and waited. He wouldn't dare walk right in the way Joe had done that morning at Christophe's; he could imagine the welcome reserved to him if he did. There was no answer, so he knocked again. That was strange. Emily's car was there.

He stood silently and listened. Soft footsteps, a breath. She was home, waiting behind the closed door. Did she know it was him? He cleared his throat. 'It's Christophe.'

What was that muffled sound in response? It reminded him of an injured animal. Perhaps it was something on TV. 'Christophe from next door. Emily? I won't hold you up on Christmas Day. I just came to, uh, say a few words.'

There it was again, a strange, soft noise, but this time he realised what it was: a woman crying. Emily, his tough, independent, invincible neighbour, was shedding tears. Was that possible?

She had seemed upset in the garden, it was true, and she appeared to believe that he'd insulted her … Had he done this to her, and on Christmas Day? Guilt tightened his stomach.

'Is everything okay, Emily?' He hesitated. If it was his doing, he'd fix it. 'I'm sorry for what I said earlier.'

'Which part?' her voice cracked.

'The part where I … where you … whichever part you like. All of it. It came out all wrong. I certainly wasn't calling you a dog or an elephant. I meant I'd invited people, just people and …' He cleared his throat. 'I was hoping to make you laugh because, well, it's Christmas and it is highly recommended not to fight on Christmas Day. Please open the door.'

He knew that asking wouldn't necessarily make it happen. If Emily had decided she didn't want to see him, then she wouldn't, no matter what he said, so after a few seconds of staring at the handle in the hope that it would turn, he placed the bottle on the doormat and started up the garden path.

The door clicked.

'I'm going to need this today.'

He turned around. Emily had stepped outside and was holding the bottle of red in one hand. Her swollen eyes sent a pang of compassion straight to his heart. If he didn't know better he'd wrap his arms around her and hold her against him until he saw her smile.

Her lips curled up, as if she'd read his mind. 'Don't worry. You're not the one who upset me.'

Is there someone in her life, after all? A difficult boyfriend who gives her a hard time? He bit his lip.

'I brought this on myself,' she said, looking away. 'I made a promise to do something by the end of the year and I failed miserably. But then, it was to be expected. Set yourself impossible tasks and you are bound to fail.' She held up the bottle and waved it around a little. 'Thanks. I suppose I should say Merry Christmas.'

'You're welcome. Merry Christmas to you. And there's still time.'

'Sorry?'

'It's not the end of the year. There's time to do that thing you want to do.'

She sighed. 'Not enough for what I had in mind. But hey, today I have a roof over my head, blue skies, a neighbour good enough to bring me a bottle of wine.'

He hesitated. Maybe Joe was right. Maybe under her steel exterior Emily was a nice woman. And if not, what the heck? It was only a meal and if she was out of line, he'd stand up to her. 'Listen, it's very late notice, and I understand if you'd rather not, but if you're free today and you'd care to join us for lunch, I'd be delighted. No fence disputes mentioned, I promise. It's just a bunch of friends who weren't otherwise doing anything and, to tell you the truth, some of the guests are new acquaintances. Joe is coming though. You know Joe Marshall.'

'I sure know Joe. But I don't want to crash your party.'

'It wouldn't be crashing it.'

She gave him a look of disbelief. 'Actually, I am doing something today anyway, so ...'

His shoulders dropped with disappointment. It made no sense. It was better if she didn't come, much better. He wasn't going to invite her in the first place yet now, somehow, he wanted her to join him. No, he was *dying* for her to join him. Listening to her sob and seeing her there with reddened eyes, her shoulders rolled in, had wiped the slate clean, washing away all the animosity that had ever existed between them.

For how long remained to be seen.

'If your plans fall through, it's drinks at noon. We'll eat around one pm. And we're dressing up for the occasion. That said, I doubt if Joe will wear shoes.'

She chuckled. 'Why doesn't that surprise me?'

He couldn't help but laugh with her, not because of what they'd said, but because her giggle was contagious. And light. And lovely.

If only she could be like that all the time. Most of the time. Half the time. He'd settle for that.

'I'd better go and get ready.'

She nodded, so with a wave of his hand he left her.

Back home, as he lathered the soap up in the shower, he went over and over the conversation with Emily, wondering if she'd accept his invitation.

He probably hadn't said the right words to make her want to join him. *If your plans fall through?* Whose plans fall through on Christmas Day? And no wonder she felt she'd be crashing the party. Nobody asks you to a Christmas lunch less than an hour before it starts.

The only response possible from his beautiful, crazy neighbour was 'no' and yet slowly, somewhat reluctantly, now that he'd seen her softer side and the incredible warmth in her smile, Christophe admitted to himself how very much he would have liked her to say 'yes' just this once.

Chapter 2

Emily poured herself a glass of the red Christophe had brought over and swallowed a mouthful. It touched her that someone cared enough to come over with a gift on Christmas Day. She'd been convinced she wouldn't see a soul today. Most people knew to stay away. Shame it was her neighbour who'd paid her a visit.

Not that she'd ever known anyone better looking, with his chiselled jaw and those lips that seemed to whisper silent promises of pleasure every time she was brave enough to let her gaze settle on them.

She sprawled out on the couch, holding her glass of red, and with her free hand patted her black cat Shadow who lay on the armrest. As far as physique went, Christophe was on a par with the best-looking guys on the planet. Including Josh, her ex. If there was one thing she was sure of, it was that she'd never go down that road again. Really hot men thought they were God's gift to women and, in so many ways, abused their power over those unfortunate enough to fall for them.

Besides, Christophe didn't get on with her. He'd proven that point over and over, had probably only invited her at the last minute out of guilt, or pity, or so that he wouldn't appear heartless if others asked whether she was coming. Yes, it was nice of him to go over there with his bottle of red—and a pretty good one at that—but it was nothing more than a neighbourly gesture.

She drank some more and the warmth of the wine spread to her limbs. Through her open window she heard cars pull up, excited voices as guests climbed out. There were people next door, not dogs, not elephants, all sharing the joy of Christmas while she sat here on her own, robbed of her youth, drinking with a heavy heart. That was the only thing she was planning on doing today, that and a visit to the cemetery to see Lisa. She wouldn't spend another Christmas with her mother, wouldn't ever ring her again, not after what the woman had done. She was sure of that.

Last year, Emily had forced herself to go to her best friend Meg's house. She'd been grateful for the invitation, but she'd been a third wheel there, with only Meg's close family around, and far too much hurt in her heart to enjoy the festivities, anyway. This year, she'd made an excuse and Meg hadn't insisted, probably realising that being with someone else's loving family had only poured salt in the wound.

She finished her glass. *Christophe's party is different though, a party of friends, not family. I won't feel left out there. I can pretend it's Easter or some other time of the year. I might even enjoy being in the company of others.*

It's time I tried harder, isn't it?

And she could handle Christophe if necessary. Wasn't that what she'd been doing with him all along? Besides, there would be enough guests for her to mingle with others. *All I have to do is stay away from Mr Hot Guy and his gorgeous French accent and everything will go as smoothly as a scripted TV show.*

She glanced at her watch. They'd be eating in twenty minutes. Could she get ready in that short amount of time? Did she even have something suitable to wear? He'd mentioned dressing up for the occasion. She wasn't as bad as Joe in his eternal thongs and shorts, but she hadn't made a big effort with her appearance in a long time.

She hurried to her walk-in robe. She had clothes, for sure. Shame she didn't own anything that bore no resemblance to beach wear, gym wear or gardening clothes. Wait! She still had the dress she'd worn to Meg's wedding three years ago.

She rummaged around and finally pulled it out from the very end of the hanging rail, squeezed behind an old coat she'd kept after a holiday in Europe a lifetime ago. The dress was more floaty than she remembered, the neckline more plunging and, worst of all, it was fairy-floss pink, a colour she wouldn't have chosen if it hadn't been for the wedding theme. Although she mightn't feel comfortable in it, it would have to do.

She had a quick shower, rubbed body lotion into her legs and arms, and slipped on the dress. It still fit perfectly. That was a good start. Tinted moisturiser and lip gloss were all she had time for, and a pair of dangle earrings. As for shoes … her everyday stretched brown leather sandals were pitiful, her slip-ons, beach shoes and runners simply not suitable. She stared at the shiny Louboutins that rested in a corner, the only expensive thing she had ever bought and all because she wanted to look extraordinary at one of Josh's work parties. The one where she'd seen him run his hand up the long leg of the receptionist and steal a kiss from her in the corridor when he thought no one was looking. And then he'd had the gall to blame it on Emily.

She hadn't tried the shoes on since. She'd been meaning to sell them or donate them to a good cause but hadn't been able to bring herself to even look at them until now. She'd hidden them in the corner of the walk-in robe and they had become invisible to her there, as if they had never existed. And her ex along with them.

Well, too bad. She needed a pair of heels today and that's all the shoes would be. No sad memories, just something to clad her feet. She slipped them on. They fit like a glove and with the tiniest effort she could walk in them relatively elegantly, despite having worn only flat shoes for years.

She checked her image in the mirror and took a step back, gasping. It wasn't her standing there: it was the woman she used to be. The one who went out and about, who smiled all the time, who loved to feel sexy. For a second, she liked what she saw and then she steeled herself. She didn't want to feel feminine these days, didn't want to attract men's admiring glances. She wouldn't wear anything like this pink frothy number again.

But just for today, to join Christophe's gathering next door, she'd grin and bear it.

And throw the outfit in the bin when the party was over.

Emily cleared her throat as she rang the bell, too nervous to walk right in through the open door, although that was what most guests would do around here.

Christophe came padding down the corridor. At the sight of her, his eyes widened like a kid who'd pulled his favourite toy out of a lucky dip. Was the pink dress too much?

'Emily! I'm glad you could make it.'

It was nice of him to make an effort to be pleasant and polite. Perhaps there really would be a truce between them that would last the length of the party. Could she hope for more? Probably not, and it was just as well.

'I'm sorry I'm a few minutes late.' She wouldn't have been had he invited her sooner, but he must have known that, and she didn't want to rub him up the wrong way the minute she arrived by mentioning it.

'It's perfect timing. A few people are running behind schedule anyway, so we haven't started to eat. Even the oysters have only just arrived.'

He welcomed her in with a wide gesture, as if she were some kind of princess. Was he making fun of her again, or was that how the French did it? It didn't matter. She'd only have to exchange a word or two with him now. After that, she'd spend all her time with Joe or whoever else seemed interesting.

She held out the gift she'd brought, a box of chocolates she'd stored in case someone visited for Christmas, although she hadn't been expecting anybody.

'A gift? Thank you! You shouldn't have, Emily.'

'It's my pleasure. I would have got something better had the shops been open.' Or had she been invited sooner. Christophe's magnetic gaze met hers and she struggled to tear herself away.

He ripped the gold wrapping paper and a smile lit up his face. 'This is perfect. I love dark chocolate.'

'Something we have in common, then.' Perhaps the only thing. Was he thinking that, too? The playful expression on his face told her so.

'Yes, finally something we have in common.' He grinned at her.

She returned his smile and followed him into the family room where most of the guests were chatting around a towering spruce beautifully decorated in silver and blue. She hadn't expected a busy, single man like Christophe to have a Christmas tree, let alone one adorned with impeccable taste.

'Everyone, this is Emily. Joe, will you do the introductions? I have to be in the kitchen. And then back to the patio where we started, to take your seats, all of you. We're about to eat.'

Christophe hurried back to his food preparations, busying himself behind the kitchen counter.

Joe rubbed his nose. 'I'll do me best. My memory's not that great with names. Here's Flick. She makes cakes for the restaurant, I think. Is that right?'

Flick nodded. 'That's me.'

'And Nico who's just started working with Chris in the kitchens.'

A shy young man waved awkwardly.

'And here's Freda.'

'Freya,' the Londoner whose refined accent contradicted her relaxed mannerisms corrected him, rolling her eyes. 'A *good* friend of Christophe's,' she added with a little tilt of the head and Emily wondered how close a friend she meant.

Joe managed to recall most of the names in the end. To Emily, the introductions went by in a blur as if she had cotton wool in her skull instead of a brain. She hated how she could never retain people's names when she first met them.

Next year, she would have to look into memorisation techniques. Now that was a good New Year's resolution, much better than the one she'd made last year, a resolution she should have known would be impossible for her to keep no matter how hard she tried. The very one she was crying over earlier when Christophe had turned up at her house.

'Where are you sitting, Joe?' she asked as people took their places, suddenly worried that she might be completely surrounded by strangers for the entire meal.

'Over there, last spot before the end. There's no one facing me. Come on.'

Relief washed over her. Chatting to Joe was easy. She slipped into the seat he indicated. Next to Joe sat the girl with striking eyes

Emily thought he had called Marta during the introductions. Or was it Martha?

To Emily's right, the young kitchen hand was already scrolling through messages on his phone. He definitely wouldn't be a bother. He was so glued to his phone, she'd be lucky if he even noticed her presence. To her left was an empty place at the end of the table. Who was yet to come? Emily glanced around. Everyone was seated. Everyone except ... Oh, no! She covered her eyes with her hand and let out a sigh.

'You okay, sweetie?' Joe leaned forward, frowning.

'I can feel a headache coming on.' Why had she thought this would be better than sitting alone at home? Would she and Christophe manage to be civilised through the entire lunch? She hoped so and touched the wood of the rustic table leg for good luck.

'Ta-da!' The chef appeared carrying a huge pastry-encrusted meat dish surrounded by jellied vegetables and placed it in the centre of the table. Emily had no idea what it was called but it sure was worthy of a photo in one of those fancy food magazines.

The guests clapped. 'What is it?' asked the young woman next to Joe.

'Good question!' exclaimed Joe a little too enthusiastically.

'Pâté en croûte with vegetable aspic jewels,' Christophe announced with a sparkle in his eye. 'Who would like the first slice?'

'Don't worry.' Freya gestured for him to sit. 'You've earned some rest, Christophe. We are more than capable of passing it around and serving ourselves.'

He was passionate about his food, Emily could tell. It was nice to see, even if it was one of the very few good things about him. Her eyes lingered on his perfect silhouette before she purposely turned her attention to the classy dinner setting and fiddled with her knife.

Men weren't worth the effort, she reminded herself—especially the good-looking ones. They had only one true interest in life: chasing as many women as possible just to use them, and the more attractive the guy, all the more deadly he would be. She'd understood that the day she'd discovered the string of affairs Josh had had. December 22, two years ago, and then … And then, that Christmas evening had changed her life forever.

As Christophe took his place, pulling in his chair, Emily caught a whiff of his musky cologne and she realised how long it had been since she'd smelled the scent of a man. Well, there were plenty of other things that smelled good. Food, for starters.

He leaned closer to her and she kept her eyes on the sparkling gumnuts that decorated the table, fiddling with them to take her mind off Christophe. What was he going to say now? Would he ask her how come she'd chosen that seat? Or tell her he'd prefer someone else next to him?

'By the way, Emily, you look lovely.'

She blinked. What derogatory comment would he add in a second? Probably something like 'it goes to show anyone can scrub up reasonably well'. Or 'shame you're so pig-headed'. Or one of a million other insults. Had he finished his sentence? She looked lovely and that was it? Was that possible? The truce was lasting?

He opened his mouth again and she raised an eyebrow in expectation. Perhaps that was why he said nothing in the end.

'You've outdone yourself, mate.' Joe served himself a slice of the work of art that was the entrée. 'Such a great chef. And this guy has so many other hidden talents, Emily. You'd be surprised. A lot of talent. A real nice guy. And you're a real nice girl. I'm just saying.'

She let out a chuckle. Was Joe trying to set her up with Christophe? Surely he knew better. 'I can see he's an excellent chef.'

'And the rest,' added Joe before suddenly giving the woman beside him, who whispered something in his ear, his undivided attention.

'I'm sorry,' said Christophe. 'That was embarrassing.' He insisted on serving Emily and then himself. 'Would you like some wine?' He held out a bottle, but she covered her glass with her hand.

'No, thanks. I had some before coming over. Some of yours, actually, and a very nice one I must say, so that's probably quite enough for now.'

She took a bite of the pâté. The pastry melted in her mouth, the meat was flavoursome and she loved the contrast in textures between the chunks and the smooth morsels. She couldn't help but let out a sound of appreciation.

'You like it?' asked Christophe.

'It's amazing.'

'*Amazing?* You find it hard to believe I could cook like that? How rude of you.'

Why, oh why had she chosen the seat next to his? She was about to snap back when she noticed that his lips had curled up in the most mischievous way. 'You're having me on, aren't you?'

'I bet just now you wondered why you were sitting here with this moron.' Deep laughter rolled out of him. 'Have you forgotten we've agreed on a truce? And you brought me my favourite choco-late. I couldn't be rude to you after that. Seriously.'

'I'm sorry. I should just shut up and eat.' She glanced at Nico next to her, still scrolling his social media accounts. 'Maybe that's what I should be doing instead of opening my mouth.'

Christophe shook his head. 'How boring would that be for me? Joe hasn't said a word to me since we started eating. He's fully occu-pied, have you noticed? You are my only distraction.'

'What?' asked Joe at the mention of his name. 'You talking about me?'

'Not at all.' Christophe winked at Emily in connivance. 'We were talking about the, uh, ban-*jo*.'

'The banjo? Oh, right. Marta's a musician, did you know, Emily? Do you play the banjo, Marta?' And with that, Joe turned to the woman with the wolf-like eyes and appeared once again to forget that anyone else was at the table, in this town, in Australia even.

Christophe leaned closer to Emily and she swallowed hard as his eyes burned through her, making her heart beat faster, heat spread through her core and her head spin more than if she'd imbibed a whole bottle of wine. 'Looks like it's just you and me,' he whispered, his lips mesmerising her.

It took all her strength to pull away. She directed her attention to Nico and then Joe. 'I guess you're right.' She and the handsome French chef were invisible to the young kitchen hand who was glued to his phone, perhaps talking to a girl or a mate, and to Joe who seemed completely smitten by Marta. Everyone else at the table was fully occupied, too, making their own cheerful conversations. It might as well have been just Christophe and her at the table. To a certain extent, she felt fragile for it, exposed. Yet somehow it pleased her too, making her feel special in a way she hadn't in years. She quickly put it down to the wine she'd had before coming over. Alcohol was the worst enemy of reason and restraint.

Christophe swallowed the morsel he was eating. 'Tell me something about yourself.'

It took her by surprise. 'About me? Like what? I live next door?'

'No, not your address. Something I don't know. Something that matters.'

A memory of Josh flashed before her eyes. It was the very question he used to ask the women he fancied. Emily recoiled. 'And why would I do that?' She hadn't opened up to anyone for years.

She wasn't about to do so with the neighbour she usually fought with, no matter how charming he was trying to be today.

He leaned back in his chair. 'Just for fun. Because you're my guest and you're sitting next to me. I know, tell me about your most amusing Christmas. Or your most catastrophic Christmas ever. One Christmas, I burned my sauce and set off the smoke alarm. Luckily I had enough ingredients to start again but everyone had too much to drink before the food arrived. That was an interesting Christmas. Your turn.'

'No,' she said forcefully. 'I'm not playing that game.' She wanted to withdraw into herself like a snail hiding in its shell from a hungry bird.

'I'm not being indiscreet. It's called chatting and being sociable. You could tell me that you got the same present three times, that you put vinegar in the Christmas pudding, that your grandma got drunk and you had to take her home in a wheelbarrow. You don't have to reveal your greatest sin or any other top-secret information about your Christmases. You know what? I can see how much it bothers you to talk to me. Just forget it.'

His mouth tightened. She had annoyed him yet again. Or was he annoyed with himself for trying to be nice to her?

'Look, I'm not used to talking about myself,' she finally whispered. 'Christmas … isn't my forte.' He should understand that without her having to explain it. Sure, she'd loved it once upon a time. Back when she had family around her—a sister she adored, parents who visited regularly and a fiancé she thought would marry her. But not since everything had fallen apart. Christmas would never again be great for her.

He watched her for a few moments with the intensity of someone who is waiting for a sign of remorse, a reason to forgive. She should apologise for her snappishness and remind him that this was a particularly hard time of the year for her. She should ... She couldn't seem to find the right words. Not here, not now.

He directed his attention to the other guests. 'If everyone's finished, I'll take those plates off you.' He cleared the entrée plates and disappeared into the kitchen.

Emily tapped Nico on the shoulder. 'Hey, pass me the wine, will you?'

She filled her glass to the brim.

It was all she could do right now to cope with her inadequacies.

Chatting about her darkest moments to Christophe wasn't an option. It was too personal, too private, even if the whole town knew about it.

Besides, he would never truly understand the agony, the tears, the sleepless nights going over and over what she might have done differently. No, he couldn't understand—she was sure of it.

No one could.

Chapter 3

Christophe tried his best to focus on the turkey as he sliced it and plated it up. He barely saw the chestnuts, oranges and glazed carrots as he added them to the dish. His mind was racing. Why had he invited his prickly, puzzling, exasperating neighbour? It had been a mistake, turning an otherwise joyful occasion into an obstacle course. And why had she accepted the invitation since being here seemed so painful for her? She wouldn't even chat about something as harmless and anodyne as Christmas.

A squiggle of marmalade to decorate the plates and the meals were ready. He poured the remaining Cointreau sauce into a gravy boat and breathed in its delicious scent. Cooking and dressing plates usually melted away all his worries, transporting him to a world of peace and pleasure. Not with Emily. With her, it wasn't enough.

Nothing seemed capable of wiping away the animosity she fuelled in him. And yet it wasn't all animosity. There was something about her, a vulnerability, the way she walked, her scent, that brought out a primal need in him. It made him want to grab her and press his lips against hers—not just to make her acerbic comments stop, nor simply to woo her, but also, and more pressingly, to taste her.

He tasted a spoonful of the *jus* instead. It was well-balanced, slightly spicy with a hint of sweetness. He was pleased with himself. Yes, a hint of sweetness like Emily. Joe was right. Under that impenetrable carapace hid a lovely woman. He'd seen it in her smile. But she didn't want to let him in. Why?

He brushed off the thought. What did it matter? He wasn't about to allow any woman into his life again. In that, at least, he and Emily were similar. Sure, he might be tempted to hook up occasionally with someone, no strings attached, but he wasn't interested in more than that. He'd given his relationship with Marianne back in France his all and look where that had landed him. In Australia, all alone. Not that he was complaining about Australia. He loved the place. The wide-open spaces. The freedom. The opportunities. The sexy neighbour. Did he have to think about *her* again?

He carried a few plates out to the patio area and placed them on the table while the guests let out sounds of admiration. His gaze settled once more on Emily, the difficult, beautiful Emily, so very attractive in that flattering pink dress with the plunging neckline. He'd made every effort not to look at the perfect flesh playing hide and seek with her décolletage and he'd slipped up a couple of times, drawn to it like a lost hiker to a light in the woods in the middle of the night. Maybe that was what had annoyed her. Maybe she'd noticed his wandering eye. What did she expect? He was a man and a flawed one. A normal man.

Well, she could bet her bottom dollar he wouldn't pay her any more attention during the meal, if it cost him his sanity. Not after she'd sent him bowling when he'd suggested she reveal the most ordinary things about herself. Ordinary? He was wrong again. There was nothing ordinary about that woman.

He marched between patio and kitchen a few times, loaded with plates, and soon everyone was served. He sat and turned his chair towards Joe and, more importantly, away from Emily to limit their exchange. She must have got the message because not once did she talk to Christophe after that, although he could smell her delicious scent every time the breeze blew in his direction. But he'd finally managed to ignore her, or rather, *appear* to ignore her.

It was better that way, much more peaceful if he turned his attention away from her.

Shame it was nowhere near as exciting.

After the dessert, Christophe invited his guests to the pool area to stretch their legs as they'd been seated at the table all afternoon. And he offered them coffee, chocolates and *digestifs*.

'Dee what?' Joe wrinkled up his nose.

His puzzled expression brought a smile to Christophe's face. 'A little something to help you digest. Liqueurs, essentially.'

'Liquor! Why didn't ya say so?' Joe was the first to jump up. 'Alcohol, people, this way!'

The guests all moved down the back of the large block to the Balinese-style pool and bar, while Christophe grabbed chocolates and sweets from the kitchen before heading out to join them. As he crossed his garden he looked up at the dark line of clouds on the horizon and hoped the bad weather would hold off until after the party.

When he reached his outdoor entertainment area, Emily was standing with her back to him, close to the edge of the pool, admiring the tiny flowers of the bush he'd planted in the narrow flower bed.

He placed the after-dinner treats on the bar, inviting people to help themselves, and wandered in Emily's direction. He let his gaze settle on her slender ankles in those mile-high heels and took a step closer.

He followed the outline of her calves, her shapely thighs, and imagined her perfect derrière under her floaty dress. He came closer again. She was all woman, there was no doubt about it.

'It's a buddleia. The butterfly bush.' He couldn't help but engage with her.

She jumped, probably surprised to hear his voice right behind her, and spun around to face him, her dress catching on the bush. She bent backwards, tugging at the material, twisting at the waist.

'Here, let me.' Christophe leaned forward.

'It's fine, I can do it.'

She hastily moved away from him, stepping into the uneven ground of the flowerbed. Her high heels wobbled and before Christophe could register what was happening, Emily had lost her balance. He reached out too late, her legs flew by him and she entered the water with a splash—and a horror-movie scream.

'Emily! Are you all right?' He'd really done it now.

'Why did you sneak up on me like that?' Her hair sat flat against her face, dripping into her eyes as she swashed about in the water. 'What the hell is wrong with you?'

'I'm sorry. I didn't mean to sneak up on you. I thought you'd heard me, or rather, I wasn't thinking at all.' Liar. He'd been thinking, about her divine body and nothing else. 'Let me help you out.'

She refused his outstretched hand. 'I'm perfectly capable of getting out of the pool by myself.'

His eyes widened as she climbed out and stood before him. The pink dress clung to her like a second skin, the once frothy material so see-through it clearly revealed a pair of tiny lace panties, leaving hardly anything to the imagination. And, a blessing for him, probably more of a catastrophe for her, she wasn't wearing a bra, courtesy of that plunging neckline.

As the guests gathered to see what was going on, he quickly wrapped his arms around his wet neighbour.

'Let me go!' She thumped his chest and pushed him away. 'You're the last person in the world I want to cuddle right now.'

'Emily, it's your dress.'

'What about it? Not to your taste? You didn't seem to mind it when it was dry, I noticed.' She looked down at the transparent material around her legs and gasped, pulling Christophe to her with urgency and pressing herself against him. 'Oh my God.'

He held her tight, so close her wet breasts squeezed into him, and for an instant her heart beat into his chest, synchronising with his as if they were one. If they'd been alone, he'd have kissed her, right then. The guests gathered around them. 'It's okay, everyone. No harm done. It's all under control. Please go back to enjoying yourselves.'

'No harm done?' she hissed into his ear. 'Speak for yourself. We can't stay here like this. Do something, Christopher!'

'Oui, Madame.' He lifted her off the pavers effortlessly, his hands covering her shapely buttocks, which he guessed were showcased in lace panties under the wet see-through dress, and carried her towards the house.

'Would you mind not having a good feel of my bottom? You're really making the most of this, aren't you?'

'Not at all,' he chuckled. 'I wouldn't dare. I'm simply hiding what others might enjoy looking at if I remove my hands. Shall I hold you by the waist instead? I'd be happy to.'

'No!'

Under the patio roof, he heard the clunk of her heels as they dropped to the ground one after the other, the water from them trickling down his legs.

He glanced down. 'Shame about the shoes. They look expensive.'

'They are. Very.'

He manoeuvred the back flyscreen door open with his foot.

In the bathroom, he placed Emily gently on the floor and quickly handed her a towel to cover herself up. 'You can borrow my bathrobe, if you like.' He took it off the hook and offered it to her.

She slipped into it with haste. 'I'll return it tomorrow.'

He frowned, dabbing his wet shirt with a hand towel. 'Tomorrow? Go home and change, and come back over. The party's still young. In its infancy, in fact. I had in mind to dance all night and really celebrate Christmas. After all, it's only once a year.'

'Everyone here might as well have seen me naked, including you. Do you know how embarrassing that is? Thank you for the worst party of my life. I don't know why I came here. In any case, I have somewhere else I need to be before it gets dark.'

His heart sank. *I slipped up, I know that. But the worst party of her life?* He drew a long breath.

'Actually, I won't bother you tomorrow either, Christophe. I'll leave the robe on the fence for you.'

He felt his shoulders sag. It was better if she stayed away, much better, and yet nothing would displease him more than her hanging the robe on the fence instead of visiting him again. 'Don't do that. Come over. What about your shoes?'

'They're probably ruined. I don't like them, anyway. Give them to the Salvos or put them in the bin if they look bad.'

'Emily, I never thought you might fall into the pool,' he called after her as she headed to the front door. 'I'm sorry, Emily.'

I'm not just saying that. I'm mortified that I upset you so much.

The only good thing about his clumsiness was that he'd held her against him for a while and liked it.

Really, really liked it. More than Marianne, when we started dating. Much more.

In fact, he hadn't enjoyed anything that much for as long as he could remember.

Christophe took off his wet clothes and threw them on the bathroom floor. At least they'd cooled him down as the perfect summer weather had turned humid, and more to the point, while Emily had made his temperature soar. He slipped into a pair of shorts and a T-shirt. Many of the guests had taken off their shoes and rolled up their sleeves and pants by now, so he figured he could change into casual clothes if he wanted to. Besides, he'd lost the desire to dress up since Emily had left.

I should have gone with my gut feeling not to invite her. It would have been more peaceful that way.

'Is she okay?' asked Joe as Christophe returned to the pool area.

'She's fine. She's gone home.'

'Well, she does need to change her clothes,' Joe chuckled. 'I suppose she'll turn up in shorts and a T-shirt like you, now, while I have to put up with these bloody fancy pants.'

'She's not coming back.' Christophe wasn't sure she'd come back at all, not later tonight, not tomorrow, not ever. 'She said she'll leave my robe on the fence in the morning.' He poured himself a white wine and handed Joe another beer.

'She's offended?' Joe frowned as he took the stubby. 'It's not like you pushed her into the pool. You didn't, did ya?'

'Of course not. She slipped.' He sighed. 'I might have scared her a little, though. Apparently she didn't hear me coming, thinks I did it on purpose.'

'Maybe she was day-dreaming. Don't worry, mate. She'll be right.'

Christophe cleared his throat to make an announcement. 'We have board games on the patio, darts near the garage, and I'm on the petanque team. Anyone who wants to play French boules, follow me.'

He desperately needed a distraction to get Emily off his mind.

Joe, who aimed like a drunken soldier, still managed to trash Christophe at petanque. 'What's wrong? You're pretty distracted, mate.'

Christophe shook his head. 'It's nothing. I'm a bit tired.'

'A bit tired since you carried Emily out of the pool, I say. She thinks you did it on purpose and it's bothering you, right? So go over there and explain.'

'No can do. I have guests.'

'No one will mind.'

Christophe shook his head. 'She doesn't want to see me. In any case, she has to go somewhere, apparently. I don't know where. Probably somewhere better than here.'

Joe pulled a face. 'That'll be to see her sister.'

Christophe rubbed his chin. 'How come she was going to spend Christmas alone if she has a sister nearby?'

Joe's eyes widened. 'You don't know? You've lived here for nearly two years and you haven't heard? What planet do you live on?'

'Heard what? I only come here on my days off. You know I stay in Rainbow Cove most of the time for work.'

'She'll be going to the cemetery, Chris. Her sister's dead. Killed on Christmas Day two years ago. A couple of days earlier, Emily had broken up with her boyfriend, too. Rough time of the year for her. That's why she went travelling all over, too, for ages, to take her mind off it. I assumed you knew.'

Christophe's jaw dropped and he took a step back. 'I had no idea. No one's ever told me about that.' Maybe everyone had assumed he'd heard it from someone else, like Joe had done. Maybe Emily had assumed the same. Christophe staggered to a chair and sat. No wonder she'd been touchy! The poor woman had been through hell at this time of the year, while he kept singing the joys of Christmas to her. He'd even asked her to share stories of her worst Christmas. *Bon Dieu*, she must have thought he was an absolute idiot! Or worse, a heartless bastard.

A lump formed in his stomach as he looked over at her house. It lay in semi-darkness now, all lights out even though night was falling. Perhaps she'd already set off for the cemetery. What a fool he'd been! She was angry with him and for good reason. He'd go over and speak to her first thing in the morning to sort it all out.

He'd explain that he'd had no idea what had happened to her at Christmas a few years ago and apologise for his lack of sensitivity.

He just hoped she'd let him in.

Chapter 4

Emily threw Christophe's bathrobe on her bedroom chair and stepped into her ensuite. She tore off her wet dress with such rage that she ripped the delicate crepe fabric. It was just as well: she wouldn't wear something like that again. She'd felt Christophe's eyes on her and to her surprise had enjoyed the warmth that had spread to her body when he'd carried her into his bathroom.

She didn't want to put herself in that position again. It was dangerous, far too dangerous, especially with a good-looking man like her neighbour. He was as handsome as Josh had been, maybe even more. And sometimes, she had to admit it, he was charming too. Luckily Christophe was often tactless, always ready to fight with her. He had especially got on her nerves when he'd tried to make her see the good side of Christmas.

He couldn't force her to have fun, and after what had happened to her at Christmas time he shouldn't be trying so hard. She was angry at him for that, but mostly she was angry at herself for having accepted his invitation. How could she have thought even for a split second that she could enjoy Christmas again? She dried herself with a towel and threw on an old pair of cargo pants and a plain top.

With a wipe, she removed the mascara that had smudged a little despite supposedly being waterproof, and tied her damp hair in a ponytail. It was getting late so she grabbed a torch in case the cemetery wasn't well lit in the evening. She placed a small rag in her bag too. Would the gates be open at this time? She'd never been there so late in the day. Perhaps it was a blessing, though, that she hadn't managed to get there earlier this year. Last year she'd visited her sister's grave in the morning, and she'd bumped into her mother. She wanted to avoid that happening again at all costs, so an evening visit might equate to peace of mind.

She'd had some wine today, late morning and a little at Christophe's during the meal. Unsure how much it took to be over the limit and how long it stayed in your system, she set off on foot to the cemetery. It was only a twenty-minute stroll away anyway, and Marandowie was the safest place she knew.

Besides, she'd walked it many times, knew the way backwards, and usually switched off from her surroundings as she went on the pilgrimage to Lisa's grave, allowing her memories of happier times as a family to come flooding back. But for the first time in a long time, thoughts of a man kept jutting in. A masculine scent. A mischievous smile. A sexy accent. Christophe holding her against him in her dripping wet dress. Nice thoughts, even if she was annoyed at him for sneaking up on her like that and embarrassing her in front of everyone. His firm chest. His dark, enticing gaze. Yes, very nice thoughts. Thoughts that were a trap. Thoughts that had no place in her life.

She wished they would do the right thing by her. She wished every memory of him would go away.

And stay the hell away.

Emily rubbed the grey marble of her little sister's headstone with the rag she'd brought until it shone. 'Hello, sis. How are you doing up there?'

She sat at the foot of the grave. 'Me? Well, it's not the same without you and it never will be. It wasn't your fault, you know. It really wasn't. I'll never forgive Mum. And I certainly wish we'd never met Josh, the bastard. Can you see from up there if all men are like him? I have this neighbour, a Frenchman, Christophe. I call him Christopher just to annoy him. He's a chef, a great chef actually. You should have seen the food he made today. His eyes are like chocolate and he smells good. Before all this, I would have liked him. A lot. You would have liked him. But now, we both know what guys are like.'

The plant Emily had brought last time she visited was looking a little sad, so she pinched off the brown leaves. 'There, that's better.'

She looked around. There was no one else in view, except an old man who was standing with shoulders hunched over a grave in the far end corner of the cemetery. 'Sorry I'm visiting a little late today, Lisa. It's not because I forgot you. I never will. I was at Christophe's party. Bad idea, really. Very bad, for more than one reason.'

Emily sat in silence afterwards, her mind blank, as the deep, quiet pain of loss took over.

She stayed there, trapped between life and death, until she felt a hand on her shoulder and jumped. It was the old man from the other end of the cemetery. 'The departed know if you think of them, dear, wherever you are. You don't have to be here long, not right now. It's Christmas and it's late. You're not like me, you're young. You have a life to live. Go home, love. Besides, they'll come and shut the gates in a few minutes. And if that's not reason enough, there's bad weather coming.'

As she lifted her gaze lightning lit up the sky. 'Thank you. I must have lost track of time.'

Grateful that someone had paid enough attention to her to bring her back to life, she left the cemetery and quickly headed home, hoping to get there before the downpour that was on its way.

Emily woke to the song of the kookaburra in her garden and it put a smile on her face. What a privilege to be living so close to nature! And what a relief Christmas was done and dusted! Somehow she'd made it through another year, although not without heartache.

She climbed out of bed and peered through the window. The storm had come and gone, and apart from a few branches on the grass, there was no damage to be seen. If anything, the rain would have done the garden good.

Emily had a quick shower and tied her hair in a bun before throwing on a pair of shorts and a T-shirt. As she came out of her ensuite her gaze was drawn to Christophe's bathrobe on the floor. It must have slipped off the chair during the night. She picked it up and took it with her to the kitchen. She'd put it on the fence, like she'd told him, as soon as she'd fed Shadow and had her cup of coffee.

Thank goodness she'd thought of a way to avoid going over there with the robe. She couldn't face him today, not so soon after yesterday's catastrophic turn of events. Christophe had really embarrassed her. She bit her lip. The guy had been trying with her, except when he snuck up on her at the pool. And except for his constant stupid Christmas comments. It was insensitive of him after what had happened to her. Perhaps it was the French way: eat, drink and be merry regardless of the cards life dealt you.

Well, ignoring her own feelings didn't work for her. She couldn't slap a grin on her face like a robot and be nothing but the fun person Christophe seemed to expect, just because most people loved Christmas. Just because *he* loved Christmas.

'Shadow! Come and eat!' She emptied a small can of tuna into her pet's dish in the laundry and her beloved ball of fur came running. Emily gave her a pat and smiled at her little darling's appetite.

She padded down to the kitchen, her turn for breakfast, placed a capsule in her favourite machine in the world and pressed the green button. The scent of freshly made coffee filled the air. It was small pleasures like these that kept her going day-to-day.

She placed a slice of bread in the toaster and took a sip of the dark liquid while she waited. She used to sit at this very table with Lisa and share a coffee; hadn't shared one here with anyone since. It was there that she'd sat with her sister the very last time she'd seen her. Emily tried to imagine how she'd feel with someone else facing her now. She had no idea, couldn't even picture it, even though two years had gone by. Two years, a long time ... Was it too long to mourn someone you loved immensely and missed terribly? When guilt weighed you down like a rock tied to your middle, dragging you to the bottom of the lake? She'd tried to be normal this Christmas. That was why she'd accepted Christophe's invitation. It hadn't worked.

The toast popped up and she spread strawberry jam on it. As she took a bite and peered through the window at the peaceful green garden, the doorbell rang. She glanced at the clock, her eye twitching. It wasn't even nine. Who would come over so early on Boxing Day? It'd better not be her mother. Meg, perhaps? No, her friend would be dealing with empty packaging and excited children with too many new toys, and general Christmas overload. A salesman? Not today. It seemed unlikely.

The bell rang again. She made her way through the lounge room and placed her ear against the door. It would be handy to have a peephole or door camera even if there was no real need for them around here. Not a cough, not a sigh. Whoever it was was as still as a cat waiting for its prey.

Suddenly a loud knock at the door made her jump back. 'Emily, it's me, Christophe.'

Christophe? Had he heard her behind the door? Panic tightened her chest. 'Oh, I'll … I'll put the robe on the fence straight away.' He must have missed it when he got out of the shower this morning.

'That's not why I'm here.'

'No?' Why else would he come over first thing in the morning?

'I'm here because … Well, the thing is …' He huffed. 'Can you please open the damn door?'

Her heart beat faster at the thought of seeing him again. She wanted to open the door, her outstretched hand automatically reaching for the handle, and yet her fingers failed to turn the knob. 'I'm not really presentable.' It was the first excuse that came to mind.

'Less presentable than I've ever seen you?' He paused and she thought she heard a muffled chuckle. 'I'm sorry, I shouldn't have said that. I wasn't thinking about the wet dress, I was thinking about the baggy old tracksuit pants earlier yesterday morning and … Never mind. I'm not fussed what you are wearing.'

She took a deep breath. It wasn't about clothes.

He must have realised straight away that she didn't intend to open the door. 'I can come back later, if you like. Shall I come over in half an hour?'

'I'll be out then.'

'What about this afternoon?'

'I don't know when I'll be back.'

'Tonight? Would you like to come to my house instead? You could stay for dinner so I can make it up to you for scaring you into the pool. Not on purpose, but scaring you nevertheless. And ruining your shoes and your dress.'

Why was he insisting? 'You never give up, do you?'

'I try my best not to.'

She sighed. If she had to see him, a few minutes now was better than two or three hours spent together later on over an awkward meal. She threw open the door. 'Okay, what is it, Christopher?'

He stood there like a little boy, holding a bunch of mixed daisies, lavender and leaves from his garden that he'd placed in an empty cereal box. 'For you. Happy *Boxing* Day.' He proudly held out his offering. 'Straight from my recycling bin. The box, not the bouquet, of course. It's as fresh as they come.'

She couldn't help but smile at the sweetness of his attention. 'They're nice. Thank you.' She took the charming posy and smelled its perfume. 'Very pretty. I'll go fetch your robe.'

'No rush. Could we, maybe, sit for a few minutes?'

She rubbed her nose. How could she say no to someone who came bearing flowers and the most sincere smile? But too much time with Christophe and there was a very good chance it would turn sour. 'Okay. A few minutes. I've a lot to do.'

'Thank you.'

She led him into the family room. As they passed the kitchen he poked in his nose. 'That coffee smells amazing.'

'I was having one at the kitchen table. I like to sit there in the morning and watch the birds.'

'Let's go in there, then.'

Before she could stop him, he was at the small wooden table, beaming as he sat down. In Lisa's chair.

'You'd be more comfortable on the couch.'

'No, this is great. I can see why you love the spot with these big windows. Anyway, I came to talk about yesterday.'

Drawing a breath, she put the flowers he'd brought in a vase and placed it on the kitchen table, then made him a cup of coffee. 'Would you like some toast?'

'No, thanks, it's just coffee for me in the morning.'

She served him and sat.

He gently tapped the table. 'About the pool incident, I'm sorry. I honestly didn't do it on purpose.'

'I know. It's fine. No hard feelings.' She was over it, but for the images of him popping into her head since he'd held her against his firm body.

'I'd like to have your dress dry-cleaned for you.'

'That won't be necessary. I tore it when I took it off.'

'Oh, no.' His eyebrows shot up. 'In that case, why don't you pick a new dress and I'll buy it for you? Your shoes seem to have survived the dip. They're in my laundry drying out with newspaper in them in case you change your mind about donating them to the Salvos. You know, I feel terrible about ruining your outfit.'

That wasn't what he ought to feel terrible about. 'It's fine,' she murmured, biting her lip. 'I didn't really like the dress anyway. Or the shoes.'

He pulled a puzzled face before taking a gulp of the coffee. 'You often buy things you don't like?'

She shrugged. 'It was for a wedding. The bride chose the dress.' And the shoes reminded her too much of the ugly past with her ex.

'Ah, I see.' The cup met his lips once again. His perfect lips. 'This is really good coffee,' he added.

'Thanks.'

'Just how I like it.'

He gazed straight into her eyes and her stomach turned inside out. He was handsome, too handsome and she hadn't had a man for so long.

'Strong without bitterness,' he added without averting his gaze.

There it was, his criticism of her. She could do without that. 'There might be reasons for bitterness. Very good reasons.'

'Well, whatever they are, they are not valid.'

'That's right, be judgemental. If you came over to insult me, you should stay on your side of the rotten fence.'

His arms flew up in the air, hitting the coffee that instantly coloured his white shirt a deep brown. He stood and pulled the wet material away from his skin. 'If I can't say that I like your coffee, then you're right, I shouldn't come over.'

'You were talking about the coffee?' Emily grabbed a tea towel and dabbed at the stain on Christophe's shirt. 'Really?'

He let go of the material, which sat against his skin once again. 'Of course I was talking about the coffee. Did I not make that clear? What else?'

'I thought ...' She looked away, unable to face him and the expression of disbelief on his face. 'I feel stupid. I thought you meant I was bitter. Which I guess I am. Sometimes, at this time of the year, it gets out of hand.'

When she finally found the courage to meet his gaze, she found nothing but compassion in it, so much so that a sudden urge to sob on his shoulder overcame her. But she wasn't about to give in to it. She pretended she needed a paper serviette and fetched two from the cupboard, blinking back her tears as discreetly as she could. She wasn't the type to cry in front of others.

When she sat back down, he placed a hand on her arm, sending a shiver through her whole body. 'Emily, I didn't come over to insult you or make underhanded, disguised comments about bitterness. I came over to tell you how sorry I am for what happened to your sister. I had no idea until Joe told me yesterday, after you left.'

She scoured his face for signs he might be telling fibs—Josh had been so good at telling lies—but she saw none. 'You really didn't know?'

'No. I had no idea. I felt such a fool for trying to get you to talk about Christmas and be all cheerful. I'm so sorry. Please accept my apology.'

'Apology accepted.' She could see the shape of his rippled abdomen through his damp, coffee-stained shirt. If she let herself go, she'd place her hand on it, rest her head on his shoulder and let down her guard. She'd believe every word he said, without reservation, and follow the attraction her body was signalling, without hesitation. 'Everyone in town knows, so naturally I thought you did, too. I can't believe you didn't.'

Christophe shrugged. 'I don't come here that often, and I mostly keep to myself. Maybe everyone in town assumed someone else had told me, but no one ever mentioned it. When I bought this house, it had already been a while since … A little while, so—'

She didn't want to hear him say *so it was no longer newsworthy*, or *people thought you should be over it*, or that *it didn't matter anymore*. If the horror of her sister's death had disappeared from the collective memory as quickly as the latest fad, she didn't want to hear about it. She quickly interrupted him. 'Would you like another coffee?'

'I'd love another coffee.'

'I should be able to get the stains out of that shirt for you, if you like.'

'Really? That would be great. I like this shirt and I'm totally incapable of getting coffee out of it. I would probably end up putting it in the bin.'

'Leave it with me and I'll do my best with it.'

She made him another espresso, and they chatted for a while about washing and gardens and birds. She touched the flowers he'd brought. 'My sister would have loved these. She used to sit there, exactly where you are. In fact, no one's sat there since her.'

Christophe jumped up faster than if there'd been a poisonous snake at his feet. Emily giggled. She hadn't expected to, but she felt fine about seeing him in Lisa's chair. Perhaps her sister was trying to tell her something from up above.

'I should have sat in your family room when you told me to. Big faux pas, I suppose.'

'Don't worry about it.' It was a good thing that he had chosen to sit there. It was liberating to see that she was fine with having someone else in Lisa's seat. 'Someone was bound to sit there at some stage.'

'Funny it should be me. I always seem to do things like that.' He cleared his throat. 'I suppose I'd better let you go. You said you hadn't much time.'

'Oh, yes, I'd better get back to, uh, it.' She couldn't now say she had all the time in the world. She hadn't expected things to go this smoothly, hadn't expected him to come and apologise, and certainly hadn't realised he'd known nothing of the ordeal with her sister until yesterday.

There was one thing she'd realised, though. It was how difficult she could be at this time of the year, and Christophe had had more than a taste of it. 'Before you go, I want to say ...' She took a deep breath. 'I need to say sorry, too. Around Christmas time I can be a little touchy. I know that. I haven't been the easiest person to talk to, yesterday, or before, with the fence issue.'

'Don't worry. It's understandable. Thanks for the coffee and especially for the chat.'

'Just a minute. I'll grab your robe.' She went to her bedroom to collect it. When she returned to the kitchen, she gasped at the sight before her. Christophe had taken off his shirt and rolled it into a ball.

She couldn't take her eyes off his perfect V-shape, his flat, tanned stomach, his wide, protective shoulders. She took a deep breath and forced herself to look away so that she wouldn't give in to the irresponsible need to press herself against him.

It was one thing to have a little chat and a coffee with a neighbour, quite another to let herself be drawn into the web of another handsome man. She certainly hadn't expected him to take off his shirt then and there, hadn't expected to find herself confronted by his perfection in that way. She threw the robe in his direction, too scared to approach. 'Catch!'

He caught it with ease and threw it over his shoulder, placing his shirt on the kitchen table. 'You're sure you don't mind doing my laundry? I promise I won't make a habit of it.'

'It's fine.'

'Okay, but I owe you one. I'll cook you a meal in exchange.'

'You don't need to do that. It will only take me a few minutes to get out the stain.'

'I insist.'

'No, no.' A sense of panic grew in her again, compressing her chest like a brick about to crush her.

'A picnic, then.'

'No, thank you.'

'Drinks?'

She shook her head.

'Afternoon tea.' He rubbed his forehead. 'Although I'll be at Chez Christophe quite a few afternoons and will sleep up in Rainbow Cove if I have a morning shift the next day.'

'Yes, it's too complicated. I'm busy most afternoons, too, so it won't work.' Now that he'd realised how tricky getting together might be, especially at this time of the year, he'd drop it and leave her in peace.

'I know! How about morning tea? What could be more innocent and irresistible than morning tea? If you say no to that, I'll be heartbroken.'

She realised that there was only one way to get rid of him, his perfect muscles and the temptation that he was: to say yes. 'Okay, morning tea one day.' In the future. The very distant future.

He grinned and spoke fast, obviously excited at the prospect. 'Great. This Thursday. Because after that, we're getting too close to New Year's Eve and I'll be flat out at the restaurant, although I will drive back out here. I don't want to see the New Year in up at work. Anyway, come over around ten on Thursday. I look forward to it.' He waved a cheeky goodbye and before she had a chance to object, whistled his way out, his step light and happy.

She rubbed her forehead, stunned. What had just happened? She'd accepted to see him again and soon, far too soon—the day after tomorrow. In nothing but a neighbourly way, of course. It had to remain that way. Because there was no way she'd make the mistake of falling for a hot guy again.

Hot guys cheated, lied, stomped on you until your heart died.

And sometimes they robbed you of the people who meant everything to you.

Chapter 5

Christophe couldn't decide which cake to prepare for morning tea tomorrow with Emily: a moist vanilla cake, orange madeleines or a fruit tart on a shortbread base. What if he chose the wrong one? Nearly everyone liked vanilla, but Emily wasn't like everyone else for so many things. What if it was the same with food?

He was so thrilled his beautiful neighbour had agreed to come over that he decided to prepare all three and piled up the ingredients in his shopping trolley. He shouldn't be so happy, really. Yes, they'd had a breakthrough the other day in her kitchen. They'd talked without animosity, and he'd seen how her cheeks had turned pink when she saw him without his shirt, but Emily was hard work.

And yet something made him want to go the extra mile to get her on his side, to break that armour around her and see the smile that lit up her face whenever she let go. And her body—wow! That body in his arms was heaven, even in a soaking wet dress. She fit perfectly against him.

He let out a huff. When Marianne dumped him unceremoniously he'd decided he wouldn't even consider getting involved with anyone again, and here he was sweating over morning tea with Emily. He had to remind himself she was just a neighbour coming over for coffee and cake, and an unpredictable neighbour at that. Although she had her reasons.

Poor woman. Losing a loved one on Christmas Day had to be tough. Christophe looked for something savoury to add to the morning tea menu. He picked up some bacon, eggs, milk and mushrooms to make a quiche, paid for his groceries and strode to the car, putting them in the scorching hot boot. He'd better get the air-conditioning on fast, or the butter and chocolate would be a mess before they reached the safety of his fridge.

He nearly burned his hands on the steering wheel when he started the engine, but bursts of icy-cold air blew out of the air-conditioner and in no time he was in perfect comfort. In summer in Australia things could certainly get very hot, very fast.

It was the same with Emily.

The next morning, he checked the spread on the outdoor table, making sure the wire cake covers were on properly to keep away the flies and tugging gently at the linen tablecloth that he got out for special occasions so it sat perfectly. He rearranged the flowers, straightened the cutlery that was already straight, and came back into the kitchen to look at the clock for what must have been the twentieth time. Why had he said *around* ten? It was only six minutes past, but waiting was making him nervous.

What if she didn't come? What would he do then? He couldn't very well go and get her and drag her over to his house. Suddenly the bell rang and he let out his breath. She was here, *finally*. He hurried to the front door, slowing down to play it cool just before he reached the entrance, in case she could hear his rushed footsteps from outside.

'It's not locked.' He reached for the door handle.

As he opened the door a smile lit up her face. 'Hi.'

'Nice to see you.' He thought about kissing her cheeks, greeting her the French way with a *bise*. But if he made her uncomfortable, she'd retreat straight away like a wild animal, and he didn't want to risk losing her. As she stepped inside, he breathed in her soft floral scent. She looked so pretty, so natural and yet perfect in a simple top and shorts that showed off her shapely legs. He tried not to glance down at them.

She held out a box and a plastic bag. 'I didn't know what to bring. I thought about making something and then I figured you didn't need any help in the food department. Worse, I'd embarrass myself.' She handed him the gift of coffee beans.

'I'm sure you cook beautiful food too, Emily. There was no need to bring anything but I'm touched. And Arabica Bourbon ... I love it. Thank you very much.' He looked in the bag and found his favourite white shirt. 'Did the stain come out?'

'Yes, cold water, dishwashing liquid and white vinegar and it's like new.'

'I can't thank you enough.' He gestured for her to walk before him. 'I've set the table on the patio. I thought it would be nice to sit outside.'

'Perfect.'

His gaze wandered up and down her lovely legs as they made their way through the house. With effort he tore his eyes away from them. 'I couldn't decide what to make, so I decided on a selection of sweet things. And a quiche for something savoury.'

'Goodness, you must have been up at the crack of dawn.' They reached the patio and her eyes widened at the spread. 'All this!'

She let out a chuckle. 'The table's so lovely, with the cloth, the flowers ... You really didn't need to go to so much trouble. Thank you, Christophe.'

'My pleasure. It's the least I could do to make things up to you. Please, sit this side so you have a view of the garden and the birds.' He didn't mind not seeing any of that today. He had Emily to look at.

A smile lit up her face. It was hard to believe this was the same woman who for the past couple of months had argued with him every time he came to Marandowie. 'That's very thoughtful of you. I do love looking at the birds in the garden, as you know.'

'Please, help yourself.' He uncovered the food and gestured to it. She helped herself to a little of everything while he admired her eager eyes and rosy cheeks. She reminded him of a child in an attic, discovering a box of beautiful old toys. 'There's a pot of coffee there, and that one is tea.'

'My goodness. You didn't have to do all this just for me.'

'No trouble at all.' And it wasn't *just* for her. It was *because* of her, *especially for her*, and she was worth it because no one since his ex had dumped him had come even close to making him feel this way. At one stage he'd even wondered if he was done with women. Until recently. Very recently. Until Emily. He shivered at the realisation. Yes, when things were good with Emily, she made him feel whole again.

'I love these little cakes. They're like a shell.'

'The madeleines? It's the cake tin that's like that. It's their traditional shape.'

'Perhaps someone by the sea invented them.'

'Who knows? My grandmother used to make them for me, although with lemon rather than orange. I think every French child eats madeleines. And every French student reads about them in Proust.'

She bit into it and let out a sigh of pleasure, closing her eyes. A tiny crumb sat on her luscious lips, and it was hard for Christophe not to reach out and brush it off with the tip of his fingers. Or better still, with a kiss. 'It's delicious!' she exclaimed.

'I can show you how to whip them up, if you like.'

'You wouldn't mind? They're not too hard to make? I'd love to be able to bake something like that at home, although I'm not a brilliant baker.'

'They're not difficult at all, except for my ex-girlfriend. She couldn't bake or cook at all, not even a boiled egg. She just wasn't interested. Food wasn't her thing.' He wondered what he'd seen in her, really. They hadn't been a match made in heaven, far from it.

'I can't imagine you with someone who doesn't like food. Well, her loss. She's Australian?'

'French. We were meant to migrate together. She stayed in France.' What was worse was the reason she stayed behind at the very last minute, but he needn't burden Emily with his past.

'I'm sorry.'

'It's fine.' He smiled. He was here in the country of plenty with a gorgeous woman who seemed to have warmed to him. And he certainly wouldn't mind getting to know her, taking a chance again. He was happy now that his ex had failed to come with him. It had been painful, but look at him now.

Sometimes failure was the best thing that could happen.

'Oh, look, a rosella!' cried Emily, pointing to a bird in the garden.

They admired the colourful ball of feathers until it flew away, and then they chatted, ate and drank. It was easy, as if Emily had accepted him all of a sudden, as if she'd let down the impenetrable guard that usually kept her away from other human beings and especially from Christophe.

'Shall we make a batch of madeleines, then?'

'Now?' She rubbed her nose.

'It doesn't take long.'

Her lip twisted. He didn't want to put pressure on her. 'It's up to you, Emily. Another time, if you prefer. Or I can write down the recipe for you.'

She took a second before answering, 'Actually, I don't have to rush back. Now is good.'

'Great.' They cleared the table, each of them taking a few dishes and plates, and he led her inside.

In the kitchen he lined up flour, sugar, butter and two eggs on the benchtop. He took an orange out of the fruit bowl and a small grater from the cupboard. 'All we do is melt one hundred grams of butter either in the microwave or on the roof of your car.'

Emily's laughter warmed his heart. 'My car needs washing. I think we'll stick to the microwave.'

'Whisk two eggs with one hundred grams of sugar. Add the cooled butter and whisk. Add the same amount of flour and whisk again. Throw in a teaspoon of baking powder, a pinch of salt, the juice of an orange or a lemon, the grated rind, organic *s'il vous plaît*, and you're done. Bake in the fancy shell tin or in a muffin tray at 200 degrees. They're ready in ten minutes.'

'That does sound easy.'

'Here.' He held out a whisk and bowl for her.

'Me? I thought you'd make a batch while I watched.'

He chuckled. 'I don't need to practise. Besides, I've baked plenty this morning. It's not fair for one person to do all the work, whether in the kitchen or elsewhere, don't you think?'

She looked away and he noticed her flushed cheeks. He didn't mean to embarrass her with the innuendo. He'd just said something for the fun of it. He reminded himself he was not in France but in Australia, where sex could sometimes be taboo, rather than money as was the case back in his country of birth. There, you could talk sex all you liked but you'd make people blush if you asked them how much they earned or what they'd paid for their house. Emily didn't strike him as particularly prudish, though. It was something else that reined her in. But what?

He tried to make her more comfortable. 'All I really mean is that doing is the best way to learn. It beats watching, every time.'

She cleared her throat and took the bowl and whisk. 'And all you really mean now is that baking beats watching someone else bake, not watching them do anything else.'

Christophe laughed as he realised she was ahead of him. He hadn't even thought of the innuendo this time. 'Yes, that's definitely all I really mean.'

'You're right, Christophe. I'm perfectly capable of doing this, even in front of an accomplished French chef. No hang-ups for me.'

He smiled at her compliment and go-get-it attitude, and watched her crack open the eggs with a fork before letting them slip into the bowl. She picked up the sugar and bit her lip. He gently tapped the kitchen scales and reminded her of the amount. 'One hundred grams, nothing more, nothing less.'

She weighed the caster sugar and mixed it into the eggs, but her whisking was a little awkward, somewhat stiff, so he stood behind her, took her arm and moved it with his. 'A nice, soft circle. Relax, let go of your tension. Cooking's not just good for the belly, it's good for the soul.'

The scent of her hair, sweeter than the cakes she was baking, filled his lungs. How he'd love to kiss the golden skin of her perfect neck! As if she'd heard his desire, she turned to him, whisk in hand, lips parted, her gaze settling on his mouth. They were two magnets, irresistibly drawn together with nothing either of them could do to keep their distance.

He paused to give her the time to move away if she didn't want him. She stayed, so he lowered his face to hers.

'Would it be all right if I kissed you right now?' he whispered.

She nodded and his body tingled with excitement.

He placed his lips on hers and kissed her ever so lightly, his hands on the small of her back to draw her to him. Her body fit his as perfectly as the first time he'd held her in her wet pink dress after she'd fallen into the pool, only this time she was like warm croissants in the morning.

He didn't quite understand the sudden pain in his stomach that made him bend forward, but as he straightened up, he realised she had shoved him away with an almighty push.

'No!' She stomped out of the kitchen and headed to the front section of the house.

'Emily, wait! I don't understand. I thought you wanted me to kiss you. The way you were looking at me … I asked you and you nodded. Wasn't that a yes?'

'I can't do this. What is it they say? It's not you, it's me. I'm sorry, I'm *really* sorry, but that's the way it is. Keep your madeleines and your invitations for someone else. Someone better.' At the front door, she turned to him. 'Stay your side of the fence and I'll stay mine. That's what fences are for, keeping people where they belong. None of this warm and fuzzy neighbourly stuff that I don't need.'

A knot formed in his stomach. 'Fine, I will. And I'll put up the fence I want, whether you like it or not, and send you the bill anyway. Because you're so unreasonable about everything, there's no way we'll agree on a fence or anything else by the looks of it.'

'Perfect.' She slammed the door shut and he slumped into an armchair in his living room, all his energy gone in ten seconds flat. 'Well, that went well,' he mumbled.

He was talking to himself.

He had mess in the kitchen and an irate neighbour he couldn't figure out.

And to top it all off, a thirst for her that wasn't about to be quenched.

He couldn't understand what he'd done wrong, said wrong, thought wrong. Everything had gone so well until the kiss, the kiss she'd seemed so ready, so eager to share. Why else stand that close, lips parted, with those dreamy eyes? Why nod when he asked if he could kiss her? Had he misread her? He shook his head. Surely not. She had agreed and then changed her mind at his touch. Didn't she like the way he felt?

The morning certainly hadn't turned out as expected, far from it. It had been better, much better at first, and worse, much worse in the end, another roller-coaster of unpredictable emotions with Emily, just like Christmas lunch. He dragged himself to his feet and back to the kitchen where he stared at the ingredients for the madeleines that sat on the benchtop.

Now he had to either bake again and clean up, or throw out perfectly good food, something he simply couldn't bring himself to do. Afterwards, he had to drive up to the restaurant and start over in Rainbow Cove, preparing the evening meals all the while wondering why Emily had rejected him that way.

It wasn't exactly the nicest way to spend the day.

Quel abruti! How did the Australians put it, again? Bloody marvellous, that was it. So much for taking a chance with a woman again.

He should have kept to the original plan. No more relationships with the opposite sex, that was what would make him a happy man. From time to time, a one-night stand with a stranger he didn't have to see ever again, no strings attached. That's what he should be aiming for, nothing more. He'd do well to remember it.

He was sure of one thing. He'd no longer go looking for Emily.

Chapter 6

Emily curled up on her old leather couch with the new novel she'd bought. She couldn't think of a better way to spend her holiday than alone with a good story, a packet of crisps and a can of cola. That was decadence for her these days, and a lot safer than trying to be sociable with anyone—especially her neighbour.

She wasn't sure what had happened over at Christophe's house two days ago for her to find herself in his arms, tasting his lips. It was meant to be nothing but a neighbourly visit, a piece of cake, a cup of coffee. He was supposed to be making it up to her for having scared her into the pool, nothing more. Something had gone terribly wrong and she'd nearly fallen for those dark eyes she could easily drown in, and that warm, firm, wonderfully built body.

The attraction had been so strong that she'd let him kiss her. She wasn't proud of it, wasn't the type to lead a man on if she had no intention of taking it further, but life wasn't perfect and slip-ups happened. At least she'd found the strength to push him away and get out of there in time. Thank goodness!

She read the first paragraph of her book as she munched on a couple of crisps, but instead of a picture of the characters and the story forming in her mind, she saw Christophe and his chiselled jaw, his lips parting just a little. That image of him had popped into her head more than a few times since that fateful morning tea.

She heard his words again. *What could be more innocent and irresistible than morning tea?* Nonsense! She steeled herself and read the paragraph again. Her mind wandered once more, this time to his arms and how protective they'd felt. She slid the book onto the coffee table and stuffed another handful of crisps into her mouth.

She had to stop thinking of a man she didn't want. She didn't want an incredibly handsome man, didn't need one, would much rather be on her own, thank you very much. It was true, wasn't it? *It had to be.* And she had to ignore that niggling feeling in her stomach that gave her the impression she was sitting on a fence, about to slip off it and fall flat on her face.

The loud knock on the front door resonated in the air, shocking her out of her reverie. Who was it? She swallowed her mouthful of potato crisps. The last person to come over was Christophe, to invite her to morning tea. Would he visit again after what had happened at his house? He was tenacious but he should know better, now that she'd told him to stay away. The knock came again and Emily quickly made her way to the entrance.

At the front door, as she was about to turn the door knob, she stopped. If it was some salesman, she didn't need anything, couldn't afford anything. If it was her handsome neighbour, he would surely get the message and go away sooner rather than later if she kept quiet and did nothing. It was probably the wisest decision, because if she saw him, saw those caring eyes again, she might give in to the urge to feel his body against hers. Lively butterflies tickled her stomach, fluttering about full of life as she pictured him in front of the door. But he knocked again, once, twice, and then so quickly and insistently that Emily lost count.

Annoyed, she threw open the door, ready to blast him, to drive him away, keep him at a safe distance. 'I thought I'd made it clear …'

A woman with greying hair and bloodshot eyes stood before her and it took a split second for Emily's brain to register that it was her mother. In the twelve months since Emily had bumped into her at the cemetery, her face had lost more of its shape, her hair become dry-looking and unkempt, and her eyes had sunk a little deeper into their sockets. Although she was still in her fifties, she reminded Emily more of her grandmother's last photo, than of how she remembered her own mother.

'Hello, Emily.' Her mother's voice hadn't changed.

A nervous shiver ran down Emily's spine. 'What are you doing here?'

'I don't want to spend another New Year without a daughter. I've come to bury the hatchet.'

Confusion rushed through Emily. Was her mother here to apologise? How did she, Emily, feel about that? Was her mother still in that awful cult that controlled her every move?

Emily would have to take it one step at a time. 'Bury the hatchet? Do you mean you're sorry for what you did?'

'I'm sorry Lisa is no longer with us.'

Emily shook her head. An apology from her mother wouldn't wipe the slate clean, nothing would. Nothing would bring back Lisa. But it had to be the starting point and Emily certainly wouldn't give her mother another chance without words that showed she was sorry. 'That's not good enough. You can't sweep everything under the carpet.'

'Let bygones be bygones. Come over for New Year's Eve, and let's start afresh. I have the Leader's permission.'

The Leader's permission. So she hadn't left the Seven Temples.

'You're still being brainwashed?'

'Don't be silly. It's not brainwashing. It's the way. Look at me, Emily. I may have the Seven Temples around me but I'm a lonely old woman. I hate to say it.'

Emily gulped. Had her father passed away? He'd stood by her mother after Lisa's death, had always taken her side and stopped talking to Emily. She suspected it was to keep the peace with his nagging wife and the other members of the cult that seemed more important to them than family. Still, not seeing him ever again would pain Emily tremendously. 'Is Dad okay?'

Her mother huffed. 'His usual self. Stupid man isn't interested in anything. Never talks unless it's about fishing. You, you must be lonely, too.'

Emily breathed a sigh of relief. 'I'm fine.'

'Let's forget what happened and move on. That's what your sister would want.'

'Don't you dare talk about what my sister would want. Lisa would have wanted you to do your duty as a mother and watch out for her. She would have wanted you to love her enough to stand by her no matter what, instead of casting the first stone without even knowing what had really happened. That's what Lisa would have wanted.'

Her mother raised her voice. 'I've done nothing wrong and you can't do this to your own mother. I shall stand here until you change your mind. I'm a good mother. I always have been. I fed you. I clothed you. Sent you to school and—'

A good mother? A judgemental one who paid more attention to what her fellow members of the Seven Temples might think than to the pain of her daughters.

Her mother's rant faded into the background as Emily's memories came flooding back: the last Christmas lunch as a family at her mother's cottage, Emily coming home early with a headache and leaving them all there, her mother turning up on her doorstep in the middle of the night to tell her that Lisa ... that Lisa ... And then, Lisa's white, rigid body in the coffin. The nausea as Emily held her sister's cold, stiff hand for the last time.

'Come on, Emily.' Her mother took Emily by the shoulder and shook her. 'You'll see, if you ever have children of your own, just how hard it is. Don't be an ungrateful daughter. You'll regret it later.' Froth accumulated at the corners of the woman's pale lips as she raised her voice.

'Ungrateful? For what? For *you* destroying our family?' asked Emily coldly. 'My sister would be alive if you'd done the right thing. You knew she'd been drinking. You let it slip that night. And you called her a whore, for goodness sake. Why? Had you listened to a sermon about sexuality or something in that cult you're in? Wanted to impress your buddies by being righteous?' Emily shivered like a volcano about to explode but her voice remained steady. 'I mean, did you ever really think that you'd done the right thing, sending her off in the state she was in? No deserving mother would think that.'

'It is not a cult, I've told you before. It's a following. Lisa lacked respect when I told her what I thought. She swore. I had to ask her to leave the house.'

'She was broken because of what happened with Josh, and you kicked her while she was down. She'd had too much to drink. You don't put someone out on the street because they say a few swear words in those circumstances.'

'I didn't watch her all day to see how much she drank. I defended you and this is how you repay me. Lisa was the one who lacked morals or it never would have happened. I didn't bring my daughters up to behave like that, trying to get into bed with her sister's boyfriend.'

'That isn't what happened and you know it.'

'It was Lisa's own fault, not mine. Lisa's and Josh's. And you're just as much to blame. You're the one who chose that evil Josh and brought him into our family. If anyone's responsible, ultimately it's you!'

Emily gasped. 'I can't believe you said that, after what you did. And you're screaming at me. Stop screaming.'

'Next time, be careful who you sleep with, young lady. Not that any man would want a relationship with you now. You're a real mess in your head, I can see that, twisting the truth, blaming your own mother. And you've let yourself go, too. You used to dress nicely. You're a lost lamb, a lonely lost lamb no one will want.'

Emily clenched her jaw as her whole body trembled with rage at the injustice of it all. 'Leave. Now.' Someone cleared their throat and she looked up to see Christophe striding up the driveway behind her mother. 'Is everything okay over here?' His hands came to rest on his hips.

As Emily's mother turned to stare at him, Emily raced to his side and took his hand, smiling gratefully at him for saving her despite everything she'd said to him, every time she'd pushed him away. 'This is my boyfriend and if you don't leave immediately he will escort you off my property.'

Christophe raised an eyebrow for a split second, but he soon pulled Emily to him and planted a kiss on her lips. It was a punch to the stomach, a surprise attack that Emily could do little about, except push the flat of her hands against his rippled abdomen. Managing to free herself from his embrace, she stepped away.

Christophe stared her mother in the eye. 'Yes, I'm Emily's boyfriend, the one who will be spending a lovely New Year with her, and you need to leave.' He closed the gap that had formed between him and Emily, wrapping his arm tight around her waist.

Emily forced a smile. Christophe was certainly making the most of the situation, and she'd make him pay for that later, but it was worth it if only to see the shock on her mother's face. More than that, it was true relief to watch the speechless woman hurry up the driveway, climb into her car and start the engine.

'I heard the screaming,' explained Christophe in his sexy French accent. 'I know you asked me to stay away, but I was rather worried for your safety so I came over just in case … as a concerned citizen, if you like.'

'Thank you, I appreciate it.' Emily smiled as they watched the car drive down the street. As soon as it disappeared around the corner, she turned to her handsome neighbour and thumped him on the arm.

'Ouch! That hurt. That's how you show appreciation? I rescued you!'

'Yes, you did, and I'm grateful you came over to see if I was all right. That's why I thanked you for it a second ago.'

'And now you punch me? I don't understand women. *Je n'y comprends rien.*'

'You understand just fine. You didn't have to take quite that much advantage of the situation. It isn't what a *concerned citizen* would do.' Not that she hadn't enjoyed his lips. She had. Very, very much. That was the problem.

'Okay, I get it. You want me to stay on my side of the fence. You don't want anything to do with me, and it's probably best that way not just for you, by the way, but for me, too. I'd simply like to point out that you're the one who said I was your boyfriend. I only did what a normal boyfriend would do.' He turned his palms to the sky. 'It had to look believable.'

She couldn't help the chuckle that escaped her at the effort he was putting into justifying his actions.

'I'll go, then.' He took a few steps down the driveway.

Her heart sank. She was the one who had told him to stay on his side of the fence and yet she wanted to hold onto him. She couldn't help it. 'Wait. You don't have to rush off. I have a question I want to ask you.'

No sooner had she said the words than he turned back and hurried up to her. She giggled again at how little he needed convincing.

'What question is that?'

'Why did you say it'd be better for you, too, if you stayed on your side of the fence?'

His head bobbed about with hesitation. 'After what happened with Marianne … No woman, no cry.'

'No man, no cry.' If only her mind were in complete agreement with her physical needs and her heart. 'We agree on that much. And on dark chocolate.'

'Dark chocolate, definitely.' He thrust his hands into his pockets. 'So, that was your mother?'

Emily nodded, pressing her lips together. She wasn't proud of the woman who'd given birth to her. 'Indeed. You don't choose your family.'

'She seems the tenacious type.'

'Stubborn as a donkey. She always has to get her own way.'

'Well, now she truly believes you have a boyfriend who will protect you. That's what you wanted, isn't it?'

'It's exactly what I wanted. You're right. Let's forget about you, well, making the most of the situation.' She wanted to forget all about it, but how did you stop thinking about lips that made the earth tremble under your feet and your whole body shiver with desire? A kiss that made you remember that you are woman, and he is man, all man? Because that's what had happened with their first kiss and she was certain their second would have ended up causing just as much chaos in her mind if she hadn't shoved Christophe away so quickly.

Christophe shuffled his foot around a little. 'So I'm forgiven?'

'Of course.' She smiled. There really was nothing to forgive.

'That's a relief.'

They stood in silence for an instant, Christophe clasping his hands. He finally cleared his throat. 'I was wondering, what are you doing for New Year? If you're just hanging around here, we could get together for a glass of champagne. Or if you're not into bubbles, we could open that beautiful bottle of Grange that Xander gave me as a thank you for organising the Christmas lunch. I'll be working in the evening, but I can be back here by eleven at the latest. Very low key. If you want to, that is. And I promise I won't pretend to be your boyfriend.'

She took a deep breath. She hadn't yet accepted her friend Meg's invitation. 'I'm not doing anything. A glass of champagne seems like a reasonable way to start the New Year, and Grange even better.'

He smiled, his mouth twisting to the side. 'Great.' He studied her for a moment. 'You seem a little upset.'

She tucked a strand of her hair behind her ear for something to do with her hands. 'I suppose I'm a bit worked up. From the argument with my mother, you know.' It was true. Seeing her mother again after all this time, hearing her accusations, had shaken Emily. But in her heart of hearts she knew that wasn't the only thing that had unsettled her. Christophe's closeness was equally to blame. 'I could do with a walk to calm down. I think I might drive to the beach.'

'That's a good idea. A nice, long walk at the beach is always relaxing.'

'It is.' She hesitated. Should she ask him to come along? Would that be sending the wrong signals? The wrong signals that she seemed to constantly want to send and had to fight against her own body and her own desires to keep to herself?

He rubbed his nose. 'I love walking along the shore.'

'Me, too. It's nice to live close enough to the water to be able to do that on a regular basis.'

'I agree.' Warmth spread to her belly as he gazed into her eyes. 'Well, I'll go back home,' he finally added. 'Have a good walk, then.'

'Thank you.' She rubbed her hands together. It didn't feel quite right to send the man off after he'd rescued her from her mother and asked her over for New Year's Eve when all she'd ever done was push him away. Besides, she could do with someone to talk to. As long as it didn't turn into more than a walk, something she'd regret later. They were grown adults. They could manage that, couldn't they? 'Do you think … Would you … I mean, do you fancy coming to the beach with me, Christophe?'

'I do!' He'd answered without hesitation but then he glanced at her sideways. 'Can you guarantee you won't push me away, scream at me or tell me to stay the hell away from you? Not punch me in the arm, the belly, or anywhere else? Not change your mind about wanting me to spend time with you once we get there? Not take it out on me if you should slip and fall fully dressed into the sea?'

She laughed. 'I get it. Don't think I don't understand, because I do. I have been touchy and I'm sorry. Still, you have to agree that it's a walk and nothing more than a walk.' She couldn't afford another kiss, couldn't deal with another second in his arms or she'd give in to the incredible pull she felt towards him and take another step in the wrong direction with the far too hot Frenchman.

He drew a long, exaggeratedly laboured breath and rolled his eyes. 'So be it, if promises are required to do something as simple as go for a walk, I promise. It will be a walk, nothing but a walk, so help me God. A walk and a chat, that is. Nothing else.'

She looked into his dark, dreamy eyes and smiled. 'In that case, I agree to all of the above.'

'Great. Let's go.'

Frothy waves licked the beach white as they crashed onto the shore before disappearing into the sand. The salty air opened Christophe's lungs and he breathed in deeply. He loved the scent of the sea, fresh and invigorating yet relaxing all at the same time.

'Beautiful.' The word escaped him as he turned his gaze to Emily. The sun caught the golden flecks in her eyes and her curls danced in the breeze. Her cheeks flushed a gentle pink, and he wasn't sure if it was because of the air that whipped them or his compliment, so he quickly added, 'very beautiful, the beach.' After all, he had promised it would be a walk and a chat, nothing else.

'Oh, yes. It's always been a firm favourite of mine.' Her lips curled up into a soft smile.

'Feel like talking about what happened with your mother?' The footprints Christophe and Emily left in the sand lined up perfectly. If only they'd been a little closer. He had to remind himself that not getting involved with a woman was better, especially one so unpredictable. 'I don't know what there is to say, really. We don't get on, haven't for a few years. Not since my sister died.'

'Mmm.' He nodded, although he could tell there was more to the story, much more. And he'd overheard some of the conversation between Emily and her mother on the driveway. He'd love her to fill in the gaps, but if Emily wasn't ready to open up to him, wasn't prepared to trust him at this stage, or maybe simply wasn't able to, he had to respect that. It pained him that he couldn't seem to break through that steely exterior of hers.

He wanted to pull her to him and wrap his arms around her, to tell her that she could let go of the pain and live free from it. He wanted to make it better for her. To control his urge all he could do was thrust his hands into his pockets.

He sighed. Why did he have to keep reminding himself that he didn't need a woman in his life to be happy? As he watched their feet sink into the sand side by side, admired Emily's glowing skin and the grace of her movements, it suddenly became patently clear to him, as clear as the pristine waters of the Pacific Ocean.

He had to keep reminding himself that he neither wanted nor needed a woman in his life because it was *untrue*. Deep down what his heart wanted was for Emily to trust him and to want him. He had to admit that fact to himself. What his heart truly wanted was to be with Emily, to share his days and his nights with her. She was the first woman to make him want to try again since Marianne. The problem was that Emily wasn't ready. That was why he kept denying his attraction, refusing to see his need, so that he didn't have to deal with the fact that his beautiful neighbour pushed him away. No woman, no cry was nothing but an excuse, a bandaid for the wounds of her rejection.

He wanted her, he wanted to try with her, and today had given him hope. She hadn't let him go home when he'd found himself on her driveway. She had stopped him, had invited him along for the walk. She'd made him promise it would be nothing but a walk, so something was stopping her from going any further, but she was here, on the beach, by his side, wasn't she? Perhaps she needed more time, more confidence, more trust. Well, he'd give her whatever it was that she needed.

And he'd *show* her how to do it, even if it wouldn't be pleasant for him. He'd avoided talking about Marianne as much as possible. Until now. 'I want to tell you about my girlfriend Marianne.

My *ex*-girlfriend, let's be very clear about that. There's absolutely nothing between us anymore.' He shot her a grin. 'Shall we sit for a while?'

'Sure.' Emily lowered herself to the sand and sat with her legs folded under her.

Christophe lay next to her, propped up on one elbow, facing the ocean. He kept his eyes on the horizon as he cleared his throat, preparing to unveil his heart. 'When I met Marianne, I wasn't instantly attracted to her. She was very pretty, but there was something I didn't like about her, a certain arrogance. Maybe I should have trusted my instincts more. Anyway, she pursued me *sans fin*, uh, relentlessly, coming to the restaurant where I worked nearly every lunchtime. She regularly asked to speak to the chef, me, that is, most of the time to compliment me on the dish, sometimes to try to get me to reveal the secret ingredient, and then she'd flutter her eyelashes at me. She invited me out a few times and after a while, I began to tell myself that maybe we could get on. I finally gave in, accepting to join her one evening. That's how it started. Things seemed fine although sometimes she'd disappear for a few days at a time. She said she had to go away for work but whenever I called her she didn't answer. She called me back later, hours later, sometimes even the next day. She wouldn't give me the name of her hotel, either. She always made some excuse, said she couldn't remember it, didn't know which hotel the secretary had booked.'

Emily grimaced. 'I don't like the sound of that.'

'Neither did I, but I trusted her. It's in my nature to trust people until they give me good reason not to.'

'I like that philosophy.' She sighed. 'I like it, but it isn't always easy to live by it … Anyway, go on,' she said and Christophe knew that she owed that difficulty to whatever her ex had done to her.

'Work was okay for me,' he continued, 'although making ends meet in France isn't as easy as over here. I had a dream, that of owning my own restaurant and my own home, too. It wasn't about to happen in a hurry in France. Marianne and I started talking about migrating. It was her idea, initially. She put it to me one day after coming home from work in tears. She told me she'd had a rough day at the office and was fed up, although she didn't want to go into the details of what had happened no matter how many times I asked. The idea of going abroad to find if not fortune, a better life, took hold for me. It grew and eventually I was really keen. We decided on Australia. We got engaged and put in the paperwork to come and live here. We had interviews and two years passed while we waited for final approvals.'

'So you came here together?'

'No, that's the catch, you see. When we finally got the green light to migrate, Marianne shut down on me. I didn't understand what was going on. She finally told me she'd changed her mind. She couldn't leave France. As it turned out, she couldn't leave the guy she'd been having an affair with for a year and a half. That's when she explained she'd had an affair before, too, with someone else. Her first lover had dumped her the day she came home from the office in tears, and that's what had initially pushed Marianne to want to get away from it all and escape to Australia. Then the second guy came along while our paperwork was in, and she said nothing until it came to the crunch and we were ready to move. I don't know what she was thinking, perhaps that it might not work out with the second guy and she'd come to Australia with me in that case. For me though, it truly was a dream to come here. I thought the Australian government might not give me another chance later if I pulled out, so I decided to migrate on my own.'

Emily placed her hand on his forearm. 'I'm so sorry. I know how it feels to suddenly realise the person you are dating isn't who you thought they were. And to come here on your own after what happened and leaving your family behind in France ... Wow! It must have been incredibly difficult for you.'

He gazed into her eyes, the pull so strong that he wanted to drown in them. 'It was hard but plenty of people go through tough times, some much tougher than that. If you fall, you have to pick yourself up and keep going. It's the best way to live. *C'est la vie.*'

Emily looked out to sea. 'You're right, I know that. I think most people know that. It's just that not everyone can manage. Not on their own. Sometimes weeks, months, years go by before you get back on your feet. I'm not even sure that everyone can always go back to being exactly who they were before their ordeal.'

She harboured such deep hurt that he wanted to take her into his arms and kiss her better, wanted to protect her like he'd never protected anyone. He leaned closer to her and could almost feel the warmth of her body, the silkiness of her golden skin. He remembered the kiss at his house after morning tea, those lips he wanted to eat more than the most delicious of sweets. And then her hands on his chest, pushing him away. He'd do well to concentrate on that part if he didn't want to be rejected again. He steeled himself and inched away.

They sat in silence for a while, not a heavy, awkward one but a comfortable moment admiring the sparkling blue-green ocean and he enjoyed the closeness without words. Could he tell her that she was the first woman to make him want another relationship since Marianne? He dug his fingers into the sand. It was too soon.

'What about your ex?' he asked when Emily next turned to him.

She shrugged. 'He was an asshole.'

Christophe couldn't help but laugh. 'Straight to the point. I like that about you.' That and a million other things.

'Honesty's always been my strength. And sometimes my weakness.' Her lips curled up and the warmth of her smile sent a pang of need to his stomach. If only he could hold her …

Curiosity gnawed at his insides. 'So, what happened between the two of you?'

She inched away. 'Let's not waste our breath on him.'

His heart sank. The moment of closeness was slipping through his hands again, like sand through his fingers. 'Okay, then. So you're not going to tell me anything?'

She took a deep breath, eyes darting around before she nodded. 'I'll tell you about something more important than that idiot. I'll tell you about my sister. Things no one else knows. Can we walk?'

'Of course.' He stood, took her small, delicate hands in his and helped her to her feet.

Any part of her background she chose to confide in him would be a step in the right direction. He'd do anything for her to let him in, into her past, her life, her heart.

He'd take whatever she was able to give him, one bit at a time.

Until the pieces made up the whole of her.

Chapter 7

Emily hadn't felt like opening up to anyone in a long time, especially not a man, but a sense of calm had melted into her shoulders at the beach thanks to Christophe's trust. He had confided in her, so she was comfortable about doing the same with him. Nearly comfortable. In any event, ready to stretch herself.

The sparkling water cooled her feet as she and the handsome French chef walked side by side along the shore. She cleared her throat, ready to sink or swim, and jumped in the deep end before she could change her mind. 'Two years ago on Christmas Day, I had a headache. Literally. Things hadn't been going well with Josh, my boyfriend, and that's the understatement of the year. I'd left him the previous week.' She took a deep breath. Just thinking of him tightened the muscles in her shoulders.

Christophe's chocolate gaze softened as he turned to her. She loved his attention, his readiness to listen to her. And the fact that when she stopped, he didn't ask questions, didn't push for more, was lovely. It made her want to continue, at her own pace. 'I opened up about what Josh had done to me and told my family that it was over with him. Other women, many ...' She grimaced. She sensed she didn't need to say much more about that at this stage for Christophe to get the picture.

She crossed her arms, holding her middle. 'It was still hard for me then, less than two weeks after I'd discovered what had been going on. Telling my family had taken its toll too, so I went home early, leaving my sister Lisa with my mother and father. Lisa and I were close, very close. She usually hugged me when the going got tough, wanted to know everything, tried to find solutions for me. That night, she didn't. She let me go without a word.'

'And then she had an accident and passed away, and you never got that hug?' Christophe leaned forward with inquiring eyes.

'Yes, except that's the tip of the iceberg. A lot happened in between.' Emily fought to hold back the tears that threatened to run down her cheeks as guilt flooded her heart. She placed her hands on her belly and pressed gently to remind herself to breathe. 'I'm sorry. I'll be okay. It's just hard.' Really hard, because by telling the story, she relived the day. 'I need a second.'

His eyes filled with sadness as he smiled. 'It's fine. Take your time.'

She turned to the sea, took in its infinite blue, its eternal rhythm. It was good to know that whatever happened in her life, whatever memories came back to haunt her, there were things bigger than her, bigger than every person on Earth, things of beauty like the never-ending ocean that every generation could count on. Hopefully forever, if we miraculously managed not to destroy the world. 'That Christmas, I fell asleep on my couch, lonely and heartbroken after Josh. Still, I knew I would get over it. I was in love with him, but give it time, I'd be all right. And then the unthinkable happened. They came to the door in the middle of the night.'

She closed her eyes and stood there, frozen in time. She could hear the knocking as if it had happened yesterday. And then, she fell deeper into the memory, and it was happening right now. *Bang, bang, bang.*

She dropped her head. She wanted to lean against Christophe. If only she hadn't told him that this was a walk and nothing more, she'd let herself go and seek the comfort of his arms. If only she didn't fear the consequences of giving into her need, the consequences, potentially dire, of accepting him and everything he had to offer.

She drew a breath and concentrated on telling the story, without the shadow of a doubt the most life-defining moment she'd ever had so far and possibly the most life-defining moment she'd ever live. 'My mother, my father, a policeman, all as gloomy as forgotten prisoners, the colour drained from their faces. It was the policeman who told me. Lisa had had too much to drink and crashed the car. She didn't even make it to hospital, died before the person who drove by and found her had finished calling the ambulance. They figured she'd been there for at least half an hour on her own. She must have been in agony, alone in the middle of the night, waiting for the horror of it to end. Maybe she called for help. Maybe she called my name.'

'Oh God, Emily. I'm so sorry.' He placed his strong, warm hand on Emily's forearm and took it away almost instantly, as if he'd scorched himself on a stove.

It was a shame she had made him understand he wasn't allowed to touch her earlier, because that hand on her arm was exactly what Emily needed. In fact, that strong hand, those perfect arms around her would ease her pain a great deal.

She rubbed the tense point between her eyebrows, to find the energy to finish what she'd set out to say to him. 'The worst part was that Lisa didn't get drunk *after* leaving my mother's house. She drank *while* she was there. Her own mother, my mother, the bitter and twisted woman you saw on my driveway, was the one who *told* her to leave after hearing what Lisa had to say. My mother is the one who made her get into the car and drive off, because she's in some following, as she calls it, that's brainwashed her into putting purity of thought, that kind of rubbish, before the needs of her own children. She watched Lisa spin the wheels and zoom off, knowing that she'd downed glass after glass of whisky. It's bad enough when it's a stranger doing that. Your own mother? It's beyond criminal.'

His eyes widened. 'I wouldn't want to see my mother either, after that. Did the police charge her?'

Emily drew a sharp breath and took a step. 'Let's walk again, shall we?' Moving gave her something other than the pain to concentrate on, one step after the other.

'Sure.'

'They wanted to arrest her but determined there was insufficient evidence. My mother said she had no idea Lisa had been drinking, that there was no indication she had. She insisted that Lisa must have had a bottle in the car, stopped on the way home, downed it, chucked it in a bin or on the side of the road, and driven off again. What I know of it, what she let slip in front of me, is hearsay, my word against hers, so the case was dropped.'

She observed Christophe, the sincere expression of shared suffering on his face, his gorgeous lips twitching, his wide shoulders beckoning to her, ready to welcome her against them. If she suddenly threw herself into his arms like she wanted to, for solace, would he assume she was ready to climb into bed with him? And if in a year, a month, a week, she did give herself to him, would he break her like Josh had? Could she trust him with her heart?

She couldn't answer those questions but her need was so deep that she came closer to Christophe and leaned her head against his shoulder. It was all she had to do for him to wrap his arms around her and pull her to him. His body was warmer than the January sun, his scent fresher than the sea breeze, and she snuggled up against him without questioning the wisdom of her move.

To be with him without thinking of the future, of the potential pitfalls of a new relationship, especially one with such a handsome man, to not even think of a relationship but simply let go of her pain and her worries in his arms, her mind rocked by the sound of the waves crashing nearby, that was what she needed. Comfort, closeness, warmth and an empty mind. It was Heaven on Earth.

Perhaps she should completely let down her guard and tell him the whole story. She looked up to find his caring gaze. She would tell him everything, just not in his arms or she might give in to temptation right here, right now and kiss him. Not quickly like on the driveway. *I'd kiss the hell out of him.* Until their bodies hummed with excitement, until they both were transported to the land of maddening desire.

A ball of heat rose from her core, just thinking about it. She took a deep breath. *I'm not one hundred per cent sure I can take things further with him. It's not right to lead him on.* She'd never been a tease, didn't like playing with someone's heart. *No matter how strong its owner, a heart is always too fragile to be treated without respect.*

She gently pulled away. 'Thank you. I needed that.'

'Any time. It's a standing offer.' There was such intensity to his gaze that she knew he'd enjoyed the closeness as much as she had.

'I might just take you up on that.' She chuckled. It was lovely to say those words and mean them. *Such a relief to feel safe with someone again after all this time.*

'Thank you so much for sharing your story with me. I really appreciate it.'

'You know what? So do I. I hadn't realised how much I wanted to tell it. Everyone pussyfoots around it.' People talked of traged-ies in veiled terms, hiding behind images and common expressions that failed to reveal the reality of the victim's fate and the nightmare they left behind for a grieving family. She hadn't even told her best friend everything that had happened with Lisa. And there was much more to the story. 'I've only told you the half of it.'

'Well, go on, if you feel up to it. I'm all ears.'

He was much more than all ears. *You are all muscle, all heart, all man.* She braced herself. It was going to be hard to say everything out loud, even to someone as caring and as willing to listen as Christophe. *But I want to do it. I need to do it.*

At that moment, two giggling teenagers, or perhaps they were in their early twenties, walked by, hips swaying as their feet dug into the sand. One of them waved cheekily to Christophe, the other pretended to fan herself before whispering something in the ear of the first girl.

Christophe grimaced and without even nodding in their direction turned his attention immediately to Emily. Then a wolf whistle pierced the air and Emily dropped her head. The girls were all hot and bothered by Christophe, and clearly not afraid to express their appreciation of his gorgeous body.

'So, the other half of the story?' He reached out to touch Emily's shoulder.

'The other half … I think I've said enough for today. Actually, there isn't really anything else worth saying. Let's just leave it at that.'

This wasn't going to work. No matter how sincere Christophe was, no matter how much he tried, there would always be too many temptations for a man so physically attractive. He might seem uninterested in those girls, he might genuinely not be interested at all right now, but there would come a time when he wouldn't mind a bit of fun on the side. Emily couldn't afford another Josh in her life, flatly refused to go down that road again.

She'd already lost far too much. There was no way she'd let another chick magnet intentionally or unintentionally take her sanity. 'I have to head back.'

His eyebrows shot up and he opened his palms to the sky. 'Did I do something wrong?'

'Nothing. You did nothing.' That was the whole point. He didn't have to do anything. To attract trouble, he just had to *be*. One day or another, he'd see how far that could take him and he'd give in and follow his male instincts like Josh had always done. No, for Emily, Christophe's fate was sealed the day he was born so strikingly handsome and she had to face that fact no matter how she felt with him. 'Let's go,' she said in her most authoritative voice, all the while trembling inside.

'Emily?'

She left him behind as she hurried off in the direction of the car park. She might have had a moment of weakness at the beach, she might have nearly given in to her attraction, but those two cheeky teenagers drooling over Christophe had been a timely reminder that she was playing a dangerous game with the wrong man. Thank goodness they'd walked by!

If she ever ventured down the path of a relationship again, it had to be with someone ordinary, inconspicuous, banal. A man who wouldn't hurt her because he *couldn't*. That was the best form of insurance she'd ever find in a partner.

It was a reality check for her.

The dance with striking Christophe was over.

Never again would Emily be caught with a stunningly handsome man.

Christophe threw the pizza dough onto his floured kitchen benchtop and pounded it with the base of his palm. How else could he take out his frustration? The roller-coaster ride with Emily had reached the bottom once again and despite the excitement at the top he wasn't sure he'd ever be prepared to buy another ticket.

Not with the emptiness and the need it left in him each time. The walk down the beach had been wonderful. He'd held her against him, and every part of him—yes, *every* part—had awakened after what seemed a terribly long slumber. If there'd been a male version of Sleeping Beauty coming back to life, it would have been him on that beach pressing his body against Emily's.

Except that once you woke up, you were supposed to have found your princess forever. Not for two minutes until the mood changed wildly and you couldn't figure out what the hell you'd said or done to make it all go to pieces. Yet again.

He added a little more flour, shaking it through his hand to avoid any lumps before pounding, stretching and pressing the circle of dough into submission the way he wished he could make Emily submit to this thing, whatever it was, growing between them. It wasn't like him to think of making a woman *submit*—Emily was driving him crazy. He smoothed some tomato sauce onto the pizza base and sprinkled it with fresh thyme.

What was he going to do about his gorgeous sweet-smelling neighbour? What the hell could he do? The obvious answer seemed to be stay away. Except he couldn't, not since he'd tasted her lips and felt her body against his. How perfectly they seemed to fit together! He'd even imagined an incredible start to the New Year, waking up next to her. He'd pictured her all sleepy-eyed, warm, naked. He might have been moving too fast in his mind, but a man could dream, couldn't he?

Christophe sighed. He couldn't just drop the whole Emily issue. The only thing he could do was go over there and talk some sense into her until she told him what on earth was torturing her so much. It must have been torture. Why else couldn't she accept what had developed between them, the electricity, the awakening, the incredible pull? What should he call this thing that he felt for her? He wasn't sure, but it was too special to be ignored. Something that could be gentler than a spring morning in the sunshine, stronger than a blazing fire on an icy night. Something she could see, too, and seemed to want as much as Christophe did, until at the flick of a switch she turned and ran faster than a hunted rabbit.

He topped the pizza with chopped mushrooms, capsicum and kalamata olives. He'd made too much dough. There was enough for two … Wishful thinking.

He shook his head. He should have known better than to let himself fall for his beautiful, impossible neighbour. Because that was what had happened, wasn't it? He'd gone and fallen for her. He'd been perfectly happy without sharing his life with anyone special since Marianne, and even if he hadn't indulged much he'd been able to find a woman in a bar at the drop of a hat whenever he'd wanted to. He probably had his French accent to thank for that. So why look for complications? A million guys would love to live that way.

He placed the pizza onto a tray, about to slide it into his hot oven, when he returned it to the kitchen bench instead. The food could wait, but not him. He was going to put a stop to all this nonsense with Emily.

He wiped his hands on a tea towel. He was heading over there this very instant to make her understand how much he hated all this toing and froing, and that he needed to know where he stood. Did she want more than a neighbourly relationship with him or not? Was she open to taking it further than that? If she truly wasn't, he needed to hear it from her and she had to stop giving him enough of herself to keep him hanging on.

It would go one way or the other, there would be no in-between, no sitting on the fence after that. Either they'd share a pizza, a kiss, and when she was ready, a bed, or he'd be putting up a new fence between them faster than the roller-coaster ride Emily had inflicted upon him.

He glanced outside at the broken fence. A gate between the properties would be perfect.

In his heart he wanted to share things with Emily: walks, talks, his body and his mind. He wanted to share everything with her, wanted to give it a real shot, but he steeled himself as he turned off the oven and scrambled through his garden. He was just as capable as the next guy of avoiding someone unpredictable in the name of self-preservation and getting on with his life, wasn't he?

He hoped he was wrong, but the lump in his stomach told him Emily could very well force him to be that man.

Chapter 8

Christophe bit the inside of his cheek as he knocked firmly on Emily's door. He listened to the song of the magpie in the gum tree while he waited, trying to empty his mind and calm the knot forming in his stomach. He sighed. She was in there and not in a hurry to open up.

He knocked again, even harder this time. 'Emily, it's Christophe. We need to talk.' *Come on, Emily.*

The door opened a crack and then a little more, and Emily stood before him, lips pressed tight. She kept her gaze on her feet.

He wanted to feel her eyes on him, wanted to run his fingers through her golden mane and kiss the tip of that cute button nose, but he had to act like they were nothing more than acquaintances. He cleared his throat. 'Emily, what is going on? What is going on with you, with us?'

She shrugged. 'Nothing is going on, Christophe. We're neighbours. We went for a walk together.'

He held back a gasp. She sounded like she believed that, when there was enough electricity between them to light up an entire city. It baffled him. 'Can I come in?' He needed some time with her, to convince her that she was wrong.

She fiddled with her top. 'It's getting late and I'm pretty tired. I haven't yet eaten, either.'

It was unsettling having to reach out to her from her front porch, kept at bay like a complete stranger. How could she let him into her heart if he couldn't even make it into her home for a few minutes? Maybe she didn't feel at ease inviting him in, but what if he asked her over to his house? 'I've made too much pizza. Would you like to come over and share it? I just have to put it in the oven and it'll be ready in ten minutes.' He held his breath like a little boy waiting to hear if he'd be granted his wish for Christmas.

Her lips twisted and her face seemed to hollow. 'Thank you, but I'd rather not.'

Did she mean *not tonight* because she was tired? Or was it a permanent refusal, a *not ever* because she was once again back to doing her best to avoid him? Christophe wasn't one to insist when a woman said no, but this time something told him not to let it go. All he wanted was a chance to get things out into the open, to really understand what was going on. 'I'd so appreciate a chat about what happened down at the beach. There are things I need to say, and things I have to know or I'll lose sleep over it for sure.' That was putting it mildly. He was already in agony; the night would be torture.

She looked up at him with her beautiful doe eyes, those eyes he could drown in without hesitation, if only she would let him. 'All right. Let's sit out here for five minutes.'

His shoulders relaxed as he followed her to the old wooden bench under the jasmine-covered arbour in her front garden. Although she wouldn't lead him inside, it wasn't an outright rejection.

'Emily, I can't for the life of me understand what happened down at the beach. It was all going so well. We confided in one another.

And then, for no reason, or at least none I can figure out, you shut me out. It was like I suddenly had a different person in front of me.' A person who from one minute to the next didn't want to share one more secret, one more smile, one more brush of the hand. Someone who couldn't even tolerate him. And all that after he'd held her, and she'd *wanted him to*—for goodness sake, she was the one who'd leaned on him.

He could tell from the way she averted her gaze once more that she wasn't proud of what had happened. She rubbed her nose. 'I didn't mean to end up in your arms earlier. It just … sort of happened. I hadn't planned it, so I owe you an apology.'

He rubbed his forehead. Talking with Emily wasn't solving the mystery of her behaviour, it was adding to it. 'I'm not sure that I follow. You are apologising for being in my arms because you hadn't *planned* it?' How much planning was required? 'I thought you wanted me to hold you. You seemed comfortable in my arms.' More than comfortable, she'd felt like an angel abandoning herself to him. They had shared a moment of closeness, a moment when he knew without a shadow of doubt that they were right for each other.

'I thought I'd made it clear that it was just a walk, nothing more. In fact, if I remember correctly, you promised.'

It was his turn to look away. 'It's true, I did give you my word.' He was a little embarrassed about breaking that promise, but he'd had good reason. She'd rested against him; it had been only natural to hold her. He wasn't ashamed of what he felt and what she seemed to feel too. He gathered his strength and sought her gaze again. 'Let's not play cat-and-mouse games. You can't deny that there's something between us, something amazing. It's as clear as the blue sky above us. And it seems to me that whenever it's all going well you turn around and reject it. I can't figure out why.'

'It doesn't matter why. We are not a couple and never will be and that's all you need to know.'

He trembled as he reached out and gently brought her face towards his. 'You were perfect in my arms, Emily. Don't you want to give this a try?'

She slid to the other end of the bench. 'No, I don't. I can't give it a try.'

'*Can't?* Why? I want to understand. It isn't because it didn't work out with your last boyfriend that it won't work out with anyone else. Otherwise, I'd be doomed too, with what happened with Marianne. Hell, half the world would be doomed as far as relationships go.'

'I'm well aware of that.'

'Well, then?' He was going round in circles, maddening, puzzling circles.

She huffed, crossing her arms. 'Look, it won't work because you're not my type.'

His jaw dropped. 'Could have fooled me.' While he wasn't pretentious enough to think that he could be every woman's type, it was clear to him that Emily was more than a little drawn to him. He should probably stand and leave now that she'd reiterated that it wasn't going to happen between them, but he couldn't control the flame in his belly that pushed him to stay and fight. 'Are you denying the attraction between us?'

How could she? No one in their right mind could deny the incredible pull between them. It wasn't just a figment of Christophe's imagination. She felt it too, otherwise there would be no toing and froing, no kisses, no hugs, just a woman who wasn't at all interested in a man who found her irresistible. It wasn't like that with Emily. It was a merry-go-round of attraction and torture, hope and disappointment. It was 'yes' and 'no' at the same time.

'You're not what I want in a man, okay?' She stood, the colour draining from her face.

'That's a technique politicians use, you know that? You don't quite answer the question, which was are you denying the attraction between us? Anyway, explain to me why I'm not what you want in a man, so that I can leave you alone, if that's what your heart really desires. What is it that you don't like? That I'm a chef? That I'm French? I'm too tall? Not rich enough? What?'

'No. It's nothing like that.'

'So, I smell?'

'Don't be ridiculous. You don't.'

'I'm scentless.'

'Of course you're not scentless.'

'So I do smell.'

'Well, yes, if you really want to know. You smell of, well, if you must know, you smell of ... I don't know what it is but you smell good.'

He smiled at the first positive comment in a while. 'Help me out here, Emily.' If she didn't, he wouldn't find peace. Instead, he'd think about how much they'd be missing out on and it would eat away at him.

'Look, I shouldn't have come over to your Christmas lunch, that's all. That's where I went wrong. Let's forget about the whole thing.'

'There's a lot about me you haven't yet discovered. A hell of a lot. Are you sure you already want to forget everything?'

'I've seen enough and it's obvious to me that while you are a very, hmm, nice man, you are not for me.'

'You're not going to tell me why? Just fabulous.' A ball of fire burned in his stomach. 'Well, don't come and see me tomorrow pretending everything's fine and asking me to hold you. Don't come and offer me your lips. I can't cope with this dance we are doing, Emily. It's getting to me, it really is. It's either a yes, and we truly give it a try, or it's a no, a real no and ...' He didn't know how to finish his sentence without telling her that he'd miss out on something he knew deep in his heart could be the best thing to ever happen to him.

'The dance never should have started, Christophe, and I'm sorry if I gave you the wrong impression. It's a no, and I won't be going out with you. There. We're clear now.'

As he stood, his jaw tightened. Once at home, he'd take his frustration out on his pillow and yell into it. Or drink wine. Or watch sport. Anything to take his mind off how he hurt to the core right now, how the lump in his throat ached, how his hands would tremble if he didn't curl them into a fist and shove them in his pockets. 'Fine. So just to be *crystal* clear, are you still coming over for a drink tomorrow night for New Year's Eve, evidently as nothing but a friend?'

She took a step back. 'I don't think we can be friends. It wouldn't work. It seems to come back to this all the time. Neighbours, that's all we can be.'

He shook his head. How could he be so wrong about what he felt, the electricity, the awareness, the pull between them? But he'd pleaded with her and she didn't even want to be friends. What else could he do? 'I'll be dealing with the fence within the next couple of weeks.'

She shrugged. 'Fine. We need to sort out the fence issue.'

'I'm not having fibro.'

'We've been over this before. It's already fibro. Changing the whole thing will cost too much.'

'There are so many sheets to repair, and even the ones that aren't broken are all brittle. It wouldn't be worth changing the broken sheets to have to change more in the near future. Besides, it never should have been fibro in the first place. It isn't in keeping with the rest of the estate, isn't what the shire expects and it's damn ugly in my personal opinion. I'm putting up the same wood as I have on the other sides.'

'The wood's too expensive.'

'*C'est ça*. I didn't expect you to agree with me.'

'Why? Because I'm not capable of being reasonable?'

'Something like that. So I'll order the fencing and have it erected and send you the bill for half the cost?'

'I'm definitely not paying for labour, Christophe.'

'And how do you expect the fence to be built? I can't put it up on my own. It's too much to ask of a friend to spend their summer holidays helping me do all that because someone … Because you …'

'I'm not being difficult, okay? I simply can't afford it.'

'Saving up for fancy shoes to replace the ones that fell into the pool?' He closed his eyes. *Quel imbécile!* The frustration of not having a real shot with Emily was turning him into an ass.

'I don't give two hoots about expensive shoes. Those shoes were to my ex's taste, not mine. I'm not that superficial that I have to have designer shoes instead of fixing my fence. If you must know, I saw a lawyer about my sister's death and what happened with my mother. It's been ages and I'm still paying off those legal bills.'

Her comment cast the shadow of embarrassment over her, her shoulders drooping, her expression suddenly pained.

The pain spread to him, his stomach tightening. *You've really had a rough run*. 'I shouldn't have said that, Emily. I was out of line. Look, don't worry about it. I'll pay for the labour. You can just chip in half the cost of what fibro would be, and reimburse me whenever you're ready. I'm happy with that.'

'That's kind of you, Christophe, don't think I don't appreciate it, but I don't want to owe you. I can't put myself in that position.

You'd be paying more than half for the materials and one hundred per cent of the labour. It's not going to happen.'

'What are you talking about? You won't *owe* me.' Was she suggesting he had an ulterior motive? *I'm not that kind of person. She's impossible!* He took a deep breath. 'So what do you propose, exactly?'

'I'll put the fence up with you. I have most of January off. We can do it over a weekend or two, or a long weekend if you don't have holidays. I'm not going away.'

'You'll put the fence up with me? Did I hear that right? It's heavy work.'

'You think I'm not capable just because I'm a woman? I have two arms and two legs and I'm in pretty good shape.'

You are indeed a woman and in perfect shape. He'd noticed that, but he knew better than to comment. And putting the fence up together would give him a chance to talk to her some more, to charm her, to make her see how sweet life could be if only she let him share it with her. What did he have to lose? 'Okay. Let's do it.'

Her eyebrows shot up. 'Okay, then.' She took a few steps to the house then stopped and turned to him. 'The sooner the better, so that I'm finally able to go out in my own backyard without wondering if you'll get an eyeful of me in my nightie when I water the plants. And then you won't have to worry about offending me, either. Once it's up, you won't see me and I won't see you. We'll each have our privacy.'

'Perfect. I'll order the materials right away and let you know when they're due for delivery. I can take a few days off work if need be. The previous chef's retired now but he's happy to fill in for me from time to time.'

She nodded. 'Great. The sooner it's done, the better.'

'Glad we had this talk. Looking forward to having a nice, new fence.'

'Not as much as I am.'

He huffed before stomping up Emily's garden path, putting on a show for his golden-haired neighbour when secretly he wasn't completely upset at the turn of events. It would have been better had she wanted to see him, and she'd made it clear that she didn't, but he would nevertheless get to spend a few days putting up a fence with her, working with her hour after hour.

He still had a chance with her.

Although only until the fence was fully built. Would he, in that time, be able to break through the armour she'd built around herself and kept patching up every time he managed to put a dent in it?

He had no idea.

What he did know was that he was going to give it his very best shot.

Emily closed her front door and rested against it. The talk with Christophe had just about destroyed her. Staying outside with him had been a good move because she couldn't smell his mesmerising scent quite as much, especially with the strong fragrance of the jasmine vine that covered the arbour under which they'd sat.

Unfortunately, there were plenty of other things that had revived her attraction to Christophe, from the way he tilted his head at times to those stunning chocolate eyes. And the memory of his arms, how his warm body had fit against hers down at the beach, was nearly too much to bear. If only she could find him repulsive for some reason; if only he were rude, gross, self-centred, dirty.

No such luck. He was perfect in every way. She padded down to the kitchen and made herself a cup of steaming camomile tea to ease her nerves. How awful it was to have to put him off her that way, but it was all she could do. If she wasn't harsh enough he'd keep on coming back and that wouldn't be fair to him. Besides, it was too hard for her, too. She wanted him so much physically, every inch of her body calling out to him, longing for his arms, his warmth, his scent. It had been a long time since she'd shared her bed with a man.

Thank goodness she had a head, a strong mind that remembered every bit of what Josh had done to her and her family. And Christophe was even more handsome than Josh. She hadn't thought that possible, had never imagined a man more attractive than her ex, that traitor, and then she'd stumbled upon Christophe.

She sat at the kitchen table and sipped her drink. This time, it wasn't Lisa she remembered sitting across from her in that spot. It was Christophe with the coffee she'd made him. Christophe who'd spilled it down his shirt. And then Christophe, shirtless, his wide shoulders and toned abdomen exposed for her to drool over, his laundry in a ball for her to wash.

She had to stop thinking about the man, had to find herself someone plain without a charming accent, perhaps a little podgy or very white, sickly and willowy. Maybe with a few spots, balding and a couple of missing teeth. A man she'd be with for companionship and support and whose physique would never threaten their relationship. How hard could it be? She chuckled. A man who wasn't attractive to anyone else probably wouldn't attract her, either.

She left the table, taking her drink with her, turned on the television and hoped that its blue light and the boredom of the reality show that was playing would empty her mind of all thoughts of men, handsome or otherwise.

Christophe might have turned her world upside down but now that he'd finally understood what to expect of her—which was nothing at all—the Frenchman with his gorgeous eyes and his

attractive ways would make himself scarce and would forget about
pursuing her.

*All that's left to be done is put up the darn fence between us and then I
won't see him at all.* She'd forget all about him, would find balance
on her own again, with her cat and a good book, and perhaps a
friend she could go and visit once in a while.

That's all I really need in life, comfort and peace. Especially peace.

She'd find it the minute Christophe stopped tormenting her with
his good looks and his never-ending French charm.

Now that's something worth looking forward to.

Chapter 9

Christophe arranged his last dessert order, a tiered champagne and chocolate mousse served with tiny almond macarons, on a plate he decorated with gold stars made of sugar for the occasion. The sweet looked perfect and screamed New Year, so where was the pride and pleasure that usually rose in him when he'd created a new and successful dish? Tonight he felt none of that.

'Mousse table 17,' he cried out to be heard from the other end of the large kitchen. He placed the fancy dessert on the benchtop, ready for the waiters to take out.

One of the extras they'd hired for the busy night, a girl who looked so young he thought she ought to be at home with her parents watching over her instead of working tonight, waltzed in and picked it up. 'These are so pretty, chef. You make amazing food.'

'Thanks. Did you let everyone know we were closing the kitchens soon?'

'Yep. All the staff did.'

'Okay. So it's definitely my last order for the night?'

'It is. And mine, then? I can go after this? I told Mum I was finishing at ten.'

Christophe glanced up at the giant black and white clock that graced their north-facing wall—a chef cutting onions and crying crocodile tears that he had found amusing although some might think it out of character in the swish restaurant. Whether you liked the clock or not, it was the true master of their working hours. 'Oh, I'm sorry. I'll make sure we pay you the overtime. You go home and have a very happy New Year.'

The girl's expression brightened. 'Thanks, you too.' She hurried out with the mousse.

Christophe wiped his hands on his apron and leaned against the stainless-steel bench. The kitchen was quiet now, except for the banging of pots and pans that were still being put away. It must have been Nico, crouched down somewhere behind a counter. 'Go home, mate,' called Christophe. 'Go and enjoy yourself. We can sort anything that's left tomorrow.'

Nico's head appeared as he propped himself up. 'Yeah, thanks, boss. I've just about finished anyway. What about you?'

'Don't you worry about me. I'll be leaving soon, too.'

'Cool.' The kitchen hand raised a fist in the air as he stood. 'Time to party!'

Christophe smiled at the young man's enthusiasm. 'Happy New Year, Nico. And thanks for everything you do here.'

Nico grinned. 'No worries. It's what I'm paid for, hey? Happy New Year, boss.'

As the younger man strode out, Christophe took off his apron and threw it into the dirty laundry basket that was already full of tea towels. He rubbed his chin. What should he do now? Stick around the restaurant although the remaining wait staff were more than capable of serving drinks until the end and cleaning up the tables? Or go home like he'd originally planned, even if he didn't finish the night with Emily. Emily ... His heart sank at the thought of not seeing her tonight.

What if he just turned up on her doorstep? How wise would that be? She'd told him to stay away and if he went against her wishes it could have an impact on her mood when they put up the fence together. He didn't want to jeopardise his only remaining chance to make her see that they could be great together, that what she kept pushing away was a treasure that not everyone found. No, he couldn't spoil his only chance, however slim it might be, by going against her wishes. He wouldn't go and knock on Emily's door tonight.

He wiped a benchtop that didn't need cleaning. He had only the slightest chance with Emily, didn't he? He didn't want to think about that tonight. It was New Year's Eve, a time to look ahead to the future with enthusiasm. And if you couldn't do that, a time to focus on the present and to have fun. That's what he ought to do tonight. Focus on the moment.

He'd had a few invitations, but he'd refused them, thinking he'd be with Emily, sitting on the patio, gazing at the stars. And now that he wasn't going to be with her, he didn't feel like going to another party. If he turned up at Joe's or elsewhere, he'd have to explain why, and then all he would want to talk about would be Emily, the mad roller-coaster ride he'd been on from the beginning with her, the exasperation of it all, and the fence—his last hope to conquer her. He couldn't do that to Joe or anyone else tonight for that matter, didn't want to spoil anyone's New Year's Eve party moping about and complaining, and he simply wasn't sure he could put on a brave face. Not when he'd thought so many times about the wonderful night he would spend alone with his gorgeous neighbour.

He'd imagined them sharing a glass of champagne, and then perhaps feeding each other or eating something together, each nibbling at one end until their lips met like in *Lady and the Tramp*. Ridiculous thoughts of romance ending of course with them rolling around in bed and starting the year all starry-eyed like teenagers in love for the first time.

He'd certainly got ahead of himself there. He'd been stupid, so very stupid. He had to get a grip on things. Emily wasn't about to hop into bed with him. She had made it crystal clear that he wasn't the man for her. It would be easier if he just listened to her, wouldn't it? But why did he feel this longing in his heart? Why couldn't he simply accept that she wasn't for him and move on? Because he'd had a taste of her, and one taste was all it took for him to know that together they would be amazing.

He looked through the small windows of the kitchen doors at the people celebrating in his beloved restaurant. Where was the pride he normally felt at having created such a beautiful place with the freshest, tastiest, sometimes most surprising paddock-to-plate flavours for miles around? And why did he see nothing but happy couples everywhere, their intertwined fingers, their loving gazes, their warm kisses? They would be going home together tonight, sharing a bed and an amazing start to the New Year that many of them probably took for granted.

He shook himself. He loathed self-pity. Yes, he could trust his capable staff to finish serving drinks, clean up and close the restaurant in his absence, as planned. And he could have himself a good time, even if it wasn't with the woman who'd been on his mind for far too long. There were plenty of bars that would be open tonight. He was a young, healthy single man and he could go out and enjoy himself without having to explain to anyone why he was there on his own tonight. He was heading into town and would make the most of his freedom.

He rubbed his chin. The Black Night seemed like a good choice. He'd been there once. It had great music. Plus, it was classy with patrons around his age, neither silly, drunk eighteen-year-olds who ended the night vomiting, nor stiff sixty-year-olds in suits who danced to dated music. He left through the back door, climbed into his car and headed towards Coffs Harbour to paint the town red before the chime of midnight.

Meg and her husband Jack had decorated their house nicely for the New Year, with a sparkling silver 'Happy New Year' banner and their best table setting on display. Music filled every room, and over-excited children ran around the backyard screaming as they tried to catch each other.

They had invited two other couples, neither of which Emily knew, who seemed to be well acquainted with one another and intent on outdoing each other every time they opened their mouths, whether they talked about home renovations, cars or their children's schools.

'We're going to Venezuela next month,' said Tanya, eyes sparkling as she placed her head briefly on her husband's shoulder.

He nodded. 'If Tanya wants to go somewhere, that's where I want to go. Venezuela, here we come.'

'Oh, excellent!' answered Marie. 'We were there a few years ago. Not my favourite place in the world, I have to say, but I'm sure you'll enjoy it.'

'I agree,' added Marie's husband, Pete, as he squeezed his wife's hand. 'There are better places to visit. I really liked Vietnam. Great food, excellent service there. We're off to Barcelona this April for something different. Now, that should be good.'

Emily left the table and sat on the couch.

'Everything okay, Em?' asked Meg, who came in carrying finger food.

'Sure. Can I help with anything in the kitchen?'

'No, it's all under control, thanks, honey. You having a good time?'

'Yeah, I just moved over here 'cause I love these new armchairs you have.'

'They are excellent, aren't they? Here, have a little mango tart.'

Emily took one and nodded her thanks. 'Looks delicious.'

'Jack, honey? Give Emily something to drink, will you?'

Emily shook her head as Meg raced off to her other friends. 'No, I'm fine, thanks.'

'But you've barely had a drink all night, Em. Jack, she'll need something to toast the New Year. It's getting close. Hurry up!'

Jack raced over with a glass of champagne. 'Here you are, Emily.'

'It's nearly midnight,' screamed Meg to everyone moments later. 'Come on, kids, guys, let's get ready to count down.'

Everyone gathered in the family room. 'Ten, nine, eight ...'

The voices faded away and Emily thought of Christophe's house. That's where she would have loved to drink champagne at midnight, where she would have had the most fun and not felt out of place like here. She loved Meg and Jack to bits, but they'd been busy all evening and she'd found herself amongst couples she didn't know and whose lives were so different from hers that she had trouble imagining a single thing she and they had in common. If only she'd been at Christophe's ...

But then she reminded herself of Lisa, how her life had been destroyed because of Emily's model boyfriend, and steeled herself. Emily couldn't ever go down that road again and she knew it. It was just as well she wasn't at her French neighbour's place tonight, far too risky to go anywhere near that sexy man. Her brain knew that. Could someone *please* convince her heart?

'Two, one, zero! Happy New Year!'

The three couples each kissed passionately on the lips while Emily guzzled down all her champagne at once.

A few moments later, she gave everyone a hug and expressed her best wishes for the year. She tickled a bunch of kids, and then discreetly slipped into the kitchen where she cleaned up the mess for Meg. As soon as it was late enough to make her escape, she thanked her hosts and drove home.

Her heart beat faster as she pulled up in the driveway and looked over at Christophe's house for signs of his presence. The home lay in darkness and silence, and Emily bit her lip. Where was he? Already in bed? Or at some fabulous party, dancing the night away with a beautiful woman? Probably the latter. Her heart sank.

It was just as well, really. She otherwise might have gone over there just because it was a special day, a day of new beginnings and hope and cheer. She might have given in to the ball of need in her belly and the ache in her soul that she tried so desperately to ignore.

She might have given in to Christophe and all his Gallic charms and that was something she simply couldn't afford to do.

She opened her front door and turned on the lamp that stood in the entrance. Shadow was stretched out on the couch in the lounge room and demanded her attention with a long miaow.

'Hey, baby cat.' Emily lay next to her furry friend and patted the swirls of hair on the belly Shadow was offering her. 'Happy New Year to you, too.'

It was comforting to have a sweet cat to cuddle up to. But as Emily's heavy eyelids closed, she knew in her heart that a cat wasn't enough.

The Black Night was as classy as Christophe remembered it, although the décor had been brightened for New Year's Eve with gold garlands, confetti, hats and streamers left on the tables and at the bar for people to play with if they wanted.

Instead of his usual cognac, he ordered a pina colada, a drink that meant relaxation, fun and light-heartedness. Because that's what he would have tonight, lots of fun. He'd hardly had his cocktail in hand for a minute when a pretty woman in a black velvet dress pressed her hand on his shoulder.

'Mind if I sit?'

'Please.'

'Are you here with someone?' Her green eyes gazed into his.

'No, I'm on my own.' It was somehow strange to reveal that to her.

'I'm with a girlfriend. I mean a friend, who happens to be a girl. She's over there.' The woman pointed to a redhead in the crowd who was wriggling her bottom to the beat of the music in front of a guy who grinned ear-to-ear. 'She's found someone more interesting than me, so I'm in search of company.'

Christophe chuckled. 'I'm sure he's not more interesting than you.'

'Thank you. What is that gorgeous accent I detect?'

'French.'

She came closer and whispered in his ear. 'I love *everything* French.'

Cheeks burning, Christophe pulled away. Where did the unease come from? It might have been a cheeky, provocative remark, but he'd never been shy with women. 'Would you like something to drink?'

'Yeah. What you're having.'

He raised his hand to call the bartender, but the girl pulled it down. She picked up Christophe's glass and guzzled half of it. 'I just needed a sip. Come on!'

She jumped to her feet and dragged him to the dance floor where she twirled around in front of him, her chestnut hair flicking about. 'I'm Cilla. And you're?'

'Christophe.'

'Nice name. It's midnight, soon, Christophe. And you know what happens at midnight.'

As she swayed her hips before him the music stopped. The DJ commenced the countdown to the New Year and soon everyone joined in.

'Three, two, one, Happy New Year!'

While people jumped to kiss their lovers, partners, friends, a pang of loneliness took Christophe's breath away. He was lonely in this crowd, lonely with Cilla trying very hard to seduce him. Emily's sweet curls flashed before his eyes. He saw her in that pink dress she'd worn to his Christmas lunch, dry and then wet and oh, so transparent. He saw her in her ugly tracksuit in the garden, still able to make his heart beat faster than wild horses could gallop, and on his patio for morning tea, beaming at what he'd prepared.

Cilla's arms closed around Christophe's neck and she pulled him to her with a jolt, her lips seeking his. He quickly turned his head and Cilla's kiss landed on his cheek.

He peeled her arms off him. 'I'm sorry, I have to go.'

'What? Cinderella has to go home, huh? Are you for real? Come on, I think the two of us could have an amazingly wild and hot start to the year.'

'I meant it when I said I'm sorry. I'm not taking the easy road, believe me, but nothing can happen between us. I'm sure you'll make someone very happy this year, but it won't be me.'

He shoved his hands in his pockets and headed for the door. He didn't want to be in a nightclub with a strange woman he didn't know, no matter how beautiful and willing she was. There was only one place he wanted to be, and that was with Emily.

He picked his New Year resolution: to make Emily trust him, like him, love him. He would win her over and share his life with her.

And if he couldn't have that, he wanted nothing at all.

He sighed, his heart heavy.

He was in trouble.

In deep, deep trouble.

He wanted Emily and no one else.

Chapter 10

Emily slipped on her old tracksuit pants and a worn, loose T-shirt, all the while wondering why on earth she had insisted on putting up a new fence with Christophe.

Well, she knew why. She hadn't the money to pay for labour since she still had legal bills to settle, as well as a mortgage she carried on her own. It wasn't easy to own your own home as a single woman and you could end up in a financial tight spot even with a decent, steady job and a lifestyle that certainly wasn't over the top. Josh had been a drain on her finances, too, with his taste for luxury and all the money she'd lent him when he was in between modelling jobs, money she'd never recoup. All you had to do was hook up with the wrong person and your bank balance could change drastically from one day to the next.

She tied her hair in a ponytail and slapped some sunscreen on her face and arms. She hesitated. Should she add a little lip gloss? She did look rather dreary in old grey clothes without any make-up at all.

No. No artifice. Dreary was perfect to face Christophe. That way he would realise just how ordinary she was and would leave her in peace. If he lost interest in her, it would be so much easier for her to fight her own demons.

She glanced at her watch. A couple of minutes to nine. She'd better get over there if she didn't want to give him reason to complain. She grabbed the new work gloves she'd bought the previous day and shoved on her navy gardening cap. As she stepped out into the bright Australian summer morning, her stomach churned. It wasn't from hunger—she'd had a good breakfast to keep up her energy until lunchtime. She rubbed her belly and what she had thought was discomfort turned to butterflies. The sensation definitely had nothing to do with food. It was the idea of spending a few days in a row working with Christophe that was responsible for the knots in her stomach.

The Frenchman was already in the garden, digging along the old fence, his muscular arms glistening in the sun. 'Good morning.' He stopped for a second and rested against the shovel.

His deep voice made her vibrate even if all he'd done was pronounce the most ordinary greeting. 'Hi, Christophe. Am I late? I thought your note said nine.' She'd found a piece of paper with a few words scribbled on it in her letterbox a couple of days after New Year, giving her a day and time to erect the fence. She thought back to how she'd expected a joke, a fun sentence or a few kind words at the end of the note, how she'd read until the end with eagerness, but it had contained nothing of the kind.

Christophe wiped his forehead with the back of his hand. 'I was up, so I figured I'd start removing the old fence.'

Was that because he wanted to get this over and done with as soon as possible? The sooner the better? He'd be right to think that, and it was what was best for her too, and yet ... There was no denying that the idea disappointed her. 'What shall I do? Do you have another shovel?'

'No need, I've loosened all the sheets. That was my last one. Your timing is perfect. We now have to pull them out one by one and pile them up near the gate ready to be taken to the tip.'

'They're not asbestos, are they?'

'No, there's nothing to worry about. I checked before doing anything. It's marked on them. We wouldn't be removing them ourselves had they been asbestos.'

She nodded her agreement. 'All right, then. Let's do it.' She stood on her side of the fence, stretched out her arms and grabbed the first sheet. 'Tell me when to lift?'

'Just a minute.' He bent forward and gently uncurled her fingers, removing her hands before placing them back on the old fibro cement about twenty centimetres lower. The butterflies she'd had in her stomach since she'd arrived multiplied as if they were fighting extinction and fluttered madly at his touch. She swallowed. Hard.

'There, that's better,' said Christophe. 'You'll have more grip and strength with your arms a bit lower and you'll be able to push harder on your legs. Let's lift the sheet out together and once it's high enough I'll pull it to my side and rest it on the ground. Then you can come and grab the end I'm holding. I'll lift the other end off the ground and walk backwards and we'll dump it next to the gate.'

'It doesn't make sense for you to let go of one side only to go and lift the other end. I can walk backwards, too. No worries.'

'I was just trying to spare you the worst part of the squatting and lifting and ...' He studied her face. 'No problem, if that's what you want. I wouldn't want to be overly protective of you.'

She raised an eyebrow at the comment. His intentions were good, wanting to make things as easy as possible for her, she could see that, but she'd much rather pull her own weight. After all, she was the one who didn't want to hire labour, so why should he take the brunt of the effort?

She nibbled on her lower lip. She was telling herself fibs and she knew it. What she was worried about was letting him woo her with his sweetness and attentiveness. 'So are we going to stand here talking and planning all day, or are we going to get stuck into it?'

'And they say men are the more ruthless sex of the species.' Chuckling, Christophe placed his hands back on the sheet, a little lower than hers. 'On the count of three. Don't forget to use your legs to lift instead of bending your back. I wouldn't want to have to take you to hospital and have to look after you, all because you injured yourself doing *men's* work with me.'

She pulled an unamused face. 'I'm not a weak, silly woman who doesn't know the first thing about health and safety. And women are quite capable of doing whatever men do.' She knew that it wasn't always the case for all women, that some jobs certainly required more strength than she had, but damned if she'd say that to smug Christophe. Besides, there was plenty women could do better than men.

His eyes twinkled with amusement. 'Would you believe me if I said I agreed? I have the utmost respect for women. Okay. One, two, *and* three,' he counted.

They lifted together. Although the sheet was heavy it came out of the sand relatively easily, probably thanks to all the digging Christophe had done earlier that morning. Emily jumped over the trench, crouched down and picked up the lower end while Christophe held onto the top. They started on the way to the gate, Emily walking cautiously backwards, all the while wishing she could somehow avoid her neighbour's gaze. But the man was facing her and there was nowhere to hide to escape those dark chocolate eyes she could drown in if she let go of reason and restraint.

Even when she dropped her eyes to the fence they were carrying, Christophe's gaze burned right through her, awakening her body in ways that made her remember she was alive.

'Here's good.' He lowered the sheet to the ground and she followed his lead. 'Okay to do that another thirty times or so?'

'Sure.' She wasn't about to admit that it was a strain and her shoulders already ached, and even less that his eyes on her as they carried the materials were harder to cope with than the heavy lifting. 'That's what we're here for, isn't it? To get the job done.'

'If at any stage it's too much, let me know. I'm pretty sure I can lift a sheet on my own.'

She shrugged. 'Thanks, but I'll be fine.'

As he turned on his heels and walked back to the fence line, her eyes were drawn to his tanned, muscular legs crossing the grass in front of her. How did he manage to look so attractive in old shorts and work boots? And the muskiness of his scent, not his cologne, not his deodorant, but the wonderful scent of his body, made her want to lie next to him and take it all in, to wallow in his masculinity, to roll on the grass with his arms around her.

She let out her breath and followed him back, reminding herself to keep her mind on the fence and not think about anything other than the work that awaited her.

She had no idea how she would manage that.

She knew one thing for sure. It was going to be one hell of a long day in the face of temptation, and tomorrow she'd be confronted with it all over again.

Christophe tried to take more of the weight than Emily. He couldn't bear to watch her struggle with the heavy sheets and was ready to take it upon himself to protect her from injury. His suggestion that he remove the fence on his own if it became too much had been met with strong disapproval, and for hours she'd flatly denied the effort he could see so clearly on her face. *Her beautiful, angelic face, perfect without even a touch of make-up.*

In fact, he wondered why she ever bothered with make-up at all. She certainly didn't need any. His arm brushed against hers as they lifted what would be the last sheet for the morning, and he nearly dropped the fence, troubled by the sensation.

Emily must have noticed. 'You're getting tired?'

'No, I'm getting hungry.' They piled the last sheet onto the others. 'Ravenous, in fact. Time for lunch, don't you think?'

Emily nodded, removing her gloves and leaving them on top of the old fencing material, while Christophe did the same. 'Sounds good. What time shall I meet you back here?'

He held back the gasp of surprise that threatened to escape him. *Is she seriously thinking of eating separately when we've spent the whole morning working together? Is she that desperate to get away from me?*

She'd hardly talked to him for the past three and a half hours and he hadn't insisted, thinking they'd make up for it during the meal. And now, she was ready to part? Well, he wasn't going to let her slip through his fingers without a fight. 'It would be considered extremely rude in France to work together and not break bread together.'

'Really? Not so in Australia. Here we do whatever we want, whenever we want. We're not bound by thousands of years of traditions. What a burden that must be! Anyhow, I'm sure you could do with a rest without having to be polite and finding something to chat about.'

'Actually, that's not true. I've been looking forward to chatting. Very much so.'

'I don't have anything interesting to talk about.'

'That's where you're mistaken. It's all interesting to me. You can tell me about your New Year resolution, for example. Or talk to me about the glasses you sell, the books you read, your hobbies or anything at all, in fact.' She could explain her past, her reluctance to be with him, her dreams for the future. She could talk about what had happened when they went for a walk along the beach the week before last too, because her reactions were more often than not a complete mystery to him. *More than anything, tell me what you want in a man and I'll be it, for you.*

'In any case,' he continued, 'I've already prepared lunch for both of us and you don't even have to walk all the way around and through my front door to come and eat with me. Having the fence down has its advantages.' He grabbed her hand and led her to his back door before she had the time to think about it and come up with more reasons to go back to her place.

To his surprise, she didn't resist. She followed wide-eyed, her hand docile in his. He liked how it rested in his, soft, fragile and so very precious, like a little bird that might fly away any minute but miraculously chose to stay there. The urge to look into her eyes and share a smile with her burned through him, but he didn't dare, in case he scared her off. *The warmth of her fingers, her precious fingers, curled around mine has to be enough.*

'We could sit on the patio, but it'll be a lot cooler inside,' he offered.

'Some cool air would be nice.'

Soon, too soon, she tugged gently at her hand so Christophe let it go. He opened the door and gestured for her to enter ahead of him. 'I've prepared a *salade niçoise*. A splash of vinaigrette over it, and it'll be ready.'

Her smile lit up his world, his heart beating faster for it. 'You're very organised, Christophe. I think I've had that kind of salad before. What's in it, again?' She removed her cap, her curls framing her face like rays of sunshine, and dropped it onto the small bookshelf near his back door.

'Green beans, lettuce, tuna, boiled eggs, olives, anchovies, capsicum, boiled potatoes and a few other things. There are many different recipes for *salade niçoise*. This is mine. I don't mix it. I serve it with all the elements separate, deconstructed if you like. That way, if there's something you don't fancy, you don't have to fiddle around trying to separate it from the rest, or worse, eat something you don't like.'

'It sounds perfect, and I love all of those things.'

'How about a drink first? Wine, or a cocktail maybe? I can rustle one up in two seconds flat.'

She chuckled as he pranced around, pretending to shake a cocktail. 'Water will be fine or we'll never finish the fence. I do appreciate the little dance, though.'

'Glad to entertain you.' *I'm so happy to see her smile. She's a different person when she relaxes, a person I just can't seem to get enough of.* He took a bottle of water out of the fridge and grabbed a glass off the shelf. 'One Mississippi Greenland cocktail coming up.'

'I really don't want a cocktail.' Her face creased as she understood. 'Oh, Mississippi, cold water, okay. I was a bit slow with that one.' She giggled.

He placed the glass in her hand. 'There's nothing quite like water when you're thirsty, is there?' *And nothing quite like Emily's laughter to warm my heart.*

He served himself a glass of it too, and they both drank up. It was exactly what they needed after working outside, even if they'd both had a water bottle with them to stay hydrated.

He brought out the food and placed it on the table in the family room, a place less formal and somehow more intimate than the dining room that seemed just right for a meal with Emily. Less formal and more intimate was exactly what he wanted to be with her.

She helped him by gathering the plates and the cutlery. Watching her move about his kitchen, looking for what they needed to set the table, melted his heart. There was something comfortable and familiar about it, and a sense that she belonged there, in that kitchen, in that house, with him.

She opened the fridge. 'The bread?' she asked.

He pointed to a cupboard. 'I know that a lot of people keep it in the fridge over here but I can't get used to that. I like it warm, fresh from the bakery. That's how you eat it in France.'

'Sounds very nice, I have to admit.'

Once they were seated and served, he ventured to ask about her New Year celebrations. 'So what did you end up doing to see in the New Year?'

'I was at my friend Meg's house. She had a few friends over.'

'Nice.'

'It was, although ...'

Had she not enjoyed herself? Had she, like him, longed for that glass of champagne they were supposed to share together, just the two of them, to see in the New Year? 'Although?' he ventured.

She cleared her throat. 'Nothing. I don't want to sound ungrateful because it was lovely of my friends to invite me.'

'It wasn't what you expected, though?' More than that, if she was anything like him, it wasn't what she wanted or needed.

'That's it. It was quite noisy, with lots of kids, and I didn't know any of the people Meg and Jack had invited. And I was the only single person.'

'That can be difficult.' It had certainly been a difficult evening for him, although not for those reasons. 'Did you eat a lot to make up for it?'

'I'm not sure. It was finger food.'

'Yes, it can be hard to tell how much you eat when it's not in a plate.' He watched her place a piece of potato in her mouth and had to tear his gaze away from her luscious pink lips.

'What did you do, Christophe? Did you stay at your restaurant?'

He wondered how much to tell her. It was better to err on the side of caution. They had a couple of days work ahead of them. If he told her how much he'd missed her on New Year's Eve he could easily scare her away. 'I went out for a drink after work. It was fairly uneventful.'

She smiled. 'Uneventful can be a good thing.'

'I suppose so. You don't want it to be eventful for the wrong reasons. So what was your resolution for the year?'

She quickly shoved more food into her mouth, as if looking for an excuse not to talk, as if needing to delay the inevitable.

Christophe sat back, half amused, half exasperated. 'Take your time. I can wait.'

She finally swallowed. 'Mmm, what was the question, again?'

She knew perfectly well what the question was. 'Your resolution.'

'Oh, yes. That. I decided to throw out all my old clothes.'

'You mean, what you're wearing today, for example.'

'Yes, amongst other things.'

'That's a good resolution. I do like that pretty pink dress you wore to my party better, although that outfit's now ruined.' If he got her going she might actually reveal something about herself.

'I can't even wear a bra with that dress! As you know. I'd look pretty stupid building a fence in that.'

'You'd look pretty spectacular.' He laughed at the way her eyes had become as round as saucers. 'So when are you planning on throwing out your old clothes? Have you already started?'

'What's the rush?'

'Procrastination isn't good.'

'What would you like me to do? Get undressed and put what I'm wearing in your bin right now?'

He laughed harder. 'I wouldn't say no. The thing is you can't leave it until the last minute to follow through with your resolutions or what happened last year might happen again. You'll end up in a panic a week before the end of the year, wondering if you are going to manage to achieve it.' He still didn't know what she had decided to do last year. All he knew was that she was upset over it on Christmas morning, enough to make her cry.

'I picked something easier this year, Mister Smartass.'

'*Mister*, huh? Nice to be treated with respect.'

'You really ought to concentrate on the Smartass part.'

'Did you manage to achieve last year's resolution before the end of the year, by the way?'

She shovelled the rest of the food into her mouth, swallowed and stood, pushing in her chair. 'Better get back to it.'

'Excuse me? What do you mean? We've only been inside for twenty minutes. Where's the rest of my lunch break?'

'We're not in France, Christophe. We don't have two hours for lunch every day. I'll see you out there.'

'You haven't even told me what your resolution was last year. Why won't you tell me?'

'Let's start with you, Christophe. What was *your* resolution last year?'

'I actually can't remember.'

'So what's your resolution for this year?'

'I, uh, well … Mmm.'

'I tell you what. Let me worry about my resolutions and you worry about yours. Let's get this fence up.' She picked up her cap and pushed it firmly onto her head. 'I'll see you out there. Playtime is over.'

And so it was. A good part of the job was done now that all the old fencing was gone but he'd still made no progress at all with Emily.

At this rate, the job would be finished long before he found the way to her heart.

Chapter 11

As Emily arrived at the fence line between her property and Christophe's, she realised that she hadn't the faintest idea what to do next. She and Christophe had pulled out the old fence and carted it to the gate that opened to the driveway, leaving an empty trench all along the dividing line between the two homes. What now? Did they just stick the wood panels that lay in the garden into the hole where the grey pressed cement sheets had been? Would she manage to cart one there on her own?

The pine sheets didn't look that heavy, certainly lighter than the pressed cement, so she slipped one off the heap enough to grip it with both hands. She pulled it towards her, her stomach muscles contracting as she bore most of the load. She suddenly bent backwards under the weight and stumbled. Not only were the damn things heavy, they were too big to handle easily on your own.

Christophe came running out of the house waving his arms about like a train master trying to avoid a derailment. 'Put it down! You're going to injure yourself.'

The problem was, she couldn't see her own feet, the ground or anything around her below eye level. And bending forward to make sure she cleared the area where she stood was like asking her to perform a circus act. 'I can't!'

Miraculously, the weight was lifted from her arms before she collapsed. Christophe had taken the sheet off her and held it on his own as if it were barely heavier than a small sack of potatoes. He placed it back on the pile of new pine fencing. He'd chastise her now, she knew it, and she'd probably never hear the end of it.

He put his arm on her shoulder. 'You really scared me, Emily. I thought you were going to fall with the fence on top of you.'

Warmth spread to her from where his fingers rested, so much so that her worries about being told off melted away. 'They're really awkward to lift on your own.'

'They are, and you don't need to do anything on your own. I'm right here.'

She smiled, grateful that he refrained from telling her how stupid she'd been, grateful for his compassion and patience, and not just today. He'd been lovely towards her on more than one occasion, she was only too aware of that.

'Anyhow,' he continued, 'we're not putting in the pine sheets today. We have to set some posts in the ground in concrete before we can put up the new fence.'

'Why is that? There weren't any posts holding the old fibro.'

'You're right. But these are a different shape, different weight, different system.'

She bit her lip as she remembered seeing pine fences with vertical and horizontal posts holding them together. She looked over at the bundle of posts next to the piled up pine materials and felt silly for not noticing. 'Of course. I knew that. I mustn't have been thinking clearly.'

What had she been thinking? That she wanted to show Christophe how capable she was, and that she meant business, that's what.

She'd wanted to show him that she wasn't mucking around with a two-hour lunch, not after he'd started pressing her about her resolutions as if she were someone who simply couldn't see a resolution through. But her eagerness to prove her worth had backfired.

'You're okay, that's the main thing.' He held out a measuring tape. 'How about you measure up the fence line and every metre and a half mark it with a stone or something? I'll dig a hole then in that spot, and after we'll mix up concrete and stick in the posts before the day is over.'

'Sure. I can do that.' Earlier she would have hated him giving her orders, would have ignored him or, worse, perhaps even done the opposite of what he asked of her. But he'd saved her from possible injury and been most gracious about it. How could she resent him taking charge? She didn't. In fact, she admired the way he did so, with kindness and care, and just how competent and comfortable he seemed with a shovel in hand.

She liked a man who could fix things and build things, even if that wasn't his job. And she liked a man who was tolerant and forgiving, someone who could look past her own shortcomings, perhaps even understand them. She sighed. It was no use liking him.

She bent down and gathered a few pebbles from a nearby garden bed. She measured the first metre and a half along the trench and placed her first stone there. As she uncurled her spine and stood, she felt Christophe's hand on her back and she shivered, the awareness of his presence running through her whole body and placing it on full alert.

'You can save a pebble and take that one to the next hole. I know where to dig the first one.'

His enticing scent filled her lungs and that deep voice in her ear could very well make her steel resolve to avoid handsome men melt. She swallowed, hoping he didn't notice the effect his presence had on her, and quickly measured another metre and a half, hurrying this time to leave the pebble there and move on to the next hole.

She simply couldn't afford to let Christophe catch up with her again.

Christophe dug a hole for the next post as fast as he could, but there was no way he could get the job done as speedily as Emily moved along the dividing line, measuring up and placing pebbles for him to mark the future holes. If he didn't find a pretext or a ruse of some sort, he'd miss the opportunity to feel her close, smell the coconut scent of her golden curls and gaze into those angelic eyes of hers.

He wouldn't get a chance to talk to her either, if she stayed down the end of the block once she was done, and that would be even worse because it would afford him no opportunity to convince her to let him into her life and give this thing between them a shot, the shot it deserved. He just knew that they'd be fabulous together. He could tell from the way her scent made him dizzy, and how she warmed his heart whenever she opened up to him. Or smiled at him. Or made him laugh.

If only she could see that too.

As he reached the next pebble, he glanced over at Emily who was busy measuring the last portion of the block. He discreetly moved the pebble ten centimetres to the left, taking care to cover the mark it had left in the sand where it had initially been.

He stood. 'Emily? Could you check this one again? It looks a little out to me.'

He watched her walk back to him. How those hips swayed! And the sun on her golden arms made him want to grab them, kiss every inch of glowing skin and wrap them around him. She was stunning in the worst of clothes and without even a dab of make-up, truly beautiful without any artifice, the kind of wholesome beauty he admired most.

'How can it be out? I measured it all so carefully.' She frowned as she examined the distance between the last hole and the pebble to which Christophe was pointing. 'It does seem a little short.'

Christophe dropped his shovel. 'Here, let me help.' As his fingers wrapped around the end of the measuring tape, they brushed against Emily's and his heart skipped a beat. The sun caught the golden flecks in her eyes and he had to tear himself away from them, away from her. It was a shame he couldn't let himself go and drown in that gaze, a shame he couldn't take Emily in his arms and kiss those pouty lips until she lost her mind. Or he lost his, more likely. He rubbed his forehead, trying to concentrate on the task at hand, and placed his end of the measuring tape on the pebble while Emily crouched down and read the centimetres at her end.

'You're right! It's only a metre forty. I don't know how on earth I managed that. What about the one before and the one after?' She checked the previous one. 'This one's fine. I'll have a look at the next one.'

As she passed Christophe on the way to the next measurement, he stopped her, placing his hand on her forearm. 'Let me. You're doing all the crouching down and kneeling.'

She took a sharp breath. Was it his touch that had affected her? At times, she seemed just as taken by him as he was by her.

'It's no problem. You're the one doing the really heavy work.' She checked the distance to the next pebble. 'If you move that one forward ten centimetres it will be okay. I don't understand. If it was out by ten centimetres there, it should be out all the way.'

He had to think fast or she'd be onto him. 'Maybe I accidentally kicked it. Or maybe you did, when you were walking to the next one.'

Her eyes narrowed as she studied him. And then her mouth twisted. She was onto him all right—as always. 'In that case, I would have kicked it forward, not back.'

He couldn't help the chuckle that escaped him. 'I'm sorry. I was feeling lonely up here. I may have moved it. Just a tad.'

She shrugged. 'You could have simply asked me to come and chat as soon as I'd finished.'

'Really? You would have?'

'I never said I would have. But it would have saved you messing around trying to hide stuff from me. Well, I've finished taking the measurements down there. How long will you be digging?'

Why? Was she going to suggest they have a rest and a drink together? 'Probably another twenty minutes or so.' Possibly more. 'Unless I take a break now. I have no objections to that.'

'So twenty minutes. And then what happens?'

'Then I have to double-check the posts, make sure they are the right size. I might have to saw one or two to bring them to length. Let's say another half hour for that. Then mix the concrete. I'll get you to hold the posts in place while I pour in the concrete.'

'Perfect. Twenty minutes or so plus half an hour plus GST. That gives me an hour to check my emails and do a few things around the house. And maybe have a little lie down to rest my back since you were so worried about me injuring myself.'

'You're going home?' She'd backed him into a corner and now he was trapped. 'You'd leave me here on my own for a whole hour? I thought you'd keep me company.'

'I'm not going to hold your hand while you do things I can't help you with. I'm not your girlfriend.'

No, she wasn't. Unfortunately. 'Well, we have kissed.' He knew she wouldn't like him reminding her but he couldn't resist teasing her about it.

She placed her hands on her hips. 'And who is to blame for that?'

To blame? More like to thank. 'Your mother?'

'Nice try.'

He gazed into her eyes, her beautiful, mysterious eyes that sparkled in the sunshine. Her lips, luscious and pink, called out to him. He bent forward, remembering how they had tasted the first time he'd kissed them.

Those perfect lips parted once more but only to let out a cry. 'Seriously? You're going to try to kiss me again?'

He jumped back. 'I'm sorry. I don't know what got into me.' He was too taken by her, too desperate to touch her, smell her, feel her, so eager to be with her that he got carried away at the slightest opportunity, imagining that she wanted exactly what he wanted right here, right now.

'Listen, I'm going to make this crystal clear. I am not your girlfriend. I have no intention of becoming your girlfriend. It's not going to happen. I've already told you, you are not my type. Remember?'

He ran a hand through his hair. 'I do. Except that you never told me why.'

'I don't have to tell you why. I don't have to tell you anything.'

'I know, but ... Come on, help me out here. If you want me to accept this, I need to understand it. The only thing you've told me is that I don't smell bad.'

She shook her head, holding it with both hands and let out a cry of annoyance. 'All right. You win. I find you too attractive, too handsome, okay? You're too perfect in every way.'

He gaped at her. Too attractive? Too perfect? What the hell was she talking about? 'I didn't think that was possible.' And he certainly never thought she'd feel that way about him. 'Correct me if I'm wrong, but isn't finding someone attractive a good thing?'

'Don't question it, just accept it. We are not negotiating a relationship. You wanted to know and now you do and you can move on.'

'Nobody is too handsome.' He certainly wasn't. He'd never particularly liked his nose.

'Whatever. I'll leave you to it.'

'Whatever? You're going, just like that, after delivering the shock
of my life? How am I going to concentrate on my work now?'

'You'll be fine, Christophe. I'll see you in an hour to help stick
the posts in the concrete and we won't talk about this anymore.'

He sighed. She'd dashed his hopes of becoming her boyfriend
and slipped through his fingers once again. Now all he could do
was count the minutes until she returned and pray that he found
more convincing arguments to change her mind about him.

Emily giggled as she glanced through her back window at Christophe sawing wood in his garden. It was cute how he'd tried so
hard to keep her with him, how he'd gone and moved that pebble
just to make her come near him. It had been a long time since
someone had paid her that much attention, a long time since she'd
seemed to matter that much to anyone.

He was certainly adorable. And he seemed to really want to give
it a go with her. It was a shame he was as attractive as the best-
looking movie stars. A few years ago she wouldn't have hesitated. A
few years ago, before she'd met Josh who had ruined her life, before
Lisa had died and Emily's relationship with her parents had fallen
apart. She sighed. Now she knew better than to fall for someone
like Christophe. She did, didn't she?

She tore her gaze away from the chef's perfect silhouette, poured
herself a glass of orange juice and, taking the bottle with her, went

to sit in her family room. She took a sip of the cool, sweet liquid and felt it travel down into her stomach. She'd take the drink over and give some to Christophe in a few minutes, to make sure he was hydrated. And the sugar from the juice would boost his energy. Not that it needed boosting by the look of things. The man never stopped.

Mind you, he would have rested more. It was her doing that he had shortened his lunch break. She smiled to herself again as she remembered the banter.

Suddenly a scream pierced the quiet afternoon air. She shook her head. What had Christophe come up with now to get her back over there before her hour to herself was over? Would he say that he'd just seen a big brown snake? Or that a wild dog passing by had decided to attack him and run away? Or a zombie had appeared out of nowhere? She was certain he'd have the most outrageous story to tell.

She'd humour him and go back to his house. She swallowed the rest of her orange juice, grabbed the bottle and made her way to her back door where she slipped on her work boots. But outside, as she looked over at her neighbour's house half expecting to see him standing there with a grin on his face, she gasped. Christophe was slumped against the pine fencing, his head tilted back, his complexion drained. Red dripped along his wrist and hand. Red. Red what?

'Christophe!' She dropped the orange juice and ran to him, her heart pounding her chest. 'Are you all right?'

He licked his lips. 'I'm dizzy.'

'Let me see that.' She held back a cry at the sight of his slashed wrist. She couldn't tell how deep the cut was but it was messy and blood dripped down his hand. Her head spun and she had to hold onto something, anything. She placed a hand on the pile of wooden sheets and breathed in deeply. Although she'd always hated the sight of blood, she couldn't afford to faint. Christophe needed her.

Steeling herself, she checked her surroundings for something clean, a towel, a cloth. There wasn't anything, and there was no time to fuss. If the cut was deep, it was possible to bleed out, wasn't it? It had to be, since people slit their wrists to commit suicide. She took off her top, wrapped it around Christophe's wrist and tied it securely.

He glanced up at her, still as pale as before, and yet the mischief in his eyes was undeniable. 'The one time I can't move at all, my vision has gone blurry, and you go and take your top off.'

She smiled despite the panic in her heart. He was hurt, badly, and she couldn't stand the thought of anything bad happening to him. 'Can you walk to the car? It'll be quicker if I drive you to Saint Andrew's. You know how long it can take to get an ambulance around here.'

He nodded. 'Take mine. It's closer. Keys ... in the dish on the bookshelf near the back door. T-shirt on the washing line.'

She pulled Christophe's top off the line and slipped it on, rushed inside, found the set of keys, locked the door and ran back to Christophe. She helped him up and he leaned on her, his weight reassuring, not a burden but a gift. He was here, next to her. And he wasn't going anywhere. She couldn't let that happen.

She managed to press the button on the key ring, open the door for him and help him into the front passenger seat, placing his wrist upturned on his lap. She quickly slipped the seat belt on him and hopped into the driver's seat, fastening her own seat belt and taking off down the street like a rocket.

She didn't care about speeding or losing her licence today. Making it to hospital to save Christophe was the only thing that mattered.

Besides, if the police stopped her, they might even help her, escort her so that they could get to Saint Andrew's even faster. She zoomed around corners and rushed through amber lights praying that they didn't turn red.

'How did it happen?' she asked, glancing over at her injured companion. 'They'll need to know that at the hospital.' And she wanted to know too.

'I was sawing the end of the post and I guess I mustn't have been concentrating … I don't know … The saw slipped, that's all I remember.'

She frowned. Clearly, something had distracted him. It had nothing to do with her, though. Nothing to do with what she'd said to him earlier. It didn't, did it? She swallowed. She'd be mortified if it did. 'You can't remember what you were thinking about?'

'It doesn't matter.' Christophe moaned like a dying animal.

Her stomach twisted. She couldn't bear to see him like that. If she could have taken away his pain, felt it instead of him, she would have. 'Are you all right?'

'I think I'm going to …' His eyes rolled back.

'No, no, no! Christophe! Stay with me. Christophe! *Please.*' The hospital was just a few minutes away now. He would make it, wouldn't he? He had to make it. She stretched her arm and touched him on the shoulder, gently shaking him.

'I'm still here,' he blurted between laboured breaths as he opened his eyes again.

She had to keep him conscious, had to find something to hold his interest. 'You know how we were talking about New Year resolutions? Last year, what I did wrong was that I picked something unachievable.'

'You were crying about it.'

'Yes. It was silly of me.' The only thing crying was good for was emotional release. It never solved any problems. She took a deep breath. 'Last year my resolution was to find the right man for me.' To be happy again. To move on. It had been too much to ask.

He turned to her slowly, grimacing with effort. His glassy eyes settled on her. 'You could … could do that this year.'

'Maybe.'

'And find a man who's …' He opened his mouth wide and breathed through it. She frowned. It wasn't just the pain that was getting to him. He was struggling to draw air into his lungs. 'A man who is not like me,' he murmured.

'I wouldn't say that. I'd say a man who is like you, except ugly. Or plain. Or at least not too good-looking.' A man exactly like him in fact, sweet, considerate, a great cook, helpful, kind, fun, amusing, interesting, resourceful … She could go on and on.

He managed a grunt and a grimace that she realised was meant to be a smile. As she finally pulled up in front of Emergency, Christophe's eyes rolled back and then his head fell forward onto his chest.

Emily jumped out of the car, screaming. 'Help! He's badly injured. We need help!'

Two nurses came running, one with a wheelchair, and they lifted Christophe into it.

'He slashed his wrist cutting wood,' mumbled Emily. She hoped to God it wasn't because he'd been thinking about what she'd said earlier, that she had no intention of ever becoming his girlfriend. Had she done this to him? She gritted her teeth.

The hospital staff carted Christophe inside where they transferred him in two seconds flat to a stretcher. 'The doctor will need to know whether he's left or right-handed.'

'Right-handed.' Emily kept her eyes on Christophe's pale face as a medic and a nurse wheeled him through double doors.

Another nurse called out to her from behind a desk.

'Can you come and fill in a form for him, dear?'

Tears quietly rolled down Emily's face. 'Okay.'

Anything. She'd do anything for him. A lump the size of a tennis ball formed in her throat and the ache spread to her chest. She ran her hand over the T-shirt she was wearing, much too big for her, creased, ordinary. But it was Christophe's T-shirt and it felt good to have something of his, something she could hang onto, because she cared. She cared about the annoying, incredibly handsome Frenchman. It wasn't ideal. It wasn't what she wanted. But she did care for him, very much so.

Where had that come from? When had it started? She wasn't sure. She'd been so busy pushing him away that she hadn't noticed. All she knew was that she needed Christophe alive and back by her side. She needed him to smile at her, to make her laugh with his antics, to tease her. She needed him to irritate her, to fill her mind and her dreams. And right now she'd do anything at all for him— anything, as long as they saved him.

Chapter 12

After a three and a half hour wait that seemed like an eternity, a grey-haired male doctor in scrubs finally came to Emily in the waiting room. She stood, eager for news, scouring his face for signs that he was happy with the turn of events—a slight smile, a peaceful gaze. Instead the doctor's face was as blank as a robot's. Why did the medical profession always do that when people were desperate for reassurance?

'Hello. I'm Doctor Fielding. I operated on Mister Duval. The cut wasn't a clean one, far from it because of the jagged edge of the saw, and although it wasn't terribly deep, it took longer than expected to repair. Miraculously the median, ulnar and radial nerves were all missed. He's a very lucky man. We've been monitoring his blood pressure carefully. He's stable. The scarring should be minimal and I'm happy to say that unless there are any unforeseen complications, he will recover all functionality.'

A cry escaped Emily. 'Thank you so much, Doctor.' She wanted to jump up and down and scream with joy at the top of her lungs, but she was in a hospital and there were people around who weren't as fortunate as Christophe.

'I must emphasise that although it's his non-dominant hand he'll definitely need physiotherapy. And let me be clear about this, no lifting whatsoever until it's completely healed, which I'll tell him, but I always make sure I inform the patient's wife, too. The wives are the ones who tend to make the men keep with the program.'

Emily couldn't wipe the grin from her face and not because of the doctor's sense of humour. Christophe was okay! He'd have to have physiotherapy, but he would be fine. Such sweet relief ... 'I'll take good care of him, Doctor. Can I go and see him now?' Her heartbeat quickened at the mere thought of it.

'He's still in the recovery area. I'll arrange for a nurse to call you as soon as he's in a room. It could be a little while longer.'

She nodded, her shoulders dropping. She couldn't wait to see Christophe, to hear his sexy accent, to gaze into those chocolate eyes and tell him how happy she was that he was going to be fine. Shame there was nothing she could do to hasten the process. She was a prisoner of the hospital system and she had to grin and bear it.

While she waited, the doctor's words resonated in her mind. *Wife*. He'd said *wife*. She was far from being Christophe's wife and yet the word brought her so much pleasure.

Christophe struggled to open his eyes, and no sooner had he managed that his heavy lids closed again against his will. He tried once more and this time took in a glimpse of his surroundings. A bed. White sheets. Grey floors. A television set above his head. His wrist bandaged up and propped up on a pillow.

It all came flooding back, the sharp saw against his skin, the excruciating pain, the blood. And Emily driving him while he struggled to stay conscious.

His mind jumped back to the previous hour when he'd cut the wood while she'd gone home. He'd been thinking about her and what she'd said, her words ringing in his ears. *I am not your girlfriend. I have no intention of becoming your girlfriend. It's not going to happen. I find you too attractive, too handsome, okay?* Then he'd thought he'd heard her approaching, had turned around brusquely only to realise it was a kangaroo hopping behind his block in the bush. He'd felt a pang of disappointment, an emptiness, and at the same time the saw had deviated, slashing into his flesh, stealing his attention away from the ache in his heart.

Too handsome. She'd accused him of being too good-looking. It wasn't like being too loud or too quiet, too focused on work or too much of a party animal. Those were all things you could work on and, with effort, eventually change. How did you change your looks? Not your clothes, or your hairstyle, but your actual physique? You couldn't. It was impossible, unless you underwent plastic surgery and then what surgeon would intentionally make you ugly? And what might seem ugly to Christophe and any surgeon prepared to disfigure him may not be ugly enough for Emily.

He moaned. He couldn't believe he was actually thinking about plastic surgery. It was absolute madness. He was born with this nose, these eyes and this mouth, and if she couldn't accept that, there was no hope for him and Emily.

The door swung open and the woman of his dreams, the woman who had told him ever so clearly that she would never be his, rushed in. 'Christophe! I'm so glad you're all right. I spoke to the doctor and he said you're going to be just fine.' She grinned at him.

Christophe grunted. He didn't know if he could face her cheerfulness right now. He took in those lips he couldn't have, those curls he couldn't roll around his finger and looked away.

'How are you feeling?' Her voice was as soft as a cat purring in his ear.

'I've seen better days.' And he didn't just mean physically. He glanced at her sideways. 'Thanks for helping me, for carrying me and driving me here so fast.' He rubbed his nose with his good hand. 'You were awesome in action,' he mumbled. She was always awesome to him. Even when she drove him nuts.

Her laughter was like sunshine on a mountain creek. 'I didn't carry you. You simply leaned on me to get in the car, and the nurses lifted you out. And I rather enjoyed the fast driving.'

He could see what she was doing. She was making small talk, playing it down. She hadn't really enjoyed the ride. Even in his agony, he'd noticed the panic in her eyes. 'I hope you won't ask me to injure myself again to give you another excuse to speed.'

Her beautiful laughter filled the room once more and saddened him. How could he not be sad? She was here because he was injured, otherwise she wouldn't be by his side. Once the fence was up between their properties, the roller-coaster ride he was on with her would be on its way down and she'd become elusive. That much was clear to him.

'What's wrong?' she asked. He caught a whiff of her coconut scent as she pulled up a chair and sat close to the bed.

'Nothing.' Liar, liar, pants on fire. And he hated lying.

'Something, not nothing, is wrong. I mean, apart from your injury. I can see it.'

He steeled himself before looking her in the eye. 'To tell you the truth, I've been thinking about what you said.'

'What did I say?'

'That nothing will ever happen between us.'

Her chest lifted as she took a deep breath. 'Yes. I did say that.'

'It's been on my mind ever since. I can't concentrate on much else.'

She gasped. 'Is that what distracted you when you had the accident? Please tell me it isn't.' She covered her face with her hands. 'I'm so sorry.'

'Don't worry. I wasn't thinking about anything at all just before it happened.' It wasn't strictly a lie because his mind had gone blank for an instant while his heart ached, he remembered that much. Besides, he didn't want her to feel guilty. What was the point? 'Accidents are accidents. No one is to blame for this.'

'Thank God.' She looked around. 'Can I get you anything? A drink of water?'

'I'm okay, thanks.'

'I can go buy you a magazine or something, if you like.'

'I don't need anything, Emily. In fact, you've been here for ages as it is. You should go home. I'm sure you have lots to do.'

'Like what?'

'I don't know. Like look for the right man. You said you would this year. A plain man as you put it.'

'Before your accident I'd probably have agreed.'

He frowned. 'But not now?'

'No. Not now.' She fiddled with his sheet, rolling its edge between two fingers.

'I don't understand. Why? Did it make you realise you could lose that plain man in an accident?'

'It made me realise that life can change in an instant.'

'It sure can.' He fell silent for a while and she waited patiently by the bed. It wasn't his intention to break that silence but he had no choice, the need to know gnawing at his insides. 'You seemed to like me enough at the beach. We were walking side by side, one minute you were so close to me and the next ... The next you changed into someone so distant. We had to come back immediately and I can't for the life of me figure out what I said that was offensive. We'd just passed those two girls. Wait a minute ...'

She pushed back against her chair and crossed her arms.

'Those girls! They had something to do with it, didn't they? You're jealous. That's what it is. You have a jealous streak.' He laughed. All this time he'd failed to see that she was possessive. Possessive of him. Jealousy wasn't the best of personality traits, but it meant she felt something for him, didn't it?

Her cheeks flushed and although she looked all the more charming for it, it spelled danger for Christophe. If he embarrassed her she might stop talking when he wanted her to open up even more. He was finally getting to the heart of the matter; it wasn't the right time to put it all at risk.

She stood. 'I'll see you in a little while.'

'Emily, no! Don't go. We need to talk about this.'

As she opened the door to leave, he pushed himself up with both hands, forgetting about his injury until the agony of using his wrist reminded him why he was in hospital. He let out a cry of pain before he could call Emily's name again, but it was too late.

She was gone.

Emily took a sip of the lemonade she'd bought at the hospital cafeteria and munched on a handful of marshmallows. Comfort food was the only thing she could think of to steady her trembling hands.

She should go home. She was already exhausted after the emotions of the day and all the waiting around to see if Christophe was all right, and his last remark had finished her off. Yes, she'd have her drink and leave.

Was she a jealous freak? She hated to think of herself that way but maybe that's what she was. She took another gulp of her lemonade and stuffed the remaining marshmallows in her mouth. No, she wasn't a freak. Christophe had no right to make her feel that way. He knew little of what she'd been through with Josh. He probably thought Josh had had a wandering eye, that was all, and perhaps had made the occasional mistake. Now he might even be thinking that it was Emily who had driven her ex to cheat, with her jealousy.

She couldn't stand the idea. She placed her empty lemonade bottle and marshmallow pack in the bin and marched back to room 116. She threw open the door and stood at the end of his bed. Christophe's eyebrows shot up at the sight of her although he was wise enough to hold his tongue. Perhaps he could see how upset she was.

'I'm not an excessively jealous or possessive person. I need you to understand that. I'm not a freak.'

'I never thought you were.'

'I'm reacting to circumstances, things that have happened in my life, horrid things, that I couldn't bear to live through again.'

He nodded. 'Sure. I understand.'

'I wasn't like this before. And it's not jealousy. It's more self-preservation. I'll go now.'

'Why don't you sit down? Come on the bed next to me. Talk to me.'

She drew a breath. Could she trust him? She wasn't sure, but she had to try. If she didn't try with him, then who? She sat at the end of the bed. Too close, and she wouldn't be able to concentrate and she needed to, to get through this. 'Josh was extremely handsome. He was a model, in fact.'

'Ah! I see. And so you don't like handsome men?'

'Not anymore. We met at a café one day. I was there on my own when he walked in. He sat at a table facing mine and kept smiling at me. Eventually he came over to me and asked if he could sit for a while. I don't know why I said yes. It was probably because he was so attractive.'

'That's a pretty normal reaction for a single woman.'

Emily shrugged. 'I suppose so. Anyway, we chatted for a while. Suddenly he said, *Tell me something about yourself. Something that matters.*'

Christophe moaned. 'I remember asking you that.'

'You had no way of knowing. I told you that Josh had many women.'

Christophe nodded. 'I'm sorry.'

'He had a string of affairs, and I caught him with his hand up the skirt of a secretary at his office. When we broke up he told me that I was being ridiculous, that of course he'd been with other women, after all he was only human. The women were throwing themselves at him because he was so good-looking. He'd been in a couple of magazines, he'd done a few advertisements, and that was his excuse.'

Christophe burst into laughter. 'I'm sorry. I'm not making fun of you. It's just that his excuse sounds so pathetic.'

Christophe's reaction warmed her heart. It was the best form of support. 'Thank you. I guess it does sound pathetic, doesn't it?'

'Yes. You're absolutely stunning and I bet you didn't sleep around just because men were available.'

She smiled. She'd never really looked at it from that angle. She'd always thought of Josh as the beautiful one, the one who had to resist temptation all the time. Christophe was right. There had been plenty of men interested in her over the years and she hadn't gone and slept with them all. In fact, she'd never given any of them, not one of them, the time of day. 'That's true.'

He winked and she melted at the sight of the little dimple that formed in his cheek. 'There you go.'

She wrung her hands. What she had to say next was the hardest part. She thought back to that Christmas evening and her eyes filled with tears. She quickly blinked them back. 'You know how I told you about Lisa's car accident? My mother stayed at my house for a while after the police left. At first I thought she was there to comfort me, or so we could comfort each other. It wasn't the reason she stayed.'

Emily's stomach muscles contracted, tears streamed down her cheeks and she let out a deep moan at the memory of that night. She covered her face with her hands, to shield it from Christophe, to hide from the whole world.

'Hey, come here.' Christophe leaned forward and took her hand, tugging at it gently for Emily to sit next to him.

She inched a little closer and took a deep breath. 'I'm sorry. I didn't mean to cry.' She was always overwhelmed by the memory of that fateful night. The best she could do to remain in control was to not think about it anymore, but she needed to tell Christophe once and for all. Then he'd understand. Hopefully. 'My mother stayed to tell me that my sister had been kissing Josh and Mother being Mother insinuated that it must have been much more than that. I found Lisa's diary later when I was helping clear out her place. Josh had thrown himself at her, nearly forced himself on her. Yet *she* was a mess, all because she'd felt attracted to him at some stage. She never would have gone further, she wrote that and I know it's true, and I also know Josh. He thinks he can take whatever he wants whenever he wants it.'

'I'm so sorry, Emily.' Christophe reached out and placed his hand on Emily's. The touch comforted her.

'Now you understand why I didn't want to be with someone too handsome, and why ... and why I am the way I am.' Wounded, somewhat dysfunctional at times. For the time being, in any event.

She hoped that one day she'd heal properly and trust someone completely again. In the meantime, Christophe deserved better, a normal, easy relationship.

'I can see why you'd feel that way. In my defence, not everyone is like Josh, though.'

'I don't want you to think that I'm naturally very jealous.' She wondered if anyone was *naturally* jealous. Was it always an imbalance that formed as a result of being badly treated?

'You're not irrationally jealous, you're just scared,' he whispered.

He was right. She was scared of the past repeating itself. She was scared of the future.

'But you deserve a life, Emily. A good one. That won't happen by running away from what you want.'

All she could do was shrug despite the wisdom of his words. 'I'm sorry, I have to go,' she murmured. She couldn't stay here in the state she was in, with a man she'd come to care about and whose words were challenging her to reach for what she'd been forbidding herself. She stood.

'Would you mind giving me a ride home when I'm due out? I'm without my car since you brought me here, and I'm not sure if I'll be able to drive straight away anyway.'

She hesitated. She should really tell him to ask someone else, but something stopped her. 'Okay, then.'

She wiped away her tears with the back of her hand, waved goodbye and quickly slipped out the door before she forgot about reason, gave in to the longing in her heart, and held onto Christophe for dear life.

Chapter 13

Christophe waited near the glass doors of the entrance to the hospital, scanning the car park for signs of Emily. He'd told her he was being discharged around four pm today. Would she come and get him?

He breathed a sigh of relief when he saw her silhouette in the distance. She walked up to the hospital, her glorious hips swaying softly, her curls shining in the sun. The little floral dress she was wearing danced teasingly around her body, following her every movement. It must have been one of the new pieces she'd bought as her New Year resolution.

He made his way through the double doors and called out to her. 'Emily, over here.'

A timid, uneasy smile lit up her face for a split second before disappearing like sunshine behind clouds. 'Hello, Christophe.'

'How are you?'

'Fine. I should be the one asking that question.'

'I'm fine, too.' Now that she was here he could breathe again.

She studied him, frowning. 'You haven't shaved.'

'Not since I've been in hospital.'

She made a sound of surprise before wrinkling her nose. 'You haven't washed your hair, either.'

'No, I haven't. Had a shower, though.' He had his limits.

'Give me that.' She took his bag off him. 'You shouldn't be carrying anything.'

'It's okay. It's my left hand I can't use for a while. Nothing wrong with the right one.'

'It's better if I take the weight off you.'

'If you insist.' He gave her the bag, pursing his lips with guilt at having to let a woman look after him, at not being the one to protect her. 'Thank you.'

They reached Emily's hatchback and she put Christophe's belongings on the back seat. 'Hop in. Do you need me to close the door for you?'

'No, I've still got one good arm, thanks.'

Emily drove for a few moments without a word, the awkward, heavy silence weighing Christophe down more than his injury. 'So, what's new?' he asked once it was clear to him that she wouldn't speak if he didn't make her.

'You know Marandowie. Nothing much happens.'

'I meant with you.' He sought her gaze.

She kept her attention on the road until they stopped at traffic lights. Then she turned to him and he struggled not to drown in her beautiful, almond-shaped eyes, washed away, never to return to shore. 'Same with me,' she answered with a shrug. 'Nothing much, except …'

The light turned green and she accelerated. Except what? Wasn't she going to finish what she'd started? Was she happy to leave him dangling? He sighed. He'd been waiting for this moment, waiting to see her again. He hadn't pictured it this way.

'Except that I've done a lot of thinking,' she finally mumbled.

'Good thinking or bad thinking?' *Good. God, let it be good.*

'It depends on your perspective, doesn't it?'

'Hmm. You've got a point. I'll rephrase that. What have you been thinking about?'

'Too much to tell you in the few seconds left until we reach your house.' She pulled up in front of Christophe's as she ended her sentence.

'Want to come in?' He held his breath. If she refused, he'd shrivel up and die.

She blinked slowly, her expression so serious that it couldn't augur well.

'It's okay. Whatever it is, Emily, whatever you want to say to me, it's fine. It'll be all right.' His heart would shatter into a million pieces if she told him she still didn't want him, that she knew without the shadow of a doubt that she never would. It would break like never before, because this time she would have put some serious thinking into her decision, not blurt it out on a whim. Still, he had to let her know that he wouldn't pressure her into anything. When he said it would be okay, he meant it. He'd make it okay—for *her*.

Her lips curled into a barely perceptible smile. 'Thanks.'

He unlocked the door, held it open for Emily with his right hand and followed her in like a lamb on the path to slaughter. Was he doomed? Maybe. If she told him she couldn't be with him, ever, that she'd put much thought into it this time and was absolutely sure of it, he'd accept her decision. After everything they'd been through, he'd have to.

But not before he showed her exactly how he felt.

Emily sat on Christophe's couch with the glass of orange juice he'd brought her. She tapped her foot on the gleaming wooden floor.

How did she tell him what was in her heart? How did you reveal this sort of thing after all their ups and downs? She hadn't found the right words in the car.

'Are you sure you don't need a hand in there?' she called out to Christophe, who had returned to the kitchen.

'Nope. I mean no, I don't need help, and yes, I'm sure.' He came out with his own glass of juice in his right hand and a packet of biscuits under his arm. 'Sorry about the presentation. Carrying plates would be a bit tricky.'

'It tastes the same out of the packet.' She liked how Christophe usually presented everything beautifully, appreciated the effort he put in, but he didn't have to do it all the time and certainly not when he'd just come out of hospital.

'If you don't mind, I'll go and get changed.' He was still in the clothes he'd been working in before she'd driven him to hospital.

She felt a pang of guilt at not having brought him fresh clothes. She'd been so preoccupied, she hadn't thought to ask him if anyone else had provided him with a change of clothing.

Christophe gestured towards his bedroom. 'I'll be quick.'

'Sure. Take your time.' She wasn't about to ask him if he needed help with *that*.

She sipped her drink and stood, gazing through the back window at the pile of wooden fencing. A magpie landed on it and carolled. Emily smiled. She loved that sound. And the pile of wood was going to be there for a while, a special place for the bird.

She heard footsteps and turned around. Her jaw dropped when she saw Christophe. He was wearing an orange and green Tahitian-style shirt that would have been perfect for fancy dress, teamed with a pair of baggy pants about ten centimetres too short for him. With his dirty hair and stubble on his cheeks and chin, he could have been mistaken for a homeless person.

She looked away to hide her astonishment, and pointed to the backyard. 'I was just thinking that the fence wouldn't be up for quite a while.'

'No.' He clicked his tongue. 'Is that a problem?'

It certainly wasn't for her. She shook her head. 'Not at all.'

They returned to the sitting area and Christophe gestured to the biscuits. 'Help yourself.'

'Thanks.' She took a biscuit for herself, then another that she offered to Christophe. 'Would you like one?'

'Yep. Actually, would you mind tearing open the pack? It'll be easier for me to eat the rest.'

'Oh, sure.' The biscuits might go soggy though, by tomorrow. Perhaps he thought that preferable to not being able to get into the packet with one hand.

He munched on the first biscuit quickly and swallowed. He took another two and stuffed them into his mouth.

'You're starving! Didn't they feed you at the hospital?'

He nodded, his mouth still full, before swallowing in haste. 'They fed me, but you know what hospital food is like. Well-balanced, calorie-controlled and all of that.'

He took another three biscuits and she let out a sound of surprise. 'Christophe, would you like me to prepare you a sandwich?'

'No, it's fine. There are more calories in these. Actually, I'll just go and grab some chocolate, too.'

She bit her lip. He'd soon have enough energy for a triathlon.

He slipped into the kitchen and came back with three blocks of chocolate. He placed them on the coffee table and opened one with his good hand before she had the time to jump up to help. He sat back down, broke the block in half and gestured to it. 'Please, take some.'

'I'm fine with a biscuit. I had no idea you had such a sweet tooth.'

'Not usually. I'm getting into it, though.'

'They didn't give you anything sweet in hospital?' That would explain his sudden craving.

'The normal desserts. Apple crumble. Chocolate mousse. Out of a packet, I reckon.'

She covered her mouth with her hand. This wasn't the Christophe she knew, the suave, polished, classy man who was a true gourmet, not a rubbish bin for food. What had got into him?

He polished off the rest of the treats and sat back, rubbing his belly. 'Well, I've probably put on a kilo with all that.'

'I'll say. If not more.' She wouldn't be surprised if he was overcome by nausea.

'You know how you said that you'd done a lot of thinking, Emily?'

'Yes?'

'So have I.'

She wondered if it was about the same thing.

Christophe grimaced. 'Might have been a bit too much chocolate. Anyway, before you say what you have to say, I'm going to get in first. On New Year's Eve, I went to a bar. There was a girl there.'

He'd met someone. He was going to tell her how wonderful this new person was. He was about to say that he'd been wrong, and Emily right. It never would have worked between them and he certainly wouldn't bother Emily anymore. Her heart sank. It was too late. She'd left it too late. She'd messed up, big-time.

'She was so pretty, with long dark hair and a fabulous figure. She was all over me. Nothing happened that night when clearly it could have. I came home, alone, because I was thinking of you.'

Nothing happened that night, but since then he'd understood that Emily wasn't for him while the brunette with the long hair was perfect. The woman was probably a lot less complicated and knew exactly what she wanted from the minute she laid eyes on Christophe. Emily wiped the moisture off her hands and onto her dress. Her hands were never sweaty. She didn't understand.

Christophe smiled and the dimple Emily had come to love appeared. 'You told me nothing could ever happen between us because I was too handsome for you.' He laughed.

A lump the size of Western Australia formed in Emily's throat. How stupid of her, to turn down a man as perfect as Christophe! She'd thought she wanted to be on her own; she'd believed it, too. She'd thought she couldn't risk being with a man as attractive as Christophe, and then the accident ... The accident had forced her to acknowledge her feelings for him. 'I understand. I don't know what to say.' She shook her head. What could she say? It was too late. She stood.

'I'm not sure you understand. Let me finish.'

'You don't have to. I'll just go home. Make sure your new girl-friend takes good care of you with that injury.'

'That would be nice.'

As she moved towards the door, Christophe's hand landed on her shoulder. 'You need to hear this, whatever the outcome. And I need you to hear me out.'

She turned to him, frowning. Was he trying to punish her? The eagerness in his gaze told a different tale. 'When I was with that brunette, it became as obvious as the sun in the sky that for me, it had to be you. No one else would do. I wanted you. If I don't look the way you want, I'll try to be that man. I'll put on ten kilos, I'll dress like a dork, I'll let my hair grow. I'm willing to accelerate all the things that will come naturally if you bear with me. I'm going to age anyway. Give me a few years and I'll be all grey with wrinkles and yellow teeth, and I'll still want you. I don't know why, I don't quite know how this happened, but I can't be with someone else. It won't work for me. I'm not Josh. I'm not going to run off with other women. Hell, I don't even notice them. Chances are you still won't want me, but there you have it. For me, it's you. It's only you. And always might seem like a long time, but it will always be you.'

Her throat ached as if it had been scorched from top to bottom while tears streamed down her cheeks, tears of joy because he'd stood by her when she'd messed him around and been a complete idiot. He'd waited for her. He'd put up with her inadequacies. He'd tried again. And now, thanks to his persistence, she'd struck gold. 'I'm so sorry, Christophe. I don't know what I was thinking. I should have known from the day we met. It's just ...'

He drew a sharp breath. 'It's just what?'

She threw herself into his arms and rested her head against his firm chest. 'I was so afraid of being with anyone, of relying on someone. I still am, but your accident scared me even more. I knew then. I knew I had to take a chance because ...' She looked up at him, at those gentle, caring eyes. 'I didn't want to lose you. I needed you. You were the one for me, too. There's no one else. You *are* the one.'

His fingers curled around her face and he slowly drew her to his lips. His kiss was soft and tender. He stopped for an instant, an instant of longing and desire so intense for his arms, his warmth, his breath and everything that was him that her need devoured her. She sought him this time, and he kissed her back with the fire of a man who had been on the longest of pilgrimages and whose prayers had finally been heard.

When Emily came up for air, she grinned at him. 'You can wash your hair and wear your usual clothes and I'll be proud of how handsome you are. I might slip up at times, but I trust you. I want to trust you. I have to learn to do that all over again.'

He let out a deep laugh. 'That's a relief. Otherwise I was going to have to buy an all-new wardrobe, the opposite of yours, and I hate shopping, except for food.'

She smiled, his laughter warming her heart. It was lovely to see him happy and to know that it was because of her. 'Guess what I'm thinking about those clothes?' she whispered in his ear. 'I'm thinking they're hurting my eyes so much, I might just have to take them off you right now.'

He ran his hands down her arms. 'If you're sure. If you're ready.'

'I'm sure.' The butterflies in her stomach flitted around joyously, free at last to stretch their wings. Life was falling down and picking yourself up. It was about hurting and healing, and finding happiness in between, for long stretches at a time. Perhaps even forever.

If there was one thing she knew with absolute certainty, it was that she was ready to find her happiness with Christophe and to hang onto it for as long as she breathed.

The magpie outside carolled and Emily glanced out at it. 'That bird seems to have found its place on our pile of fencing.'

Christophe wrapped his fingers around hers and led her to his bedroom. 'Why don't we humour it and leave the stack there until it tires of it?'

Emily nodded. 'Fine by me.'

The fence could stay there until it disintegrated, as far as she was concerned. She pressed her body against his, until his heartbeat resonated in her chest as if it belonged to her, as if they were one and always had been.

And that was exactly how she liked it, him and her together, no divide between them. It had been a long, winding road to Christophe. Now that she'd found him, she wouldn't let anything stand between them ever again.

Acknowledgements

Thank you to my precious husband and daughter for your undying love and support. I couldn't do what I do without you. I couldn't do anything without you.

Thank you to my amazing critique group, Claire Boston, Anna Jacobs, Juanita Kees, Teena Raffa-Mulligan and Susanna Rogers. It's because of you that I continue to grow as a writer.

Thank you to my wonderful commissioning editor, Nicola Robinson, for your guidance, support and insight; to my editor, Linda Nix AE, for adding shine to my work; and to the entire Escape publishing team for making the publication process a breeze.

To the other writers in the 2019 Rainbow Cove series, Susanne Bellamy, Renée Dahlia and Shirley Wine, thank you. It's been such a pleasure to work with you. Let's do it again soon!

Last but not least, thank you to my readers. This amazing journey wouldn't be possible without you.

About the Authors

Alissa Callen

When USA Today bestselling author Alissa Callen isn't writing, she plays traffic controller to four children, three dogs, two horses and one renegade cow who believes the grass is greener on the other side of the fence. After a childhood spent chasing sheep on the family farm, Alissa has always been drawn to remote areas and small towns, even when residing overseas. She is partial to autumn colours, snowy peaks and historic homesteads and will drive hours to see an open garden. Once a teacher and a counsellor, she remains interested in the life journeys that people take. She draws inspiration from the countryside around her, whether it be the brown snake at her back door or the resilience of bush communities in times of drought or flood. Her books are characteristically heart-warming, authentic and character driven. Alissa lives on a small slice of rural Australia in central western NSW.

Janet Gover

Janet Gover grew up in outback Australia, surrounded by wide open spaces, horses … and many, many books. She is a self-confessed 'bit of a geek girl'. When not writing novels she works in IT—in really dull places like Pinewood Movie Studios, Puerto Rico and Iraq. When her cat lets her actually sit in her chair, she writes stories of strong women, rural communities and falling in love. Her novel Little Girl Lost won the Epic Romantic Novel of the Year Award presented by the Romantic Novelists' Association in the UK, and she has won or been shortlisted for awards in Australia and the USA. As Juliet Bell, in collaboration with Alison May, she rewrites misunderstood classic fiction, with an emphasis on heroes who are not so heroic. Her favourite food is tomato. She spends too much time playing silly computer games, and is an enthusiastic, if not always successful, cook. Janet loves to hear from readers—so do drop her a line.

janetgover.com
facebook.com/janetgoverbooks
Twitter: @janet_gover

Jacquie Underdown

Jacquie resides in coastal Central Queensland, Australia. On permanent hiatus from a profession she no longer loves, she now spends her time wrapped up in her imagination, creating characters and exploring alternative realities.

Jacquie has a business degree, has studied post-graduate writing, editing and publishing at The University of Queensland and earned a Master of Letters from Central Queensland University. She is the author of many published romance novels, novellas and short stories.

Juliet Madison

Juliet Madison is a bestselling and award-nominated Australian author of multiple books in fiction and self-help, an artist and colouring book illustrator, and an intuitive life coach who creates online courses for writers and those wanting to live an empowered life.

She likes to combine her love of words, art, and inspiration to create books that entertain and empower readers to embrace the magic of life and love.

Living on a coastal farm in Australia, Juliet loves to hang out with her family and pets, read, watch movies, play board games, bake, and of course write books, while doing her best to avoid housework.

You can find out more about Juliet, her books, and her courses at julietmadison.com and follow her on social media at Facebook www.facebook.com/julietmadisonauthor and Instagram @julietmadisonauthorartist.

Nora James

Nora James has had a diverse career, from working in a pâtisserie in France as a student to jet-setting the world as an international lawyer. She now writes novels and teaches English in a small town in coastal Brittany where she lives with her husband, her daughter and a menagerie of furry friends.

When Nora isn't working you'll find her in the kitchen cooking up a storm, or outside tending to her garden. She also loves interacting with readers. You can contact her through her Facebook page www.facebook.com/authornorajames and check out her website www.norajames.com.au.

talk about it

Let's talk about books.

Join the conversation:

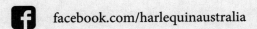 facebook.com/harlequinaustralia

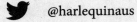 @harlequinaus

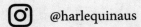 @harlequinaus

harpercollins.com.au/hq

If you love reading and want to know about our
authors and titles, then let's talk about it.